# Gloriel

# Gloriel

Angel to the Lord

Marguerite Cone

Copyright © 2009 by Marguerite Cone.

ISBN:	Softcover	978-1-4415-1636-7

All rights reserved. No part of this book may be reproduced or transmitted in any form or by any means, electronic or mechanical, including photocopying, recording, or by any information storage and retrieval system, without permission in writing from the copyright owner.

This is a work of fiction. Names, characters, places and incidents either are the product of the author's imagination or are used fictitiously, and any resemblance to any actual persons, living or dead, events, or locales is entirely coincidental.

This book was printed in the United States of America.

**To order additional copies of this book, contact:**
Xlibris Corporation
1-888-795-4274
www.Xlibris.com
Orders@Xlibris.com
59168

# Prologue

The small figure lay motionless and silent on the glassy golden surface. A heart-shaped face, framed in a mist of sleek amber curls, shone whitely through the vapor. Soft gilt lashes shadowed her cheeks. No breath of life stirred her breast or touched her flesh.

Softly, tenderly, the Lord God breathed His Spirit into this exquisite creation. Rosy color slowly suffused the ivory cheeks and lips, and her breast heaved as the breath of God filled her lungs. She stirred slightly, eyelids fluttering.

A voice, gentle and low, whispered into her consciousness, filtering slowly through the awareness of light and shadow, ethereal, yet almost tangible.

"Gloriel . . ."

Dimly aware of a shimmering, incandescent glow permeating her eyelids, she smiled as a warm sense of reassurance flowed slowly over her.

"Gloriel! Wake up!" The voice urged her, "Open your eyes!"

Bit by bit, her soft lashes parted to reveal deep golden eyes, innocent and bewildered. She blinked against the light.

*That glorious glow! I can almost reach out and touch it,* she thought. The warmth was increasing, and an incredible feeling of joy flooded over her.

*What's happening?* Her eyes widened and searched the surrounding mist. Tentatively, she stretched out one arm, but it only passed through the sparkling haze, without sensation.

"My child, stand up!"

She sat up, stretching out both arms. A tingling sensation rose up in her chest, slowly spreading to hands and fingers, legs, feet and toes. Unsteady at first, she rose swaying to her feet. A faint smile curved her lips, as her heart lifted on a powerful wave of delight.

She blinked her golden eyes, as borne faintly on the bright particles of haze; the murmur of distant voices reached her ears. Music tinkled softly as she turned her head slowly from side to side, exploring the soft-hued golden vapor.

*Where are the music and voices coming from?* The air around her seemed faint and gauzy, infusing the atmosphere with an entrancing fragrance. She closed her eyes and inhaled the sweetness.

"Gloriel..."

Her lips parted, "Y-es?" She shook her head in bewilderment, startled by the sound coming from her mouth.

She turned toward the voice, gazing curiously around her. *That amazing voice! Where...*

"Welcome to Life, Gloriel." The voice stirred a response deep inside her.

Awareness of a loving, comforting Presence touched her body and spirit, and the sense of warmth increased.

Suddenly, deep within, she knew!

"My Lord!" The words burst unbidden from her lips.

"Yes, Gloriel!"

An even brighter light spread throughout the golden vapor like ripples in a vast lake of gold.

Her eyes widened as if to draw the luminosity into her very being.

"Lord, I can't see you! Where are you?"

"No, not yet, Gloriel. But I AM here."

Glancing down, she became aware of her own embodiment. A diaphanous pale blue tunic flowed in soft folds over her small figure. The cloth appeared to be woven with a kind of radiance within its strands.

She wiggled her toes. Shining golden sandals reflected the surrounding glow.

Reaching up with both hands, she touched the glossy curls framing her face, her fingers tracing down her neck, over her breasts and down her hips.

"But, I can see me, Lord."

"Yes. This is the form you will take as needed, Gloriel," the Lord replied. "You will know when and how to do this." With these words, the loving Presence faded away.

Gloriel glanced around, searching her surroundings curiously. Gradually, the distant voices and the music grew louder.

The glittering mist parted, and a figure appeared and stood before her. He was of medium height, and slender. Short, dark auburn hair curled over his ears and broad forehead. Large, wide-spaced hazel eyes framed by thick short lashes lowered their gaze to study her. His kind mouth curved up slightly at the corners. A short, bright green tunic with a broad belt of gold encircled his waist, covering his lithe frame.

Gloriel gasped. A magnificent pair of ivory-colored wings gleaming softly in the golden light framed his body.

He stood, feet wide apart, in sandals laced to the knees. Hesitantly, he held out a long-fingered hand to her, smiling.

"I am Gabriel," he said quietly, moving closer. "Who are you?" His voice was warm, his behavior friendly. There was a slightly luminous aura about him, a faint gold shifting of the air around him.

Shyly, Gloriel touched his outstretched hand. It felt warm, firm and reassuring.

*Mmmmm . . . What a wonderful sensation,* she thought. *Does my touch feel like that to him, I wonder?"*

"I-I'm Gloriel," she murmured timidly. She looked intently at the magnificent figure, her eyes wide and questioning. "I don't understand what's happening, Gabriel. Where are we? Who are we? Have you spoken to the Lord?"

"I know, Gloriel. I was confused and didn't understand anything either, when I first opened my eyes." He grasped both her hands in his. "I do know that God has given us Life! This place is called Heaven, and it's filled with other beings just like us!" he exclaimed, laughing aloud.

*What an amazing sound!* Gloriel thought, smiling.

"This place is called Heaven? But who are we, and why are we here, Gabriel?" she questioned, eyes bright, eager, and enormous with awe. *Where did we come from? I don't remember anything before I woke up a little while ago."*

"The Lord spoke, and created us out of nothingness, Gloriel. I've been told that we are here to serve Him, glorify Him, and proclaim His holiness," Gabriel replied, squeezing her hands and smiling down at her. "But I still don't fully understand," he whispered.

Puzzled, Gloriel looked around. "'Holiness'? I don't know what 'holiness' is. What do you know about it, Gabriel? Who told you about it? Where can we get it?" Bewilderment shadowed her features as the questions tumbled forth.

Gabriel's grasp was warm and comforting. He fixed her amber eyes with his marvelous penetrating gaze.

"These are things the Lord told me, Gloriel. You'll understand better, soon. We're called 'angels', 'the holy ones,' 'ministers of God;' I am an archangel."

Gloriel's lovely face turned up and she looked full into Gabriel's eyes with her honeyed gaze. "Archangel? Minister? Gabriel, what do these things mean? I'm so confused," she sighed, shaking her head in an effort to clear it. She felt as though there were no end to the questions flooding her mind.

"I am not really sure, Gloriel. The Lord hasn't explained everything to us yet."

The fog began to dissolve, evaporating in the incandescence surrounding the two angels. All around them, the sparkling light expanded, pulsating, swirling and dancing. It was brilliant, and yet it did not hurt their eyes. It seemed full of life, to BE life, as it enveloped and filled their flesh with deep and vibrant warmth.

Gloriel raised her eyes, and drew in her breath with a gasp of delight. Soaring through the glow, pearly wings of light flashing, a form swooped and glided low over their heads.

The radiance emanating from it was too bright for the two angels to discern any distinct shape. Hovering in a ring of even more dazzling light, the flashing wings seemed to expand, growing until they filled the angels' vision.

Gloriel turned her head quickly toward Gabriel. His face was glowing brightly as he stared wide-eyed at the shimmering wings of light overshadowing them.

"Gloriel . . ." Gabriel's voice was an enthralled whisper in her ear. "It is the Lord . . . the Holy Spirit."

As suddenly as the vision appeared, He was gone, melting silently away into the light.

The two angels stood silent, enchanted and breathless.

Gloriel turned to Gabriel whispering faintly, "Please, Gabriel, how do you know all this?"

"The Most High, the Father, told me, Gloriel. You will soon be gifted with this 'knowing', too."

The radiance on Gabriel's fine features was fading slowly. Gloriel wondered if her face also reflected that astonishing illumination.

The low murmur of voices swelled around them, as the ethereal music of lutes and harps caressed their ears.

Gradually, other angels gathered around them, many wearing the same confused and puzzled expression as Gloriel.

*There are so many!* She marveled to herself. Standing motionless among them, she gradually became aware of a sense of belonging, of companionship, and love. It was a stunning sensation, and she found herself smiling at all the angels surrounding her.

"Hail, my brothers and sisters!"

The gathering of angels turned toward the voice, as a figure approached through the light.

"It is I, Michael."

A strong-featured face wearing a broad smile appeared in front of them. Gleaming ebony hair crowned his head, and black eyes sparkled beneath heavy brows. His body was solidly muscled, and tall. His tunic was similar to Gabriel's, but of a heavier, pearl gray material. The belt around his waist gleamed silver in the light. A circlet of silver crowned his broad forehead. Like Gabriel, his robust build was enhanced by the amazing wings framing it.

*I wonder why all the angels don't have those stunning wings.* Gloriel pondered.

"Welcome, my brother!" Gabriel exclaimed, in the same warm tones that had greeted Gloriel. "I'm Gabriel, and this is Gloriel," he said, indicating the small angel beside him. I don't know the names of our other companions here," he said, pointing out the other angels with a sweeping gesture. "We were just discussing why we are here, and what we're supposed to do, Michael. Do you know?"

Curious, the other angels drew closer, murmuring softly among themselves.

Michael's dark eyes twinkled with warmth, and he smiled at the ever-growing crowd of angels.

"The Lord has appointed me Captain of his Hosts, Gabriel, and I'll be the guardian of His Chosen People."

*Chosen People? Who are these Chosen People?* Gloriel wondered silently, her mind swirling with unanswered questions.

Michael turned to her. He leaned down, took her hand, and whispered softly, "You, Gloriel, are destined for the most awesome ministry of all the Lord's angels." A broad smile curved his mouth, as he squeezed her hand.

Filled with wonder and astonishment, Gloriel felt too shy to question him. *What is this 'ministry' Gabriel and Michael keep talking about?*

She smiled shyly at Michael. *What a penetrating gaze he has,* she thought. *It's almost as if he can see inside me.*

She glanced at Gabriel. His features still retained a faint aftermath of the glow which suffused them a short time ago. He smiled disarmingly, reaching out both hands to Michael.

"I've been informed that I will be leader of the Lord's Messengers, Michael. Although I'm not quite sure what that means," he said with a chuckle, looking down shyly.

"Oh yes, Gabriel. You are among the most beloved of the entire Heavenly Host! Did you know that your name means 'God is my strength?' An exceedingly wonderful name," Michael added, white teeth flashing.

Gloriel's eyes widened with wonder as she listened to the exchange between the two powerful beings. More and more angels gathered about them, their number swelling rapidly, until the Heavenly Host filled her vision as far as she could see. She felt a growing excitement infusing the crowd surrounding her.

Suddenly, Michael's expression changed, growing absorbed and serious. His powerful voice rose up and flew above the myriad angels gathered.

"Praise Him, all His angels, praise Him! Shout for joy, for the Morning Star will soon rise!" he exclaimed.

He extended his arms high above his dark head as the heavenly chorus raised their voices in acclaim.

The faint tinkling music that first reached Gloriel's ears as she awakened grew steadily in volume as numberless silvery sweet voices filled the shining air.

Dulcimer tones of harp, lyre, and trumpet swelled in indescribable harmonious beauty, joining with the joyful voices of the angels. Although each voice and instrument sang a different song, they blended together into one marvelous chorus of praise.

A thrill of joy shot through Gloriel's heart as it vibrated to the sound of the pure melodies.

"Praise the Lord! Praise Him in the heavens and the heights! Bow before His radiant throne and give Him all glory and honor and praise!" Michael's rich voice rang out.

The voices were like thunder now, the music swelling and throbbing until it filled the dome of Heaven, and each listening heart brimmed with awe. The golden light, burst into an ever brighter and more stunning display, cascading like flowing water down upon the gathering of angels.

God was well pleased with His first creation, the angels; spectacular beings who were such a beautiful expression of His love.

#

So the angels came into being. The Lord God created them to love, serve, and glorify Him. Sometimes, they would be a visible presence among His creation. He rejoiced in these awesome holy creatures, exalting them highly. These angels, the very first beings to receive His love, basked in the light of the Lord God's pleasure.

As part of this great heavenly company, Gloriel received life from the hand of the Lord. She soon realized that she and her companions were objects of the Lord's love and grace from the very moment of their creation.

Walking around rejoicing among her brother and sister angels, her heart was entranced with the beauty and grace of the incomparable creatures all about her.

Gabriel and Michael approached her, and each of them, without a word, took her by a hand, leading her through the heavenly throng.

She continued to marvel at the Heavenly Host, as she walked along with Michael and Gabriel. All were different in feature and form, but were alike in one way . . . their obvious joy.

Here and there amongst the multitude, a pair of gleaming wings stood out like shining sentinels.

Gloriel looked around curiously as she and her two friends walked slowly through the midst of the other angels. She wondered where Gabriel and Michael were taking her, but was too captivated with watching the others to ask questions.

Gazing about, she noticed that although the angels' clothing was of many different colors and hues, that same characteristic of light which shone in the fibers of her own garments, was common to all.

"Gabriel," she said as she gathered her thoughts, "where are we going?" She regarded him with big, uncertain eyes.

"We've been summoned to the Throne, Gloriel," he said quietly, auburn hair gleaming in the light.

"The Throne? God's Throne?" Gloriel asked, breathless with excitement.

"Yes, God's Throne, Gloriel," Michael interjected, grinning over her head at Gabriel.

She glanced down at her feet and gasped sharply. In the shifting, mysterious light, they seemed to be walking on a sea of glass, which sparkled like crystal. Translucent and gleaming with fiery golden particles, it appeared vaporous, and yet it was solid.

*How strange! But how beautiful!* She thought to herself.

The breath-taking splendor of their heavenly home enraptured Gloriel, and her heart celebrated the goodness of the Lord God.

All around them, talking softly among themselves, the countless Host of Heaven moved slowly toward the Throne.

In the distance, faint outlines of towering golden structures that looked to be part of the light, and yet of solid substance, glistened and gleamed. A massive cupola of light rose high above the other buildings.

The walls around the city appeared to be fashioned of crystal-clear jasper. Standing out like giant sentries, broad and high against the horizon, they glowed in the light.

As they approached the great city, Gloriel counted twelve massive gates. She could see that each one was formed from a single, softly shimmering pearl. *How magnificent!* She thought.

Without warning, a mighty trumpet blast split the air, and a booming voice proclaimed

"I AM the Alpha and the Omega, the Beginning and the End!" Sonorous and clear, the voice thundered through the multitude of angels. "I am the One Who is, Who always was, and Who is still to come!"

All the angels surrounding Gloriel began sinking to their knees. Suddenly, so close she could almost reach out and touch it, the massive golden Throne appeared, gleaming and flashing with gemstones. Through the mist, rubies, sapphires, diamonds and emeralds flashed their mixture of rich colors into the mist.

Flowing from the side of the Throne, a sparkling stream of crystal-clear waters bubbled, singing an ecstatic melody. It surged out across the sea of glass toward the great city, vanishing in the distance. Along both sides of the crystal river, near the throne, grew two magnificent bright green trees. Their heavy branches arched low, laden with glowing orbs of golden fruit.

Gloriel hardly dared breathe. A burnished cloud of light, with an incredible heart of gold, drifted above the Throne. Suddenly, the Lord God totally filled their sphere of vision. They could not discern any form or features, only the spectacular light.

Bliss overwhelmed Gloriel, and she was transported with joy. Filled with inexpressible delight, she shivered with awe and fell to her knees.

On either side of her, Michael and Gabriel bowed low to the ground in adoration, their luminous wings folded about them.

"Arise, my children; don't be afraid." The voice of the Lord was loving, and pleasing to their ears.

"Michael and Gabriel, come up here."

The two angels quickly arose and walked forward, faces shining.

"Lucifer!" The voice rang out again. "Come forth!"

Gloriel glanced around curiously, searching the throng around her. Hushed voices whispered.

Slowly, the crowd parted, as a tall figure approached, striding confidently. Gloriel had not seen this angel before, and was struck by his great beauty. Pale golden hair framed patrician features, and imperial blue eyes, like liquid sapphires, gazed straight ahead at the Throne.

Lucifer continued advancing, looking neither to right nor left. His handsome face was set; his shining wings folded in a regal, cape-like fashion. He took his place with Michael and Gabriel standing before the Lord, his manner radiating self-assurance.

In the wake of his path, Gloriel noticed that several angels followed him through the crowd.

It was almost as though someone whispered their names in her ear, for suddenly she knew that these who followed Lucifer were called Imamiah, Azazel, Nizrock, Moriah, Asmodeas and Jezrel.

Their eyes remained fixed on Lucifer, as if spellbound by his great beauty and power. All were tall, and almost unapproachable in brilliance.

"Lucifer has enormous power; and he is greatly loved by the Father," someone whispered in Gloriel's ear.

Gloriel turned around, slightly startled. A jolly face that seemed familiar, peered back at her. Yet she knew she had not seen him before this. He was not much taller than she, but sturdily built. His face was merry, his smile dimpling the dark skin of his plump cheeks. His nose and chin were round, and black eyes twinkled under thick brows.

"My name is Samuel." He added in low tones.

"Hello Samuel, I'm Gloriel," she replied softly, reflecting back his smile.

*How does Samuel know so much about Lucifer?* She wondered.

She turned and gazed again at Lucifer. *He's so beautiful! It's hard to keep my eyes off of him.*

Exceptionally tall and powerful of build, he stood ramrod straight, garments shimmering in the light. His robe was brilliant, flowing snow-white and glistening around his towering form. Flecks of white fire radiated from it. A jet-black belt gleamed in the light. Unlike the short garments Michael and Gabriel wore, Lucifer's robe was long, just brushing the top of his black leather sandals.

*His face is breath-taking, more so than that of any angel I've seen, and it's like the light itself is sleeping in his hair,* Gloriel marveled.

The three angels drew closer to the Throne. She could hear the Lord's voice speaking in low tones to them, but could not discern His words.

Michael walked to the right of the throne, and Gabriel took his stance on the left. Lucifer, powerful wings outspread, rose up to hover behind and over the throne. Engrossed in his beauty, Gloriel could not tear her eyes away from him.

She wondered briefly why she felt such a sad pang arise in her heart as she stared, fascinated, at him. Her knees felt weak, and a curious restlessness stirred in her breast.

Again, the Lord's voice rang out, filling the heavens. "Uriel, Chamuel, Zoakiel and Japhiel, stand forth!"

Gloriel stared out across the sparkling sea of glass as it shifted and parted before four burly angels. She felt very small in comparison to their powerful bodies.

Drawing near to the throne, they bowed low before the Lord, their wonderful wings folded closely around them.

*These angels are so extraordinary in appearance, so dazzling!* Gloriel mused. *It's really hard to keep my eyes focused on them.*

"You seven will be the mightiest of the Heavenly Host, my Archangels. You shall carry out my will among my earthly children, shielding and caring for them. You are the leaders of the Seraphim." The voice of the Most High was somber, filled with power and intensity.

*'Earthly' children? What does that mean?* Gloriel wondered curiously.

Then the Lord God summoned the remaining innumerable angels before the throne. He divided the Heavenly Host into nine groups, which He called "Choirs." Gloriel waited eagerly to hear which Choir would be hers.

Once again, He addressed the angels. "You are my Holy-Elect. Although I have created you as pure spirits, there are no limits to the forms you may assume when you decide it is necessary.

The Seraphim are foremost among you. They will reflect my Glory to all those whom they serve, and they will stand nearest to my Throne."

Gloriel listened spellbound as the vibrant voice continued.

"You Cherubim! Come forward!"

She felt euphoric as the atmosphere around the Throne of God grew vibrant and blissful.

As the Seraphim stepped aside, except for Michael, Gabriel and Lucifer, a number of angels stirred the golden sea of fiery glass as they walked to the Throne.

All wore robes of pure golden silk. The soft fabric caught and reflected the glow of the air around them.

"You, my Cherubim," the Lord continued, "are the Keepers of Heaven's record books. Your wisdom and power will be very great. You will document the life stories of each of my earthly children. Cherubliel, Orphanuel, and Zaphiel shall be your leaders."

These three stepped forward out of the group, bowing low before the Throne, faces solemn.

Next, the Lord called forth the Thrones, Dominations, Virtues, Powers and Principalities, explaining their various duties and responsibilities to each group.

Watching closely, Gloriel noticed that every Choir, although they differed in appearance, had some characteristics which were shared among their own groups.

Finally, as the last of the nine choirs, the Lord summoned the Angels. These He charged with being the special protectors of His earthly children.

Then He instructed them carefully in how to love, attend, and glorify Him. Gloriel was overjoyed to hear her name called by the Lord God to be a member of this choir.

The numberless throng of stunning creatures gathered around the Throne. Lifting their hands and voices in praise, they proclaimed the supremacy of the Most High. Heaven echoed and re-echoed with their stirring, beautiful music.

Gloriel felt her heart would surely burst with joy.

Soon her attention returned to the three angels standing closest to the Throne. The Lord was again murmuring in low tones to Michael, Gabriel, and Lucifer.

She stood watching, enthralled, when without warning, Lucifer spun around and strode away through the midst of the angelic throng assembled around the throne. They hastily opened a pathway for him and his companions following closely behind.

*What's wrong?* Gloriel wondered, her jaw dropping in surprise.

Suddenly, the mystery in her mind cleared as she fully understood that Lucifer, great in intelligence and beauty, was truly much-loved by God, as Samuel had said. This "Bearer of light" was one of the most powerful of the Lord's beloved Seraphim.

*But what could have caused him to turn and walk away from the Lord like that?* She questioned, shaking her head.

Puzzled and perplexed, she faced Samuel, who was standing quietly by her side. "Why . . ."

"Hello." The voice was sweet and hesitant. Gloriel turned around toward the delightful sound and blinked in surprise. The young child standing before her was exquisite. Her beauty pierced Gloriel's heart with an aching sweetness. Burnished golden hair curled softly down her small back. Her fair skin glowed with an inner radiance, staining her dimpled cheeks with a rosy hue. Round blue-green eyes peeped shyly up at Gloriel from under long velvety lashes.

"My name is Sariel. What's yours?" The childish voice was just above a whisper.

Gloriel smiled at the small face with the upturned nose. The golden light of Heaven reflected on the charming features.

"I'm Gloriel," she replied softly. "Oh, you're so lovely, Sariel!"

Sariel's face lit up with a radiant, innocent smile. "I was told that I will minister in this form, Gloriel"

*Minister?* Gloriel felt bewildered. *There's that word again. Why haven't I been told about this "ministry" others are talking about?* She asked herself.

She was about to ask Sariel, when Michael and Gabriel materialized beside them. Both the angels looked a bit mystified.

"Gloriel! Sariel! Samuel! We've learned so much from the Lord!" Michael's deep voice thundered the compelling fire of God's love in his heart. His eyes glowed as he grasped Gloriel's hand.

"Gloriel, do you remember when I told you that I am to be the Guardian of God's Chosen People?"

"Well yes, Michael," Gloriel replied, "I do remember, but I really didn't understand what you meant." She peered at him curiously, eager for answers to all the questions engulfing her mind.

"The Lord is going to create a wonderful new world; settled with creatures He calls 'human beings'. He said that like us, these humans will be made in His image, and have the same free will as we. This new world will be called 'Earth,' and it will be a wondrous place of great beauty." Michael's eyes danced with black light, as he paused to catch his breath.

"These 'human beings' will love, worship, and serve the Lord, as we do. They will give Him great pleasure. We are to protect, guide and comfort these people, looking after their needs, ministering to them. Sometimes, we'll appear among them in these forms, which are like theirs will be, so that we will seem familiar to them."

Gloriel listened intently to what Michael was saying. A small frown drew a line on her smooth forehead. *So this is what a 'ministry' is! I have so much to learn!* She thought. *I am truly blessed to stand so close to God's throne. Yet, I still don't know what I'm supposed to do.*

Sariel and Samuel were silent, looking slightly stunned with the enormity of the responsibility Michael had outlined for them.

#

There followed a time of intense education and study for all of the angels. Each one was trained in his or her position from the mouth of God himself. All of them were flawless in character, yet totally different in nature from one another. Each individual angel developed a loving, personal relationship with the Lord. He called each of these numberless creations by name, rejoicing in their beauty and purity. Heaven was blessed by their presence.

There was no time, as such, in this amazing place called 'Heaven,' and none of the inhabitants grew any older, only wiser.

#

"My friends!" The voice, which sounded both close at hand and far away, created a joyful ambiance around the little gathering of angels.

Each head in the small group turned quickly toward the deep voice that vibrated the strings of their hearts with its warm tones.

A figure radiating flecks of silver fire stood before them. Gloriel could see his form, but the light shone far too bright to distinguish any features. She stared wide-eyed at the radiance, suddenly longing to hurl herself into it. Incredible love emanated from Him. A burning desire to drown in that love arose in her soul.

Then, amazingly, in her innermost core she became aware of the figure's identity. He stood in the golden nucleus of light; Father, Son and Holy Spirit, the Godhead. Three persons, one God, and this was the Son!

She clasped her hands together in adoration, basking in the blessedness of understanding.

She felt as though she had known Him even before the Father called her into being. *How could that be?* She wondered. Again, an overwhelming and soul-searching sense of love flowed from the figure of light and swept over Gloriel. Bright tears welled in her golden eyes, and rolled slowly down her cheeks.

Almost as one, the angels fell to their knees, bowing low before the dazzling light which shone forth from the eternal Son.

"Get up, my friends." The wonderful voice resounded with love. "Come, share in our joy as the Beginning dawns."

Silence enveloped the Host of Heaven. No sound was heard, no word spoken. So palpable was the silence, that Gloriel felt she could almost reach out and touch it. No movement disturbed that perfect and absolute stillness.

Her eyes were drawn downward, and she saw a deep, permeating darkness, suffused with an undulating, boiling, yet soundless movement. She could distinguish no forms, no outlines, just a far-flung, impenetrable blackness. Then something began moving over the surface of the dark void.

"LET THERE BE LIGHT!!" The voice of God, like thunder approaching, boomed out the Fiat lux.

Great billows of sound swelled, amplified, filling the heavens with a commanding timbre. The enormous rolling waves of sound echoed and re-echoed, fading slowly away into the vast reaches of space.

Gloriel's eyes grew huge in her small face. Within that enormous void of darkness, little by little at first, then swiftly spreading, pale gold streaks of light explored the blackness, fingering it and pushing it aside.

Without warning, a tremendous roar shook the universe. Gloriel covered her ears and closed her eyes against the blinding, illimitable light borne on the wings of the explosion.

And so there was Light.

Her eyelids parted slowly, and she gasped at the spectacle below. An immense ball of light glowed where moments before were only darkness and a formless gulf; as a Word from God set the unruly mass into motion.

"It is good!" God said.

A rising excitement rippled like a wave over the hosts of angels, but none dared speak.

A staggered bolt of lightning suddenly forked from the glowing figure standing beside them. It sliced between the light and the darkness, dividing them in half.

"The Light shall be called 'Day,' and the darkness 'Night,'" the awesome voice rang out again. These two together completed one day.

Peering down upon the globe, half dark, and half light, Gloriel noticed that underneath the light, a spectacular body of sapphire blue heaved and gleamed, reflecting the radiance.

God said *"Let there be space between the waters, to separate water from water. This space shall be called 'sky.'"* Genesis 1:6 NLT This was the second Day.

Gloriel's heart pounded, leaping in her breast. She found it hard to breathe. Looking around, she again became aware of her companions.

Michael's black eyes glowed with a fierce new fire, and Gabriel's dear face looked awestricken. Sariel's small hands clasped over her breast; her fair skin blanched to ivory. The enormous blue-green eyes shone lustrous with wonder.

Samuel's sturdy figure seemed carved from stone. Still, no one spoke. All around them, God's angels gazed with astonishment upon this breath-taking manifestation of their Creator's power.

The voice of the Lord once more broke the silence with its powerful timbre. *"Let the waters beneath the sky be gathered into one place, so dry ground may appear."* So it was. Genesis 1:9 NLT

Ru-ach, the Spirit, the Wind, blew over the face of the waters, as they divided before the marveling eyes of the angels.

The deep blue water below seemed to climb up and pour in upon itself. Then a rich, deep brown soil, obeying the command of the Word, burst forth where the waters divided. God named the dry ground "land," the water he called "seas."

"It is good!" God exclaimed.

*"Let the land burst forth with every sort of grass and seed-bearing plant. Let there be trees that grow seed-bearing fruit. The seeds will thus produce the kinds of plants and trees from which they came,"* God said. Genesis 1:11 NLT

Once again, it came to be. This all happened on the third Day.

Thus the world began, as God brought it forth from disarray and formless void, revealing His Power, His Holiness and His Majesty.

Gloriel glanced around. Her eyes fell on the commanding, graceful figure of Lucifer, standing to one side of the group of angels. In sharp contrast to the joy and awe on the faces of Michael, Gabriel, Samuel and Sariel, his countenance was dark and glowering. His eyes shone wild and glittering, flashing blue rays.

A chill swept over Gloriel, as her flesh quailed with a sense of foreboding. Quickly, she turned back to watch the earth below.

Again the thunderous voice spoke to the heavens. *"Let bright lights appear in the sky, to separate the day from the night. They will be signs to mark the Seasons, the Days and the Years. Let their light shine down upon the earth."* Genesis 1:11 NLT

So it was.

Into the nothingness of never-ending space, the hand of the Supreme Being flung an enormous, vaporous orb of dazzling incandescence to light up the Earth below. The blue waters of the seas reflected its face in myriad flashes of blazing brightness. The sun stretched out warm fingers of orange, yellow, and gold to touch both land and sea. God hung this great globe of fire in the sky to oversee the Day.

Gloriel and her companions trembled with awe at the miracles unfolding before them. Their hearts soared in praise as untold varieties of plants sprang up in wild, colorful abandon. The trees stretched out green leafy arms to the great light in the sky, as God blessed the earth with radiant color. Blue, violet, green, scarlet, yellow and various tones of all these hues, spread slowly across the expanse of fertile brown soil. The angels gazed enthralled as a heavy mist of fragrance rose up to the heavens.

On the other side of the budding earth, shadowed from the sun, another light came forth, flooding the sky with its splendor. It appeared to Gloriel to be a soft reflection of its larger brother. In contrast to the sun, the moon's light glowed cool, bathing the countryside in silver. Overseeing the night, this globe of shimmering light turned its serene face upon the mountain tops and the blue-green oceans below.

"Its light is glorious!" Gloriel whispered to Sariel, entranced with the moon's glowing countenance. Sariel smiled, her small face reflecting the radiance of the great ball of silver.

*God set these lights into the heavens to light the earth, to govern the day and the night, and to separate the light from the darkness. And God saw that it was good. This all happened on the fourth Day.* Genesis 1:17-19 NLT

The Most High's awe-inspiring Word spoke yet again, and Time was born on the new Earth. This was the beginning of days, weeks, months, years and seasons. God's voice reached out, touched, and put into motion the meticulous timing and intricately detailed workings of His universe.

In precise order, the stars, twinkling balls of blazing light, soared flaming from the mighty hand of God to take their places in space. The planets, other worlds of His making, also bloomed in the measureless heavens.

All around Gloriel, the angelic host began raising their arms in praise, awestruck and adoring. The silence was broken by a rising crescendo of song, as Heaven delighted in the creation of Earth.

A tall and striking figure stood silently to one side of the throng. The perfect features of Lucifer's face twisted in anger, and his powerful fists clenched at his sides. No light reflected from his face as darkness suffused his skin.

Then God said, "Let the waters swarm with fish and other life. Let the skies be filled with birds of every kind."

It seemed to Gloriel that they drew even closer to the earth. Details grew clear to their wondering eyes. Many-colored flocks of birds slowly ascended from the vivid green earth. They ranged in size from a wee bit of brilliant feathers whose tiny wings hummed in the air, to an enormous creature with magnificent golden wings casting a great shadow on the ground below.

The melodies of these feathered creatures rose up to Gloriel's ears, and her heart thrilled to the concert of joyful sounds. She watched as the birds settled into the shadowy foliage of the trees and began to assemble their nests and choose their mates, all the while voicing their glorious songs. Dipping low and gliding over the surface of the blue-green seas, white-winged gulls shattered the salt air with their raucous screeching.

Beneath the waves of the emerald oceans, Gloriel saw huge, mysterious forms gliding, now and then breaking the surface, glistening in the sunlight.

Before the astonished eyes of the angels, there sprang up a multitude of inhabitants of sea and air, both great and small.

So God created great sea creatures and every sort of fish and every kind of bird. And God saw that it was good.

Then God blessed them, saying "Let the fish proliferate and fill the oceans. Let the birds increase and fill the earth." This all happened on the fifth Day.

Sea, sky and soil all swarmed with new life as the angels looked on, delighted and amazed. Every bird, each leaf, blossom, and blade of grass was lovingly shaped by the Word of God. Everything in Time, and all through the deep reaches of the universe designed and fashioned by His hand, showed forth His Glory clearly.

A sense of immense portent began filling the atmosphere around the angels. Tears trembled under Gloriel's eyelids as her heart fluttered ecstatically. The awesome Glory of the Presence standing beside them was almost more than she could bear. She was deeply aware of His great tenderness and love.

Endless space, brimming with the Lord's splendor, spread out before her enthralled gaze. She wondered what could possibly be any more marvelous than the amazing things they had already witnessed.

A great quiet fell again upon the Host of Heaven.

God said "Let the earth bring forth every kind of animal—livestock, small animals, and wildlife." And so it was.

Now it seemed to Gloriel and the other angels that they hovered just above the earth's surface, able to see even the minutest details of the miracles unfolding.

Slowly, materializing before their eyes, all forms, sizes and colors of living creatures appeared. Large, small, and all sizes between, rapidly multiplying in numbers now, they leaped, waddled, galloped, scampered, shuffled, stomped, and crept; slithering among the grasses, trees and rocks of the blooming world. Almost with one voice, they trumpeted and bellowed, squealed, chattered, peeped, grumbled, roared and growled, lifting their voices joyfully to the Creator. The earth vibrated with life and energy. Just as swiftly as the cacophony started, it faded away, and creation grew silent.

Gloriel's lips parted, and she felt breathless with anticipation. Michael, Gabriel, Samuel, and Sariel stood mute with awe, staring wide-eyed at the wonders wrought by the hand of God. The wonderful ambiance of peace and silence deepened.

Then God spoke, *"Let us make people in our image, to be like ourselves. They will be masters over all life—the fish in the sea, the birds in the sky, and all the livestock, wild animals and small animals."* Genesis 1:26 NLT

The stillness in Heaven and on earth was profound, as all of creation paused to see the supreme wonder of all taking shape under the hand of the Lord.

Gloriel's breath caught in her throat. Among green grasses below, a puff of air stirred a small eddy in the dust of an exposed patch of rich soil. Nature held its breath. The little piece of earth bared a fruitful brown core to the small whirlwind. The cloud of soil rose up in a pillar, as the sound of rushing wind mounted up to Heaven. Suddenly, blending with the dirt, the familiar particles of the brilliant golden light of Heaven materialized. The cloud of dust and dazzling light dissipated slowly as the breath of God withdrew.

The angels gasped. There, lying inert and silent upon the soil of Earth was the crown of God's creation, Man.

The Lord fashioned a man's body from the rich dust of the earth, breathing into it His breath of life. So the man became a living person.

A deep, resounding cry of celebration spread among the angels. On Earth, nature echoed their joy with the jubilant song of birds, fierce powerful winds, booming seas, and the thunderous roaring of huge beasts.

Gloriel fixed her eyes on the figure of the man asleep in the grass. He was tall, with wavy brown hair and a well-muscled body. His square-jawed handsome face was serene.

"Adam! Awaken!" The same awesome voice that first pierced Gloriel's consciousness rang out again.

As the angels watched in fascination, a gentle zephyr stirred the soft grass surrounding the man. He lay utterly still, no life evident in the strong body. Suddenly, his features flushed, and he gasped as the breath of Life rushed into his lungs. His eyelids fluttered and opened. Bright brown eyes gazed out upon the newborn earth created for his pleasure. Slowly, he sat up, blinking against the light and the brilliant blue sky arched above him. He rose gradually to his feet, and stretched his arms toward Heaven.

*He looks a little dazed,* Gloriel thought; *I wonder if he feels as I did when the Father first awakened me.*

The man gazed around at the beauty surrounding him, delight soon replacing the bewildered expression on his strong features. Awareness of the new life coursing through his veins slowly grew within him, as the Holy Spirit whispered God's love in his ear.

*The Lord called him "Adam". I wonder what that name means.* Gloriel questioned silently. *He is magnificent!*

Truly the most marvelous of all God's creatures, Adam's form was perfect, without blemish. Muscles rippled beneath his smooth skin as sunlight reflected in the rich sable brown of his hair. No clothing concealed the beauty of his lithe body as the soft new air caressed it. His eyes grew wide with awe, and innocence shone from his face as though lit by a light from within. Tentatively, he took a few steps, curling his toes and relishing the soft cushion of grass beneath his bare feet. Gradually increasing his pace, he stretched his long legs, sprinting across the green pasture, shouting with joy.

So it was finished. God's work of creation was complete. The heavens, the earth, and everything in them celebrated. This all happened on the sixth Day.

Elated, Gloriel turned to her companions. Delight was written on every face. Gloriel smiled at all of them, clasping their hands one by one in her own. The bright figure of the Son vanished.

"My children!" Again the great voice rang out. "Behold the earth, the seas, the heavens and all that inhabit them! Look upon the gem of my creation, the most precious of all—behold Man. In only a moment, other people will appear in many different places on the earth. All will be my children, and my greatest delight shall be in them."

"My angels, you are to guide and guard, love, keep and serve these precious beings. For this you were created, and great joy will be yours in this service. Man shall have free will, such as yours, to choose good or evil. For only in freedom can man or angel impart love. I will make myself known to him." God's voice echoed and re-echoed through the immensity of the heavens and the earth below them.

So before the eyes of His angels, the awesome, powerful Word of God brought forth harmony, beauty, Time, and Life without end upon the Earth.

*"On the seventh Day, having finished his task, God rested from all his work. And God blessed the seventh day and declared it holy, because it was the day when he rested from his work of creation. This is the account of the creation of the heavens and the earth.* Genesis 2:2-4 *NLT*

The Lord provided Adam with many different kinds of herbs, fruits and vegetables to eat. He placed him in a lovely garden. He put all the birds of the air, and every creature on the earth under Adam's authority. All the different species of animals were brought to the man one by one, and he gave them all names.

But there was none among all these creatures that was like him. He had no companion to share this wonderful gift of Life from God.

*Adam is lonely,* thought Gloriel. She looked around at the faces which had become so beloved to her. *What would it be like in Heaven without them?* She gazed at them with love, and gratitude to the Father for their companionship.

So the Lord God caused Adam to fall into a deep sleep.

"Gabriel, what's happening to Adam?" Gloriel whispered.

Gabriel's eyes revealed his bewilderment. "I don't know, Gloriel," he replied quietly, "I don't know."

The faces of Michael and Sariel reflected Gabriel's puzzled expression. Samuel stood behind Sariel, black eyes shining with wonder and curiosity.

A murmur arose from the group of angels gathered around the imposing figure of Lucifer a short distance away. Gloriel drew in her breath sharply, surprised at the expression on Lucifer's once bright countenance. His powerful body trembled; his face grew fierce and dark, nostrils flaring. Those angels who were with him before, surrounded him now, gazing in mindless fascination at his stony features. Darkness slowly suffused their faces as Gloriel watched, horrified and spellbound.

Michael placed his hand gently on Gloriel's shoulder. "Look, Gloriel!" he urged her, pointing to the drama unfolding in the beautiful garden below.

The sun blazed out of a pale blue sky, and the air lay warm and soft on the new earth. A small stream glinted silver in the sunlight beside where Adam again lay on the velvety green grass.

A murmur of anticipation swept through the crowd of angels.

Adam's eyes were closed, dark lashes shadowing his cheeks. He was deep in sleep, breathing softly. All of a sudden, before their startled eyes, the flesh over his ribs parted, rolling back like a scroll. The same bright cloud of light which drifted above the throne of God now descended and enveloped Adam in its golden embrace. They could see nothing now of the man, only that shimmering cloud, heaving slowly over the place where he lay.

The angels strained their eyes, trying to pierce the golden cloud, but Adam remained hidden from their view.

Gradually, the shining cloud began ascending, a rising pillar of light stretching back into Heaven. Everyone gasped as the scene below grew clear to their marveling eyes.

Adam lay still sleeping on the soft grass, his chest rising and falling with each breath. The opening in his side closed, leaving no mark of its brief existence.

"Ooooh," Gloriel exclaimed, as her eyes were drawn to a figure standing silent and motionless beside Adam's sleeping form.

"She is so lovely!" Gabriel's warm voice was filled with awe.

The graceful figure stood perfectly still, staring down at the man sleeping at her feet. Long, thick golden blonde hair hung straight and fine about her shoulders and down her back. Sunlight reflected in the gleaming strands covering her full breasts like a golden curtain. She stood tall and stately, her face serene and full of dignity. Silken gold lashes brushed her fair cheeks, and her white skin glowed in the sunlight. Her oval face was fine-featured, and clear, bright eyes, the color of the sea sparkled beneath golden brows.

She smiled, a dimple twinkling beside her soft mouth.

Adam stirred, eyelids flickering and parting. He looked around sleepily, blinking and yawning in the bright light.

His eyes suddenly widened in amazement as they came to rest on the lovely slender figure standing over him. He sprang to his feet, stumbling slightly in his haste. A rosy flush spread over his features and down over his chest as he stared at the vision before him.

*What . . . Who is this exquisite creature?* He wondered silently.

Her smile widened as her gaze traveled over Adam's sleek muscled form and handsome face. The bewildered brown eyes gaping back at her began to clear as realization took place. His hand moved slowly over his ribcage. For a long moment, the two gazed unwavering at one another.

"At last, here is one who is bone of my bones and flesh of my flesh. I will call her 'woman', for she came from her man." Adam's voice rang out in joyful tones.

Tentatively, he reached out and touched the satin skin of the woman's cheek with his fingertip. Looking up and raising his arms to Heaven, he praised God in a trembling voice for this marvelous gift standing by his side.

A cloud of white birds circled the azure sky, catching the sunlight in their wings.

God blessed the couple then, his voice coming to them in solemn instruction.

"Be fruitful, multiply, fill up all the earth and tame it. Govern over the fish of the sea, the birds of the sky, and all living creatures that live on earth." So it was. God saw that all he had made was indeed wonderful.

Heaven rejoiced for Adam, who was no longer lonely.

All the angels exulted in the wonders of God's creation.

Except for one, who along with his companions, grew more and more angry and rebellious. The once dazzling face now darkened with pride, as the patrician features blazed fierce with rage; and the blue eyes sparked fire.

The leading ones among his followers, Mariah, Jezrel, Arioch, Azazel and Abigor stood close by his side, gaping in awe at the wrath twisting his face. Slowly, their own features began reflecting Lucifer's poisonous expression.

"Lucifer!" The voice of the Lord suddenly thundered and reverberated throughout Heaven.

Startled, Gloriel turned toward her companions. Michael's black eyes were gleaming with anger, their sharp gaze fixed now on the rebellious angels.

Lucifer's stunning face, veiled with fury, turned slowly toward the Throne, his eyes now mere slits of blue, glimmering wildly.

*Oh, his face looks like it's carved from stone*, Gloriel thought.

The faces of his companions were now mirror images of the sinister and glowering features of Lucifer.

"Lucifer! Come to me!" The Father's voice again rent the heavens with its powerful tones.

Lucifer's voice rang out, insane with rage. "I will not!! I will NOT serve those weak and puny creatures of yours! My power is great, and I am as you are! This 'man' should bow to me!"

Raising his clenched fists, the furious angel faced the Lord God Almighty in fuming defiance, scowling, his mouth twisted into a grimace.

Mariah stepped forward and stood at Lucifer's left side.

"Neither will I serve this thing you call 'man', which you have made," he muttered angrily.

Azazel stepped forward and stood by Lucifer's right side.

"Nor will I bow before this insignificant creature, 'Adam'! He is but a speck in my eye!" He shouted defiantly, a sneer curling his lips.

Gradually, more and more angels gathered around Lucifer's towering figure as their fellow angels watched in amazement.

Bewildered and stunned, Gloriel noticed that most of these angels were from the choirs of Principalities, Powers, Dominations and Thrones. Lucifer's massive wings were outspread now, glowing in the golden light.

Gloriel's jaw dropped in disbelief as the group surrounding Lucifer grew in number before the shocked eyes of the rest of the Heavenly Host.

Milling angrily, the mutinous angels took up Lucifer's daunting stance. Their murmuring voices grew louder as defiance swept over the muttering, cursing angels gathered around the seditious Archangel.

"Lucifer! Stand forth!!" The booming tones filled the heavens.

Gloriel's heart grew faint within her breast. *How can Lucifer stand in defiance of the Lord God who created him with such love?* She questioned silently.

All the other insurgent angels, surrounding Lucifer in great numbers now, raised their arms with the same insolent gestures.

*There must be at least a third of our number standing with Lucifer now.* Gloriel sensed a strange melancholy overtaking her spirit, and she felt sick at heart. *How can this be? Lucifer, Bearer of Light, beloved by God, rising up in raging rebellion against his Creator . . . Why is this happening?*

She turned to Gabriel, whose face reflected her own emotions. She grasped his arm tightly, whispering, "Gabriel, what are we to do? What's happening to Lucifer and the others?" She felt the scalding sting of tears beneath her eyelids.

"Lucifer! Surrender now to the Lord our God, Creator of Heaven and Earth!" Suddenly, Michael's strong voice boomed out, steely with anger. His dark eyes glittered large in a face pale with wrath. His majestic wings unfolded and spread out in powerful splendor around him. Muscles rippled beneath his dark skin as he assumed a threatening stance. Neck bulging with cords of tension, he stared fiercely at Lucifer.

Angels close by involuntarily shrank back from his frightening expression.

They all gasped in astonishment as a large sword materialized suddenly in Michael's hand. It picked up the golden light of Heaven, as if fire burned within its steel.

In an instant, his raiment changed before their startled eyes. The gray tunic was replaced by one of glistening white. A splendid armor covered his broad chest, gleaming white, and glowing with a light of its own.

"Lucifer, you must repent before it is too late! Do not turn your back on our God!" Michael bellowed, his voice resounding throughout Heaven.

Lucifer's eyes were now mere glittering slits of blue ice between the yellow lashes. Standing tall in silent defiance, he turned an ominous stare upon Michael. Frenzy was written over the once handsome features, very dark now, contorted with a strange look which Gloriel could not interpret.

Suddenly, he threw his head back and raised his powerful arms, fists clenched tightly. Roaring in speechless fury, he shook his fists at Michael.

He strode toward the Throne as his voice rang out in harsh and trembling tones, "I will never bow down before your puny Man! It is he who should kneel before me! My power will rule over him! I come against You now!" he bellowed.

Gloriel stared, incredulous, as all light drained from Lucifer's form and countenance. She shrank back in horror as the "Bearer of Light" became enshrouded, buried in darkness. The shining white robe faded away. In its place appeared one of deepest black, adding to his ominous look.

The dark form turned again toward Michael, advancing menacingly, roaring like a lion.

The gleaming sword seemed to spring to life in Michael's hand. Flashing in the golden light, its blade slashed the air between the two powerful beings. The muscles of his body swelled and arched as Michael's great wings lifted him up, and his voice rang out throughout Heaven.

"LUCIFER, BE GONE!! You and your minions are cast out from Heaven and the presence of the Lord God! You have chosen wickedness, and are eternally separated from all that is good! You shall no longer be called Lucifer, Bearer of Light. From henceforth you will bear the name SATAN, Angel of Darkness, the Enemy, the Evil One, the Adversary! Flee now to those outer expanses of darkness called Hell!"

Michael, noble ruling Prince of the Archangels and the Seraphim, Chief of the choir of Virtues, angel of mercy and Prince of the Presence, stood forth against Satan in all God's blinding grandeur.

Gloriel grew conscious of a fine trembling throughout her body. How could Lucifer—no, she must not call him that—how could Satan reject their Father's love and choose the darkness of pride and defiance? She looked around at her companions, whose faces were frozen in shock.

Gabriel and Raphael quickly took their places on both sides of Michael, other angels gathering behind them.

Satan's companions, contemptuous and dark-featured, advanced to stand shoulder to shoulder behind him.

The glistening sword flashed, whistling in a blinding arc, and once again slicing through the air, singing as if it had discovered a voice of its own.

Suddenly, a blinding flash of lightning flew from its tip, cutting through the golden surface where they stood. It cut like a great scythe through the firmament on which Satan and his angels gathered.

A huge black chasm appeared in place of the golden surface. Another bolt of lightning flashed with an explosion of fire and light.

Gloriel gasped, her blood running cold, as Satan and his followers fell headlong, shrieking, into the great valley of darkness.

As quickly as it had appeared, the cavernous wound in the heavenly firmament closed.

A profound and stunned silence shrouded the remaining Host of Heaven, though Gloriel's heart thundered in her ears.

*How could this have happened?* She wondered dazedly.

She felt numb. This great and powerful being, foremost in knowledge and beauty among God's angels, he with the stunning brilliance and matchless intelligence, cast out of Heaven forever, in but a moment.

Her heart ached, thinking of how this wonderful angel was turned by his pride into a rebellious and evil creature. Stripped of light and goodness, he had fallen screaming, along with his followers, out of God's holy presence into utter blackness.

*Yes, he had great knowledge and power, but what became of the love and charity in him?* She wondered.

She bowed her head and wept for the Lucifer who had been, and for all those angels who fell with him, choosing the desolation of darkness instead of God's marvelous light.

*Are they regretting already this terrible choice?* Deep in her being, Gloriel knew that there would be no more choices for these lost angels, forever banished without hope, without joy or peace. They were now bound throughout time without end by their foolish, disastrous choice. *There will be no turning back, ever.*

She thought grimly of the others who had fallen. Amy, an apparently stalwart member of the order of Powers, always seemed to be content with quietly serving the Lord. Asmodeus of the mighty Seraphim, his face often appeared angry and disgruntled with his companions, Gloriel recalled now. Azazel, a strong protector, or so he had seemed; gone, all gone,—never to return.

*What will they do without the Lord?* Gloriel felt the hot burn of tears coursing down her face, as a long shudder flowed through her body.

She glanced around at those angels she loved, gathered close by. Michael's eyes were like dark stars in his pale face. He threw down the gleaming sword, as if it had suddenly grown red hot to his touch. Sariel looked stunned. Her round cheeks seemed carved from alabaster, the blue-green eyes enormous in her childish face. Gabriel's usually kind mouth was pressed so tightly together it was a thin, sharp line. His eyes gleamed with unshed tears. Samuel's ordinarily merry countenance looked sorrowful and pained.

The music in Heaven ceased. The thick silence was broken by the voice of the Lord, no longer thundering, but gentle and heavy with sorrow.

"My children; do not despair." His tone was warm and comforting. "Lucifer and his companions have chosen the way of pride, which leads only to eternal destruction. You must not grieve. They now begin their struggle against everything that is holy and good. They will seek to deceive, corrupt and destroy my human children. Deliberately and willfully, they have chosen their destiny. There will be neither light, nor love, joy nor peace for them, ever again. The "Bearer of Light" has become the "Prince of Darkness," Satan, the Great Deceiver, shall perish at the end of Time." He spoke quietly and reassuringly.

The gentle voice continued, a little louder now. "Lift up your hearts! Your work will soon begin, and you shall see my plan come to fulfillment through the ages. Now watch, as the story unfolds before your eyes . . ."

Suddenly, the remaining members of the Heavenly Host, Angels and Archangels, Cherubim and Seraphim, thronged the golden atmosphere as they rose up and proclaimed in chorus, "Alleluia! All praise and honor and glory are yours!"

And so God, wishing to make Himself known to mankind, began writing Earth's long story . . .

# Chapter One

*They are so happy!* Gloriel reflected as she watched Adam and his lovely helpmate strolling hand in hand through their lush Garden. As they passed through the shadow of a date-bearing tree, Adam reached up to pluck a bunch of the luscious sweet fruit. Smiling, he held a sugary morsel to the soft mouth of his companion. His face shone as he gazed at the woman with the sparkling green eyes almost on a level with his own. He adored her, this wondrous creature whom God had given him. Her fine features glowed as she reached up and stroked Adam's square jaw. She gently brushed aside the brown hair curling moistly over his forehead, bestowing her dimpled smile on him.

Gloriel smiled, as they wandered through the beautiful countryside of the Garden east of Eden, enjoying their close relationship with God. She knew that God the Father spoke with them often, usually in the cool of the evening, when the soft air was perfumed, and the shadows grew long. She did not know what he said to them, but she could see their faces radiate in the twilight. *Does He talk to them about His plans for them and the future of the Earth?* She wondered to herself.

As time passed on the verdant, beautiful earth below, Gloriel continued growing in knowledge, wisdom and grace. Many of her angel companions were already pursuing their ministries to the growing population. Still, she knew no more about her own ministry than when she first awoke to the Father's call.

Two beautiful angels, Araziel and Damiel, began their watch over the man and his wife. *When will I be called?* Gloriel wondered, constantly. Still, she rejoiced for those angels already ministering to their charges.

Sometimes her thoughts would wander to Lucifer, now called "Satan." Since their lightning fall from Heaven, she had not seen him or his companions. Her face clouded, and she shuddered as the awful scene rose up in her memory. *Where are they now? Are they roaming the earth below?* She speculated. Quickly she turned her thoughts to the wonderful companionship and love that she shared with her fellow angels here in their heavenly home.

Daily, Gloriel basked in the golden glow of God's love, sitting close beside the glistening Throne, listening to His teaching. He gifted the small angel with great wisdom and insight. Her heart expanded with unbounded joy as the finger of God touched her mind. His presence consumed her being and ignited a passionate life within her. She grew increasingly eager to begin the mysterious ministry the Lord was preparing for her.

Gloriel loved the great City of God, with its golden streets and magnificent gates of pearl. The walls, with their sparkling jeweled bases of jasper, sapphire, agate, emerald, onyx, carnelian, beryl, topaz, and amethyst, glistened softly in the distance. The Glory of God lit up the city, and no other light was needed. Flowing down the center of the main street, a glittering crystal-clear river shimmered in the pristine light. Enormous trees rose up through the golden mist along its banks. Gloriel often reclined beneath them, stretching out on the green grass and dreaming of "the Day", as she came to regard it, when the Lord would divulge the secret of her ministry.

Beds of fragrant flowers of every imaginable color and hue spread their heady fragrances throughout the green grass edging the golden streets. Each huge building in the Holy City was a splendid model of architecture. Towering pillars of gold, with jeweled ceilings reflecting every color imaginable ornamented many of the buildings. Though each was unique in design, when Gloriel looked at them as a whole, the mansions seemed to blend together, delighting her eyes with their grandeur. *The beauty of the earth is so great, but it can't compare to the glories of Heaven,* she marveled. She loved to stare into the awesome sea of glass, where golden particles glistened and twinkled in incessant motion. Walking over the glittering surface filled her with reverence for its Maker. Sometimes her whole body trembled with adoration at the glory of God encircling her.

The Heavenly Host lived in perfect harmony, revealing and demonstrating God's love to one another. No rivalry or selfishness, jealousy or hatred marred the relationships among the angels. Each loved the others with a pure and holy love.

Gloriel delighted in discovering more and more of God's great Plan. She matured steadily in wisdom, insight and knowledge, as she waited to enter into service at the appointed time.

Sometimes, Gloriel and her companions allowed their bodily forms to fade away, so that they might worship the Lord as pure spirits. During these times, their ecstasy heightened, and indescribable rapture seized them. Bliss and shining solitude with the Lord made her spirit soar to unimagined heights, unbound and unshackled by flesh.

"Oh, dear Lord! When will I begin my service?" she cried out one day to God, as she sat at the foot of the great Throne.

"My child, you must learn patience. You have been created for a very special ministry, such as none of your companions have known, or ever shall know," the Holy Spirit answered gently.

His voice was soft and melodious. Gloriel felt mystified by His words, but His reassurance assuaged her yearning, and she was content for a time.

#

Below, the earth matured in beauty as God's creatures multiplied. Adam and his wife worshipped their God, continually thrilled by His companionship. Their love for each other and all of creation grew steadily with the passing of days filled with delight and joy.

Magnificent trees grew everywhere in the garden, laden with many varieties of fruit. Globes of sweetness hung low on their heavy boughs, where Adam and his wife could reach them easily.

In the very center of their Garden, the Lord placed two majestic, towering trees, which differed from all the rest. One, God called the Tree of Life. Its branches reached toward Heaven, as if trying to enfold the Lord in its deep green, leafy embrace. Its leaves stirred and rustled constantly, even when no breeze disturbed its fellow trees. Standing tall and strong, it was laden with a golden fruit unlike any other in the Garden.

Beside it grew another tree, also extraordinary in appearance. Massive, shorter than the Tree of Life, broad and sturdy-limbed, its thick, glossy leaves gleamed in the sunlight. The fruit of this tree was sparse. Red satiny spheres tempting to the eye, shone amid the leaves here and there. This tree, God called the Tree of Knowledge of Good and Evil. Curious, Gloriel was not sure what that meant, but she did not question Him.

A wide river swirled and twisted its clear waters through the fertile Garden, providing drink for trees and grass, blossoms and animals. The woman loved to cup the cool silver water in her hands and drink deeply of its sweetness.

Outside the Garden, the river divided into four branches. God called these rivers Pishon, Gihon, Tigris and Euphrates. The glitter of gold lay beneath Pishon's bright waters.

The Lord instructed the man to take care of the lush Garden. Adam loved their beautiful home, and cared for it diligently, spending many hours cultivating its fruits and vegetables in the warm sun. His body grew tanned and hard muscled. The heady fragrances of ripening harvest and rich soil delighted him.

One day, God told Adam, "You may eat as much as you want of all the fruit in the Garden. But you must not eat of the Tree of Knowledge of Good and Evil. If you disobey me, and eat this fruit, you will surely die."

*What does it mean to "die"?* Adam wondered silently. But he did not question the Lord.

Adam's angel, Araziel, whispered quietly in his ear, "It means that you will lose your life, your very being, and walk no more in this glorious Garden with your wife, if you eat the forbidden fruit."

Adam shook his head, chastened and puzzled.

Araziel loved walking in the Garden, always watching Adam closely, and revealing God's love to him. He didn't disclose his human form, so Adam was not aware of Araziel's presence. His angel spoke to Adam's spirit, inaudibly, just as his fellow guardian angel Damiel did with the woman.

Adam called his wife to his side, and told her what the Lord God had said.

"We have so many delicious fruits to eat, Adam," she replied, smiling sweetly at him. "We don't need that fruit."

Adam drew his wife close in the circle of his arms. "Of course we don't," he murmured in her hair, nuzzling her ear. "Anyway, you are the sweetest fruit of all."

The perfume of flowers and fertile earth rose around them like incense. The woman basked in the glow of her husband's love and admiration, leaning her head back to gaze into his warm brown eyes. Their angels watched, smiling at one another.

Adam and his wife loved each other deeply, and adored the Lord their God. They were happy and contented, and Peace and Joy lived in the beautiful Garden of Eden.

But outside the Garden, peering through the branches of an olive tree, glittering hate-filled eyes watched the two people closely. The face grew dark and twisted with rage. Two other creatures crouched beside the figure, breathing heavily and muttering deep in their throats. Azazel and Mariah, once beloved servants of the Lord, turned their contorted features to gaze on their new "god," Satan.

In the beginning, these fallen angels were beautiful, radiant creatures of light. Now they were only ugly caricatures of their former selves, demons lurking in the shadows. Although still recognizable, evil had altered their countenances with a vicious hand. Darkness and malevolence lurked in eyes that once looked on the beauties of Heaven, and no spark of light survived.

The woman loved to walk through the silken grasses of the Garden, gathering armfuls of fragrant blossoms. She would place them around the soft grass bed where she and her husband slept at night. Often, while Adam slept, she lay curled in the circle of his arms, gazing at the luminous stars in the velvet black of the night. She could smell the warm fragrance of the Garden under dew, and her heart rejoiced in contentment.

In the mornings, when the sun rose, it spread its golden splendor, enveloping the Garden in a radiant mist. Adam tended the Garden, his heart enraptured with its beauty.

Animals joined the woman strolling through the meadow grass, as it rippled in a gentle breeze. She especially loved the great tawny lion, with a magnificent black mane framing his gentle face and soft golden eyes. He paced beside her, rubbing against her legs, and purring loudly deep in his throat. She stroked him gently, gathering the massive head in her arms and whispering softly in his downy ear.

She laughed and clapped her hands as she watched the little woolly white lambs, gamboling together in the green pasture. The tiny creatures often frisked around her and the great golden beast at her side. She laughed delightedly when the lion's huge rough tongue reached out to lick a small curly head, knocking the lamb off its feet with affection.

*What a glorious place this world is,* the woman thought as she lay down on the velvet carpet of green at her feet. She stretched out, folding her arms behind her head, her movements fluid and graceful. The warm sun shone its way through leafy overhanging branches as they swayed in a soft, sweet wind, against the blue-green sky.

Thoughts of Adam filled her mind as the woman watched soft white tufts of clouds floating lazily overhead. *I love him so much!* She thought, smiling to herself. His tall, strong body was a delight to her eyes, and just the sound of his voice could make her heart melt. Closing her eyes, as the sun caressed her white flesh to a rosy blush, she slept. Her angel, Damiel, looked down on her, a bright smile lighting her face.

The great honey-colored lion stretched out beside her, nuzzling his soft nose into the fine satin of her hair. Suddenly, his round ears twitched. He raised his head and gazed toward the thick trees surrounding the pasture. The soft purr in his throat swelled into a low, deep growl. Startled, the woman woke abruptly. She put her hand on the lion's head, wondering at the ominous sound coming from her companion. She strained her eyes to see the object of his stare.

Sunlight reflected on the softly fluttering leaves of the trees in the Garden. The clarity of the air made details snap into sharp focus as her eyes searched the trees. A deer faded in and out of the shadow pools. The lion was quiet now, though he continued to fix his eyes on the trees. She buried her face in the long soft fur of his mane. Deep among the trees, glittering eyes watched and waited.

# Chapter Two

Now the serpent was a very beautiful creature that lived in the Garden. His skin was soft and satiny, glowing with rich, deep colors. He stood tall and handsome among others in the Garden. He loved the cool shade of the trees, and often sat among their branches where he could observe all the other animals and the two human beings as they moved about the Garden.

One day, the serpent was watching Adam and his wife as they strolled hand in hand among the flowers. A perfumed breeze blew softly, caressing his skin. He yawned, stretching his beautiful body. Suddenly, he felt a strange trembling in his flesh. His tongue grew dry, and rose to stick to the roof of his mouth. He shook his head, bewildered. Breast heaving, he became aware of his blood slowing to an icy trickle in his veins. A weird blackness crept bit by bit through his body, invading his heart. The darkness grew, expanding until he was no longer aware of who he was, or his surroundings.

Slowly, Satan took over the serpent's body, assuming his very being. Sadly, Araziel and Damiel, guarding Adam and his helpmate, failed to notice the transformation in the serpent.

Adam stopped to kiss his wife's soft lips, then sauntered away through the garden, whistling cheerfully. He glanced back at the woman. Her pale hair caught the light of the sun in glints of gold. An enormous masculine tenderness touched Adam's heart. *Her hair is so beautiful in the sunshine,* he reflected dreamily. Some distance away, he knelt by the river, raised the cool water to his mouth in cupped hands and drank, savoring its refreshing taste. Gratitude to the Lord for all the beauty surrounding him, for the wonder of life, and most of all for the lovely helpmate He had given him, filled his heart.

The woman's green eyes followed Adam until he disappeared through the trees, the lilt of his whistle fading away in the warm air. Tilting back her head, she closed her eyes and listened to the multitude sounds of nature. The bleat of lambs came from the nearby flock, and doves murmured among the trees. Sweet scents filled the air everywhere. A solitary eagle soared effortlessly overhead, his head switching from side to side, wing-tips stretching wide into the warm lifting thermals.

Extending her arms toward Heaven, she lifted her voice in praise.

"Father, the earth and sky are full of your glory!" she sang, exulting in the wonders all around her.

Suddenly, a soft, beguiling voice interrupted her prayer.

"Is it true?"

Startled, the woman dropped her arms to her sides. She turned her head quickly, searching the trees and bushes for the source of the velvet tones. Damiel stood close by, unseen. *Oh! It's the serpent. How strange*, she frowned; *I've never heard him speak before.*

Inching closer to the handsome creature who sat on a low branch nearby, she asked, "Is what true?"

"Did God really say you must not eat any of the fruit in the Garden?" He questioned; his voice honeyed and seductive.

Uneasy, Damiel moved closer to the woman, alerted by the serpent's query.

A broad smile dimpled the woman's cheeks. "Of course we may eat it!" She laughed gaily at his ignorance. "All except for the tree at the center of the Garden, the one right over there." She pointed to the sturdy Tree of Knowledge. Its leaves gleamed in the soft sunshine. "We must not eat its fruit. God said that if we eat it, we will die. He assured us we may eat the fruit of all the other trees in the garden though," she said, a little defensively.

The serpent clicked his tongue, a look of disdain on his striking face. "Really! You really believe that? How foolish you are! You will not die!" he scoffed. "Actually, God knows that if you eat that fruit, your eyes will be opened," he sneered.

Unseen, Damiel took a stance between the woman and the serpent. She whispered into her charge's mind, desperately; "Do not listen to his words! He is evil!"

The woman shrugged one shoulder and closed her eyes briefly.

The serpent slid gracefully off the branch, dropping lightly to the grass below. Walking over to the Tree of Knowledge, he gazed upward into the thick foliage. He reached up and plucked one of the glossy red fruits, pushing aside the dark leaves. He brought it to the woman, and dropped it at her feet.

She shrank back from the fruit as it rolled toward her. Gazing at its succulence gleaming red in the dappled sunlight on the grass, she whispered "What do you mean, our eyes will be opened? My eyes are open!"

She turned her green gaze from the fruit to the serpent. Her eyes were wide open, the pupils huge and dilated. He nudged the fruit toward her with one foot. Damiel's voice in the back of her mind grew more urgent. *"Don't touch it! God has forbidden it!"*

The serpent's tones were honeyed and silken to her ear. "The eyes of your soul will be opened wide, and you will become just like God, knowing both good and evil. That's why He said you must not eat the fruit. He doesn't want you to be like Him," the beguiling voice continued.

Damiel was frantic now, and in desperation willed herself to take on her bodily form. Nothing happened. *Lord God, what's wrong? Help me! I must stop her from eating!* Fear for the woman surged through Damiel's heart on a riptide.

*Oh! It looks so delicious and fresh and juicy, and I will be so wise!* The woman thought.

Damiel was pleading now, *"No! No! You must not listen to him!"*

Shutting out the fading voice inside her, the woman succumbed to the serpent's guile. She bent over slowly, picked up the fruit, and raised it to her lips. *Oh, it smells so sweet . . . maybe just a small bite. Probably, God will not even notice.* Biting into the juicy flesh of the fruit, its sweetness running out the corners of her mouth, she reached greedily for her legacy before the appointed time.

*Lord God, have mercy!* Damiel cried, helpless and distressed.

Swallowing the juicy morsel, the woman glanced up and saw Adam approaching. Invisible to their eyes, Azariel walked closely beside him. A sense of foreboding rose up inside the woman's breast. Looking around, hoping for the serpent's support, she realized that he had disappeared.

"What are you doing!?" Adam exclaimed, horrified. "God told us we would die if we ate that fruit!" He stared at his mate incredulously.

"B-but the serpent told me I would not die! See, I'm not dead, Adam! And the fruit is so delicious!" she cried, holding the sweet flesh up to him.

Azariel pleaded, *"Adam, you must not eat!"* But his words went unheard.

Hesitating, Adam looked into his wife's smiling face. *Well, nothing has happened to her,* he reasoned to himself, *perhaps the serpent is right.* Surrendering to the urging of his wife, and the sweet alluring fragrance of the fruit, Adam ate.

As they looked down upon the tragic scene playing out below, the hearts of Gloriel and her companions grew heavy with sorrow. How could this be, that Adam and his wife, the very crown of God's creation, could fall into disobedience, mistrusting and rebelling against the Lord? *Why didn't they listen to their angels?* Gloriel wondered. Sorrowfully, she realized that the man and his wife could no longer be heirs and participants in the life of God. She wept, then, a great wail for Adam and his wife building up inside. She took a deep breath and pushed it down. *What will become of them now? Will they become children of the Evil One?*

Azariel and Damiel suddenly appeared in the midst of the Heavenly Host. Her face visibly darkened with pain, Damiel cried out passionately "Adam and his wife were living happily, in harmony with You, Lord, and with creation. Now they have given it all up for a bite of fruit! I couldn't reach the woman. She would not hear!"

Azariel's bright head bowed in sorrow, and grief etched his fine features. "Adam would not hear me, either. Oh, Father! We have failed in our mission! We were not able to protect Adam and the woman!"

On the Earth below, as Adam swallowed the tasty bite, he looked questioningly at his wife. She returned his gaze, her eyes wide and stricken. A foreign feeling swept over both of them, an alien emotion unknown before that moment. Suddenly overwhelmed with a sensation of profound loss and sorrow, Adam stared at his wife's nakedness. His face and chest grew hot, as if the sun had struck them. He became overcome with shame.

The woman's bright green eyes brimmed with tears as she returned Adam's stare. Gleaming drops began rolling down her cheeks, and she hid her face in her hands.

The man and his wife, filled with embarrassment at their nakedness, hurriedly plucked large leaves from a nearby fig tree. Trembling, they twisted them together around their hips, and the woman covered her pale breasts with her yellow hair. A flaming fire of guilt suffused their faces with scarlet as they tried to cover themselves.

"Adam!" The woman's voice was tremulous. "We must hide before the Lord sees what we have done!" Her lovely face blanched chalky with fear.

A great stillness enveloped the Garden. Birdsong ceased, and no animal stirred. Adam seized the woman's hand, turned and ran, strong legs pumping in panic. Dragging his terrified wife behind him, he dove into the thick bushes along the path. Fear dug its taloned fingers into his gut as his heart filled with an unfamiliar chill.

*What will happen to us now?* He wondered silently. *We have disobeyed the Lord.* He felt the hot burn of tears fill his shadowed eyes. *What is this awful feeling?* Until now, the couple had only known happiness and peace, constantly rejoicing in the beauty of the world God had made for them.

His wife stood staring at him as her pale face flushed again. Adam returned her gaze, heat bulging in his breast. Escalating feelings of outrage and fury rose up in his heart.

"It's all your fault!" Fury shone in his eyes like a smoldering fire "You enticed me to eat the fruit!"

The flush drained from the woman's face, and she pushed back her disheveled gold hair with shaking fingers. She felt small, alone, and utterly abandoned. "It-it was the s-serpent! H-he beguiled m-me!" she stammered, eyes darting about nervously.

"ADAM!!" The powerful voice of the Lord thundered, echoing throughout the silence of the Garden. "Adam! Where are you?"

Petrified, Adam looked askance toward his shivering wife as she covered her ears at the sound of the Lord's voice. "Adam! Come into the open!" The leaves on the sheltering bushes around them stirred as though a breeze swept through them.

"I-I'm here, Lord." Adam answered, his voice cracking. Slowly, rigid with terror, Adam and the woman stepped out of their hiding place. They stood whimpering fearfully in the presence of the Lord. "I h-heard your voice in the Garden, Lord, a-and I was afraid . . ."

"Why were you afraid, Adam?" The Lord's voice was subdued now.

"Because I was naked, so I hid." Adam clutched the scant covering of leaves around his loins, bowing his head in shame.

"Who told you that you were naked, Adam?" The Lord asked sternly. "Did you eat the fruit of the forbidden Tree?"

"I-it was the w-woman . . . she gave me some of the fruit from the tree, and I ate it."

The voice of the Lord grew weighty with sorrow as he questioned the woman. "What have you done?"

A chill worked its way up the woman's spine. "B-but Lord, it wasn't my fault; it was the s-serpent. He-he tempted me. He t-told me I wouldn't die if I ate the fruit. It looked so delicious, Lord! So I ate it," she whispered. A goiter of fear filled her throat.

Watching the drama unfolding below, Gloriel, Azariel, Damiel and the others stood close together, stricken with sorrow. Adam and his wife had disobeyed the Lord. The handsome serpent in his brightly colored coat had deceived them.

Gloriel saw the wily creature standing in the shadows behind the disgraced man and woman. The Lord summoned him.

*"So the Lord God said to the serpent, 'Because you have done this, you will be punished. You are singled out from all the domestic and wild animals of the whole earth to be cursed. You will grovel in the dirt as long as you live, crawling along on your belly. From now on, you and the woman will be enemies, and your offspring and her offspring will be enemies. He will crush your head, and you will strike his heel."* Genesis 3:14-15

The angels looked on in amazement as the tall, striking figure of the serpent seemed to melt, the bright colors merging and slowly dissolving to the ground in an ugly, muddy conglomerate. His features lost their clarity and beauty. For a moment, the once powerful and cunning creature was formless, lying inert and unmoving on the green grass of Eden.

Adam and his wife exchanged quick looks. The woman pressed the back of one hand to her lips to still their trembling.

Then, before their incredulous eyes, the serpent's body began to re-form. Twisting and sinuous, a limbless, scaly, elongated body lay at the feet of the two people. Its ugly flat head appeared to be one with the body, the eyes narrow and lidless. A forked black tongue flicked in and out of the serpent's mouth, which suddenly opened wide to reveal long wicked-looking fangs. A hissing sound came from the gaping maw.

Startled, the couple sprang back away from the ugly creature. Twisting and slithering, the serpent moved away through the grass, disappearing into the lush undergrowth of the Garden.

Stunned, the two people stared wordlessly at one another. The woman fell shuddering to her knees as a sudden blast of icy wind flashing and clattering through the trees, brushed her pale skin with frigid fingers. A mammoth thunder cloud appeared in the dreary sky overhead, spreading rapidly from horizon to horizon. A chill rain began falling, as thunder echoed and re-echoed through the electric atmosphere.

Adam stood gazing with awe at the sudden turbulence surrounding and permeating their once peaceful and sunlit Garden. His heart leapt in his chest, and his body shook like the leaves in the storm-tossed trees.

The woman bowed her head low on her breast as the voice of the Lord rang out again.

"You will bear children with deep pain and suffering. You may want to control your husband, but he will be your master."

To Adam He said, "Because you listened to your wife and ate the fruit I told you not to eat, I have placed a curse on the ground. You will struggle to scrape a living from it. It will grow thorns and thistles; but you may eat of its grains. Every day, you will sweat to produce food, as long as you live. Then you will return to the ground from which you came. For I made you from dust, and to dust you will return."

Weeping bitterly, the man and his wife prostrated themselves before the Lord.

The angels looked on the dark scene below, and Heaven wept with the man and woman. This is how Death entered the world.

Then the Lord fashioned clothing from animal skins for Adam and his wife. Shame-faced, they covered their trembling bodies with the skins.

Sinking to the ground, the two people lay on the wet grass for a long time, sobbing for their lost innocence. The voice of the Lord was silent now, and they were alone with their sorrow.

Finally, Adam rose to his knees and looked around. The world around them looked so different! The sky above them was boiling with dark clouds, shifting and glowering on the sad earth below. The gray rain drifted against the trees.

Suddenly, he felt a sharp pain in one of his knees. Jumping up, he looked down at the grass where he had knelt. A small black insect crawled through the blades of grass at his feet. Rubbing his knee, Adam noticed a red welt rising up on his skin. It burned and itched. *Did that small creature cause this strange and very unpleasant feeling?* Adam wondered, silently.

The rain was still falling, but no longer pelting them with icy fingers. Adam reached down and grasped his wife's cold hand, helping her up from the wet ground. As he gazed at her ravaged face, melted and ruined with grief, his love for her arose again in his heart.

*The Lord said that she would bear children. I must give her a name,* he thought. *She is the first of all women . . . so I shall call her "Eve," the mother of all living.*

Cupping her cold face in his hands, he brushed aside the clinging wet wisps of golden hair.

"Eve, my wife, we have sinned in the sight of the Lord God. I don't know what will become of us now."

They stood shaking in each other's arms, in the middle of the Garden. Strange bushes and trees surrounded them, bushes with thistles among their branches, instead of fruit. Trees with long and deadly sharp thorns spiking out from between the leaves seemed to reach out and grab at the tender flesh of the disgraced man and woman.

Nearby, the Tree of Life still stood. *Even it looks different,* Adam thought. Leaves no longer stirred. Its branches hung low, drooping toward the ground beneath.

A short distance away, the Tree of Knowledge even now rose broad and massive, but its gleaming red fruit had disappeared.

Above the weeping earth, the Lord God called the Heavenly Host to gather before the Throne. The great throng of angels stood in the presence of the Most High, some of them still mourning for Adam and Eve.

"My Angels, weep no more now. Adam and Eve have forfeited their inheritance. But do not grieve for them. I will have mercy and compassion on their descendants. They shall be rescued from death, and become my children once again. The man and woman have become as we are, knowing both good and evil; so we must banish them from the Garden east of Eden, lest they eat the fruit of the Tree of Life, and live forever."

The voice of the Lord grew stern. "Raphael, come forth!"

The multitude of angels parted slowly. Gloriel watched the glossy black curls of the Archangel Raphael moving through the angels gathered around the Throne. He knelt before the Lord, his indigo blue eyes gleaming in the dark skin of his oval face.

"Raphael, I charge you with the task of banishing Adam and Eve from the Garden of Eden. Arise!" the Lord said.

Raphael rose to his feet. He wore a short, dark blue tunic, and a golden belt circled his waist. The beautiful massive pearl white wings of the Cherubim framed his body and his thick shoulder length black curls.

Those angels close at hand gasped and moved back as a mighty sword suddenly appeared in Raphael's hand. Orange, yellow and red flames danced along its gleaming gold blade, engulfing it. The light from the flames reflected in Raphael's eyes and the faces of those angels surrounding him. The multi-colored jewels of the great Throne flashed in the red glow.

"You must guard the path to the Tree of Life, Raphael, and close the gates of the Garden to the people of Earth forever." The Lord spoke softly as he charged the stalwart angel with this sorrowful task. "Go now."

Off to one side of the Throne, Gloriel noticed the figures of Damiel and Azariel, faces drawn with sorrow. The Lord called them to stand before the Throne. Their heads bowing low, the two angels drew closer. God spoke to them in hushed tones, and Gloriel could not hear his words. As the Lord talked with Damiel and Azariel, their heads lifted, and the marks of grief withdrew from their features.

Raphael was gone, and the red glow faded from the golden mist.

Meanwhile, Adam and Eve stood bewildered in the midst of the Garden, waiting whatever was to happen to them next. The gray rain ceased, but thunder still crashed from the dark clouds above, lightning flashing over the nearby hills.

Eve clung to her husband in terror as a deep roar resounded through the trees, and a dark form glided through the bushes. Suddenly, the massive head of the golden lion appeared among the leaves.

"Oh! It's the lion!" Eve exclaimed, delighted. She held out her arms to the great beast, her long-time companion and friend. The golden eyes gleamed from beneath the thick mane. It was no gentle gaze, however. Eve gasped and shrank back as the huge jaws opened and bared long, sharp white fangs. A low growl started deep in the beast's throat. His huge head tilted to one side as a great roar burst forth, echoing throughout the Garden. Eve screamed in terror and buried her face in Adam's neck.

"Eve, he's gone." Adam whispered in her hair.

Raising her head, she searched the bushes with a stricken gaze. "Adam, what has happened to him?" she cried out, her eyes blazing silver with grief.

A staggering bolt of lightning split the gray atmosphere, illumining the sky, followed by a tremendous crash of thunder. Standing in a bright circle of light a short distance away, a mighty angel appeared, flaming sword in hand. His great wings unfurled, glowing even in the gray air.

Adam and Eve fell to their knees in fright. Fearfully, Eve buried her face in her hands, not daring to look at the angel.

"I am Raphael, servant of the Lord!" The angel's clear voice rang in their ears. "Get up! The Most High has sent me."

The couple arose, breathless and shaking with fright.

Peering between her fingers, Eve stared at the wondrous figure before them. His grave features reflected the red-orange flames of the golden sword in his hand. Through a shining blur of tears, Adam gazed transfixed at Raphael.

The angel's voice, pure and sure and strong, continued. "You are banished now from the Garden that the Lord God gave you. Because you have disobeyed him and eaten of the forbidden fruit, you must go out into the outside world, and never return. Go now!"

The great wings spread until they seemed to fill the Garden. Raphael raised the flaming sword aloft and dark clouds above caught the dancing light, reflecting with an angry red glow.

The thundering ceased as absolute silence crept over the Garden. No signs of life moved among the vegetation. No birdsong or bleating of sheep cleft the air. For a moment, Time stood still. Adam and Eve stood transfixed.

Raphael's clear voice rang out once more. "Go now!" he repeated.

The terrified pair looked at one another in bewilderment. Eve's pale flesh seemed translucent, like mother-of-pearl. Adam's bronzed skin glowed in the light from Raphael's flaming sword. His eyes held a bleak look, confused and dark. Clinging to one another, the couple turned and fled the beautiful Garden, stumbling and staggering blindly in their grief and terror.

The rumble of thunder began again, as the black clouds burst open with torrents of icy rain, pelting the fleeing man and woman. Glancing back as the heavens resounded and echoed the wild beating of their hearts, they saw the brilliant form of Raphael in the distance, flaming sword still held high overhead.

Adam and Eve, no longer beneficiaries of the Kingdom of God, were reduced to a life of labor, poverty and exile. So closed the door to the beautiful Garden of Eden, forever.

# Chapter Three

Gloriel thrived, growing in grace, love, and understanding as the centuries on the Earth below passed. One by one, her companions received their assignments to care for their human charges. As each one left, she felt a twinge of sadness, even as she rejoiced for them. *Oh, Father . . . When?* She appealed in her heart.

It was times such as these, when often, she would raise her eyes, and the bright figure of the Son walking across the sparkling surface of glass appeared in the distance, the golden mist silhouetting the radiance of his form; and her heart would grow peaceful once more.

After the tragic fall of Adam and Eve, when Man lost his authority over the Earth, the angels looked on helplessly as people grew ever more fearful, envious, and full of greed and senseless hatred. God's human children began to blame others for their own sins, becoming subject to anxiety, greed, arrogance, and selfishness. Wickedness escalated, and vice flourished throughout the whole world as a result of the fallen angels' evil sway.

It seemed to Gloriel and the other angels that people were becoming unable to deal with even the ordinary trials and pains of life, and their hearts were saddened by this.

But gradually, Gloriel noticed that God always remained loving, forgiving, and faithful to His plan, no matter how much people on earth rebelled; and for this she felt grateful and encouraged.

God's human children, having inherited the punishment of Adam and Eve, began passing through the door of Death.

All the angels wept in sorrow on that terrible day when Adam's and Eve's son Cain murdered his brother Abel in a fit of jealousy. Until God's plan could unfold, Abel became the first to enter the special place the Father prepared for the souls of those who would die before they could be redeemed.

Adam and Eve, growing old, mourned the loss of both their sons, since Cain was sentenced to wander the earth the rest of his life with the mark of the murderer emblazoned on his forehead.

But the Heavenly Host did not grieve over this. The Lord God assured them, that one day these souls would be given the opportunity to choose where they would spend eternity.

The angels began to see God's marvelous design taking shape, like many-colored pieces of an intricate puzzle.

They realized that some people responded to the Father with respect, trust and love; while others reacted with disobedience and defiance, grieving the heart of the Holy Spirit.

Self-righteousness, greed and resentment spread unbridled among the Father's earthly children. But still, Gloriel and the other angels kept hope for the people alive in their hearts.

Those among the angels who had not yet received their assignments, continued to look down on the great globe of the Earth with close attention and eagerness.

They recognized the influence of Satan and his minions, as evil continued to spread and thrive among the people.

The years flew by swiftly, in the twinkling of an eye, it seemed to Gloriel. Her heart constantly reached out with love for God's struggling, vacillating people on the aging Earth.

Yet, God's plans for her own personal ministry remained a mystery. Sometimes she felt frustrated, because she realized that although Michael and Gabriel knew her destiny, when she questioned them about it, they avoided answering her queries.

Sariel, too, had not yet been assigned her guardianship; and so her fervor and anticipation grew, along with that of her friend.

One day, as she and Gloriel were sitting on the grass, laughing at the antics of some playful children on the Earth below, Sariel was summoned to the Throne. Her eyes flashed with excitement as she jumped to her feet, curls bouncing.

"Gloriel! Do you think . . . ?"

Gloriel smiled brightly at the dimpled, pink-cheeked angel standing over her. She rose quickly, laughing and giving Sariel a gentle push in the direction of the Throne.

"Go! Hurry!" She responded,

Her golden eyes followed the little angel as Sariel moved swiftly through the bright mist, her hair blending with the sparkling light, until she disappeared from view.

Her spirit exulted for her friend. *Surely the Lord is calling Sariel now for assignment to one of his human children.* She returned her gaze to the frolicking little ones below. *Will I ever be allowed to have one of these in my charge?* She pondered wistfully. Sighing, she closed her amber eyes and dreamt of small chubby hands, dimpled cheeks, and childish laughter.

#

Sariel smiled softly as she stood beside the mother and newborn child. The room was small, almost bare. The woman lay on a mat on a hard-packed dirt floor. Her dark hair clung to her forehead in wet strands, and her rosy face shone, damp with heat and exhaustion. In her arms, a baby girl lay snuggled in swaddling clothes, her small rosebud mouth making sucking motions. Fine eyelashes fluttered on the tiny silken cheeks, like moths in the lamplight. An oil lamp sat on a low wooden table, casting its flickering light and dancing shadows on the mud brick walls.

Stars, like chips of diamonds, winked in the dark cloaked night sky. The small town of Nazareth, climbing the foothills of lower Galilee, lay under a heavy atmosphere of quiet. Here and there, firelight threw shadows across rock walls and grottoes. Small houses with flat roofs huddled together.

Inside the room where Sariel kept watch over her newborn charge, a bird-like little woman hovered over the pallet, twittering brightly.

"Anna, she is such a lovely child!" She dipped a cloth into a basin of water sitting on the floor beside the young woman. Wringing it out, she handed it to her patient. "Wipe your face now, dear, and I will bring your husband in to see his new daughter."

Sariel gazed lovingly at the newborn child. *This wondrous gift from God is destined to be the most blessed of all womankind,* she thought. She beamed at the baby lying tiny and helpless in her mother's arms.

"Aunt Miriam," Anna replied, clearing her throat, "please help me with my hair." Her voice was faint with fatigue. Sariel smiled again, watching the older woman dry the new mother's hair with a rough towel. *She really is like a little brown sparrow, chirping over her charge.*

Anna kissed the tiny pink face peering up at her with soft eyes reflecting the yellow lamplight. "Joachim will be so proud of his beautiful new daughter," she whispered. "What shall you be called, my little one? Esther? Sarah?"

Miriam chose a strip of blue cloth from several looped over her belt, and tied back Anna's damp black hair from her face. "There now, Anna, you look presentable for your husband," she said, her little dark face crinkling in a smile.

Pushing aside the rough textured brown material hanging over the doorway, she fluttered into the cooking area of the small dwelling.

Anna's husband, Joachim, paced nervously, wringing his hands as he awaited word of the delivery of his third child. He was tall and agile, with wavy light brown hair and beard. Dark blue eyes shone clear and candid in his angular face.

"Joachim," Miriam said in solemn tones, although her eyes danced merrily, "I bring you good news of great joy, for unto you is born this day, a daughter."

The ancient words of address to the father of a newborn child fell joyfully on Joachim's ears. Stumbling slightly in his eagerness, he entered the room where his wife and new daughter lay.

"Anna . . ." his voice was husky, and a little hoarse. "Anna, my love . . ."

"My husband," Anna whispered, her ripe pretty features alternately lit and shadowed in the lamplight. "I present to you, your daughter. What shall she be called?" She placed the child gently in his arms.

Joachim's face lit up with a joyful smile as he studied the sweet sleeping face. "I think . . . Susannah, my mother's name, God give peace to her soul."

He stared adoringly at the precious gift from God laying his arms. Leaning down, he kissed Anna's moist brow, and then the child's downy pink cheek.

Unseen, Sariel whispered in Anna's ear.

"Mary! Her name is Mary!" The words, uncalled, burst forth from Anna's lips.

A puzzled, faintly shocked expression came over Joachim's kind face. It was ancient custom for the father to name the child.

"My husband, forgive me, but she must be called 'Mary'," Anna pleaded.

"But Anna, we already have our Mary Elizabeth," he replied, bewildered. Then, looking down at the earnest, beseeching face of his beloved, Joachim's heart melted.

Sariel watched as Joachim's angel, Ezaniel, laid a hand on his charge's shoulder and whispered in his ear. Joachim's heart expanded painfully with love, and he smiled down at his wife.

"So be it, then. Her name is Mary."

Kissing the tiny face with trembling lips, he placed the precious bundle back in her mother's arms.

"Mary . . ." Anna whispered in her daughter's tiny pink ear. "Mary . . ."

Speaking the name softly, like a caress, she wondered what lay ahead for the baby clutched firmly to her breast. She vowed to shower this infant with love as she learned to smile, to walk, and talk. She and Joachim would teach her how to be a loving, happy young woman, instilling in her the qualities of compassion, honesty, and mercy.

Anna drifted quietly off to sleep, dreaming of a lovely young woman, fair of face, and beautiful in spirit.

Seeing the tender scene unfold below, Gloriel sighed.

"When, oh when, Lord?" she breathed softly into the incredible brilliance of the golden light surrounding her.

No answer came, and yet her heart was touched by a secret, consuming joy. Soon . . .

#

So Gloriel and her companions kept their watch over the thriving earth. The passing ages brought the country of God's chosen people, Palestine, under Roman control. Israel was His special people, whom He chose out of all the nations of the earth to be his treasured possession. It was to them He revealed Himself, and His special plans.

A decree of Caesar Augustus in Rome appointed Herod as king of Judea. Herod was a talented architect with a sharp intellect, an experienced hunter, horseman and archer.

However, he also committed many pitiless, brutal atrocities, with deliberate cruelty and malice. A jealous, suspicious, lustful man, he had an insatiable hunger for power.

The people of Palestine, Gloriel noted, had changed their beliefs drastically. King Herod's luxurious, decadent lifestyle reduced them to abject, hopeless poverty; and so they grew steadily more rebellious.

Some of the people were watching and waiting eagerly for the Savior, the promised Messiah, to appear and deliver them from the cruel domination of Rome.

Gloriel remembered the great prophet Isaiah's words regarding His coming:

*"All right then, the Lord himself will choose the sign. Look! The virgin will conceive a child! She will give birth to a son and will call him Immanuel—'God is with us'."* Isaiah 7:14 NLT

Although at first the Jews did not believe in a bodily resurrection on Judgment Day, many of them came to believe in it. The Pharisees readily accepted this belief. This reminded Gloriel of what the prophet Ezekiel had said:

*"Now give them this message from the sovereign Lord: O my people, I will unlock your graves of exile and cause you to rise again. Then I will return you to the land of Israel. When this happens, O my people, you will surely realize that I am the Lord."* Ezekiel 37:12-13 NLT

The Jews searched and pored over the sacred scriptures intently, looking forward to the promised Deliverer, anxiously awaiting signs of the Lord's Plan for His people.

The Heavenly Host looked on as the Jewish people in rural villages tilled the soil; while in the Holy City, Jerusalem, their priests offered sacrifices to the Lord God.

One by one, Gloriel's angel companions were granted guardianship over the people on Earth. As the years passed, they were reassigned when their charges died and went to the Place of the Dead.

Still, there was no assignment for Gloriel. Sometimes she felt sad, but mostly she worshiped and adored at the great Throne of the Most High. The joy she experienced there far out shadowed any anxiety she had for her role in the Lord's great Plan.

After the Assyrian conquest, aliens settled among the Jewish population; so half of Palestine's populations were Jewish at the time of Mary of Nazareth's birth. The other half was a mixture of people from many nations. Babylonians, Greeks, Arabs, Egyptians, Syrians, and Persians mingled among the Jews.

At this time, Palestine was divided into five provinces by the Romans: Perea, Galilee, Judea, Idumea and Samaria.

The Samaritans were hated most of all. They weren't allowed to take part in the rebuilding of the Temple after the Jews returned from their exile in Egypt. So they built their own temple on Mount Gerizim. This caused even more strain, conflict, and hostility between Samaria and Jerusalem.

Because the Jewish people were increasingly subjugated by the Roman invaders, they grew extremely bitter and resentful toward these foreigners who were taking over their Promised Land.

Some waited patiently for the promised Deliverer. Others, mostly in the hills of Galilee, formed little groups of patriots, planning an armed revolt. They were waiting and watching for the day when the Lord would drive out the pagan invaders and establish His Kingdom throughout the whole Earth.

Some believed that Elijah the prophet would return to earth to proclaim the coming Kingdom. Still others were constantly watching for the Messiah, who was to be born of King David's line, according to the Sacred Scrolls. They believed he would restore freedom to his Chosen People, revealing the Most High God to them.

#

It was in this atmosphere, that one day Gloriel watched as Gabriel appeared to an elderly priest called Zechariah. A good and upright man, he lived in a small village called Ein Karem, outside of Jerusalem. Zechariah served in the Temple at Jerusalem. A member of the priestly order of Abijah, one of 24 priestly divisions, he was serving his one-week rotation. This happened only once every six months, so Zechariah felt honored to be chosen by lot to burn the incense offering in the Sanctuary twice daily.

A tall man, even in his old age, he bent his silver head in prayer, standing in the dim light of the Sanctuary. His thin face was deeply lined, his sparse beard still black, although flecked with silver. His gray eyes closed as he lifted his heart to the Most High.

Much to his sorrow, he and his wife had no children, and yet they persisted in faith. He had prayed long and hard for a son, but the Most High had not seen fit to grant his petition. Now he was advanced in age, and hope was fading, in reality almost gone.

Zechariah's mind wandered from his prayer, and he thought of his wife, Elizabeth, who was from the priestly tribe of Aaron. Her once dark brown hair was silver now, and her round dimpled face a mesh of fine lines. Still, her smile was merry, and her short, plump body a comfort to him as they lay in their soft bed at night. Elizabeth's shame at her barrenness had only increased as their years together flew by. She still longed and prayed for a son. But Zechariah loved her dearly, and treasured their life together. As one, they walked blamelessly before the Lord. In his mind's eye, the old priest pictured his beloved Elizabeth awaiting his return from service.

Candles flickered slightly in the silent Sanctuary as the sweet scent of incense filled the air. The veil between the Holy of Holies and the Sanctuary whispered softly, rippling as if touched by an unseen hand. Zechariah's eyes flew open. *What's happening?* He wondered silently. *No breeze can reach the inner Sanctuary, and yet . . .*

Gloriel smiled as Gabriel, standing to the right of the incense altar, revealed himself to the startled old man. The angel's clothing glowed softly in the shadowed Sanctuary. His fine features shone with the Glory of God, as his auburn hair reflected the candlelight.

Zechariah's skin paled to alabaster. With a sharp intake of breath, he stepped backward quickly, almost stumbling on the long robes of his priestly office.

Gabriel's voice was quiet but firm. *"Don't be afraid, Zechariah." God has heard your prayer, and your wife Elizabeth will bear you a son! You are to name him John. You will experience great joy and gladness; and many will rejoice with you at his birth, for he will be great in the eyes of the Lord. He must never touch wine or hard liquor, and he will be filled with the Holy Spirit, even before his birth. And he will persuade many Israelites to turn to the Lord their God. He will be a man with the spirit and power of Elijah, the prophet of old. He will precede the coming of the Lord, preparing the people for his arrival. He will turn the hearts of the fathers to their children, and he will persuade disobedient minds to accept godly wisdom."* Luke 1: 13-17 NLT

Bewildered, terrified and awestricken, Zechariah sank to the floor of the Sanctuary, his weak knees no longer able to support him. *How can this possibly be?* He thought to himself. *I cannot believe that my aged wife could be blessed as Sarah and Hannah were when they miraculously gave birth in their old age!* So, Zechariah doubted, and asked Gabriel for a sign, questioning him.

"How can I believe this will happen? After all, I am a very old man now. My wife Elizabeth is also old, and barren!" Zechariah's voice cracked and quivered as he doubted and distrusted Gabriel, seeking some kind of proof that all this would come to be.

Then the angel said, "I am Gabriel! I stand in the presence of God. He sent me to bring you this wonderful news. But now, since you don't believe what I said, you will be struck dumb, until after the child is born. For my words will indeed come true at the right time." Gabriel's voice was stern, and his brows drew together in a slight frown.

Zechariah's bent form bowed low in acquiescence to the Lord's decree. Looking up, he saw that the bright figure of the angel had disappeared, and he was once more alone in the Sanctuary. He trembled as he stumbled his way outside the Sanctuary, where the people awaited him. They were murmuring among themselves, wondering what was taking him so long. Appearing in the doorway of the Sanctuary, Zechariah tried to speak to the waiting crowd, but it was as if his vocal chords were frozen, and no sound escaped his lips. He gestured wildly, attempting to describe his experience in the sanctuary. He grew frustrated, and great tears rolled down his withered cheeks, coming to rest glistening in his silver-flecked beard.

Finally, a voice from the back of the crowd cried out.

"He must have seen a vision in the Temple Sanctuary!"

Zechariah nodded vigorously, sobbing, and lifted his hands to bless the people.

The old priest remained in the Temple for several more days, until his time of service was over.

#

The moon was a pale, nebulous shadow far down in the sky as Zechariah hurried along the rough road toward home. The winter night held its breath in silence. He walked quickly along the narrow unpaved street that led to the square in the center of town. Pausing to rest a few minutes, he leaned heavily on his staff, breathing deeply of the crisp night air. He thought about the joyful announcement of the angel Gabriel, and smiled to himself as he began the climb up the steep pathway to his home high on the mountainside.

Terraced hills rose above the lush and verdant valley, hushed now in the stillness of the night. *Can this truly be, that God would perform the same miracle for Elizabeth and me that He did for Abraham and Sarah, Elkanah and Hannah, and Manoah and his wife?* Zechariah pondered as he climbed.

Then he recalled the words of the Lord to Abraham:

*"Is anything too wonderful for the Lord?"* Genesis 8:14 NLT

Zechariah swung open the heavy oak door of his home, breathing heavily from the long climb. He was overjoyed to be safe inside. He removed his sandals, walked quietly over the polished marble floors, and entered the bedchamber where Elizabeth lay, snoring softly. A solitary candle flickered dimly, its light burning low. The bed looked warm and inviting. He undressed quickly and climbed in beside his sleeping wife. Elizabeth wakened with a start as his cold feet touched her warm ones.

Zechariah tried in vain to explain to her, without benefit of words, the wondrous thing that had occurred.

Elizabeth, bewildered by her husband's muteness, grew increasingly frustrated, upset, and a little angry.

At last, Zechariah took his aged wife in his trembling arms, and Gabriel's prophecy was fulfilled. Elizabeth's shriveled womb, long barren and unfruitful, became suffused with warm blood and healthy tissue. New life was planted, and the Herald of the Lord was conceived.

# Chapter Four

She hummed softly to herself as she walked the winding path to the well. *What a glorious day it is,* she mused. Flowers were blooming, brought forth by the first rains of the season. The stony mountainsides of Nazareth shone radiant with the scarlet of anemones. The green and soft limestone hills beyond were dotted with age-old silver-green olive trees. Her small village lay nestled in the hills at the northernmost edge of the Plain of Esdraden.

Mary glanced over her shoulder at the huddled square houses a short distance from the main road. Verdant pasture lands and orchards stretched out below. The song of birds sweetened the soft morning air with melody, lifting her heart.

She loved her small, humble but comfortable home. She thought of her parents, Anna and Joachim; her brothers and sisters, Mary Elizabeth, Salome, Jacob and Elias, how dear they all were to her young heart!

She breathed deeply of the scented air. A large clay water jug balanced precariously on her shoulder, as her sandaled feet gracefully picked their way through the small stones strewn along the path. Her clear complexion, lightly browned from the bright sunlight, shone with the fresh glow of youth. Bright, light brown eyes, framed by delicately winged eyebrows, absorbed the beauty of the morning. Her lithe form gave her rough linen tunic an almost regal look. A wide leather belt complimented her slender waist. Draped softly over shining golden-brown hair, a linen mantle the color of sand and edged in blue bordered her lovely face.

Mary of Nazareth was 13-years-old, already wed to her beloved Joseph, although they still lived apart, as custom dictated, since the nuptials had not yet been performed. Smiling to herself, she daydreamed of Joseph. *He is so wonderful, and handsome, with his dark brown hair and shining eyes,* she thought. The heavy beard curling against his olive skin made her heart skip a beat whenever she came near him.

Beautiful words from the Song of Songs came to her mind as she reflected dreamily.

*"Let me see your face, let me hear your voice, for your voice is sweet and Your face is beautiful."* Song of Solomon 2:14 NLT

A soft glow crept over her delicate features. *Mary!* She scolded herself, *Be about your duties now!*

Her guardian angel, Sariel, smiled at her young charge's thoughts. *What a delightful young woman the small babe has grown to be,* she thought, remembering the heart-warming scene of Mary's birth.

Mary rounded a bend in the pathway, and joined the chattering girls and women gathered about the town well with their jugs and skins. The well sat squarely in the center of the small village. Beside it stretched a watering trough, where a few livestock were drinking deeply of the cool water. She swung the earthenware jug down from her shoulder to the smooth hard-packed ground beside the well.

Here the women of the village came every day to shop in the dusty open-air market, and to draw water from the communal well. Small shops edged the marketplace, where a carpenter, a potter, a weaver and a blacksmith pursued their trades or sold their goods.

Mary looked up at the warm sun picking its way through the leafy branches of a tree arching overhead.

"Good morning, Mary!" Rachel, her very dearest friend, greeted her with a radiant dimpled smile.

"Good morning, Rachel." She returned her friend's smile, brushing back a wisp of soft hair from her eyes.

"How is Joseph?" Rachel whispered, lowering her head and gazing up through thick golden lashes at her friend. Eyes the rare clear blue-green of turquoise sparkled at Mary. The girl's figure curved plump and rounded under her deep blue tunic. Her fair skin glowed rosily in the warm sun. "Did he visit you last evening?"

Mary flushed, a slow tide of pink rising to cover her neck and face. Swinging the bucket over the lip of the well, she lowered it into the cold sweet water.

"No. No, he didn't," she replied reluctantly, shaking her head. She had not heard from Joseph in four days.

*Have I displeased him in some way? Has he changed his mind?* She wondered to herself. *Oh, Joseph! No, the covenant has been made, the Contract of Marriage completed, the vows spoken before the rabbi.*

Mary recalled how Joseph's fingers trembled as he placed the betrothal veil over her shining face. They belonged to each other now, according to the ancient laws. Only the Wedding Celebration remained, when Joseph would come to take her away to his home, accompanied by his family and friends and the Matrimonial Banquet could begin.

Pulling hand over hand on the thick rope, Mary slowly raised the heavy bucket, creaking to the top of the well. She set it on the rocky ledge, then sloshed the sparkling water into her earthenware jar.

The other women and girls murmured among themselves, exchanging the latest gossip. The ancient well was a gathering place for the female population of Nazareth.

Glancing across the well, Mary noticed a young girl whose face seemed familiar, and yet she was a stranger. She found herself staring at the sweet face framed in long golden curls. Clear blue-green eyes returned her gaze shyly. *She's as lovely as a dream! Her hair looks like spun gold, and her eyes . . .* Mary felt drawn into the clear depths of those eyes. A sense of peace flowed through her, and she returned the dimpled smile offered by the exquisite child.

"Mary, when did you last see Joseph?" Startled, Mary snapped out of her reverie and turned to look at her friend. Rachel's round face was clouded, and her brow furrowed with concern.

"Oh, Rachel dear, it's only been a few days, and I'm sure he will come tonight," Mary replied confidently.

As she spoke the words, her heart believed them. She felt marvelous! *That lovely young girl! Her eyes . . .* Mary turned back quickly, eager to look into them once more. Her gaze searched among the women and girls surrounding the well. The beautiful child had disappeared.

"Rachel, did you see her?"

"See who, Mary?" Rachel's voice was puzzled.

"That beautiful young girl with the golden hair, standing right over there," Mary said, pointing across the well.

"No, I didn't see any young girls, except Naomi and Sarah," Rachel replied, nodding toward two prattling girls on the far side of the well.

Mary shook her head in bewilderment. *Have I seen an apparition?* She wondered silently. But she smiled at Rachel as the sense of peace once more surrounded her.

"Well, I must be seeing things!" she chirped brightly, sitting down on the edge of the well.

Sariel stood across the well from her young charge, her bodily form no longer visible. She lifted her heart in prayer. *"Father, please bless our sweet Mary, and hold her in the palm of your hand."* She watched as Mary shouldered her jar of water and started down the pathway toward home, her friend Rachel at her side.

"Gabriel, she is ready now!" Sariel whispered excitedly.

Mary shifted the heavy jug to her other shoulder. She bid Rachel goodbye as she approached the modest mud brick house where she lived with her mother, Anna, her father Joachim, and her sisters and brothers. She hurried inside to finish her chores for the day.

The Shabbat, the Sabbath, would begin at sundown. A bit breathless, she hastened into the cooking area, greeted Anna, and set the earthenware water jug on a low table.

"Mary, we must prepare the bread for the Sabbath," Anna smiled at her lovely young daughter, feeling nostalgic. Too soon now, she must watch her Mary leave their house and start a new household.

"Oh, and perhaps we might fry some sweet cakes, too, and bring out a skin of our best wine for supper." Anna's brown eyes twinkled as she watched her daughter's face.

Mary's skin was flushed from the walk home in the warm sun, and her hair clung to her damp forehead, spilling over her shoulders.

"Emi, sweet cakes and the best wine! Are we having a guest for Sabbath supper?" Mary asked, her sweet voice slightly husky.

She took some barley from a storage pot, dipping a wooden scoop into the un-ground grain. Her fingers trembled slightly as she turned to face her mother.

"Mother, is Joseph . . . ?" She breathed slowly and deeply as her heart skipped a beat.

Laughing, Anna circled Mary's slender form with her plump arms, and drew her close.

"Yes, my child,-Joseph. Mary Elizabeth!" Anna called out to her elder daughter who was on the roof making curds from goat's milk in the goatskin churn.

Mary Elizabeth climbed down the short ladder which led to the roof, her dark curls bouncing. She was 14 years old and soon to celebrate nuptials with her bridegroom, Clopas. The year of betrothal was almost over.

"Yes, Mother?" Joachim's dark blue eyes gazed at Anna from beneath dark brows in Mary Elizabeth's rather solemn face.

*Mary Elizabeth, always so serious,* Anna thought to herself. *Unlike Mary, whose laughter and bright spirit light up the household.*

Salome, their eldest daughter, already wed to Zebedee, and mother of two sons, James and John; was more like Mary, light of heart and merry . . .

"Mary Elizabeth, help your sister grind the barley, please. And you might add a little cinnamon today," Anna directed.

Mary and her sister ground the barley kernels between two rasping millstones, gradually filling a large bowl with the coarse meal. Mary Elizabeth took a small portion of fermented dough saved from the day before and crumbled it into a small bowl of water. Gradually adding the liquid to the barley meal, the two girls kneaded the dough, covered it with a cloth and left it to rise. Later on, it would be shaped into large flat disks and baked in the big household oven.

Sariel watched, unseen, her heart swelling with anticipation of the marvelous event about to occur.

Mary's face shone rosy, dewy with perspiration. It was mid-day, and dust motes danced in the pale rays of sunshine steaming through the small window in the kitchen.

*So many chores to be done yet*, Mary sighed to herself, wiping her brow with a towel. Her whole being thirsted for the sight of Joseph, and she felt the hot blood rise in her cheeks at the thought. Her soft brown eyes grew luminous with anticipation. *Dear Joseph . . . his eyes speak love for me.* Her gentle mouth curved into a secret smile. *He really is the most handsome man in Nazareth!*

The three women worked together in the silence of the full noontide heat, each caught up in her own thoughts.

The bright afternoon hours wore on, the sky burning hot and brilliant blue overhead.

Finally, the table was set, the bread baked, and the delicious aroma of roasting fowl hung in the warm air. A pewter plate of cheeses and ripe fruits rested in the middle of the low table; the finest oil lamp stood ready at the head. The three Sabbath meals were prepared, and all the lamps were filled with olive oil. Tall jugs brimmed with fresh cool water.

*The table looks lovely, but I can't say the same for myself*, Mary thought. She put her hands up to her hair, which clung in damp curly strands to her flushed forehead and neck. Pouring some water into a wooden basin, she sponged her face and neck with a wet towel. *Maybe I'll wear my blue tunic tonight.* She smiled, knowing that Joseph loved to see her in the soft, flowing blue garment. But first, a short walk in the cool shadows of the olive grove . . .

The aged, wind-shaped and silver-leafed olive trees shimmered in the late afternoon sun. Shadows, elongated and darkening, formed a cool sanctuary for the weary young girl. Sitting down on a large rock, she closed her eyes and leaned back against the gnarled bark of an olive tree. Listening to the stillness laced with a few sleepy bird songs, she dozed.

Sariel, ever watchful, beamed as she stood watching the lovely face relax in the dappled, waning light.

"Mary . . ."

Her eyelids were too heavy to hold open. *It's so cool and quiet here*, the thought penetrated her sleep. The birds stopped singing.

"Mary . . ." The voice, a little louder now, was like warm honey, flowing softly through her consciousness.

Sighing, she opened her eyes slowly, fine eyelashes fluttering. She gradually became aware of a shaft of white gold light directly in front of her.

"Hail, Kecharitomene, full of Grace, favored one!"

Mary's eyes flew wide open, their golden brown depths startled.

Her surroundings, the olive grove, the birds, the brown earth, all faded away in the brilliant white light emanating from the shining figure standing before her. Magnificent wings, glowing like pearls in the light, framed his form.

*I am dreaming of an angel*! She said to herself. Her heart beat wildly in her breast. She felt dazed and perplexed.

*What a strange form of greeting! I've never heard it used before, and everyone knows how important the greeting is.* Amazed and startled, she felt confused, because no one she knew had ever uttered such a greeting. *What does "full of Grace" mean?* She rose slowly to her feet, feeling slightly faint.

The light grew even more dazzling. Mary shaded her eyes with one hand. She could see curly auburn hair reflecting the light, and large, shining hazel eyes gazing at her tenderly. She gasped sharply. His face was more beautiful than that of any man she had ever seen.

"Don't be frightened, Mary," the angel told her, "*for God has decided to bless you! You will become pregnant and have a son, and you are to name him Jesus. He will be very great and will be called the Son of the Most High. And the Lord God will give him the throne of his ancestor David. And he will reign over Israel forever; His Kingdom will never end!*" Luke 1: 30-33 NLT

Unseen, Sariel stood behind Mary, touching her lightly on the shoulder. The fear left the dazed young girl, replaced by a feeling of wonderment

Just then, Mary remembered the great respect for marriage that her parents had instilled in her. *How can I have a baby?* She wondered silently.

Startled, she heard herself asking the question aloud. "B-but how can I have a baby? I am a virgin." Her voice was ragged, almost inaudible

Gabriel smiled at her, and replied "*The Holy Spirit will come upon you, and the power of the Most High will overshadow you. So the baby born to you will be holy, and he will be called the Son of God. What's more, your relative Elizabeth has become pregnant in her old age! People used to say she was barren, but she's already in her sixth month. For nothing is impossible with God.*" Luke 1:35-37 NLT

As the angel spoke, Mary wondered to herself, *is he talking about the Messiah? Why has God so honored me? I am only a simple country girl.*

All the angels in heaven leaned down to listen as the Creator of the universe waited for Mary's consent to clothe Him with her own flesh.

Responding with simple trust and pure faith, she bowed her head and whispered humbly, "I am the Lord's handmaiden. I am willing to accept whatever he wants. Let everything you have said happen. I am ready." Her voice trembled, and the golden brown eyes gleamed with silver tears. She placed her hand upon her breast and bowed, in the ancient sign of admission that she was willing to obey.

The moment her "yes" to God passed her lips, a tremendous sensation of peace flooded Mary's being. She felt as if her heart would burst.

*It's as though a basin of warm water is being poured over my head,* she thought with a thrill.

Light engulfed her tingling and trembling body as the Holy Spirit overshadowed her. She became aware of a pungent perfume in the air. Sinking to her knees as wave after wave of joy washed over her, she became one with the brilliance. Her soul took wings and soared into the Heavens as the Love of God was made known to her inmost being.

So in one incredible moment, a simple young girl became both spouse and mother of the Lord, forever changing the path of history.

Unknown to Mary, the Host of Heaven looked down on the miracle unfolding, bowing low before the power and the glory of the Lord God.

Gloriel and her companions raised their voices in praise as God's Plan of salvation continued to unfold. They rejoiced as Mary entrusted herself, with absolute faith, into the hands of her loving God.

Slowly raising her head, Mary opened her eyes and looked about. The angel was gone. The light, that wonderful transplendent light, had disappeared. She felt as if she were floating, her body light and weightless. She gazed around at the olive trees, the rock, and the ground beneath her. *Have I been dreaming?* Instantly, she knew deep within her soul, that this was no dream.

Sariel remained unseen by Mary as she walked slowly back to her home, still feeling a bit dazed. *What will happen now? What do I say to my parents? And Joseph! Dear Lord God, what do I tell Joseph?* The questions came crowding into her mind, jostling one another, vying for the most importance. She still felt a bit faint from the enormity of what had happened to her. And yet, the joy-the peace . . . "Oh God, take my yes to you, and bring about all your plans and intentions for my life," she breathed softly.

Placing her hands on the flat plane of her pelvis, Mary thought of the new life just begun. *The Son of God!?* The enormous consequences of her commitment washed over her in great waves. *Will Joseph believe me? Will he reject me?*

She trembled as she thought fearfully of the ancient customs surrounding the breaking of the betrothal vows: the Writing of Divorcement, the Trial of Bitter Waters, where a woman caught in adultery was subjected to public trial and shame, and forced to drink the bitter waters. Sometimes the woman was even sentenced to death by stoning! *Oh, dear God . . . stoning! Lord, what do I do? Help me, please!* She prayed silently. As she approached her house, Mary's steps slowed with fear and reluctance.

Her unseen guardian placed her hand on Mary's head, whispering in her ear.

*"Even when I walk through the dark valley of death, I will not be afraid, for you are close beside me. Your rod and your staff protect and comfort me.*

*You prepare a feast for me in the presence of my enemies. You welcome me as a guest, anointing my head with oil. My cup overflows with blessings. Surely your goodness and unfailing love will pursue me all the days of my life, and I will live in the house of the Lord forever."* Psalm 23:4-6 NLT

The beloved Psalm of King David echoed in Mary's heart.

*Gabriel said I will have a son, a King, Son of the Most High! All young Hebrew girls dream of being the mother of the Messiah, the Deliverer, the Healer of the Nations,* she thought, elated. Dazedly, she shook her head, overcome with wonder at the honor God had bestowed on her.

The air beamed with warm gold as the sun prepared to vanish below the hilltops. A warm breeze blew softly against her pale cheeks as Mary approached the humble home she loved. *It's time for hadlakat neirot, the lighting of the Sabbath lamp, before the sun sets,* she thought, feeling strangely calm and at peace.

Soon the first evening star would appear. Then the Hazan, the cantor, would announce the beginning of the Lord's Day of rest with three sharp blasts of the Shofar, the ram's horn trumpet, from the roof of Nazareth's small synagogue. Taking a deep breath and straightening her slim shoulders, Mary entered the house.

## Chapter Five

Mary's young body ached with exhaustion. It was the sixth day of the long journey from Nazareth to Ein Karem, and it was taking its toll, even on her youthful vigor. The rocky road was rough, and her sandaled feet were dirty, sore and aching.

Gloriel looked on, fascinated, as Mary's arduous trip drew close to its end. She spoke frequently with Sariel regarding the unfolding drama in the land of Judea below. Sariel's face reflected a radiant serenity and her eyes filled with glory as she shared the joy of her watch over Mary with her friend.

*How much longer, oh Lord?* Gloriel prayed silently even as she celebrated with Sariel.

Mary's thoughts returned to the ordeal of the days just before she began the journey to visit Cousin Elizabeth. A lump rose in her throat just thinking of the pain and distress in Joseph's eyes, and how his face became strangely still and gaunt when she revealed her pregnancy to him and her parents.

In her mind's eye, she could still see her parents' faces glazing with shock, the veins standing out in ridges along her father's temples and throat.

At first, Mary was afraid that her mother, her dear Emi, was going to faint. Anna's face blanched to a sickly white, her eyes closing quickly, as if to shut out what she had just heard.

*Joseph, dear Joseph,* there was ice and pain in his voice as he bid them an early goodnight, rushing out the door as if trying to outrun the raging emotions within.

As the night wore on, her parents finally believed her, as she described the angel's announcement in the olive grove.

Anna dried her brown eyes as her practical spirit came through. "We must make plans," she insisted. "First, Mary, you need to visit Cousin Elizabeth. If it was truly an angel, and you were not dreaming, if Elizabeth is actually with child, then we will know that you are indeed most blessed among women, my daughter."

The stunned expression on her father's face as he nodded, wordlessly agreeing to Anna's plans, burned in Mary's memory.

Joachim made arrangements with his cousin Boaz for Mary to travel with him and his family to Jerusalem. They were leaving in ten days, and there was much to do. She did not see Joseph again before she left with Cousin Boaz' caravan.

When she bade her parents goodbye as she embarked on her journey, Joachim laid his hands gently upon her head in the ancient blessing: "Ye simcha Elohim k'Sarah, Rivkah, Rachel, v'Leah. May God make you as Sarah, Rebbekah, Rachel and Leah."

Recalling this tender gesture from her father, Mary's eyes overflowed with tears. *Avi, my dear father, I'm so sorry for your pain.*

*I must not dwell on this.* She shook her head as if this would make the painful thoughts flee.

*I have to find out if Cousin Elizabeth is truly with child in her old age. I have to be sure I was not dreaming.* She lifted her hair from her damp neck, and brushed away the beads of perspiration which stood out on her soft upper lip and along her high cheekbones. Her nose was burned a deep rosy pink by the long hours in the sun.

*I'm so tired. Emi, Mother, I miss you. Joseph, Joseph, have I lost you?* Tears etched their gleaming pathways down her flushed cheeks.

The little caravan camped beside the road for the night. Mary tried to join in the conversation around the warm campfire, but her thoughts kept straying, and her weary body cried out for sleep. Excusing herself, she lay down on her pallet inside the goatskin tent. The desert night was chill and silent, except for the low murmur of voices outside the tent.

"Oh, Lord Most High, I'm so afraid. My heart is failing within me. Uphold me with your strong right arm," she whispered, voice trembling.

At the head of the pallet Sariel knelt unseen, placing her hand tenderly on Mary's furrowed young brow. *"Sleep, sweet Mary, the Lord hears your cry. Rest now,"* Sariel whispered deep in the young girl's consciousness.

Slowly, the brow under Sariel's hand relaxed, growing smooth and soft beneath the angel's touch. Mary's weary eyes closed, the thick lashes shadowing her cheeks. She slept, dreaming of her home in Nazareth, her parents, her sisters and brothers, and Joseph, dear Joseph . . .

#

Cousin Boaz settled his family in Jerusalem, and escorted Mary to the small village of Ein Karem, nestled in the rolling hills just beyond the Holy City.

*This valley is so beautiful!* Mary thought, as Boaz lifted her atop the little donkey she had grown to love during the long journey. She had named him

Ezra. Most of the time, during the long trek, Mary walked, not wanting to burden the small ass any more than necessary. But she was so weary, and the ascent to Elizabeth's and Zechariah's home looked so steep and long.

Boaz bid her goodbye, eager to rejoin his family in Jerusalem. At Mary's insistence, he left her at the foot of the wide path which led upward. She embraced her cousin, thanking him profusely for his kindness in bringing her this far. This was the seventh day of their journey.

The view was breath-taking. Terraced hills rose above a lush green valley, blending into the natural landscape. The air gleamed clear and bright with golden sunlight. Below, farms, vineyards, and lush vegetation covered the valley floor. Peering up the steep grade, Mary could see small homes along the way. An abundance of brilliant-colored flowers and greenery softened the edges of the pathway.

As the little ass labored up the path with his precious burden, Mary prayed.

"Oh Lord Most High; grant me strength and courage I need to walk the path you have prepared before me. I am sick with longing for my home, and frightened, though in my heart I know you are with me always. I am your handmaiden . . ."

She guided her small mount around a large rock lying in the path. Patting his warm rough neck, she encouraged him, "Just a little farther, Sheli, little friend."

The lane began to narrow a bit as Mary urged her companion onward. Sariel kept guard over her precious charge as they approached Elizabeth's home. *There! The last house along the path, just as Emi said,* Mary rejoiced.

At last, the long weary journey ended. Soon she would know without doubt whether she had been dreaming or not when the angel Gabriel appeared to her in the olive grove. Deep in her heart, she knew it was true, and not in her imagination. Still, it would be good to have her convictions reinforced. Her heart pounded like a drum in her chest.

A drop of sweat rolled down her small nose and dripped off the end. The rough gray linen travel tunic was clinging to her body in the hot afternoon air. How good it would be to rest her dusty, travel-weary feet, and bathe her aching body in cool water.

Elizabeth's and Zechariah's house was magnificent. Two terra cotta planters of huge red begonias flanked the front door of the house.

Mary knew that her cousins were quite wealthy, and that their home was perhaps the finest in the village of Ein Karem. But this had not prepared her for the sight of the beautiful structure rising before her. The facade of the house was white-washed stone, and several windows shuttered in golden oak peered out upon the valley stretching out below. The door was finest oak, intricately carved, polished and gleaming in the sunlight. Centered in the door, a bright brass knocker flashed.

Mary slid gracefully off her little brown donkey's back. Suddenly, she felt shy, reluctant to approach the huge door.

She stood on the stone step, trembling in anticipation, trying to bolster her courage. There had been no way to send a message to Elizabeth and Zechariah before she left home, so they were not expecting her.

She was only a small child the last time her kinsfolk saw her. Vaguely, she remembered the visit they paid her parents several years ago. She recalled being surprised, even at her young age, that they had no children. Elizabeth's kind face loomed clearly in her memory, but she could remember nothing about Zechariah.

*How will they receive me, a strange young girl suddenly appearing on their doorstep? Surely they will not recognize me as the small child they saw so long ago!*

Mary's tired brown eyes welled up with tears of homesickness and exhaustion. One bright drop slowly rolled down her flushed and dusty cheek. Dashing it away with the back of her hand, she scolded herself. *I must have courage now. I have made a covenant with the Most High. I must trust in Him!*

As she raised her trembling hand to grasp the bright brass knocker, the heavy door suddenly started to swing open. She gasped sharply, startled. Taking an involuntary step backward, Mary widened her eyes to peer into the shadowed interior.

A plump form stepped forward into the sunlight. *Cousin Elizabeth!* Mary remembered the deeply dimpled round face, and the kind brown eyes which now gazed at her curiously. She was about to speak, when Elizabeth's expression changed abruptly. It seemed as though a lamp had been lit behind her face and eyes. Mary's own eyes grew wide in astonishment as Elizabeth stood enveloped in light before her, hands outstretched.

"Peace be with you, Cousin Elizabeth!" Mary cried. She stepped forward over the threshold, and Elizabeth clasped her in her chubby arms. Mary's voice trembled as she greeted the elderly woman, whose already plump body sagged, heavy with child.

Elizabeth gave a glad cry and exclaimed to Mary, "You are set apart by God far above all other women, and your Child is holy. What an honor this is, that the mother of my Lord should visit me! When you came in and spoke to me, my baby jumped for joy the instant I heard your voice! You are most blessed, and so is the Fruit that you bear in your womb, because you believe that the Lord will do what He said."

Instantly, incredible joy flooded over Mary. "It's true! I haven't been dreaming!" She cried out.

Her heart felt as if it were melting in her chest. Unbidden, words of praise began to spill from her lips, and a song for all the ages was born.

> *"Oh, how I praise the Lord.*
> *How I rejoice in God my Savior!*
> *For he took notice of his lowly servant girl,*
> *and now generation after generation will call me blessed.*
> *For he, the Mighty One is holy,*
> *and he has done great things for me.*
> *His mercy goes on from generation to*
> *generation, to all who fear him.*
> *His mighty arm does tremendous things!*
> *How he scatters the proud and haughty*
> *Ones!*
> *He has taken princes from their thrones and*
> *exalted the lowly.*
> *He has satisfied the hungry with good things*
> *and sent the rich away with empty hands*
> *And how he has helped his servant Israel!*
> *He has not forgotten his promise to be*
> *merciful.*
> *For he promised our ancestors, Abraham and*
> *his children,*
> *to be merciful to them forever."* Luke 1:47-55 NLT

As Mary uttered these words which were destined to live forever, Sariel's heart warmed with pleasure and gratitude to the Lord for the privilege of caring for this beautiful and holy young woman.

Mary remained with Elizabeth and Zechariah for about three months, caring for her elderly cousin in the final stages of pregnancy, and helping prepare for the birth of Elizabeth's child.

As the weeks passed, Mary delighted in her own child growing inside her virgin womb. She felt both eagerness and apprehension about returning to her home in Nazareth, to her family, and to Joseph. She wondered in her heart how he would receive her. How would the people of the small village react to her pregnancy, which would soon be obvious to all?

Since it was not proper for a young virgin to remain in a household where a birth was to take place, Mary took leave of her elderly cousins and began the long journey home. She traveled with a small caravan of her father's friends, accompanied by Ezra, her dear little donkey companion.

As the small group of travelers approached Nazareth, Mary's heart grew faint with dread. *Joseph, Joseph, are you thinking adultery?*

Great tears traced down her dusty cheeks and dripped off her chin as the little hillside town of Nazareth came into view. The green olive groves glimmered with fresh silver as the setting sun cast ribbons of color over the hills.

*Gabriel said I should not be afraid . . . O, my God, don't let them cast me out!*

\#

Viewing the scene from her heavenly vantage point, Gloriel watched Sariel place her small hand on the shoulder of the girl-child carrying God in her virgin womb. As she witnessed the further unfolding of God's great Plan, her spirit was consumed with awe and joy. She rejoiced for Sariel as the small angel continued her careful watch over the young mother-to-be.

\#

Joseph woke with a start, his body trembling and drenched in sweat. "Mary!" Her name sprang uninvited from his lips.

The night was hot, the darkness thick and clinging. The room where he slept smelled of the sawdust and chips of his carpentry trade.

Over the past few months, while Mary was visiting her cousin Elizabeth, Joseph pondered and prayed, finally deciding on a just, yet compassionate plan. If he hid her sin, he would be fighting against the ancient Law of the Lord. If he exposed her, would he be delivering her up to death? His love for her was true and deep; he could not bear the thought of a public trial and humiliation, perhaps even stoning for this lovely young girl, still so precious to him. Sorrow rocked his heart at the thought of all he had lost, and tears were his constant companions in the long, sleepless nights.

So Joseph had decided to divorce Mary quietly, according to the laws of his religion.

Although gone more than three months now, she was never far from his thoughts. This night, exhausted from the weight of his decision, Joseph fell into a deep, dreamless sleep. An unnatural stillness pervaded the house.

Outside, night had fallen, warm and lush. The atmosphere grew heavy, and heat threw a blanket over Nazareth. An army of fierce black clouds stood guard overhead, as a deep, gloomy night veiled the earth.

At first, Joseph lay motionless on his pallet, breathing heavily, bewildered by his sudden awakening.

*A dream! The Most High sent an angel to me as I slept!* Jumping up from his pallet, Joseph stumbled in the darkness. He felt his way across the room and stepped outside into the black cloak of night. His night garment was damp, clinging to his sweaty body. Dizzied, he shook his head to clear away the cobwebs of sleep.

Slowly, the angel's voice and the message he brought flooded Joseph's consciousness. *What was it the angel had said?*

Strangely, there was no shadow of doubt in Joseph's mind that he had been visited by a Messenger from the Sovereign Lord. The angel's face and form were clear in his mind's eye. His heart bounded and his soul expanded as he recalled the angel's words.

*"Joseph, son of David,"* the angel said, *"do not be afraid to go ahead with your marriage to Mary. The child she carries has been conceived by the Holy Spirit. She will bear a son, and you are to name him 'Jesus', for he will save his people from their sins"* Matthew 1: 20-21 NLT

Joseph remembered the brilliant light surrounding the angel and reflecting off his auburn hair, the golden belt around his waist, and the huge glowing wings framing his form.

Gazing intently at the bewildered Joseph, the angel had smiled as his bright figure slowly faded from view, vanishing in a flash of light and a flurry of wings.

Hot tears coursed their way down Joseph's face as he raised his eyes to Heaven in thanksgiving. He understood, deep in his heart, the calling to be head of the Holy Family. Awestricken with the knowledge that the Most High had chosen him for such an awesome responsibility, he sank slowly to his knees.

Unseen beside him, his angel, Samuel, he of the merry face and twinkling black eyes, placed his arm around Joseph's broad shoulders.

As she watched Joseph and her dear friend Samuel, Gloriel felt a sharp pang of longing. Quickly, she turned her face towards the shining Throne of Glory, and a sense of comfort and joy swept over her.

#

*Home! Am I really here at last?* Mary's young, vigorous body was weary and soiled from the long journey. Almost four months into her pregnancy, her small form already seemed out of balance and puffy. She felt both eager and uneasy.

"What kind of reception awaits me?" She whispered to herself. She had received only two messages from home during her stay with Cousin Elizabeth and Zechariah. Both were from her parents, speaking only of their longing for her return, with little news of her family, and nothing about Joseph.

Ezra plodded along steadily, bearing his sweet burden without objection.

"Mary!"

*Am I dreaming?* Her heart leapt in her breast at the sound of the familiar and beloved voice. Her eyes, weary from travel and smarting from the dust, strained ahead.

"Mary!" Again the voice rang out.

There . . . standing by the roadside . . . Joseph! Mary slid slowly off Ezra's back.

Joseph stood gazing wide-eyed, as if enchanted, unable to move as he drank in the vision before him. "Mary, my Mary, home at last—beloved, blessed, beautiful Mary!" His voice quivered.

Standing before her adored Joseph, tremulous with apprehension, Mary raised tired brown eyes and gazed full into his dear face.

A shaky smile touched Joseph's lips and a tear slipped quietly down one cheek. *My love and pain I offer you,* he thought, as he stared at the dream standing before him.

"Mary, my wife, welcome home!"

At these words, there was a flutter in Mary's womb, like faint whispers of butterfly wings, proclaiming new life.

# Chapter Six

Gloriel watched closely as an order came forth from the king, Augustus Caesar, that the entire world must be registered, each man in his own city. She knew that at a council in Rome, Caesar had learned that many of his subjects were dishonest, and were avoiding paying their taxes. So, his advisors suggested that there should be an accurate count of the populations of all the provinces, and this was why he ordered the census.

The Romans were excellent administrators, and one of their main functions was tax assessment, Gloriel noted.

*Ah, so the real purpose of the census will not be just to count the people, but to make sure that the most important source of revenue, the conquered provinces, are properly taxed. This means that Mary and Joseph will have to comply with this edict.*

The decree made it imperative for all those who for any reason were away from their home towns, to return to their own districts so that the census could be taken. Even married women had to obey this ruling.

Samuel and Sariel grew concerned about the toll this would take on Mary, now heavy with child. Joseph tried to get excused from the census because of Mary's advanced pregnancy, but he was informed that absolutely no one would be excused for any reason.

The young couple prepared to make the journey to Bethlehem; as Joseph had originally come from this small hillside community, and his family owned property there. The town lay about five miles beyond the Sacred City of Jerusalem.

As they prepared to begin the journey, Joseph carefully lifted Mary onto Ezra's sturdy back.

She leaned forward and patted the little donkey's neck, whispering into his soft ear. "We have a long journey ahead, Sheli, little friend." Ezra lowered his head and snorted, as if nodding in agreement.

It was early on a bright and sunny morning in the season after the first rains, when they embarked on the long journey to Bethlehem in Judea. Soon the familiar hills of Nazareth were left behind.

Sariel and Samuel accompanied their charges, keeping close watch over them, while Gloriel observed from her Heavenly home.

Joseph planned to take about six or seven days for the trip, as he did not want Mary to become too weary on the road. They traveled lightly, with only enough provisions for the journey. These were tied securely behind Mary on Ezra's brawny back, with freshly filled water bags hanging on either side. Joseph carried a stout staff, along with a knapsack over his shoulder. Both Mary and Joseph wore sturdy sandals and warm cloaks.

Although the sun shone brightly overhead, a newborn cool breeze stirred the trees, and the air sparkled, sharp and clear.

Mary turned to look back at the sun-sweetened green hills of Nazareth. *Soon,* she thought, *they will be bursting with color, when the wildflowers poke their bright heads through the soil.* Pensive, she considered all of the events of the past few months, and a flock of memories spiraled up within her. *So much has happened.* Her heart felt fragile and delicate, brittle like glass.

Sariel listened closely, following Mary's racing thoughts. *She seems so utterly defenseless,* she thought.

Mary was thinking about the gossiping tongues, whispering behind her back. She had held her head high, dwelling in her mind on the words of the angel *"Hail, full of Grace."* Even Rachel had acted withdrawn and reticent. Though her friend had tried to reach out to Mary in support, her face flushed whenever her eyes were drawn to Mary's thickening waistline. Her dreams of serving Mary as her bridesmaid turned to ashes.

There had been no beautiful wedding procession, no songs to celebrate the beauty of the bride, no music or dancing, no flowers; only Joseph, dressed in his multicolored Sabbath robes, knocking on the door.

Mary wore her finest linen tunic, a gift from Cousin Elizabeth. A pale, almost iridescent blue, edged in silver threads, it fell in soft folds from her shoulders. A long mantle of the same fine material draped over her shining brown hair, held in place by a circlet of silver, a wedding present from Zechariah.

There was no fine wedding chair for Mary to sit in to await the coming of her bridegroom. There was no joyous wedding procession. She recollected how Joseph's brown eyes had glistened with tears when he gazed on her, dressed in her wedding finery. Mary had felt her cheeks grow hot under his gaze. Quietly, they walked together down the dusty path, through the town square to Joseph's modest house. No crowd of celebrants awaited them, no rich food and wine, only a simple meal, alone together.

Mary smiled as she remembered how Joseph cupped her face in his hands and tenderly kissed her goodnight as they lay down together on their first night in his house—their house.

*Dear Joseph!* He had taken her home as his wife, refusing to subject her to ridicule and punishment, perhaps even death.

Remembering, Mary's heart swelled with love for her husband.

Sariel beamed at Samuel, who walked unseen close by Joseph's side.

Ezra plodded steadily, bearing his precious burden without complaint.

As they trudged along silently, lost in their own thoughts, Joseph, too, was remembering. He recalled that wonderful day, that seemed so long ago now, when his parents and Mary's agreed during a formal discussion, that Joseph and Mary would be married. Soon afterward, the qiddushin, the formal betrothal, had taken place. Even though the marriage ceremony had not yet happened, Joseph's heart had rejoiced in knowing that Mary was now truly his. Nothing could dissolve their union then, except divorce.

All through the engagement, Mary remained in her parent's house, awaiting that glorious day when Joseph would come to take her home to live with him.

Then came that shocking day, full of anguish, when Mary stood before him and her parents, gazing into his eyes. This had filled him with apprehension, as it was usually considered bad manners in Judea to stare directly into the eyes of another, even one's betrothed.

Then, lowering her shadowed eyes, she had whispered, "I'm going to have a baby."

He had been shocked beyond measure. His very flesh felt weighty on his bones. A foreboding shadow darkened his thoughts. He loved this beautiful young girl with all his heart and he dreamed of a long and happy life together. It was as though she had plunged a dagger deep into his heart. Sorrow sat like a stone in his chest.

Mary tried to say more then, but Joseph's ears were closed in trauma. He uttered not a word, but turned and silently left Mary's house, his dreams shattering to pieces with each step.

His thoughts then turned to the night of the angel's visit, and the tremendous relief that had poured over him at Gabriel's words. It was then he had found out that it was not shame that covered his beautiful bride, but great honor.

Shaking his head to clear away the memories, he glanced back at Mary. She had slipped off Ezra's back, and was walking beside the small donkey. *How lovely she is!* He thought. *Even in the final days of her pregnancy, she glows as if lit by a lamp from within.* Her sweet face radiated a wise serenity. Great with child, her chin held high, there was still grace in her step. Joseph smiled at her, and was rewarded with a flash of white teeth between the rosy lips he loved to kiss.

As the day wore on, Mary grew deeply fatigued, the precious burden in her womb pressing heavily in her pelvis. Her body ached, but she did not complain.

When the sun stood high in the azure sky, they stopped beneath a few bent and gnarled pine trees along the wayside. Joseph spread a blanket for Mary, and she drank deeply of the cool liquid in the water bag. The knapsack yielded a small loaf of flat bread and some goat cheese. Their appetites were whetted by the long walk, and Mary dug out some dates and nuts from a pouch hanging from her belt.

She curled up on the blanket after they had eaten, "just to rest for a few minutes." She laid her head in Joseph's lap and closed her drowsy eyes. As he watched his beloved slip into a quiet sleep, a great wave of tenderness welled up in his heart. He stroked the soft curve of her cheek with the back of his hand, brushing her silky hair away from her pale brow.

"Oh, Lord Most High, please help me care for this precious gift you have given me," he breathed quietly.

#

Looking down from Heaven on the tender scene, Gloriel smiled warmly.

Samuel and Sariel each stood close by their charge, keeping careful guard over the young couple soon to become the Holy Family.

Gloriel's heart swelled with emotion, and again she yearned for a young soul of her own to protect and guide. Heaven's beauty and peace surrounded her, and yet she felt a great void inside. Turning toward the Father's throne, she breathed a silent prayer.

*Lord God, Most High, your ways are so mysterious. I know your plans are perfect, and your love is endless. Please allow your servant the privilege of loving and protecting one of your earthly children. My heart is longing for this.*

For a brief moment, it seemed to Gloriel that the cloud of light above the Throne grew even brighter, and the gemstones adorning the Throne glittered in brilliant sparks of reflection. Peace returned to her heart once more.

#

Joseph and Mary continued their journey through the boggy plains and hills of Esdraelon. The soft grazing lands spread out a brilliant green carpet, spongy from the recent rains.

Swaying gently back and forth on Ezra's back, Mary's thoughts turned to the child, heavy in her womb. *What will he be like? Will he free us from the Roman tyrants? How can he become a King, being born to a simple country couple? Will he lead an army against the enemy as King David did?*

As they traveled, Joseph and Mary encountered more and more pilgrims, most of them trudging along on foot. They arrived in the city of Bethsheun, close to where the lush and fertile Jezriel and Jordan valleys met. Newly sprouted fields of wheat lay bursting with life.

They stayed overnight in the small Jewish sector of the pagan city. In the morning, they stopped to marvel at the wide thoroughfare where Greek and Roman temples of pure white marble rose in splendid tribute to their many gods.

That afternoon, they stood in awe of the massive stone fortresses, looking much like sentries, keeping tall, silent guard high above the city.

Mary and Joseph rose early the following morning, somewhat refreshed. Heading south on the road which edged the western hills, Joseph chose the path which seemed much more level and straight than the one which followed the twisted course of the Jordan River. The day grew warmer, silent, and breathless. On either side, rose the barren mountains of Ephraim and Gilead.

When the sun extinguished itself in a deep red haze, there were no more towns along the way, and campfires spurted at the foot of the surrounding hills. So Joseph and Mary camped off to one side of the dusty road, under a few naked and spindly trees.

Other travelers also spread out their pallets on the bare ground, or erected small tents for shelter.

A soft breeze was blowing, and a chill gradually crept into the air with the coming of night. A great canopy of luminous stars arched overhead, winking and sparkling.

Mary snuggled in Joseph's arms, bone-weary and homesick. The skies were an awesome wonder to their tired eyes as the gleaming radiance of the evening star beamed down on them.

Sariel and Samuel kept their silent watch.

Mary woke with a start. A caravan was passing by, laden with heavy treasure. Camels bearing their burdens of gold, carpets, and silk brocades lumbered along, complaining loudly.

Dawn, red-drenched and gold, tinged the eastern sky, and the hills were a colorful mosaic in the early morning light.

Her body was sore and aching, and she dreaded the long day's journey ahead. Another wave of homesickness washed over her. Her thoughts strayed to their small humble home in Nazareth, which seemed already so long-ago and faraway. The child in her womb stretched and turned heavily. She groaned softly.

Whispering in Mary's ear, Sariel bent low over her sweet charge.

*How precious are your thoughts about me, O God! They are innumerable! I can't even count them; they outnumber the grains of sand! And when I wake up in the morning, you are still with me!* Psalm 139:17-18 NLT

The words of the treasured song of King David flooded Mary's mind, and comforting warmth spread throughout her weary body.

Joseph stirred and stretched his cramped arms over head. Yawning, he rubbed his eyes. "Good morning, my wife." His voice was husky with sleep.

"Good morning, dear husband," Mary responded warmly.

Joseph gazed at his young spouse. Blue shadows smudged her brown eyes, and their usual clear light seemed dimmed.

*This journey is too hard and long for her*, he thought uneasily. Rising, he opened his knapsack and handed Mary some figs and a chunk of goat cheese. A small piece of cold broiled fish wrapped in flat bread and a cup of tepid water completed their breakfast. Joseph fed Ezra some oats and poured water into a tin for him. The little animal drank deeply, long ears twitching.

The third day of the journey wore on. The landscape grew brown and barren as they walked. Rock formations smoothed and carved by centuries of wind were scattered close to the dry undergrowth of the hills a short distance away.

Joseph kept close watch on Mary, insisting that she ride on Ezra's back for most of the day.

The shadows were growing long when at last the landscape began to grow greener, and lush palm trees appeared here and there. Mary gasped as Herod's gleaming white marble summer palace loomed ahead. It stood in stark contrast among the thick palm groves surrounding it. And there, just beyond, rose the ancient city of Jericho. More lush, heavy stands of palm trees surrounded the city, in green contrast to the long range of red granite rocks lining the hills beyond.

"Some say that this is the oldest city in the world, Mary," Joseph said, taking her hand.

Off to the west, a sheer cliff rose stark against a darkening plum-colored sky. From the dusty road, they could see numerous grottoes dotting the cliff sides. The deep purple Judean hills rose steeply westward toward Jerusalem and their destination.

Joseph and his young wife camped overnight outside of Jericho, resuming their journey in the cold gray early light of dawn on the fifth day. They joined the ever-growing crowd of Jews on the road to their ancestral homes. The young couple, footsore and weary, set their faces toward Bethlehem.

Joseph became more and more anxious about Mary. In the pale chill of morning, her face held a ghostly white pallor; and deep purple shadows underlay her brown eyes, now deep-set with exhaustion. Her mouth was pinched and drawn, her lips bloodless and pale, although she managed a faint smile for Joseph.

"My love, it will not be much longer. We shall be in Bethlehem by tomorrow night, I promise you." Joseph kissed his wife's brow tenderly.

As he helped her onto Ezra's back she moaned softly. *Lord God on high, be with us through this day. Keep my Mary safe in the shadow of your wings.* Joseph's silent plea rose to the Father's Throne, and the Heavenly Host looked on as Salvation's Plan unfolded below.

Gloriel was acutely aware of the growing excitement among the angels surrounding her. Soon, very soon now, the Son would be born upon the very Earth which was the work of His hands.

Sariel and Samuel, ever watchful over Mary and Joseph, sometimes chose to appear among the crowd in their human forms.

The road now wound through a desert floor which seemed like a great sea of white goat's milk to the couple's tired eyes. The surrounding hills provided a play of colors against the cerulean heavens.

As the day wore on towards sunset, the noise and the press of bodies on the swarming road grew more unbearable for Mary. A weary Ezra stumbled, almost dislodging his precious burden. Mary cried out in pain, and the pallor about her tense mouth increased. Joseph hastily led the little donkey to the side of the road, pushing through the complaining crowd. As he struggled to break loose from the press of humanity around them, he noticed a short, stocky man with a pleasant round face, making way for them ahead. Suddenly, they were in the open alongside the road. Joseph turned to thank their benefactor, but he had disappeared among the throng.

Joseph led Ezra into a small clearing where there were a few bushes, and the insects were not so bothersome. Out of view of the teeming road, Joseph gently lifted Mary down to the ground. He held up a sheltering blanket so that she could relieve herself. Quickly, he spread out a pallet on the sandy ground for her. She slumped in his arms, groaning softly, then leaned wearily back against a large boulder.

Her eyes were heavy-lidded with exhaustion, and although she tried, she could not hold them open. Her skin was a translucent white in the gathering twilight.

"My love, my sweet love," Joseph murmured against her damp brow. He felt sick with anxiety. "Mary, we will go no farther today. You must rest now," he said. She nodded, tears forming along the lower lids of her eyes.

Joseph unloaded the supplies from Ezra's tired back, fed him some oats, and tethered him nearby. Digging through his knapsack, he found some dried salted fish, goat cheese and flat bread for their supper. There was no meat. He filled a cup with the lukewarm water remaining in the goat skins, and pressed it to Mary's quivering lips, rousing her to drink deeply. He coaxed her to eat, breaking the bread and fish into small pieces for her.

"You must eat, my love, for the sake of the child."

Mary raised herself up, trembling, on one elbow. She ate slowly, washing the morsels down with the water.

Joseph built a small fire with some dry branches lying nearby. He removed her veil, and gently brushed Mary's heavy hair. Wringing out some cloths in a little water from the skin, he bathed her face tenderly. A faint dusting of color began to flush her cheeks.

Refreshed, Mary raised her eyes and looked about her. Suddenly, her eyes widened with surprise. A short distance away, like a vision in the twilight, a lovely child stood smiling at her.

*It's the same child I saw at the well in Nazareth!* Blinking her eyes in disbelief, Mary gazed in amazement at the beautiful young girl. A final beam of sunlight gleamed behind the golden curls, turning them into a halo of light.

Mary turned toward Joseph, crying out excitedly "Do you see her?"

"See who, my love?"

"Standing over there, that lovely child!" Mary turned and gestured.

She was gone. Mary looked around in bewilderment.

"She was right over there! I have seen her before, at the well in Nazareth. She must be traveling with her family for the census. Where did she go?"

Mary's receding pallor had given away to a full rosy glow. Her eyes gleamed bright and alert with excitement.

"Mary, hush, hush now, my dearest. You must rest. We'll start out early in the morning. Lie down, please. There is no one there now," Joseph replied, stroking her brow.

Reluctantly, Mary lay down, and Joseph covered her gently with a blanket. She fell asleep almost immediately, a faint smile curving her lips.

The sixth day dawned in a soft hue of rose. A chill still filled the air as Mary and Joseph prepared for the last day of their journey. After a meager breakfast, Joseph loaded Ezra with their belongings, along with the most precious burden ever to honor an animal.

They joined the throng on the dusty road, blending in with rich Greeks traveling in sedan chairs on their way to trade with wealthy Jews in Jerusalem. All around them, the jostling crowd swelled, as they approached the great city.

They paused to rest in the early afternoon, as Mary grew more and more fatigued. Her back ached cruelly, and at times she felt as though she was sitting on the child's head.

Sariel whispered comforting words in Mary's ear as the girl closed her drooping eyes and rested against Joseph's strong shoulder.

Their rest was all too brief as Joseph roused his exhausted bride. His feet Were sore, his body unbelievably weary. *How much more so must my beloved be,"* he thought as he stretched his sore muscles.

"Mary, we must move on now. We are almost there, dear one."

"Oh, Joseph, I know we must go on, or the child will be born by the roadside." She smiled wanly. She noticed that Joseph's eyes were bloodshot and darkly ringed, his dark hair powdered with white dust.

The sun sat low in the western sky, a flaming pink, fading to smoky lavender. Mary and Joseph crested a small rise, and there appeared to their thankful eyes, the Holy City. Even from a distance, the great dome of the Temple gleamed in the setting sun. This Temple of the living God, restored by the despised Herod hoping to appease God's chosen people, stirred an array of emotions in the young couple.

Joseph found himself breaking into song. The familiar psalm of David for the ascent into Jerusalem sprang forth from deep in his heart.

*"Those who trust in the Lord are as secure as Mount Zion; they will not be defeated but will endure forever. Just as the mountains surround and protect Jerusalem, so the Lord surrounds and protects his people, both now and forever.* Psalm 125:1-2 NLT

Some in the crowd stared as the strong young voice rang out. Mary and Joseph could see a solitary translucent cloud hovering over the Mount of Olives. Their hearts lifted, and suddenly the weariness was forgotten in their joy at the sight of the great city. Joseph quickened their pace, and even Ezra seemed to find new strength for the last leg of their long hard journey.

# Chapter Seven

The holy city of Jerusalem! Here the sages and prophets of old had lived. The patriarchs; Moses, Daniel, Saul and Elias once walked these narrow walled streets. Mary and Joseph passed through the massive gates, marveling at the watchtowers far overhead.

"Mary, do you remember how Ezekiel called Jerusalem "the center of the earth?" Joseph asked, sweeping his arms in an arc overhead, and grinning. "Surely, it must be!"

The street swarmed with market rabble, even in the twilight. Women shrieked and men shouted; children, the blind, the crippled, were everywhere. Beggars sitting against the walls wailed, rattling their tin cups. The tiny little shops, sunken into the walls, and crowded with wares, began closing down. Many pilgrims took shelter for the night within the great walls. Myriad aromas assaulted the couple's nostrils as they hurried through the teeming streets. A multitude of languages battered their ears.

A pain, no longer vague and fleeting, struck deep in Mary's pelvis. She drew in her breath quickly. This was different, somehow, from those little nagging sensations which had plagued her throughout this last day. It was gone now. *Has the time come?* She wondered to herself. *Joseph said we still have about five miles to travel.*

"Oh Joseph, we must hurry!" Mary exclaimed, clutching at her round belly.

Joseph urged Ezra onward through the throng, his heart pounding. He stumbled several times in his haste. The weight of the pack rode heavy on the weary muscles of his legs and back. *Oh Lord God, help us find shelter soon,* he prayed silently.

The crowds were thinning, and as they left Jerusalem they were able to travel a little faster. The noises of the city began to fade away in the distance as they hurried along the shadowed road. Sariel and Samuel stayed close beside their charges.

Another contraction rose slowly to a peak, like a bellows, and Mary found it difficult not to cry out. Ezra struggled, breathing heavily, his precious burden shifting. Fatigue sank its fangs deep into the little donkey's muscles, but still he picked his way carefully.

"Ezra seems to know how precious a burden he carries," Sariel commented to Samuel.

"I believe he does, Sariel," Samuel responded, nodding.

Nausea gripped Mary as Ezra swayed and stumbled occasionally in the deepening dusk. "Oh, Lord, have mercy," she prayed under her breath.

Sariel leaned close, tenderly placing an unseen hand on Mary's pale and sweating brow. Gloriel and the great Host of Heaven anxiously watched the crisis taking place below.

Few pilgrims were still on the road now, most having camped or found shelter for the night. The stench of humanity and the acrid taste of rising dust were left behind. The dark road grew steeper as they approached Bethlehem.

On either side of the road, Joseph and Mary could see the flickering campfires of shepherds. The surrounding hills stood in stark black silhouette against the fading azure of the western sky.

"Joseph, please hurry!" Mary cried out again, as pain rolled through her pelvis and back. Increasing in intensity, it rose to a climax and gradually faded away. The weary girl bowed her head down on her chest as sweat began to bead her forehead and pale upper lip.

"My dearest, we cannot go much faster, lest Ezra stumble in the dark. It won't be much longer," Joseph replied miserably. His usually vigorous voice was husky and a little hoarse.

Darkness fell, and the long wing of night settled over the road ahead. Two gleaming stars appeared as the sky turned from amethyst to a velvety black.

The road climbed ever steeper as they pressed on. They all bore a burden uniquely their own; Ezra his precious onus, Joseph his great responsibility, and Mary her pain.

Sariel and Samuel remained close at hand, seeking to comfort and encourage the young couple. Samuel guided the small donkey around stones and holes in the now barely discernible road. Sariel whispered a soft lullaby in Mary's ear.

Mary moaned softly. A shepherd's flute trilled faintly from a darkened hillside as they drew nearer to their destination. Numberless stars gleamed brightly in the soft curtain of night.

The road leading into Bethlehem curved, climbing steadily. Perched on two hills, the little town lay surrounded by orchards and olive groves. Rounding a bend in the road, Joseph could see flickering torchlight a short distance away.

The gates of Bethlehem with two Roman soldiers on guard rose up before his tired eyes.

Oblivious now to her surroundings, the young mother-to-be felt dazed and faint with nausea. *I have to hang on until we find shelter,* she told herself. *Oh Lord God, please help us. Emi, I need you!*

They arrived, finally, at the gate. Some people were resting beside the road. Joseph spoke briefly with the soldiers stationed at the entrance. Mary's pains were closer together now, and of longer duration. *Oh, Lord Most High, I can't go on much longer,* Mary prayed silently, biting her lower lip to keep from crying out.

Ezra's sides heaved from the exertion of the long climb to the hillside community. His head and ears drooped in exhaustion. Mary felt pity for her dear little companion, but she knew she would not be able to walk any distance.

Joseph led Ezra through the gate and into the little town. It was pitch-dark now. The streets lay silent, as most of the inhabitants of Bethlehem were preparing or eating their evening meal. Joseph stayed on the main road, which had two small streets crossing it.

"Mary, the soldiers say there is only one inn, and it is most likely full now. But I will go inside and inquire. Do you want to get down, my love?" Even in the flickering and shadowy light, he could see pain etching its mark on his wife's white face. Her eyes were deeply shadowed and her mouth trembled.

"No, Joseph. I will be fine. Please hurry."

"My dearest, I am sure we will have no trouble finding lodgings. Especially because of the baby," he assured her, patting her hand.

He noticed a lamp swinging on a rope across an opening in the wall at the top of the steep hill. Surely, this must be the inn, he thought. He pulled again on Ezra's bridle strap. The little ass lowered his head and started bravely up the hill, flanks heaving.

As they approached the inn, Joseph's heart sank. There were several families sleeping outside the entry to the inn. Disheartened, he reluctantly entered the door. It was the usual "khan," a long rectangular walled space. Unharnessed animals stood around the room. Men, women and children lay sleeping on the earthen floor.

Threading his way among the prostrate figures, Joseph finally found the proprietor. He was a wizened little man, wearing a sour expression and an air of frigid unconcern.

"Sir, my wife is expecting a child, and her time is upon her. Is there a small private place for us?" Joseph asked. Nausea lay pallid in his stomach, with fear of the proprietor's response.

The proprietor glared at Joseph from beneath ragged gray eyebrows. "There are people from all over the country here, people here for the census, people here with the usual caravans from Egypt, people here just because. Now where would I put a woman to have a baby?!" he snapped, gesturing angrily.

A chill sweat broke out on Joseph's forehead. "Sir, please, do you know of anyplace we can go?" He was pleading now, his voice trembling.

Unseen, Samuel placed a hand on the innkeeper's shoulder, and whispered in his ear. A strange expression crossed the irascible old man's face. His austere mouth softened, and his dark eyelids flickered in surprise. He placed a grimy forefinger on his lower lip, tapping it lightly.

"Well," he said, pausing thoughtfully, "there is one place . . . Outside, there is a pathway to the left. Go down it, and you will find a cave, where the donkeys, goats and cattle are kept. That's the best I can do."

Relief flooded over Joseph's taut features.

"Thank you, sir! We are so grateful. May the Most High God bless you!"

"Humph! Well, you will find some fresh straw in the manger. You may use that for a bed for your wife," the innkeeper replied gruffly. His expression had warmed somewhat.

Joseph returned to Mary outside the inn. Reluctantly, he told her there was no room for them.

"However, my love, the innkeeper has agreed to let us stay in the stable," he said quietly, hanging his head.

Mary smiled at her shame-faced husband. "Oh, Joseph, it's all right. It will be warm in there with the animals, I am sure," she said, leaning down and patting his cheek. "The Most High is with us. Come, we must make haste." Pain once more held the young girl in its relentless grip, leaving her breathless.

The path ran along the side of the hill, leading to the entrance of the cave. Joseph pulled steadily on Ezra's bridle, hurrying him along. He lit the lamp before entering the cave. Glancing up at his wife, he was startled at her appearance. Despite her exhaustion and pain, there was a serene expression in her eyes, and she smiled down at him tenderly.

He lifted her gently down from Ezra's back, and she clung to him briefly. He led her into the cave, raising the lamp high. The room was separated into two parts, the upper for people and the lower one for animals. The walls and roof were bare rock. The pungent odor of animals filled the air, although there were only a few, as the cave was not large.

Joseph hung the lamp on a stable peg and looked around quickly. The feed boxes contained some clean straw, and he prepared a bed for his wife, plumping the straw and covering it with a blanket. Suddenly shy, he asked Mary what he should do. According to the ancient Law, a man should not witness the birth of a child. It was the custom for a midwife or other woman to be in attendance.

"My husband, please go to the inn and see if there is a midwife close by. The time is very near." Mary's mouth drew tight. The pains were increasing rapidly, one following on the heels of another. Joseph helped her lie down on the straw pallet. She was perspiring heavily now, sweat beading her forehead and running down her flushed face.

Feeling awkward and helpless, Joseph did as Mary bade him. He hurried out into the night, stumbling in the dark. The animals grew silent, watching with soft eyes glowing in the lamp light.

Ezra nuzzled Mary with his soft nose, as if to comfort her. Sariel knelt beside her blessed charge, singing a soft song into Mary's ear.

As the pangs of approaching birth struck deep into her trembling flesh, Mary whispered the words of an ancient Psalm.

*"Lord, hear my prayer! Listen to my plea! Don't turn away from me in my time of distress. Bend down your ear and answer me quickly when I call to you, for my days disappear like smoke, and my bones burn like red-hot coals."* Psalm 102: NLT

The old prayer rose to the Father, and Mary thought wistfully of Anna. *Oh, I need my Emi now! But the Lord is with me. It is his Child I bear, and he will not abandon me in my travail,* she reasoned hopefully.

Joseph rushed into the cave, sweating and breathless. His voice trembled as he told his wife that there was no midwife available.

His eyes were blinded with tears as he knelt beside Mary. "What should I do, beloved? What can I do?"

Mary's expression turned momentarily serene as she placed her soft arms around his neck.

"The Lord is with us," she replied calmly.

Joseph cradled her in his arms, wishing he could bear her pain. He wiped her glistening forehead with his sleeve as she cried out on the rising tide of another contraction.

*So close together now; the time is nearly upon me!* She rode the crest of the pain, like a wave bearing her helpless in its gigantic clutches. An involuntary scream tore its way through her clenched teeth.

Joseph burst into tears; wringing his hands, frantic with worry. Never in his young, strong life had he felt so helpless.

As the pain subsided, Mary lay gasping and limp in his arms.

"Joseph! Go now! Please do as I bid you!" Sweat drenched her exhausted young body, and her long hair clung to her neck and face in wet strands.

Joseph laid her gently back on the straw bed, kissed her dripping face, and hastened outside the cave.

A windless deep quiet had settled over the hillside. It was as if the night held its breath in profound silence.

Thinking that he might obtain some warm water at the inn to save some time, Joseph walked quickly up the path, breathless in his anxiety.

The innkeeper's wife was kind enough to give him a jar of warm water, and he hurried back to the cave, stumbling, and almost spilling the water. He grabbed some soft cloths from Mary's pack and hastened to her side.

She was sitting up now, her back pressed against the hard rock wall. Her sweet face was pinched and contracted. Joseph hastily poured some of the warm water on a cloth and bathed her flushed and sweating face.

Her back arched in the cruel grasp of another contraction. "Joseph," she whispered raggedly, as tears flowed down her cheeks. "Bring me the swaddling cloths, quickly!"

He sprang to his feet, startling the animals, which began to stir restlessly. Ezra brayed softly, and Joseph realized he had not fed the little donkey. Tearing articles out of the pack, he found the swaddling cloths, so carefully prepared by the young mother-to-be. Wrapped with the cloths was a small knife. He brought them to his wife. He was sobbing now.

"Dear Lord, please help her!" he prayed aloud. Samuel placed his hand on Joseph's trembling shoulder.

Mary looked up at her husband. "Go now, Joseph. You must leave now." Her voice was raspy.

Reluctantly, Joseph left her at last. Just inside the entrance, he built a small fire to warm more water, and to prepare some warm broth for Mary with some onions and herbs left in his knapsack. He could not see her from the entrance, as the animals hid her from view; but he could hear her moaning, and calling upon the Most High. The smell of the animals mixed with that of the broth beginning to steam in the pot. The fire flickered and reflected off the shadowed rock wall. Hands trembling, he fed Ezra and bedded him down.

Joseph prayed then, pleading with the Lord to deliver his Mary safely through her travail. *This is the Lord's Son*, he thought to himself. *He would not allow anything to happen to the Mother of his Son.* He paced back and forth outside the cave entrance, as fathers had since the beginning of time.

Inside, Sariel ministered to Mary in every way she could. She longed to take on her human form, but she knew this could not be, at this time. The night lay very still and silent outside the cave.

Suddenly, Mary gave a loud cry, sustained and high-pitched. Joseph's heart leaped into his throat at the sound. "Mary! Mary!" he called out, trembling with fear. It was all he could do, not to rush to her side.

Then there was silence, profound and deep. Even the animals did not stir. "Mary!" Joseph cried. Tears flowed freely down his anguished face.

Then, a new cry filled the air, sweetly. The cry that has filled the hearts of parents with joy from time immemorial rent the heavy air with gusto. "Joseph!" Mary's voice, tired but elated, called out to her husband. "Wait just a few minutes, my husband."

Relief flooded Joseph's heart. He laughed aloud, and raised his arms to heaven in thanksgiving.

Samuel and Sariel rejoiced together, celebrating the Event that would forever change Time on the Earth.

#

Meanwhile, the entire Heavenly Host gazed enraptured at the miracle which had just occurred in the tiny town of Bethlehem, in Judea. They knew that the long awaited fulfillment of the Lord's Covenant was happening as they watched.

*How wonderful for Sariel*, Gloriel thought, *to be present as the Creator takes on the flesh of His creation!*

Watching Gloriel, Gabriel and Michael grinned at one another, looking much like co-conspirators.

Suddenly, the voice of the Father rang out. "Gloriel! Come to me!" As always, His voice brought a thrill to her heart and soul as the little angel hastened to stand before the Throne. The warm golden light enfolded her as she stood before the Almighty One, bowing low in His presence.

"Gloriel," the voice was soft and low now. "Come closer." Trembling with awe, she tentatively stepped forward. The golden mist was thinning, reflecting in her searching amber gaze. For the first time, Gloriel could make out a figure sitting on the Throne. The glittering gems set in the Throne flung their varicolored rays into the mist. The figure seemed to be part of the light, and yet was distinctly discernible, although Gloriel could not distinguish any features.

Her very being was suddenly pierced by an indescribable love. It flooded her heart, soul, and body with warmth, peace, and incredible joy. She sank to her knees, overcome with bliss. In the presence of His Glory, everything else minimized to triviality, like a speck of dust.

"Gloriel, my child, arise. It is time now for your mission to begin." The voice was part of the golden light, surrounding her with its tenderness.

Rising to her feet, she stood trembling as she waited. That which she had so longed for was about to be revealed. *Am I dreaming?* She wondered to herself. Heaven was totally silent, waiting for the revelation of Gloriel's ministry.

"Gloriel, you are most blessed among all the angels. The eternal Son at this moment is taking on the flesh of his mother, and of all his people. You, my angel, shall be his guardian for all the days he walks the earth. You will protect, nurture, and guide him from the moment of his birth until he returns to Heaven in glory. Keep watch over my beloved Son, Gloriel. Go now, with my blessing upon you."

The figure on the Throne increased in brilliance, and power flowed from the Lord God into the small angel trembling before Him. She felt strength flowing, growing, inside her, a marvelous sense of the Lord's sanction.

She became a shining figure of light before the eyes of her companions, her face and figure a shimmering white. In the twinkling of an eye, she vanished from among them in a flash of dazzling light.

# Chapter Eight

Benjamin was content this brisk early spring night. His belly was full, his flock dozing quietly in the field. He reclined against a boulder, knees drawn up, his arms crossed over them.

Nearby, Zadok, Tobias, and Joshua kept guard over their sheep. The soft melody of Zadok's flute faded away, and all was silent. Benjamin's staff stood propped against a nearby rock. The campfire danced gaily, and his eyelids grew heavy. Yawning, he ground the heels of his palms into his eye sockets. *Even the sheep are unusually quiet,* he thought to himself. He stretched his long gangly arms over his head.

Benjamin ben Ephraim was 17 years old, and this was his first flock. Zadok and Tobias were in their thirties. *Old men, now,* he thought, smiling. Joshua was 23, and newly-wed. Not quite so old.

Shepherd's campfires dotted the hillsides, though none were close by, except for those of Zadok, Tobias, and Joshua. By day, the flocks wandered Judea's hills and grasslands, drawing a little closer to Jerusalem each day. The great city was the best market for sheep. Some were sold for shearing, some as sacrificial animals, or for food.

Benjamin's flock huddled quietly together in the night chill. Slowly, the young shepherd's sharp chin lowered to his chest, and he dozed.

Suddenly, the sheep began stirring restlessly, and the lambs bleated. Benjamin jumped to his feet and grabbed his staff. *Is it a lion come down from the far hills*? So far, the youth had not needed to defend his flock from any predators. His heart beat hard in his thin chest. He could faintly distinguish Tobias, Zadok, and Joshua standing next to their campfires. He called out to Zadok, who was nearest. "Do you see anything?"

Zadok's husky voice cut through the cold night air. "No, nothing!"

Picking up his torch which lay nearby, Benjamin quickly ignited it in the fire. He circled the flock, his black eyes searching the shadows.

A melodious murmur reached his ears. *Where is it coming from?* The darkness seemed to be lessening. "How can this be?" he wondered out loud. "There is no moon, and it must be close to midnight." He glanced up at the night sky. Myriad stars gleamed and winked down at him.

Before his wondering eyes, the black curtain of night began lifting, split with light. Straight overhead, a strange glow began growing far in the depths of space. Slowly at first, then gathering speed, it filled his vision, growing ever more brilliant as it approached. It was clear silver, so bright that he wanted to shield his eyes, but found he could not raise his hand. The torch fell from his grasp, and he was consumed with heart-stopping terror.

As Benjamin stood frozen with fear, an angel descended from within the light. Gabriel's great wings spread their magnificence directly over the petrified youth's head. The Glory of the Lord surrounded the shepherds, and they were struck speechless by an overwhelming fear.

*"But the angel reassured them. 'Don't be afraid!' he said, 'I bring you good news of great joy for everyone! The Savior—yes, the Messiah, the Lord—has been born tonight in Bethlehem, the city of David! And this is how you will recognize him: You will find a baby lying in a manger, wrapped snugly in strips of cloth!'"* Luke 2: 10-12 NLT

Before the stunned gaze of the shepherds, thousands upon thousands of angels materialized in the sky overhead. The countryside lay bathed in dazzling light. Both sheep and shepherds stood struck dumb with awe.

The murmur which had begun a few moments before the appearance of Gabriel, swelled into a magnificent burst of heavenly melody. Glorious voices filled the surrounding countryside with their joyous proclamation:

"Glory to God in the highest Heaven, and peace on Earth to men of good will!"

The shepherds remained paralyzed with fear, as terror shot a cold bolt through Benjamin's chest. His head whirled with the spectacle before his startled gaze. A multitude of colors and hues shot through the silver light, glimmering like thousands of rainbows, in hues of a richness he had never seen before.

The praises of the angelic host rose heavenward. As the song of the angels and Gabriel's words penetrated the shepherds' hearts, the fear began to diminish, and elation rose up within them.

As suddenly as they appeared, the host of angels returned to Heaven. The glorious light faded away, leaving the shepherds dumbfounded and motionless. As they stood gazing into the heavens, jaws agape, another light appeared over the hillside where the little town of Bethlehem nestled in the darkness. It increased steadily in brilliance, yet did not light up the surrounding countryside. A beam of soft silver light focused on one spot in the town.

Benjamin shook his head, as if waking from a dream. He tried to gather his wits about him as he hurried over to Zadok's camp, where Tobias and Joshua joined them.

Did you see what I saw?" Benjamin exclaimed. Dazed, the older shepherds nodded, still unable to speak. "What should we do?" Benjamin asked, his voice cracking and trembling.

Regaining his power of speech, the soothing voice of Joshua reassured them. "We should go and see this wonderful thing which has happened, as the angel said."

Leaving their sheep in the care of the Most High, the little group of shepherds walked across the valley and up the hill. Tobias clutched a small lamb close to his chest. They hurried up the dusty road to Bethlehem, growing breathless, and stumbling in their haste and excitement.

When they reached the gate to the town, they wondered how they might find this Babe of which the angel spoke.

"Let's follow the bright star and its beam," Benjamin suggested, voice still shaking. His black eyes reflected the dancing torch light, and his boyish face was shining.

The others agreed, and hurrying through the quiet streets, they tracked the cold fire of the star overhead.

When they reached the inn, they turned aside on the narrow path leading to the manger. They were slipping and sliding on the pathway now, in their eagerness to see the Babe, as they approached the entrance to the cave.

Inside, the new mother rested quietly, dozing on and off. The created one clasped the Creator tenderly to her breast.

The steamy breath of the animals and the small fire at the entrance warmed the shadowy cave. Joseph stood guard, fiercely protective of his little family, even in his exhaustion.

Approaching Joseph eagerly, Joshua spoke first. "Sir, a host of angels appeared to us in the sky as we watched over our flocks in the fields. A huge number of glorious beings, all singing praises to the Most High, told us about the birth of a King, the Messiah, in Bethlehem. Then they disappeared, and an enormous, flaming star led us to this cave," he explained, pointing to the gleaming star overhead. He was breathless after such a long speech. Inhaling deeply, he continued. "May we come in and worship the Child?"

Joseph studied the four shepherds solemnly, but did not reply right away.

Mary listened closely to the shepherd's words. She gently laid her tiny Son down in a feeding trough lined with fresh straw.

"Joseph, bid them come in, please." Her soft, melodious voice broke the silence like the call of birds at daybreak.

Benjamin started to step inside then, at Joseph's bidding. Suddenly shy, he motioned to Tobias, the eldest, to enter first.

Tobias solemnly approached the young mother and child, setting the little lamb down at Mary's feet. He sank to his knees in adoration of the tiny bundle lying in the manger. The sweet smell of straw, barley and oats surrounded the Babe.

Hesitantly, Benjamin, Zadok and Joshua shuffled forward in awed silence and knelt beside Tobias. Joseph and Mary smiled at them in encouragement.

Zadok reached inside the folds of his tunic, slowly withdrawing his flute. An achingly sweet melody filled the small cave, a poignant song of love, of joy, and praise. The animals were silent and still, ears twitching, as Zadok's tribute to the newborn King caressed the night air. Mary's sweet smile rewarded him.

After the shepherds left, Mary continued to ponder their words, remembering Gabriel's announcement to her all those months ago. In her quiet, reflective spirit, the night's events became a precious treasure to her, stored safely and forever in her memory.

Gloriel, Sariel and Samuel looked on with delight, rejoicing in this glorious event. Gloriel's heart sang with joy as she stood beside her blessed charge, gazing in adoration at the small bit of humanity and divinity placed in her care. The long ages of waiting, leading to this moment, seemed such a small cost to pay for the ecstasy she enjoyed now.

The Father smiled down upon his newborn Son. The Beginning and the End were born in that moment. The story of Earth was struck with such power and force that it was forever ripped in two; Before, and After.

#

That same night, far away in a distant land, three men observed the brilliant Star in the eastern sky. They were very rich and wise, scholars and astrologers of Persia, called the Magi, the wise ones.

Intrigued with the bright new Star, they wondered from whence it came to grace the night sky like a luminous diamond. Was it but a single star, or a rare conjunction of two or three stars? They could not agree, so they searched all the ancient astrological writings available to them, both Greek and Persian. Nothing seemed to apply to the Star. Finally, they discovered a very old prophecy in the Jewish Scriptures, about a Star which would rise out of Jacob, and a Scepter spring up from Israel.

After much thought and discussion, they reasoned among themselves that this must mean that a Savior had just been born to the people of Israel. Was it possible that this Messiah had come not only to the Jews, but to the entire known world?

Hastily, the three wise men, Gaspar, Melchior and Balthazar, packed supplies for a long journey on the backs of three camels. Each one carried a gift for the infant Messiah.

Moving across arid, scrub covered desert in the still of night, they followed the incandescent light set before them. During the day, they pitched their tents and rested. Each night, their shining sojourner beckoned them on toward their destination. Resolute in their mission, the three passed through great sand dunes, ranges of red granite hills, and soft grazing lands.

#

Meanwhile, Joseph and Mary remained in the small cave for eight days. On the eighth day, as was the custom, Joseph took the baby Jesus to the Synagogue in Bethlehem to be circumcised. He asked the rabbi if he might circumcise his son himself.

Gloriel watched, smiling at Joseph's nervousness. Samuel placed his hand on Joseph's shoulder as the rabbi guided the young father's hand.

Jesus, the Christ, shed his first tears as Gloriel kissed the top of his small head. "Jeshua, little Jeshua," Joseph whispered, trying to soothe the infant's pain.

When they returned to the cave, Mary cried softly as Joseph placed her baby in her arms, trembling in her own flesh for the pain in his. *This pain has to be,* she thought, *for the Father's glory and as a sign of the Covenant.* But her mother's heart cried. She kissed her little son's satin cheek. The tiny bundle in her arms yawned and blinked up at her.

*So his mother worships the Savior of the world with a kiss,* Gloriel thought to herself as she watched the tender scene.

Sariel smiled and touched Mary's hair gently.

The next day, the little family moved out of the stable into a small house on the outskirts of Bethlehem. Joseph's brother Abner arrived in Bethlehem with more of their belongings, remaining with them only long enough to register for the census.

They settled in the meager quarters, and Joseph found employment assisting a local carpenter. Mary was confined to the house until the 40th day after the birth of her son, the time of his Presentation in the Temple.

#

Gloriel never left Jesus' side, watching over him with adoring eyes, delighting in the little changes each day brought.

*His face is so sweet, his cheeks like satin,* she thought one day. A little shiver thrilled through her, as she traced the curve of his face with her finger. She was not sure exactly what lay ahead for this Holy Child, but she did know that he was destined to fulfill the Father's Plan of Salvation for his people.

# Chapter Nine

Simeon was a very old man. His beard was long and white, growing scraggly in his great age. His eyes were rheumy, his sight growing dim. Though he appeared frail, his heart was young. He was a Prophet of the Lord, one who speaks God's word to His people, speaking only as God directed him. Simeon had received guidance and nurturing from the Holy Spirit, transforming him into a prophetic voice. For many years, his heart longed for the promised redemption by God. He was so faithful and devout, that the Holy Spirit revealed to him that he would not taste death until he gazed upon the face of the Messiah.

Over the long years of waiting, he was present every morning in the Temple, attending the Presentation of firstborn sons.

By praying and pondering the Holy Spirit's promise to him, Simeon's relationship with the Most High blossomed into an intimate friendship. No matter how long he waited, he cherished the promise that he was to see the Messiah with his own eyes. Every day, he wondered if this was the time for the promise to be fulfilled. Many times, he asked "Lord, am I hearing you correctly?"

Simeon longed with all his heart for the coming of the Messiah who would fulfill the Most High's Plan for his people.

Seeing the worsening state of God's people, numberless times, he had cried out: "How long, O Lord, until we see your comfort? Bring your consolation to us!" But still, as the days, months, and years passed with the promise unfulfilled, he held firm in faith.

This particularly beautiful, bright morning, he felt an odd stirring within his breast, like the fluttering of butterfly wings. He placed his ancient bony hand over his heart. *Do I have a touch of indigestion?* He wondered silently.

Sariel and Gloriel were absorbed in watching, as in another part of the Temple, in the Women's Court, a devout widow, a prophetess, clasped her wrinkled hands in prayer. She spent every day in the Temple, fasting and praying, awaiting the fulfillment of the Most High's promises.

Anna was fully mature in the Holy Spirit, intimate with God, His thoughts, and ways. She knew His grace and His Plan to redeem his people. She had been a widow for 84 years, and was very, very old. No one was sure just exactly how old.

Suddenly, she felt a gentle flutter in her chest. A sensation of warmth spread slowly from her breast, up over her neck and into her soft wrinkled cheeks. "Go to the Presentation" a voice whispered in her ear. Startled, she looked around. No one was near her.

Rising to her feet slowly, she drew her frayed mantle close under her chin. Anna, daughter of Phanuel, of the tribe of Asher, urged her creaking joints toward the Court of Presentation.

#

Mary stood quietly in the court reserved for women. As she waited, she prayed, and in her heart, treasured the things God had done for her. The incense was kindled on the Golden Altar, and smoke rose, filling the air with a heavy and oppressing odor.

She stood surrounded by women who had recently given birth. Patiently, they all waited together for the Purification rites.

Out in the courtyard, Joseph, with Jesus in his arms, purchased two young turtledoves. This was all the young couple could afford, though the best offering would have been an unblemished lamb.

A line of goats and bleating lambs was being herded into the outer court to be sold for sacrifice.

Mary and the other young mothers ascended a curved flight of stairs leading to the Nicanor Gate. Here they were met by the Temple station men, who helped them with all the ceremonies involved in the Purification Rite. The young women were then declared ritually clean, as the incense rose into the bright morning sky. Now they would be allowed to join in the sacred offerings.

Joseph and Mary gave Jesus into the arms of a Temple priest. Mary's heart exulted as she watched the priest turn toward the altar with her son in his arms.

The magnificence of the Temple, the holiness of the moment began to overwhelm Jesus' young mother, and her lips trembled. Smoke was thick, mingling with the dizzying fragrance of incense. The burning of wool, hair, and flesh permeated the air with a heavy odor. She felt slightly faint, and clung to Joseph's arm. Crowds of people pressed close in on them.

Mary's eyes moved over the faces surrounding them. They were drawn to a lovely young woman standing to her right. *I don't think she's one of the new mothers. I didn't see her at the Purification Rite. She's like a shimmer of light, so exquisite and alluring—so beautiful!* Mary thought to herself. The gleaming amber hair was glossy and polished. The young woman's golden eyes fixed on Mary's child in the arms of the priest, shining with unmistakable love. *How strange*, Mary thought.

As the priest turned toward the altar with Jesus in his arms, the old man Simeon approached and peered into the blanket folds around the tiny face. His watery eyes widened, and he voiced a wordless cry. All eyes turned toward Simeon as he took the babe from the arms of the startled priest.

Since Simeon was well known in the Temple as a Prophet, the priest did not protest. Gazing into the wide, shining eyes of the infant, Simeon crooned softly. Unbounded joy and excitement filled him as he raised the child up in his wiry arms toward Heaven. His voice, now strong and clear, sang out to the Most High:

*"Lord, now I can die in peace! As you promised me, I have seen the savior you have given to all people. He is a light to reveal God to the nations, and he is the glory of your people Israel."* Luke 2: 29-32 NLT

Tears streamed down his aged face as he gently placed the baby back into the arms of the priest.

Joseph and Mary stood watching, wide-eyed with awe and amazement. Turning to the young parents, Simeon blessed them. He looked deep into Mary's brown eyes and said, *"This child will be rejected by many in Israel, and it will be their undoing. But he will be the greatest joy to many others. Thus, the deepest thoughts of many hearts will be revealed. And a sword will pierce your very soul."* Luke 2: 33-35 NLT

A chill and a thrill coursed through Mary's body. She turned to Joseph questioningly. Unseen, Sariel placed her hand on Mary's arm.

Joseph's face mirrored Mary's own bewilderment. *What could these words mean?* The young mother wondered silently.

Gloriel watched the dramatic scene with eyes only for the precious baby in her care. How she adored him! He was sleeping again, blissfully unaware of the prophecy unfolding.

Simeon slipped away in the crowd, filled with joy and looking forward eagerly to being with the Lord. The priest then concluded the ritual, and the baby Jesus was presented to the Lord.

Mary was thinking about the words of the old man, when there was a stirring among the murmuring crowd. An ancient face appeared among the people surrounding her. It was a tiny face, crosshatched with deep lines and wrinkles. A wisp of fine white hair had escaped from the coarse brown mantle, and lay damply across her forehead. The priest bowed his head slightly in deference to the old woman.

Someone standing behind Mary whispered, "It's Anna the prophetess. Everybody knows she is one of the holiest of women. No one knows how old she really is."

Anna's bent shoulders and back made her appear even smaller than she was. The priest lowered the baby so that Anna could see the small pink face.

She burst into praise, her voice husky and a little hoarse.

"These old eyes have seen the Glory of the Lord! Praise his holy Name!" Moving slowly back into the crowd, she spoke to all in her path, telling them that the promised King had finally come to save Jerusalem.

So, Anna and Simeon, after long years of waiting, of making the Temple their home, after decades of prayer and fasting, were rewarded with a glimpse of the Salvation of mankind. They saw the Promised One of God, who would bring light to the whole world.

The priest then placed her baby son back into Mary's arms. She looked down at the small innocent face, flushed from the heat. "Jeshua," she whispered, "my precious little one . . . Messiah?" Gloriel smiled.

Joseph took Mary's arm and led them back to where he had tied Ezra. Glancing around, Mary looked for the beautiful young woman who had been standing by her side. She had vanished in the crowd.

The late afternoon sun shimmered in a pale blue sky as they left the great City of David and headed home to Bethlehem.

Gloriel, Sariel, and Samuel accompanied their charges, watching the evening fold darkly over them as they entered Bethlehem.

#

Soon after Mary and Joseph settled in their humble home, Gaspar, Melchior and Balthazar arrived in Jerusalem. The Star, standing directly overhead now, had not yet reached its full nighttime brilliance. Stepping into the Court of the Gentiles, the three inquired of one of the Temple priests as to the whereabouts of the newborn King. One of Herod's spies, who stood nearby, mingling among the people, overheard the conversation.

"We have come from a distant land to worship him. We have followed his Star in the eastern sky," Gaspar told the priest.

The High Priest was then summoned. He asked them searching questions, and then informed them that he knew nothing about a Star, or a newborn King. He was about to go back into the Temple, when he paused, stroking his long silver beard. "There is a prophecy in the Sacred Writings which mentions Bethlehem as the birthplace of the Messiah." He gazed searchingly at the Three.

Gaspar, Melchior and Balthazar thanked the High Priest, who heaved a sigh and turned away once more. Only instead of returning to the Temple, he hurried to King Herod's Palace, eager to report the news of the mysterious three strangers seeking a newborn King. Unbeknownst to him the spy had already carried the news to Herod.

The three asked directions from the Temple guard, and immediately set off for Bethlehem. The Star was now gleaming in full glory overhead, shimmering, flashing, and sparkling in a sky the color of amethyst.

Gloriel knew that Herod the Great was an evil and cruel tyrant. She had followed the life of this despotic ruler closely, as she knew that somehow he would play a part in God's Plan.

Herod was not a true Jew, but an Idumean, whose ancestors had been forced to convert to Judaism. Gloriel recalled that he had been installed as King of the Jews by a decree of Caesar Augustus, and remained dependent on Rome. He was extremely fearful and anxious, insanely jealous of any threat to his position. For over 30 years, he continually drained away the very life-blood of his people.

He favored the Greek culture, and was an inexhaustible builder, skilled in architecture. In the fifteenth year of his reign, he rebuilt the Jewish Temple at his own personal expense.

Gloriel was aware that the heart and character of Herod the Great allowed for no mercy, or any sign of softness. He had five wives, and had executed two of them in fits of rage. Even his children were not safe from Herod's wrath, for he killed three of his sons because of rumors that they were scheming to take over his throne.

This was the man to whom the High Priest hurried with the news of the three strangers and their puzzling questions. He passed through the massive gates where Roman soldiers stood guard in watchtowers overhead. His priestly robes billowing behind him in his haste, he was admitted to the royal presence.

The Jews had special privileges, and were allowed to manage their own affairs, so the High Priest considered himself a friend of Herod.

Sitting on his throne to receive the High Priest, Herod postured and posed, his robe shimmering in shades of crimson and gold. Precious jewels flashed brilliantly from his thick neck and heavy arms. Herod was a short, heavy man with an enormous paunchy belly. His mouth was small and cruel, his heavy-jowled face pockmarked.

Lamplight gleamed on columns of variegated marble, and the soft muraled walls gleamed as the High Priest bowed low before Herod. He breathlessly related his news, which fell on ears already on fire from the spy's disclosure. Herod listened, his face growing steadily darker, his hooded gray eyes steely.

"Where did the prophets say the Messiah would be born?" he asked the High Priest.

"In Bethlehem, your Majesty," he replied, bowing again deferentially.

Herod began to fume, as anger, bright, hot, and galvanizing flowed through him. Even though he was dying slowly of an incurable disease, the thought of a usurper of his throne infuriated him. *I will wait until the Magi return, and then I will deal with this child "king", this upstart,* he thought to himself.

He summoned a slave, and ordered him to pursue the three strangers and deliver a message to them. "Ask these three "wise" men to return to Jerusalem when they have found the new-born king, so that we can go ourselves to pay him homage. Go quickly now, you idiot!" he shouted at the cowering servant.

#

The swarming streets began to empty. The reeking scent of hot grease still filled the air as Gaspar, Melchior and Balthazar passed through the Gate of Damascus. The great Star preceded them, its cold fire gleaming through the gathering gloom as night deepened around them.

Jerusalem was now far behind them. As their camels labored up the winding road to Bethlehem, the Star stood directly overhead, its radiance palpating and glowing.

All three paused outside the gate to change into rich silken robes, intense in color; green, red, and white, with beautifully embroidered details. All of them wore the soft, pointed Phrygian cap of the Far East. They dug into their saddle pouches and withdrew the gifts they brought to honor the new King.

As they entered the city gate, the Star remained fixed over a small house nearby. The few people on the street stared rudely at the trio as they dismounted from the camels. These onlookers gazed at the strange saddle rugs and bridle ornaments on the camels. Believing that these were rich gentiles, the people were not inclined to speak to them freely.

At the entrance to the small house built into the side of a cave, Joseph appeared in response to Gasper's soft call.

"Greetings, sir. We have come from a far distant land to adore the new King. We have followed his Star to this place. We are overwhelmed with joy to have found him." Gaspar's voice trembled, and he was startled to feel hot tears brim in his eyes. He introduced his companions to Joseph, who was wide-eyed with wonder.

Joseph bowed to his guests, excused himself, and went to speak with Mary. He was back in a moment, bidding the three to enter the humble abode. Ezra, tethered nearby, peered at the visitors curiously.

Mary was sitting on a low stool beside a small wooden cradle. She looked up and smiled as the three approached.

"Peace be with you," she murmured. Her lovely face was serene, her brown eyes reflecting the flickering lamplight. Gloriel leaned unseen over the cradle.

Melchior asked if they might approach the child to pay homage. Mary nodded and reached inside the cradle to arrange the blanket so the face of her precious baby might be seen clearly.

All three men dropped to their knees, their rich robes standing out in sharp contrast to the hard-packed dirt floor. Although they could not fully grasp what had taken place at the birth of this boy child to a simple Galilean couple; by some mysterious gift of faith, they recognized his authority, and worshipped him.

The baby was awake, gazing placidly out at them with large, intelligent dark eyes. His hair was a soft downy nimbus of pale gold in the lamplight.

Bowing their foreheads to the ground, the Magi adored him. At that moment, they gave up their worship of the stars, to worship the One who had hung those points of light in the night sky.

Gloriel bent low, whispering in Jesus' small pink ear. He smiled, and a dimple appeared in one round cheek.

Balthazar stood up and reached inside his robe, bringing forth a small box made of teakwood, ornately carved. Lifting the lid, he placed it beside the cradle. The heady scent of frankincense filled the small room. "To honor his Divinity,' he murmured. He bowed low and moved aside as Gaspar took his place.

Gaspar's dark hair and beard shadowed his face as he withdrew a large pouch of soft leather from inside his robe. He opened the pouch with trembling fingers, and scooped out a handful of gleaming golden coins.

"For a journey you will soon undertake, and to honor the baby's Kingship," he whispered to Mary.

She turned her clear eyes, liquid in the lamplight, upon the youngest of the Magi. "A journey? But we have just settled . . ." Her voice trailed off into silence as she gazed into Gaspar's wine-brown eyes, glowing like topazes.

Melchior, his dark skin like polished mahogany in the flickering light, knelt down once more beside the cradle. He gazed at the blessed infant, who was sleeping now, lashes lying on his cheeks like the softest shadow.

He took an ornate alabaster jar from the rich red folds of his robe and placed it at Mary's feet. As he lifted the lid briefly, the heavy fragrance of myrrh, a rare perfumed unguent, mixed with that of the frankincense.

Mary and Joseph smiled, and thanked the visitors for their gifts, their faces glowing in the soft light.

Gathering their bright silken robes about them, the Magi turned to get one last glance of the sleeping babe. They bowed low before him, and backing slowly out the door, withdrew in silence.

Once outside, the three sages decided to spend the night in Bethlehem, and return to Jerusalem in the morning. They recalled the message from Herod, brought to them by his servant; *When you have found child, return to me. I wish to go and worship him also.*

The great gleaming Star had vanished from the night sky. While they were sleeping, Gabriel appeared to each of them in a dream, warning them not to return to Herod, who was determined to destroy the child.

In the morning, after discussing their dreams, they packed their belongings and set out on the return journey to their homeland, by a different route. As they passed through the narrow streets of Bethlehem, curious eyes again watched from behind latticed windows.

Leaving the hills, they entered on the great open desert, content at heart for having seen and worshipped the infant King.

#

That evening, as Mary and Joseph settled down for the night, they discussed the three strange visitors.

"Ba' ali, my husband, what do you think the Most High would have us do with the gifts those men brought for our baby? Gold, frankincense, and myrrh are very costly things. Should we take them to the Temple?" Two tiny lines furrowed the smooth skin between Mary's brown eyes as she questioned Joseph.

"I don't know, my love," he replied. "Let's get some sleep now, and we shall pray for the Lord to make his will known to us." He yawned and stretched out on the pallet Mary had prepared for them.

Nearby, the baby lay tucked snugly in his cradle, breathing softly and making sucking noises.

Mary sighed deeply, snuggling her head between Joseph's strong jaw and his shoulder, and draping her arm across his chest. She lay in the curve of his arm, thinking of the strange events of the day. In moments, she was asleep, the furrow gone from her brow.

Joseph lay awake, praying for guidance and strength to bear the awesome responsibility now his. Soon his eyelids grew heavy, and he slipped into a deep sleep.

Once again, as Joseph slept, Gabriel appeared to him in a dream. "Joseph! Get up! You must take the child and his mother and flee to Egypt, for Herod is going to try to kill the child. Hurry! You must stay there until you are told to return!" Gabriel's tone was urgent.

Joseph woke with a start and sat bolt upright, flinging Mary's arm off his chest. He was filled with a chill of fear, and his heart beat like the wings of a frantic bird.

Mary cried out, shaken from her deep sleep. "Joseph! What is it?"

"Mary! Get up! Quickly! We must leave this place now! I have had a dream, and the same angel who spoke to me before has come again. We have to leave for Egypt this very night, for Herod seeks to kill our child! We must go now. Gather up only what we shall need for the journey, Mary. I will get my tools, and saddle Ezra. Hurry now!" Sweat beaded Joseph's forehead, and his dark eyes gleamed with fear.

Mary sat stunned, still half-asleep. She parted her lips as she gazed at Joseph in astonishment. Sariel touched her lightly on the shoulder.

"Mary! You must get up now!" Joseph's voice was loud and stern.

Rubbing her eyes, Mary rose quickly then, startled into action by her husband's rough voice. Never before had he used this tone with her.

Quickly, they prepared for the journey. Leaving many of their belongings behind, they loaded Ezra with the necessities of the trip.

Mary wrapped the baby Jesus securely in soft woolen cloth, and looked sadly around the small house. She was loathe to leave this humble place where their life as a family had begun. Joseph carefully put the gifts from the Magi in a soft pouch and placed it in his knapsack.

The night sky was black, the stars glittering, as they hurried along the narrow dark street. The fragrance of fig and olive trees lay heavy in the air.

Unknown to the little family, their three guardian angels were close at hand as they began the flight from their native land. Gloriel wondered what lay ahead for them in that strange land, where God's people were once enslaved. Gabriel's appearance had happened so swiftly, and he was gone before she could speak to him. She had not appeared before the Father's throne since the birth of the holy Child. Because of the long and urgent journey which lay ahead, she did not think she should leave her charge to visit the Father. Soon, perhaps, the Most High would make His will known to her.

Heading south, they hurried as fast as they could, Ezra's small hooves making puffs of dust in the soft dirt road. The lonely desert stretched endlessly toward an unseen horizon and an unknown future.

# Chapter Ten

King Herod fumed as he angrily paced the marble floor of his bedchamber, unable to sleep. Ten days had passed since the Magi left Jerusalem. His servant had delivered the message to the three on the first day. Still, they did not return to tell him the whereabouts of this newborn "king." He was certain that this so-called king would be a political one, perhaps even a demagogue. His beefy face grew red, as anger stained his cheeks ominously.

"This man is carnal minded, lewd and lustful, and there is no spirituality in him," Michael observed to Gabriel as they watched the scene below.

Hatred and wrath ruled in his heart. The more he paced, the angrier he became. In a rage, he summoned a servant. "Bring the astrologers here! Now, you lazy son of a camel herder!" he roared, scowling at the hapless man.

In a matter of minutes, the three palace astrologers stumbled sleepily into the room, rubbing their eyes. Herod glared at them, fixing his hard gray eyes on the unfortunate men.

"Where are the Magi? They were supposed to return here to tell me where the newborn supposed "king" is. They haven't come back! How long has that accursed Star been over Bethlehem?"

The astrologers lowered their eyes, frightened and bewildered. "Sire, we know not where they have gone," said one hesitantly. "It is said they returned to their homeland a different way from whence they came. But it is only a rumor, your Majesty. The strange Star is now gone from the heavens, also."

A suspicious glint entered Herod's fiery eyes. "It's a plot to steal my throne!" he raged. "The child must die!"

"But-but, your Majesty, w-we don't know which child in Bethlehem," one of the astrologers stammered, quaking.

Herod breathed heavily, apoplectic in his fury. "Then they shall ALL die, every single newborn male child! No, wait, every male child under two years old! They shall all die by the sword! Now!"

The infuriated tyrant stumbled about the room, tearing the rich draperies from the marble walls, and screaming as spittle dripped from his beard. "Tell the soldiers that none is to be spared, not even their own children, if they live anywhere near Bethlehem!"

So began the slaughter of the Innocents. Babies were torn from the arms of their screaming mothers, massacred, and slaughtered like lambs before their eyes. Bright red blood splattered on earthen floors and dusty streets and soldiers tunics.

Stabbing viciously with their short swords, whipped to a fanatical frenzy by the awful viciousness of their actions, the soldiers moved down like a pack of slavering wolves upon the small town. Searching every house, cave, and barn, they unsuspectingly fulfilled Jeremiah's ancient prophecy.

*"A cry of anguish is heard in Ramah—weeping and mourning unrestrained. Rachel weeps for her children, refusing to be comforted—for they are dead."* Matthew 2:18 NLT

Gabriel and Michael and all the angels in Heaven looked on helplessly and wept, as did Gloriel, Sariel, and Samuel, when this terrible deed was made known to them.

*Bethlehem, the House of Bread, is now the House of Sorrow*, Gloriel thought as they led their charges to safety.

#

An uncertain future lay before them, in a strange land, the land of Moses and the Pharaohs. The little family slowed their pace as soon as Joseph felt it was safe to do so. Trekking across fertile valleys, hot and sandy desert areas, and through verdant hills, Joseph and Mary fled the tyrant Herod. They followed the coast of the Mediterranean Sea until they came to the River Nile.

Using some of the gold which the Magi had given the baby Jesus, they crossed the wide river by ferry. Ezra was very nervous on the voyage, voicing his complaints at not having solid footing for his small hooves.

At last they set foot on the soil of Egypt, the land of the Pharaohs. Joseph and Mary found a green spot shaded by tall date palms, where they rested and washed their tired dusty feet in the cool water.

Mary bathed Jesus' small face with a wet cloth, kissing his damp rosy cheek. Gloriel's heart ached with love as she touched the wet curls lying golden on his brow. He could not feel her touch, she knew, and yet he lay very quietly in Mary's arms, dark eyes sparkling.

Joseph found out where the small Jewish community in Alexandria was by inquiring of a caravan lumbering by while they rested by the riverside, refreshed by food and cool water. He spoke with a short, friendly man with twinkling black eyes, who gave him directions to the settlement. He thanked the man profusely, thinking to himself, *this man looks so familiar. Could I have seen him before?*

Samuel grinned, dimples flashing in his round cheeks, and slipped away among the caravansary.

While talking to a traveler from Jerusalem in the caravan, Joseph learned of the terrible, bloody atrocity which had been committed in Bethlehem. Bile rose in his throat. He felt nauseated, struck to the heart. He determined not to tell Mary this horrific news.

Voicing his sorrow for the lost Innocents and their parents, he paused also to give fervent thanks and praise to the Most High for delivering their precious babe from the hand of the monster Herod.

Moving on, they took the main road to the great city of Alexandria, and were now in the heart of Egypt. The young couple grew homesick as they realized how very far they were from home and everything familiar.

Finally they arrived at the splendid city. It was filled with riches and wonders. Almost every wall poured with red and purple flowers and vines. They were awestruck by all the treasures and splendors around them. Mary exclaimed over the beautiful palaces with gardens stretching down to the very edge of the sea.

"It is said that this great metropolis rivals even the famous wonders of Rome," Joseph said to his wife.

Alexandria was a great trade center, a hub of the studies of medicine and literature. The temples of learning and the great sports arenas dazzled the young couple's eyes as they walked slowly through the great city.

They passed at last through the narrow, crowded streets of the Jewish settlement, and their long journey came to an end.

Using more of the gold from the leather pouch, Joseph found lodging for his family for the night.

Mary noticed that the people in the settlement were very different from the people back home. They were much noisier, laughing and joking in a loud and boisterous manner. They wore more ornate clothing, often with sparkling jewels and gold arm bands. The young people of the city were scantily clad, girls in sheer, light, airy gowns, and boys in very short, colorful tunics.

"We will look for a quieter place to live, Mary," Joseph promised. "I have heard there is a small village just outside the city, not too far from here. Tomorrow, we will take Ezra and look for a suitable home where I might find employment."

Mary smiled wearily at her husband, and nodded. She clutched the sleeping Jesus to her breast, her usually bright eyes shadowed with fatigue.

They were both tired and hungry, so Joseph and Mary found a nearby inn where they enjoyed a delicious meal of duck stuffed with herbed rice, steaming bowls of barley soup, and sweet meats. Mary held Jesus on her lap, loosening his swaddling bands as they feasted. He looked around at all the people, his great dark eyes wide and luminous. Looking across the low table at Joseph, his lips curved into a smile. Joseph beamed back at his tiny son.

"Jeshua, my little one, the Most High has brought us safely through our long journey, praise Yahweh!"

Jesus' smile widened and he waved his small fists in the air and squealed.

In the morning, Joseph, Mary, and Jesus left the vast city and walked to a small village just a short distance away.

Leaving Mary and their baby to rest in the drowsy shade of some spreading oak trees, Joseph set out in search of a home for his family. He returned soon, grinning from ear to ear.

"Mary, I have found a small but comfortable home for us, with a room in front which will serve for a carpentry shop." He took his son from Mary's arms and clutched him close to his chest. Jesus smiled brightly, gazing up into Joseph's beaming face.

"Oh, Joseph, that's wonderful!" Mary exclaimed, clapping her hands.

They were soon able to make a cozy home, using more of the gold coins. Though desperately homesick for the far away hills of Galilee and their loved ones, Joseph and Mary settled down to provide a happy family life for their little son.

As the months passed, the baby Jesus grew into a chubby toddler, his parents' joy and delight.

In the evenings, he would shriek with glee as Joseph played his favorite game of toss-in-the-air. Then he would sit on Mary's lap, giggling as she nuzzled his soft neck and played pat-a-cake.

Gloriel hovered over him, with a strange tenderness she had never felt before, as he took his first wobbling step. He plopped down on his round bottom, laughing as Mary coaxed him to try again.

Scooping her baby boy up into her arms, Mary kissed the tip of his nose. "It's okay, Jeshua. Soon you will be running all over!"

Jesus grabbed her face with his chubby hands and planted his first wet kiss on his mother's soft cheek. *So, he loves her first, before he loves any other in his human flesh,* Gloriel mused. *Only His mother can worship her Creator with a kiss.*

His little face, rosy and brown from the sun, glowed with love and innocence.

#

At this time, Gloriel left her little charge in the care of Sariel and Samuel for a short while. She returned to Heaven to stand before the Father in awe and thanksgiving. She bowed low before the shimmering cloud of Light, her heart leaping with joy. The wonderful old sense of bliss and sweet assurance of love filled her soul once more, as she delighted in the Lord God.

"Welcome, Gloriel, most blessed of all my angels." The familiar voice, vibrant with love, caressed her spirit. "Refresh yourself for a little time with your companions, my child. Then you must return to my Son. Take care of him, guide him, love him, and keep him from all grave harm, until his appointed time."

Sinking to her knees, Gloriel lifted her arms in praise and thanksgiving, and rested before the Lord. All awareness of her surroundings faded away as she basked in the blessing of her Father.

#

On the earth below, King Herod's despotic reign was coming to an end. Wasted and eaten away by disease, he lay on his deathbed. There was no one who really mourned his passing as he cursed those around him with his dying breath.

At last, he went to the Place of the Dead, to await God's judgment. Another assumed the rule of the oppressor who could not save his throne from the eternal robber, Death.

#

Meanwhile, the young Holy Family settled into the daily life of the small village outside of Alexandria.

Mary often paused in the midst of her never-ending wife and mother chores, to dream of their families so far away in their beloved homeland.

*Emi and Avi, are they well? Are my brothers and sisters safe and happy? What about Elizabeth and Zechariah, and their baby, John?* She wondered to herself.

She thought of Joseph's parents, and the rest of his family. Jesus was over two years old now, and had never known the joy of a grandparent's love, or the companionship of a large family of aunts, uncles and cousins. Although life in the village was good, and they had become fast friends with their neighbors, it was not like being with family, surrounded by the rolling hills of Nazareth.

Outside the door of their small home, Mary listened to the palm trees rustling in a light breeze, their branches heavy with clusters of dates.

She sighed as she looked down at her small son in his short blue tunic, playing close-by with the little wooden ball which Joseph had carved for him. His chubby fingers caressed the smooth surface. Looking up at her, he smiled, his great dark eyes shining.

Tenderness welled up inside his young mother, so acute that she was almost overwhelmed. Her heart always melted when he bestowed that wondrous smile on her. The dimples were less pronounced now in the round cheeks, but still worked their magic on his Emi.

Gloriel, too, grew hopelessly entranced by her little charge. Her angel's heart wanted to protect him from every bump and bruise, but she knew she must not interfere with the lessons of life for a little child. She was aware that she should protect him from serious harm, and was vigilant in her care for him. She remained always nearby as little Jesus accompanied his mother on the short trip to the marketplace, where they exchanged greetings with other mothers and their children.

Even though Mary shortened her stride, and walked slowly, Jesus' short legs pumped hard to keep up as he clung to her hand.

Gloriel smiled tenderly as she watched the small face light up at the sight of the other children.

Still clutching his beloved wooden ball, he loosened himself from Mary's grasp and toddled quickly toward the small group of children gathered by the village well.

"Jesus! Wait for Emi!" Mary called after him, laughing at his eagerness.

He plopped himself down on his little bottom, chubby legs out-stretched. Immediately, a small boy of about three years approached him. The child sat down beside Jesus, his black curls gleaming in the bright sunlight. Jesus bestowed a wide grin on him. The boy reached out to touch the toy in Jesus' hands, smiling.

"Ball," Jesus said in a clear voice. Mary stood close-by, watching.

Gloriel waited to see what Jesus would do. The older child's small hands closed around the toy.

"Let me see," he said, tugging slightly on the little ball clutched in Jesus' protective grasp.

The smile on Jesus' small face faded, and the great dark eyes brimmed with tears as he looked up at his mother in bewilderment. "My ball," he sobbed.

"Jesus, it's all right. Let the boy see your ball," Mary said quietly.

Unseen, Gloriel whispered in Jesus' small ear, and kissed the top of his head. A gleaming tear rolled slowly down his flushed cheek, but he released his grasp on the precious toy.

"It's good to share, my son." Mary crouched down beside her little boy, and hugged him.

The other child sat down beside Jesus and stroked the smooth surface of the ball.

Jesus' round chin quivered slightly, and his eyes never left the little wooden treasure. Drawing in a ragged breath, he said "My Avi made ball."

"What's your name?" the boy asked, peering at Jesus with curious bright black eyes.

"Jesus," he replied, breathing easier now.

"My name is Seth." The boy grinned at Jesus. "My father made a ball for me, too. It's at my house. I'm three years old. How many are you?"

Jesus wiped the tear away and held up two chubby fingers. "This many," he replied, his smile returning.

"Seth, give the boy back his toy, now."

Mary looked up into the face of a lovely young woman, haloed by the bright rays of the sun behind her.

"Now, Seth." Her voice was light, but firm. The boy slowly handed the toy back to Jesus, who clutched it to his chest and clung to Mary's skirts. Mary stood up and smiled at the young woman.

"My name is Mary, and this is my son, Jesus."

"Good morning, Mary. My name is Leah, and of course you know this is my son, Seth." She returned Mary's smile.

Leah was tall, and very slender, with raven black hair framing a face of strong but delicate bone structure.

"I have seen you here at the well with your little one many times. I'm sorry we haven't spoken before this," she continued.

The young women turned to watch their little sons now playing happily together on a patch of grass beneath a large fig tree. The figs were ripe, and their rich scent filled the air.

Gloriel and Sariel watched the warm scene, content, and filled with tenderness for their charges.

#

The news of King Herod's death spread swiftly in the provinces of Galilee, Judea, and the surrounding countryside. Many rejoiced at his passing. Laughter, music and singing rang through the streets of Jerusalem.

The crowds clapped their hands and chanted gleefully "Herod is dead! Herod is dead!"

#

Far away in Egypt, however, it took almost two months for the report to reach the Jewish settlement in Alexandria, and the small village where Joseph, Mary, and the child Jesus lived. The news that another cruel despot, Herod's son Archelaus had ascended the throne had not yet arrived.

By this time, Mary and Leah were fast friends, and Mary's homesickness had eased. Jesus and Seth played happily together every day, the older boy assuming the role of big brother to the toddler Jesus.

Joseph was kept very busy in his trade as a carpenter. The villagers and the Jewish settlement inside the city walls soon recognized the quality of his work, and his reputation as an honest and righteous man was well known.

One balmy night, the air was deep and still as Joseph lay down beside his beloved Mary. He dozed off quickly, exhausted from a busy day in the carpentry shop. As he drifted into a deep sleep, he became aware of a bright light beneath his eyelids. Once again, the angel Gabriel appeared to Joseph in a dream. He recognized the angel's face immediately.

"Get up and take the child and his mother back to the land of Israel, because those who were trying to kill the child are dead." Gabriel's voice was light, and he smiled at Joseph.

Joseph woke with a start, his heart dancing in his chest. "Was it real?" He whispered to himself. Rising up on one elbow, he looked down at Mary. She was sleeping soundly, breathing deeply, her face relaxed and serene.

"Mary," he whispered, not wanting to wake the child who slept close by. She stirred, and smiled in her sleep. "Mary, wake up."

The brown eyes, heavy with sleep, opened slowly. "Joseph, what is it?" She yawned.

"I've had another vision in a dream," Joseph replied quietly. "The same angel as before came to me. Herod is dead, and we are to return home." He still felt a little dazed and unsure.

Sariel whispered in Mary's ear, reassuring her.

"Oh, Joseph! Home! We can go home!" Mary was instantly wide awake. Sitting up, she threw her arms around Joseph, knocking him off his elbow.

Across the small room, Jesus rubbed his sleepy eyes with chubby fists and sat up, looking bewildered. When he saw the bright smile on his mother's face, his own lit up.

#

"Emi go home?" He clapped his hands and laughed sleepily.

Gloriel smiled. She knew the little one had no idea what 'going home' meant, but he loved to see his mother laugh.

"Come, we must start packing!" Mary cried, throwing aside the blanket and jumping to her feet.

Gloriel, Samuel, and Sariel looked on, delighted.

"My love," Joseph laughed. "We have much to do before we leave. It will surely take a day or two to prepare for the journey. We need to pack up our belongings, buy supplies, and bid our friends farewell. We also have to look for a caravan, and sell much of our goods."

Mary's bright face sobered. "Oh, Joseph. We have to leave Leah and Seth, and all our good neighbors. I will miss them terribly. Jesus loves Seth so."

"I know, my dear, I know." Joseph replied. "But think how wonderful it will be to see Bethlehem again."

Mary looked intently at Joseph, her smile fading. "Bethlehem?" Sariel knew that in Mary's heart, Nazareth was home, not Bethlehem.

"Yes, my love, Bethlehem."

"Joseph, are you sure Herod is dead?" Mary said, pensively.

Her husband looked at Mary solemnly. "Mary, the angel Gabriel told me. Do you question him?"

Instantly, Mary recalled her own blessed encounter with Gabriel. She lowered her eyes, and the subject was closed.

*Dear Lord, please let us go home to Nazareth*, she breathed a silent prayer.

Three days later, the young family was packed up and ready to leave. Joseph had sold the last of the myrrh and frankincense, and a few gold coins remained, the gifts of the Magi. After tearful good-byes with friends and neighbors, Mary, Joseph and Jesus joined a caravan leaving for Judea.

When they were three days into the journey, travelers in a caravan from Jerusalem reported that Herod was indeed dead. His kingdom had been divided among three of his sons. Herod Antipas was now the ruler of Galilee. The cruel Archelaus had begun his reign of terror by massacring 3,000 Jews. Joseph and Mary were sobered and sick at heart on hearing this news.

"My husband," Mary said quietly, "Don't you think we should return to Nazareth? It will not be safe for Jesus in Bethlehem." Joseph bowed his head in thought. He was silent for a few minutes. Samuel whispered in his ear, unseen.

"Yes, Mary. We shall return to Galilee," Joseph replied.

Deep in her heart, Mary rejoiced. Holding Jesus close to her breast, she buried her face in the soft flesh of his neck, and silently thanked the Most High for His wonderful, mysterious ways.

The journey was slow and arduous, for the summer season was upon them, and they had to walk through hot, cloying sand.

Jesus sat astride Ezra's broad back, along with their goods and provisions. His little legs stuck straight out on either side. Clutching his beloved wooden ball, he watched the people in the caravan, wide-eyed.

Once, on a particularly hot day, the child grew weary and miserable. Sweat beaded his brow, and the gold ringlets clung to his face and neck. Tears rolled down his flushed cheeks, and he began to sob. Suddenly, a soft hand pushed back his wet hair, and a cool cloth was laid on his forehead. He looked up into a pair of soft amber eyes smiling at him. It was a beautiful lady with hair the same color as her eyes. She walked alongside Ezra, wiping the little one's face with the cool cloth, and humming a sweet song. Jesus forgot that he was hot and sweaty and tired. The song made him feel good inside, and he bestowed his dimpled smile on the beautiful lady.

Joseph walked ahead, staff in hand. Mary was leading Ezra, a few paces behind her husband. Both were absorbed in their own thoughts. The sun beat down mercilessly, and their clothing clung to sweating bodies.

"Joseph," Mary called. "We need to stop and give Jesus some water now." Glancing back, Mary was astonished. Jesus sat straight up on Ezra's back, eyes shining, cheeks pink, but not flushed. His golden curls were glowing in the sun, and his brow looked cool and dry. He was smiling at his mother.

"Get down, Emi?" he asked.

Leading Ezra to the side of the sandy road, Mary gently lifted her little boy down to the ground. She removed the water pouch from her belt, and let Jesus drink deeply. She smoothed his cool forehead with a warm, damp hand. Joseph joined them, drinking from his own water bag, and sweating profusely.

"Jeshua, my son, are you hot?" he asked.

"Not hot, Avi," the little one replied. "Where is the lady?"

"What lady, son?" Joseph asked, puzzled.

"The singing lady," the small voice chirped.

Joseph and Mary looked at one another quizzically. There was no "singing lady" anywhere to be seen.

Gloriel, Sariel and Samuel smiled at one another.

## Chapter Eleven

Mary stood in the doorway of her humble home. She pushed aside the heavy brown linen curtain which hung across it to keep out winter's chill fingers.

*The days are getting warmer*, she thought to herself. *Soon I must ask Joseph to hang the light curtain.*

She gazed out at the damp hills of Nazareth. Puddles from the late spring rains dotted the landscape. A pale gold sun was shining. Her eyes were drawn down the road to a wall covered with newly green vines and budding red blossoms. The hillsides were beginning to burst with color as the wildflowers poked their brilliant heads out among the grasses.

Mary breathed deeply of the pure and balmy air. She smiled and turned away from the doorway, letting the curtain drop back into place. Sariel watched as her beautiful young charge walked slowly around the room. *She lights up the house with her smile*, she thought. *How the Lord has blessed me with this ministry.*

The house was little, the walls a pale dun color. There was one main room, and a smaller one with an alcove where Mary and Joseph slept. Two small windows were cut into the walls, and covered with bleached linen curtains. The floor was hard-packed dirt. Joseph had added clay and ashes to the soil, which made it very hard and smooth, almost like wood. A low wooden table stood beneath one of the windows. An oil lamp nestled in a niche carved into one wall. Several earthenware jugs were lined up in a corner next to a lamp stand which held yet another oil lamp. In a far corner, a small pallet was rolled up. A spinning wheel stood near the center of the room.

In the smaller room, the household oven, which kept the little family warm on frosty nights, gave off the inviting fragrance of baking bread. It was quite large, about three feet by six feet, and two feet high.

Mary loved her modest home. It was warm with love, and beautiful in her eyes. Her heart sang with joy as she looked about the room.

These were happy days for Mary and her little family. It had been almost four years since they returned to Nazareth from their exile in Egypt.

Mary and Joseph had decided to give Jesus as normal an upbringing as possible; not mentioning the miraculous circumstances of his birth to any, outside of those who already knew.

According to ancient law and customs, between the ages of one and five, a male child should be instructed in fundamental truths about the Most High, and also in the sacred Law. This was mothers' work in all of Judea. When she was a child, Anna and Joachim had taught Mary about the Scriptures and the Law, along with how to run a household and care for a family.

Accordingly, Mary began Jesus' education as soon as they returned to Nazareth, though he was not yet three years old. Now her sweet boy would soon be six years old, and starting classes at the synagogue next week.

Mary smiled to herself as she thought of her small son's excitement and joyful anticipation of the big day. She and Joseph had already taught Jesus the Sh'ma, the ancient prayer recorded in the sacred scroll of Deuteronomy.

Lifting the curtain once more, Mary walked outside to the wooden ladder which led to the roof. A short wall, about 18 inches high ran all around the edges of the roof. Joseph had fashioned the roof from a mixture of straw, mud and lime, packed and hardened.

She stepped over the parapet and gathered up the clothing which she had washed in a nearby stream early that morning, and laid out to dry on a rack in the warm spring sunshine. Raising Jesus' short linen tunic to her face, she breathed deeply of sunlight and fresh air, and lingering little-boy smells.

From her vantage point, Mary viewed the small village with pleasure. She gazed at the surrounding hills, like sentinels standing guard, dressed in their bright green garb. Grottoes hewn out of rock shadowed the hillsides.

Very few caravans or travelers came through the little town because of its position in the valley and on the hillside. Even though it was a rather unimportant little place with fewer than 200 residents, many of them part of their extended family, it was her home, and most dear to her.

At the highest point on the lower hill, stood the synagogue. Mary could see the marketplace at the village entrance, where Joseph plied his carpenter's trade in a small shop.

Glancing over the parapet at the rear of the house, she saw Jesus playing happily with his friend Jacob, who lived a short distance down the lane. The two little boys were enjoying a game of leap-frog, squealing and laughing with glee.

Unseen, Gloriel stood close by, keeping watch over her precious charge. She laughed at the boys' antics. Jesus' sturdy arms and legs were still pale from the winter sun's weak rays. His golden hair had darkened somewhat and was now a shining light brown. The ringlets were gone, replaced by soft waves.

"Jesus," Mary called from the roof, "come, we must go to the marketplace now."

"Oh, Emi, can't we play a while longer?" Jesus pleaded. He was exhilarated by the game, and reluctant to leave Jacob when they were having so much fun.

Mary smiled. "Just a few minutes, Son," she replied. "As soon as I put the clothing away, we need to leave."

She climbed down the ladder and went inside the house. Humming to herself, she folded the clean clothes placing them in the beautiful wooden chest which Joseph had made for her. It was precious to her. Wood was scarce in a land almost denuded of lumber.

She ran her hand over the smooth wood, and thought of her dear husband, who worked so hard for them. She loved him even more today than she had when they were first betrothed.

The memories of those wonderful and awful days were still fresh in her mind. The visit from the angel Gabriel, the trip to visit Cousin Elizabeth, the fear and anxiety, the long journey to Bethlehem, and the flight to Egypt, all seemed so long ago now. But they remained crystal-clear memories, and she often thought about them and wondered what the future held for her little family.

Carefully, she removed the fresh-baked bread from the oven and placed it on the table, breathing in the delightful fragrance.

She fastened her purse to the leather belt around her still slim waist. Today the local farmers would be gathered at the market place with their fresh produce. Her shining hair was a nimbus framing her face. Smoothing it back, she draped a light brown, rough linen mantle over her head, then checked to make sure her simple tunic was not soiled.

As Mary walked around the side of the house to fetch her young son, she was greeted by a crooning chorus of doves sitting in a nearby olive tree. Jesus and Jacob were watching the purple-breasted birds ruffle their soft plumage and coo to one another. Mary smiled at the sight of the two little boys so deeply engrossed in the flock of birds.

"Jesus, we must go now," she called. Startled, the doves took flight with a low rush of wings.

"Emi, you scared the pretty birds!" Jesus cried.

"I'm sorry, Son, but we have to get to the market place. We have things to buy for the Sabbath day," Mary replied, pushing back the soft hair from his forehead. "Tell Jacob goodbye for now."

"'Bye, Jacob," the boy waved at his friend reluctantly.

"G'bye, Jesus," the dark-haired little boy replied.

Taking Jesus' hand, Mary led him around the house to the pathway leading to the market square.

"Look at the beautiful day the Lord has given us, Son!" As they strolled along the narrow path, Mary pointed out the terraced hills with their burdens of cypress and olive trees. The late spring day was pale gold, and the sun warmed their skin as they walked.

A cloud of noisy, chirping swallows swooped low over their heads. Jesus pulled loose from his mother's grasp and chased them, whooping with delight.

"Look, Emi, look! I want to fly, too!" He cried out as he stretched his small arms out like wings.

A sharp pang struck Mary's heart suddenly, and she felt a shadow move over her soul. Her surroundings faded away until only her small son with arms outstretched and silhouetted against the light, was left in her tunnel-like field of vision. Her heart beat with a vague fear, and there was a sudden sick drop in her stomach.

Then, as quickly as it had come, the fear left, and her vision returned to normal.

Bewildered, and a little dazed, she called out loudly, "Jesus! Wait for Emi!" Her voice was sharp, and Jesus turned to look curiously at his mother, surprised at her tone.

As Gloriel observed the scene between mother and small son, she said to Sariel, "What happened?"

"Something frightened Mary, but I'm not sure what it was," Sariel replied. The two angels followed their charges closely now, vigilant for any dangers along the pathway. Taking Jesus' hand, Mary smiled at him reassuringly. Her heart was still pounding, and she felt bewildered by the frightening experience. She struggled not to show her fear to her small son.

"Jeshua, let's walk together. Soon you will be going to school, and I will miss having my boy with me all the time."

"All right, Emi. Let's race!" Jesus tugged on his mother's hand, laughing.

Mary looked down at the small shining face, and the fear melted away. Gathering up her skirts with her free hand, she ran down the dusty lane, laughing at her little one's delight.

Sariel and Gloriel smiled at one another, and followed their beloved charges into the village marketplace.

#

"Joseph, here is Jesus' lunch. Please make sure he asks the teacher where to keep it, so he doesn't lose it."

Mary stood outside the doorway to their small home. Handing the pouch to Joseph, she smiled at Jesus, who was hopping from one foot to the other in his eagerness. He was wearing a new white tunic, which Mary had made for his first day of school. A small brown leather belt, a "first-day" gift from Joseph, circled his still slightly rounded stomach, the last vestige of toddler-hood.

Mary stooped to kiss his dimpled cheek. "Son, Emi loves you. Be a good boy," she whispered in his ear.

"Yes, Emi. Let's go, Avi, we'll be late!" he pleaded, pulling eagerly on Joseph's hand. Goodbye, Emi!"

Mary watched the two beloved figures marching up the path. The one tall and straight, the other small and bouncing with excitement, tugging on his father's hand.

"And so your life apart from me begins, my little one," she whispered softly, bright tears rolling down her cheeks. Crooning a soft lullaby to herself, she thought about the joys of his baby-hood, of watching him grow stronger each day. She remembered the first smile that lit up his sweet face, the first wobbling steps, feeding him, changing him. How many times had her heart sung with happiness as she fondled him and talked to him, even when he could not understand her words.

A memory came rushing to the surface then, of sitting on a big stone beside the well, undressing her baby boy, and bathing him in the warm Egyptian sun. A sob caught in her throat. The image of her small, helpless infant waving his chubby arms and legs as she bathed him on her knees, faded slowly away.

"Lord God Most High, set your angels guard around him," she breathed a quiet prayer.

Sariel placed an unseen hand on Mary's arm, while Gloriel and Samuel accompanied Joseph and Jesus up the road to the small synagogue on the hill.

All boys in the village from the age of six attended school six days a week in the white-washed synagogue. Father and son approached the simple, one-story building, Jesus still tugging on Joseph's hand. As they started up the flat, narrow steps, Jesus suddenly stopped pulling on Joseph, and his pace slowed almost to a stop.

"Avi . . ."

Joseph looked down on the small upturned face. Two large dark eyes, brimming with tears, gazed up at him.

"What is it, my son?" Joseph asked, kneeling down on one knee beside the boy.

"Avi," the small voice was choked. "Will you stay with me?" Jesus' little chin quivered slightly.

Joseph put his arms around the boy, and hugged him.

"Jeshua, Avi can't stay with you now, but Emi will come to get you when school is over. You must go in now. The teacher will be waiting. You will learn many new things today, and you can tell us all about them tonight. Take your lunch and go in now, Son."

Gloriel whispered then in Jesus' ear. Still looking up at his father, the boy sighed deeply and smiled through his tears. Turning, he marched resolutely up the few remaining steps. Joseph grinned, watching the small shoulders straighten. As he entered the synagogue door, the child looked back over his shoulder, and waved to his father.

Inside the synagogue, Gloriel watched as Daniel ben Abijah, ruler of the synagogue, greeted his students. He was dressed in a long white tunic, with a tasseled prayer shawl over his graying head. His thin, aquiline face was solemn.

She looked around the hall, which served as a schoolroom, and also for evening and Sabbath services. Wooden benches stood along the walls. The ancient sacred scrolls were stored in the Tebhan, the ark of the apse, at the far end of the room. Ever-burning ruby-colored oil lamps stood in front of the chest.

Jesus, his dark eyes huge in a slightly pale face, took his place in a semi-circle of boys sitting on the bare floor. He looked around at the usually noisy and crowded room. It seemed so empty, with just the teacher and the small group of boys of various ages. The teacher ascended a platform in front of his students, the four tassels at the corners of his prayer shawl swinging. Seating himself, he looked down at the fresh young faces before him. Jesus swallowed nervously as the teacher's eyes came to rest on him.

"Before we begin the studies this morning, we have a new student among us," the teacher's voice was deep and sonorous. "Jeshua ben Joseph, stand up."

The boy scrambled to his feet and smiled tentatively at the stern figure looming above him. Already, he missed Emi and Avi. Gloriel stood behind Jesus and placed her hands on his shoulders, her heart swelling with tenderness.

"Jesus, you are welcomed into the sacred school," the teacher intoned solemnly, "sit down now."

Jesus plopped down on the hard floor, as if his sturdy little legs had suddenly given away.

The master stepped down from the platform and walked to the Tebhan in the back of the room. Pushing the curtain aside, he removed the scroll of Leviticus, third book of the Torah. He carefully carried the leather case back to the platform. Inside the case was the linen-wrapped sacred scripture.

Gloriel noticed that Jesus' eyes were shining as he gazed at the linen wrappings. Joseph had taught him to love the sacred papers, pointing them out to him every Sabbath, when the family attended services at the synagogue. The master sat down and removed the linen wrappings from the sacred scroll.

Jesus' heart beat fast with the excitement of being so close to the holy writings. The teacher's sharp black eyes again sought out the new pupil.

"Jesus, will you recite the Sh'ma for us this morning, please?" The room was silent as all eyes fixed on the little newcomer.

"Yes, sir," the small voice quivered slightly. The boy rose to his feet slowly. He stood tall and straight, as Mary had taught him. *"Hear, O Israel! The Lord is our God, the Lord alone. And you must love the Lord your God with all your heart, all your soul, and all your strength."* Jesus paused, slightly breathless, then continued. *"And you must commit yourselves wholeheartedly to these commands I am giving you today. Repeat them again and again to your children. Talk about them when you are at home and when you are away on a journey, when you are lying down and when you are getting up again. Tie them to your hands as a reminder, and wear them on your forehead. Write them on the door-posts of your house and on your gates."* Deuteronomy 6:4-9 The young voice rose clear and lilting as he finished his recitation.

The master smiled down then at his newest student. "Well done, Jeshua. You may sit down. Boys, where do we begin our studies today? Which scroll is this?" The teacher's black eyes darted from one upturned face to another.

"Leviticus, Teacher." The boy sitting on Jesus' right side answered quickly.

"Yes, very good, Andrew. And what is the most important thing we learn from Leviticus?"

"It teaches us about sacrifice, and the presence of the Most High among us. It calls us to be holy," a tall boy seated at the far end of the semi-circle intoned solemnly.

Daniel ben Abijah nodded his head. "Yes, Jesse, that is correct.

"Jesus," the teacher's gaze came to rest once again on the bright-eyed little one in front of him. "What do the scriptures mean when they tell us about the presence of the Most High among us?"

Gloriel waited expectantly for her little one's reply. *He's so small, does he understand?* She wondered.

"The Lord is here with us all the time. We can't see him, but he hears us when we talk to him, my Avi says," Jesus' bright intelligent eyes looked up into the teacher's face.

"Yes, yes, very good, my child."

He looked searchingly into each boy's face, one by one. "Leviticus is the story of how God is with us, always. Even when we act like unholy people, the Most Holy God is present. He calls us to be a holy people. But through the system and arrangement of the sacrifices which he has given us, we learn about forgiveness and atonement. So what we learn in Leviticus is about reconciliation and redemption."

Jesus looked at the master in bewilderment. *All those big words!* He thought to himself. *Will Emi and Avi know what they mean?* He was afraid to ask, because the other boys seemed to know what the teacher meant. He glanced around at them, suddenly shy. All the boys were attentive, listening carefully as Daniel ben Abijah read passages from the ancient scroll. The older boys then recited some of them by heart.

Jesus wondered if he would be able to do that some day. Avi and Emi had already taught him some things about the history and laws of their nation, and he was eager to learn more.

Gloriel noticed that although the boys spoke Aramaic at home, the classroom language was Hebrew. *So much for the little ones to learn,* she thought.

Later in the day, after lunch, the boys practiced writing. Each student was given a pointed bone, or wooden stylus, which was used to write on wax-covered wooden tablets.

Gloriel smiled at Jesus' excitement. He carefully copied the 22 letters of the Hebrew alphabet, as the teacher showed him. The older boys copied long lessons on parchment; using pens made out of reeds, and dipping them in black ink.

Jesus was eager to learn quickly, so that he, too, could write beautiful words on parchment in the shiny black ink.

As the afternoon wore on, the smaller boys grew restless, looking longingly at the door. Jesus was tired, his small legs cramped from sitting so long. But his heart was happy. Already, he loved being with the other boys and listening to the master tell them wonderful things about God and his special people.

At last, in the late afternoon, the teacher dismissed his students, and they filed quietly out of the synagogue. As soon as they were outside and down the steps, however, the boys began running and jumping, wrestling with one another.

Jesus looked around eagerly for his mother. Mary was standing under a nearby Terebinth tree.

"Emi! Guess what? The teacher asked me to recite the Sh'ma! We learned that the Most High is always with us, just like you and Avi said. Why can't we see him, Emi? Will he ever show us his face?" The boy was breathless with his effort to tell his mother all about the day, and eager for answers to his questions.

Mary laughed at her little one's enthusiasm and joy. She tousled his hair, and took his hand.

"Let's go home now, Son. We'll talk at supper, and your father will answer your questions. Jacob is waiting for you. He wants to hear all about school."

Jacob would not be six years old for another 3 months, and so could not attend school with Jesus yet.

Gloriel and Sariel smiled at one another, hearts filled with love for their charges. The other boys were walking or running off in small groups now, still rough-housing and shouting, happy to be freed from the confines of the synagogue for the day.

Gloriel noticed that a few of the older boys were watching as Jesus and Mary walked down the path, hand in hand. They whispered among themselves, then burst out laughing. Feeling uneasy, she followed Jesus closely as he and Mary chattered together on their walk home.

As they approached their house, Jacob came running to meet Jesus, and the two little boys ran around to their favorite spot beneath the olive tree behind the house.

The early spring afternoon sun was warm and golden, caressing the tender blades of new grass. Mary breathed deeply of the soft air. Smiling to herself, she entered the house to begin preparing the evening meal.

#

Jesus stood on the steps of the synagogue. His chin quivered as a single silvery tear slipped gleaming down his cheek.

"Hey, baby Jesus! Why didn't your mommy stay with you?" Two boys were standing between Jesus and the synagogue door. A few others stood to one side, watching and laughing.

"Baby Jesus! Cry-baby Jesus! Can't walk to school without his mommm—my!" The taller of the two boys laughed derisively as he poked Jesus in the ribs with his finger.

"Baby Jesus, does mommy still nurse you?" the other boy, a plump youngster with a pimply face joined in with a sing-song voice. "Ba-by Jesus, ba-by Jesus!"

Stung and bewildered by the cruelty of the boys, Jesus stood frozen and silent, trying desperately to hold back his tears. Why were the boys being so mean? He couldn't understand. No one had ever made fun of him before. It hurt.

Gloriel moved between her charge and the two boys who were harassing him. She did not interfere, but stood waiting to see what Jesus would do. "He's so little, Lord, should I intervene?" she whispered a prayer. No answer came.

The older boy poked Jesus again with his finger, viciously. The little one stood still, his great dark eyes filled with tears.

Gloriel bent low and whispered in his ear.

Suddenly, Jesus sniffled, and wiped his eyes on the sleeve of his tunic. He stood up straight, smiled, walked between the two surprised bullies, and marched through the synagogue door. He sat down in his place on the floor, back straight and chin up.

One of the smaller boys sat down beside him. "Don't pay any attention to those big bully boys. They're just mean, and like to pick on new boys," he whispered, putting his hand on Jesus' shoulder.

Jesus smiled at the boy, and nodded. "Did you know that angels look after us?"

"Angels? We haven't talked much about them yet," the boy replied, lifting his eyebrows and smiling. My name is James. Yours is Jesus, right?"

"Those two boys outside told you, didn't they?" Jesus replied. James and Jesus looked at each other and laughed.

## Chapter Twelve

"He's old enough now, Mary."

Joseph and Mary were sitting on the roof of their little house, enjoying the evening breeze on an early spring day in the month of Nisan. Jesus was studying inside the house, and they were resting and talking together quietly, as was their custom.

Mary admired Joseph's strong profile silhouetted against the sky. The sun was setting over distant hills, igniting the tree-tops afire, and mowing a path of pure gold down the center of the fields. The years together had strengthened their devotion to one another, and to their child.

"I know, my husband. It's just hard to realize that our little one is growing up so fast," Mary replied, smiling a little tremulously.

Joseph took his wife's slim brown hand in his callused one. Turning it over, he kissed her palm. "It's time for him to begin learning the trade. He will still have time to play for a while after synagogue school," he said.

"Joseph, do you think he knows? Do you think he realizes who he is?"

"We have told him since he was little that he is special in the eyes of the Most High, Mary. But he thinks all people are special to Yahweh. It's difficult to know what to say to him, or what the Most High is revealing to him. But we must continue to raise him as any other child. Of this I am sure, my dearest."

Mary smiled again, reaching up to touch Joseph's dear face. "Yes, Joseph, of course, you are right."

"Then tomorrow after synagogue school, he may play for an hour, and then I want him to come to the shop to begin his apprenticeship," Joseph said, firmly.

"Yes, tomorrow," Mary replied, patting his face.

Together, they descended the ladder from the roof-top and entered the house.

Jesus was lighting the oil lamp, as it was getting darker inside. The lamp was flat, without a handle. It didn't give off much light, so it was usually placed on a lamp stand. Jesus always sat on one of the low stools to study by its flickering light.

"Good job, son." Joseph patted Jesus' shoulder. He had just recently taught the boy the elaborate job of fire-making.

During cold weather, a slow fire was kept burning most of the time in the household oven or hearth. Jesus loved making the fire, and always volunteered quickly when it was needed.

Gloriel stood watch as the little family went about their evening routine.

Mary prepared a thick lentil soup, and some dried salted fish. The mouth-watering aroma of fresh-baked barley bread filled the room. She poured wine into three cups, and placed a large soup bowl on the low table.

Before dinner began, the family washed their hands according to the ancient traditional ritual.

Smiling at his wife and son, Joseph blessed the food and wine, and they all sat down on straw mats beside the table.

Gloriel knew that Jesus loved this time of day, sharing good food and wine with his beloved Emi and Avi. They would talk about the events of the day, and Joseph always recited wonderful stories about their ancestors.

His father also used this evening time to teach Jesus the duties required of every Israelite. This night, however, Joseph cut short the story-telling time.

"Son, your mother and I have decided that now you are nine years old, it is time for you to begin to learn the carpenter's trade. We will start with just an hour a day in the afternoon, and gradually increase the time as you get older." Joseph's eloquent dark eyes shone in the flickering light. He stroked his dark beard, now shot through with strands of silver.

Gloriel smiled as excitement moved over Jesus' face. He was grinning from ear to ear, fixing his father with his bright, alert eyes shining with delight.

"Oh, Avi, really? When may I start? May I build a house first?"

Joseph and Mary laughed. "Well, Son, you should begin with something a bit simpler, I think. But one day, perhaps you will build a house," Joseph said, placing his hand on the boy's head.

Jesus broke off another piece of bread and dipped it into the bowl of lentil soup. "I have to eat a lot of food, so I can grow to be a big, strong carpenter, right, Emi?"

Mary grinned at her elated boy. "Yes, my son, very big and strong."

Joseph then recited the final prayer of thanks and praise after the meal. Getting up from the mat, he stretched his arms over his head and yawned. "I'm going to the evening meeting at the synagogue now, Mary. Jesus, would you like to come along tonight?"

"Oh, Avi, may I?" Jesus asked eagerly. Even though he spent hours at the synagogue during the day, he loved to go the evening meeting with the men of the village. He always listened closely to the discussions. Sometimes his father allowed him to ask questions. Mostly, he just loved listening to the stories the men told about the wonderful heroes and prophets of long ago.

Emi had taught him the ancient truths and the law of the Most High since he was able to walk; and although he loved the prayers that Mary and Joseph recited at home, the ones said at the synagogue meetings would always make his heart sing.

That night, after the meeting, when Joseph and he were walking home, Jesus could not contain himself. Dancing on tiptoe ahead of Joseph on the path, in delirious abandon he stretched out his arms to the sky. The moon was full and huge, burning in white fire, laying a tracery of silver along the path. The landscape was painted in a thousand shades of gray, silver, and gold.

"Yahweh, I love you!" He sang out. "Avi, I love you!"

Joseph's eyes brimmed with tears as he watched his young son exulting with pure joy in life. Suddenly, as he was watching him, Jesus' young features seemed to turn into all sharp angles and shadowed hollows in the moonlight.

A strange pang nibbled at Joseph's heart, and his breath caught in his throat. Samuel placed an unseen hand on Joseph's broad shoulder.

"Most High, please take care of our boy." Joseph murmured under his breath.

The tense moment passed, and Jesus' face was glowing again. Gloriel and Samuel looked at one another questioningly, but did not speak.

The next day, before sunrise, Mary was up and busy preparing for the Sabbath day, which would begin at sunset. She sang as she worked, in a clear and lilting voice.

She was thinking back over the past years as she mixed the bread for Sabbath, kneading it with care. The memory of a special Sabbath day rose up in her mind. It was still sharp and clear, though ten years had passed. As she worked, filling the lamps with oil, she remembered her excitement when she learned that Joseph was coming to dinner. She smiled to herself when she realized that she still felt excited when it was time for Joseph to come home in the evening. That long-ago day, so much had happened; preparing the Sabbath meal in the kitchen with her mother and Mary Elizabeth; her nap in the olive grove; the appearance of the angel and his invitation to her; the ecstasy, the fear, the anguish on Joseph's face.

*I'm 23 years old now, almost middle-aged*, she thought, smiling to herself. *Our boy, our Jeshua . . . it's so hard to think of him as the Son of the Most High.* Sometimes she even forgot about it, watching him with Joseph. *They adore one another*, she mused. *Are we supposed to tell him who he is, or will the Lord reveal this to him? How can we tell him Joseph is not his father? How do you teach God about God? What does the Most High expect of us?* She frowned thoughtfully.

Suddenly, she recalled that long ago day in the Temple, when the aged Simeon had fixed her with his kindly, faded blue gaze, and told her that one day her very soul would be pierced by a sword. *What did he mean? How did the old man know what lies ahead for my child and me?*

Watching Mary, and listening to her thoughts, Sariel knew that the Lord would not permit the blessed mother to see the entirety of his Plan, as she would be overwhelmed to be in the presence of his Son, and unable to raise him as a truly human child.

The Son of God had to be as human as his family, his friends, and his neighbors. And yet, his parents could never lose sight of his divinity, though his mission was still shrouded in mystery. So Mary still pondered these things in her heart.

#

Joseph was outside with Jesus, feeding two fat hens and a rooster. The morning was chilly, as dawn's gray eyes surveyed the mist drifting down from the hills of Nazareth.

The rooster strutted around the hens, cocking his head to look at the boy scattering grain. He stretched his scrawny neck and crowed loudly. Jesus stopped and looked at the bird. A strange sadness came over him as he gazed at the rooster, and fullness rose up in his throat. The feeling passed as suddenly as it had come.

Father and son watched the chickens, laughing at the little dance the birds performed, scratching in the dirt and bobbing their heads, sometimes in unison.

"Jeshua," Joseph said quietly.

"Yes, Father?" The fresh young face looked up questioningly.

*He no longer calls me "Avi" all the time,* Joseph thought, a little regretfully. He leaned down, resting his hands on his knees. "The Most High is like that brown hen will be after her chicks are hatched." He reached out and ruffled the boy's thick hair, flowing back from his brow in shining waves. "He shelters us under his wings and keeps us from harm when we trust him, just as the hen does her little chicks."

Gloriel listened, and smiled tenderly as Jesus slipped his slim olive-skinned hand into his father's big rough one. Looking up at Joseph, the boy's smooth young brow knitted with sudden anxiousness.

Removing his hand from Joseph's, he reached down and picked up one of the shiny-feathered fat hens.

She fluttered in his hands for a few seconds, and then grew suddenly quiet. Cocking her head to the side, she fixed one bright, beady eye on the child.

Jesus held the bird tenderly against his cheek, and then gently set her back on the ground, stroking her and murmuring softly. He grinned at his father.

"Avi, the Most High loves all the animals and birds, too, doesn't he?"

"Yes, Son, even the little sparrows."

Gloriel whispered in the boy's ear.

"But he loves us more!" Jesus exclaimed. The startled chickens scattered, squawking.

"Yes, Son, indeed he does," Joseph replied, chuckling. "Now, go tell your mother goodbye, and be off to school!"

Jesus scampered into the house and hugged his mother, whose hands were buried in soft barley dough.

"Jeshua, wait! You haven't had your breakfast!" Mary cried, turning a flour-smudged face to her son.

The boy grabbed the pouch his mother had prepared for his noonday meal. "It's all right, Emi," he said, "I'll just eat this on the way."

He scuttled out the door before his mother had time to object, racing up the path to join Jacob, who was waiting impatiently for him.

"Hurry up, Jesus! We're going to be late! The teacher will be angry!" Hands on his hips, the boy called to his friend streaking up the rock-strewn pathway.

Jacob had grown tall, his black hair thick and heavy. He stood an inch taller than Jesus, though younger by several months.

The two boys were fast friends, spending their after-school hours wandering the pastures and hills of Nazareth. They loved to watch the shepherds grazing their flocks, and the farmers tilling the rich soil.

Though they both had other friends, the bond between them had grown steadily since they first met as toddlers.

As Jesus ran toward his friend, he suddenly thought of King David and his friend, Jonathan.

Emi had told him the wonderful story about the two young men many times, but he never tired of hearing it. He thought about the great love between the two friends, David and Jonathan; how David had grieved so deeply when Jonathan was killed in battle.

Listening to her charges thoughts, Gloriel reflected, *to the young, death is impossible and unthinkable.*

Jesus slowed his pace as he approached his impatient friend. Impulsively, he reached out and hugged Jacob, who drew back in surprise, a faint frown creasing his young forehead.

"Are you all right, Jesus?"

"Sure, Jacob. I was just thinking how glad I am that we are friends." Jesus smiled.

His friend returned the smile, and then said gruffly, "Hurry up now, it's getting really late!"

Gloriel listened to the exchange between the two boys. *He's growing up*, she thought to herself. *He's not a baby anymore.* She felt the sharp pang of nostalgia in her chest as she remembered the dimpled toddler with the golden hair.

The trees around the synagogue were dressed in the pale green of early spring, and a soft breeze stirred their branches as the two boys climbed the synagogue steps and entered the classroom.

Jesus was excited. Today, he would be reciting the Hallel, the great Psalms 113 through 118. He had worked so hard at learning these beautiful poetic words; and it was an honor to recite them for his fellow students.

Now he was starting to memorize the prophetic books. It thrilled his young heart to read all the wonderful prophecies of olden times. Sometimes at night, he lay on his pallet and dreamed of the great prophets; Isaiah, Jeremiah, Ezekiel. His spirit would soar, and he was filled with deep wonderment at the great Plan of the Most High.

That afternoon, Joseph and the other men of the town put away the tools of their trades, and cleansed themselves with ritual ablutions.

Perfuming his body with scented oil, Joseph put on a clean white tunic. He was very frugal with the oil, as it was a valued commodity and quite expensive for a simple carpenter's family. He treasured each drop as it penetrated deeply into his body. He believed that it brought him strength, health and refreshment. *After Jesus' Bar Mitzvah, he can join me in the ritual*, he thought, enthusiastically.

Mary and Jesus were also preparing for the evening Sabbath services at the synagogue, dressing in freshly laundered tunics. Mary did not always attend the evening service, but tonight she would join her husband and son.

The little family was light-hearted as they ate the first of the three Sabbath meals. Mary had prepared a special treat for Jesus, fried sweet cakes and wild honey. His eyes sparkled in anticipation as Joseph recited the ritual prayers at the table.

Jesus loved the Sabbath. It was a time filled with thanksgiving and quiet joy in their little home. The three sharp blasts of the shofar had sounded when the first evening star appeared in the blue velvet sky.

While they were eating, Jesus asked "Avi, which is the most important commandment?"

"The Sh'ma, my son," Joseph replied without hesitation. "If you obey this commandment, you fulfill all the Law."

"What do all the statutes and ordinances mean, Father?"

"Jeshua, my son, we have told you the story many times of how the Lord brought our people out of Egypt when they were slaves to Pharaoh. He worked many marvelous signs and wonders against Pharaoh and his people. He had sworn to give our ancestors a land flowing with milk and honey, and so he brought us out of Egypt. Then he gave us all the commands and statutes for our good. He taught us to fear him, and to serve him with uprightness and wonder.

So we must be very careful to do all he commands us in the Sh'ma, my son." Joseph put his arm around Jesus' shoulders.

"Now, let's finish our prayers and be off to the synagogue!"

Joseph looked down at his son's shining face, knowing he was eager to hear more. *He is so bright and inquisitive*, he thought to himself. *I hope and pray we are providing him with all the knowledge he needs.*

The following morning, the Sabbath dawned bright, waking the larks to sing their sweet songs. A warm violet light lay over the earth and the distant mountains.

Mary pointed out to Jesus the trees which were covered with buds, swelling and unfurling with promissory green.

The young family breathed deeply of the spring air as they retraced their steps to the synagogue for Sabbath morning services. Jesus scampered along the path, lightly skipping and jumping over the rocks. Mary and Joseph laughed at their young son's exuberance as he ran ahead to greet Jacob and his family, also on their way to Sabbath meeting.

Jacob's younger sister, Suzanne, bestowed a dimpled smile on Jesus as he approached. She was a pretty child, with shining hair the color of a raven's wing hanging over her shoulders in two satiny braids. Her eyes were a silver gray, reflecting the morning light. She was slightly plump, but graceful.

"Suzanne thinks Jesu is a very handsome boy. I have noticed that she often watches Jacob and him from a distance as they play together," Gloriel commented to Samuel and Sariel.

Jacob and Jesus ran on ahead, laughing and scuffling with one another. Outside the synagogue, they waited for their parents and Suzanne to catch up. As they entered the door together, Daniel ben Abijah greeted them warmly. On this Sabbath morning, he was being assisted by Jeremiah ben Simon, a highly respected young member of the community.

Mary, Jacob's mother Rebecca, and Suzanne took their seats in the women's section of the synagogue, separate from the men and boys, as was the custom.

Gloriel and Samuel remained close by their charges, and Sariel accompanied Mary.

Gloriel's heart soared as the services began with a prayer and the first three of the Eighteen Blessings. She loved to join God's people in worship.

It had been a long time since she had last visited the Father. Although she knew He was with her at all times, she longed to see her heavenly home, and refresh her spirit before the Throne. She thought to herself that it was time to leave her young charge just long enough to be strengthened by a visit to Heaven.

*I'll go at sunset, when the Sabbath Day ends*, she thought, happily.

Jeremiah recited the Sh'ma in a clear, vibrant voice, standing tall and straight, his face quiet and serene.

Then several lectors, including Joseph, read from the scriptures. Jesus listened with rapt attention as his father read the ancient words. The boy's face grew bright with pleasure, his brown eyes taking on a vivid inner light.

*Is he becoming aware of who he is?* Gloriel wondered as she watched the young Jesus closely.

After the scripture reading, Jacob's father, chosen by Daniel ben Abijah, stood up and gave a homily. Jacob sat up straight and proud as his father spoke.

The congregation then lifted their voices in song after the sermon. Jesus recognized it as one of King David's beautiful Psalms. Then a collection was taken up for the poor, and the services ended with a final blessing by Daniel ben Abijah.

Jesus was deep in thought. The scripture readings for the evening were the story of the six days of creation in Genesis; and the prophecies about the new Heaven and Earth, in the scroll of the prophet Isaiah.

He was thinking of Adam and Eve, their fall into sin, and how the story was paired with the promise of salvation in Isaiah's scroll.

"Jesus!" Mary was shaking his shoulder gently. "It's time to go home, Son. Come now."

Shaking his head dazedly, Jesus got up and followed his parents out the synagogue door.

On the walk home, his father told Jesus that tomorrow, after school, he would begin his apprenticeship at Joseph's shop in the marketplace.

This would be the first time that Jesus was allowed to go without his mother. He would begin by helping to keep the small shop clean, and watching his father closely as he worked with pine, sweet-smelling acacia, and cedar woods.

Jesus still had the little wooden ball that Joseph had made for him when he was a toddler. He even now loved the feel of the wood, worn satiny smooth by the many caresses of small fingers.

"Oh, Avi, really?" Jesus' voice was filled with excitement.

Joseph laughed. "Yes, really, Son. First you will learn well by watching. Then you will learn by doing."

"May I come right from school, Avi?"

"I think your mother may need you to do your chores first, Jeshua," Joseph replied.

The eager smile faded a bit. "Yes, Father. But I'll work very fast!"

Joseph and Mary smiled at one another in the dim light of a slivered silver moon.

# Chapter Thirteen

The next morning was born silver in glistening dew-drops, as the sun rose in sparkling glory over the distant hills. Jesus bounced eagerly out of his pallet, bright-eyed with excitement.

"Emi!" He called, rubbing his eyes. "May I go to Grandfather and Grandmother's house before school?"

Mary opened sleepy brown eyes, yawning deeply. Stretching her arms overhead, she rose slowly. "Son, it's so early. The sun has just risen."

Jesus loved Joachim and Anna deeply. Although he loved Joseph's parents dearly, he felt especially close to his mother's parents.

*In fact*, Gloriel thought as she listened to the boy pleading with his mother, *he is very close to all his family; aunts, uncles, and all his many cousins are a big part of his life.*

Jesus spent many happy hours with Joachim in the fields, watching his grandfather push the plow. Sometimes, the old man would lift his small grandson onto the back of the ox, and let him ride a short distance.

Anna told him wonderful stories, and when he was very small, she would hold him on her lap as she repeated tales of their people's great heroes while he listened with glistening eyes.

*So*, Gloriel mused, *he wants to share his wonderful news with his grandparents.*

"Please, Emi, I won't be late for school, I promise!" Jesus pleaded.

By now, Joseph had roused, and was sitting on the pallet, eyeing his wife and son. "It's all right, Mary. Let the boy go, "he said, clearing his throat.

"Very well, Jesus. But wash your face and put on a clean tunic first," Mary admonished. "And don't forget to wash behind your ears!" She grinned at her young son then.

Suddenly, Gloriel felt a warm glow spreading through her breast. She was filled with joy, and realized that the Father was summoning her to the Throne now. She glanced around the room at Jesus, Mary and Joseph, and whispered "Goodbye, just for a little while."

Taking on her bodily form, Gloriel found herself standing in a field of asphodel. Its heady fragrance enveloped her, and she inhaled deeply of the heavenly perfume. She was filled with inexpressible delight, gazing across the golden field at the magnificent trees growing beside the crystal clear waters of the river flowing from the Throne.

She began walking toward the brilliant golden glow which filled her field of view now. As she walked, colorful-plumaged birds appeared, singing their numerous silvery melodies, and yet in seemingly perfect harmony to Gloriel's ears.

Flowers of a thousand hues, both soft and radiant, bloomed among the asphodel, interwoven with flowering vines. The heady fragrance rose into the air, almost intoxicating.

The sound of distant voices and melodious music came floating on the silky air, just as when she first awakened to the Lord's call.

"Gloriel, my child!" The glorious voice of the Father touched her spirit.

She stood now before the dazzling throne, gazing at the cloud of golden light resting on it. She longed to see the Father's face, to behold him in all his wondrous glory. The golden particles shifted, swirling and twinkling softly. She sank to her knees, lifting her arms toward the warm inviting glow.

"You have been faithful and loving in your care of my beloved Son, Gloriel. You must rest for a while now, and refresh yourself. There will be many times ahead in my Son's life when you will be sorely tried, and you must gather all your strength."

Gloriel closed her eyes as the golden glow enveloped her, and absolute Love caressed her being. She felt as if the Father was holding her in his arms, and ecstasy flooded her spirit. It was exhilarating, exciting, and fulfilling. She uttered a cry of jubilation.

"Go now, my child, and be with your companions. Refresh your spirit. We shall speak again before you return to my Son's side."

Gloriel opened her eyes to find herself standing on the beautiful sea of glass, with its gleaming, shifting particles of gold.

"Gloriel! Welcome Home!" A familiar voice rang out.

Looking around, she saw her dear friends, Gabriel and Michael approaching, striding across the wonderful glassy sea. Gabriel reached her first, and embraced her warmly. His auburn hair glinted in the golden light, and he was grinning from ear to ear.

Michael's black eyes sparkled with warmth as he welcomed her. "We've been watching you, dear friend. Come, let's visit the City, and we'll talk about all that has happened since last we spoke," he said, reaching for her hand.

Gloriel smiled at her two dear companions, as they strolled hand in hand toward the great golden dome in the distance. She thought of her young charge then, and knew in her heart that he would be safe until her return.

#

Meanwhile, in the small village of Nazareth, Jeshua ben Joseph was seated on a small stool in his father's shop. He watched intently as Joseph worked with chisel and hammer, making a yoke for oxen. He was meticulous, and exacting in his measurements.

"Whatever you do, Son, do your best. No job is so small that it does not deserve your very best efforts," Joseph said, looking down at the eager face. "Now take the broom and sweep up the shavings, please. Put them in the bag over there in the corner, and we will save them for your mother to start the fire in her oven."

"Yes, Avi," Jesus said, jumping up from his seat. "Then may I help you with the yoke?"

Joseph smiled to himself. "Not yet, son. First you must learn to keep your workplace clean. Tell me, Jeshua, what are the tools I am using here called?"

"A hammer and a chisel, Father," Jesus answered, sweeping up the curls of cedar and pine. The boy loved the smell of the cedar shavings especially. The floor of the small shop was hard-packed dirt, very smooth.

"You are doing a very good job, my boy," Joseph commented, nodding his approval. "Taking good care of your tools is an important part of being a carpenter."

Outside, the warm afternoon sun was lowering toward the hills, and newborn leaves glittered on the topmost branches of the sycamore trees around the village well. Birds twittered their springtime melodies. Jesus felt warm and drowsy, content just to be with his father.

As he listened to Joseph, he felt something stirring within his chest. His eyes grew heavy-lidded, and his mind began to wander. The fine skin between his eyes puckered, and his fingers and toes tingled. He felt as if he were soaring on the wings of an eagle, higher and higher into the brilliant blue sky, until the whole of Galilee lay beneath his wondering gaze. His vision grew keener and clearer, and in the far distance, the dome of the holy Temple in Jerusalem glinted in the sunlight. The aromas of dust, stone, spices, and warm fertile earth rose like incense around him, surrounding him with a windless silence.

"My Son," the voice was clear and soft, filled with love.

Jesus eyes flew open. "Yes, Avi?"

Joseph looked at Jesus quizzically. "I said, are you ready to go home now? I think that's enough for your first day. Run along now, and spend some time with your friends, or visit your grandparents. But be sure to ask your mother, and let her know where you will be, Son." Joseph smiled at Jesus, patting his shoulder. "I will see you at supper."

Jesus' cheeks were flushed, his expression dazed. He gazed at Joseph with brilliant, intelligent eyes.

"Yes, Father. Goodbye!" The boy started slowly across the market square, shaking his head as if to clear it.

"Jeshua!" Joseph called after him. "Don't forget the wood-shavings for your mother!"

Jesus scampered back to the shop and picked up the bag of shavings he had swept up earlier.

"I'm sorry, Avi. Goodbye!"

Joseph watched his young son scurry across the market square with the canvas bag bouncing on his shoulder. *Life is good,* he thought to himself, *and I am well-blessed.*

Jesus sprinted joyfully down the rocky path to his house.

"Jesus! Wait!" Jacob came running out of his house, waving eagerly at his friend. "Let's go see the new lambs in Benjamin's flock," he said breathlessly as he approached Jesus.

"All right, but first I need to take this bag to my mother." Jesus replied.

Mary pushed aside the curtain and came out the door as the boys approached. Her cheeks were rosy, and a smudge of flour powdered her nose.

"Hello, boys. Jesus, how was your time with your father at the shop? Come in and tell me about it." She wiped a floury hand on her apron, and patted her son on his arm. She didn't want to embarrass him by kissing him in front of his friend.

"Mother, here is a bag of shavings I swept up at the shop. Avi said you can use them in the oven."

Mary looked down at her son. Small beads of perspiration were shining on his upper lip, and his light brown hair was wind-blown. The golden curls were long-gone now.

"Thank you, Son."

"Mother, Jacob and I want to go see the new lambs in Benjamin's flock. May we go now?"

"Yes, Son. Would you and Jacob like a piece of fresh bread to take with you?"

"Yes, please!" Two eager voices chimed in unison.

Mary took a loaf of barley bread, fresh from the oven, broke off two pieces, and gave one to each of the boys.

"Thank you, Emi." Jesus smiled at his mother.

"Yes, thank you, ma'am, Jacob said.

A ray of sunshine beamed through the small window over the oven, glinting gold in Mary's soft brown hair, which curled moistly over her forehead and shoulders. She wore no mantle, for baking was hot work, and the day was quite warm.

The two boys started out the door, clutching the fragrant bread, and jostling one another playfully.

"Be home in time for supper, Son!" Mary called after them. She watched as the two friends ran across the green field behind the house and disappeared from sight.

"My little Jeshua, you and your friend are growing up so fast," she whispered wistfully.

Jesus and Jacob slowed to a walk as they approached Benjamin's flock. They didn't want to frighten the sheep with their exuberance. The late afternoon sunlight lay soft over the newly green meadow. The sheep were quiet, lulled and drowsy in the warm afternoon air.

Benjamin was 26-years-old, strong and sturdy of limb. He stood tall and straight, gazing into the distance, his black eyes heavy-lidded and dreamy. He was thinking of Ruth, his wife of nearly five years now. She was small and pleasingly plump, with sparkling blue eyes, and hair the color of new straw. He loved to bury his nose in her soft fragrant curls.

He recalled the marriage contract between his family in Bethlehem, and that of Ruth's in Nazareth. At first, the agreement between the two fathers, who were boyhood friends, was that Ruth would move to Bethlehem to the house of Benjamin's parents. However, in the end, it was decided that the young couple would settle in Nazareth, despite the usual customs.

So, they had settled in the small village, and Ruth's parents had gifted them with a small flock of sheep as a wedding present. In the ensuing years, the small flock had grown considerably, and the young couple was happy and content.

"Benjamin . . ." The young voice snapped him out of his pleasant reverie. He spotted the two boys approaching and raised his staff in greeting

"Hello, Jesus. Hello, Jacob. Peace be with you!" His voice was deep and friendly. "Have you come to see the new lambs?" He asked. The sheep stirred as he spoke, lifting their heads and looking toward him.

"They know your voice, don't they, Benjamin?" Jesus observed.

"Yes, yes they do. They even know their names."

Jesus and Jacob laughed. "They have names?" Jacob asked, grinning.

"Indeed they do. See the one over there with the black spot on her tail? Her name is Patches," Benjamin said, pointing to a nearby ewe. "And the one behind you is called Sheli . . . friend." He never strays far from my side." Benjamin pointed to a rather ragged looking ram. "He's getting pretty old, now."

Suddenly, Jesus felt something cool and wet in the palm of his hand. Startled, he looked down to see a curly white lamb nuzzling his hand. He laughed in delight. "Benjamin, may I hold her?" he asked eagerly.

"Yes, but be very careful. Newborn lambs are very tiny and helpless. Hold her close to your chest, Jesus."

Thrilled, the boy leaned down and gently lifted the tiny creature into his arms, cradling her against his breast. A feeling of love and tenderness spread through him like warm water as he caressed the little one, burying his face in her curly coat.

Tears welled in his dark eyes. *Why do I feel like this?* he wondered to himself. The lamb snuggled into the boy's chest and stuck her nose under his arm. For a few moments, she lay motionless in his embrace.

Her mother pushed against Jesus' leg, anxious about her baby, and bleating softly. Very gently, Jesus placed the tiny animal back on the grass, a strange expression in his luminous eyes.

The two boys chatted with Benjamin, laughing at the antics of the lambs gamboling around their mothers, and kicking up their heels. Time passed quickly, and the sun stood in the western sky, in a sea of scarlet and gold, as the boys bid Benjamin goodbye, and hurried toward home.

#

Gloriel stood before the Throne. She was filled with peace, basking in the joy of the Father's Presence. Standing in the light of his Glory, the great Earth lying below seemed as insignificant as a speck of dust to her. She bowed low before Him, as that wonderful voice which had called her into being so long ago, instructed her once again.

"Gloriel, you must return now to my Son. You are to guide his footsteps, instruct him in all wisdom, and for now, shield him from the fallen one and his demons. Whisper my words into his heart, and never leave his side until I summon you once more. Go now, my child."

Instantly, Gloriel found herself back in the little village in Galilee, where the eternal Son slept in a young boy's body, dreaming of green fields, blue skies, and frolicking lambs.

She gazed down at him, at the thick silken lashes lying soft on velvet cheeks, and the light brown hair spreading out in waves about the boy's head, like a halo. His breathing was quiet and shallow, barely discernible.

Filled with adoration and humble thanksgiving for her precious charge, she gently touched his cheek. He stirred slightly, smiling in his sleep.

Gloriel turned to greet Sariel and Samuel, who were standing watch over Mary and Joseph. The three friends rejoiced again in their calling, as the Father poured down his blessing on them.

## Chapter Fourteen

Jesus stood in the doorway of Joseph's carpentry shop, gazing out at the torrent of rain running off the eaves in tattered sheets. Thunder echoed and beat through the air. A cold front moved slowly over the village, bringing a harsh wind with the chilling rain.

It was late winter, and he longed for the warming rays of spring sunshine. He was almost 13 years old now and growing rapidly, nearly as tall as his mother. He was day-dreaming about his special day, when he would become a man spiritually.

Thinking about Passover, excitement rose up in his breast. This year, he would be presented at the Temple in Jerusalem.

His heart pounded with excitement as he dreamed of finally seeing the magnificent House of his Father. *My Father?* Jesus shook his head slightly, his thoughts suddenly perplexed. *My Father? Of course, all Jews are children of the Most High,* he thought. *But He is my Father.* Bewildered and confused, the boy pushed the thought from his consciousness.

Gloriel attended to him closely, acutely aware of his bewilderment. Jesus turned away from the doorway, feeling a bit dazed.

Joseph stood at his workbench, carefully sanding a piece of fine cedar, enjoying its fragrance as he worked.

"Son, you should go now and see to your chores. Your mother will be waiting. I'll be home soon. It's getting quite cold," he said, looking up from his work.

"Father . . ." it was almost a whisper from the boy's lips.

"Yes, Son?"

"Oh, I'm sorry, Avi. I'll leave now."

Joseph smiled at the youth's use of the familiar name. "Jeshua, don't forget your cloak, and the shavings for your mother."

Jesus wrapped the rough woolen cloak around his shoulders and picked up the familiar canvas bag.

"Goodbye, Father." The young voice suddenly cracked.

Joseph covered his smile. His boy was growing up.

Jesus dashed across the market place as quickly as the torrent would allow. The gray rain slanted icy cold, hurling itself in cascades against the walls of the marketplace. Lightning flashed, and iron strides of thunder rolled across the sodden hills.

The boy slowed his pace as he began slipping and sliding on the muddy path. Sudden darkness folded its mantle around the scene as Gloriel attended her charge.

Jesus lowered his head, struggling against the wind. Darkness lay heavy and wet on the countryside. Rivulets began cutting into the rocky soil as he strained to see the edges of the narrow path. The darkness was like a blanket covering him now. Howling wind and icy cold driving rain swirled all around him.

Blinded by the vicious storm, for the first time a wave of fear washed over him, clutching at his heart with frigid fingers. He felt lost and alone.

Gloriel placed an unseen hand on his shoulder.

"Father!" the word burst involuntarily from between Jesus' chattering teeth. "Father!"

Jesus looked full into the face of the storm. Abruptly, it was as if a mighty unseen hand swept away the rain, wind and darkness with one powerful stroke. Stunned and bewildered, the boy stared out over the early evening landscape. The air was damp, but soft. A slight breeze lifted a sodden strand of hair from his white forehead. His eyes widened incredulously. Little prisms of colored light reflected in small pools and puddles on the pathway.

"Father?" he whispered, as warmth spread through his limbs and torso. His astonished face lit up, and Gloriel smiled.

#

The opalescent early morning light stretched its pale fingers through the small window of the room where Jesus slept.

The aroma of baking bread warmed the air. Mary had risen while darkness still lay heavily on the hills of Nazareth.

It was late in the month of Nissan, and preparations for the journey to Jerusalem were completed. She was preparing a hearty breakfast for her two men-folk. They all needed strength for the five day journey. Mary peeked out the window at the road, soggy from the spring rains. A rack of gray clouds sat heavily on the horizon.

Outside, Joseph loaded supplies on the backs of their two small donkeys. He took care not to overburden Ezra. Signs of advancing years were unmistakable in the gray hairs sprinkled around his soft nose. His companion, Eli, stomped restlessly with the vigor of all young creatures. Joseph had acquired him recently by trading a low table carved from cedar for the young ass.

"Jeshua," Mary called to her sleeping son. "It's time to get up now. Your father needs your help."

Bending down, she ruffled Jesus' thick light brown locks. The soft hair of childhood was almost gone now. Their little boy was becoming a young man. A pang struck her heart as she thought wistfully of the golden curls, chubby arms and dimples of yesterday.

Jesus rubbed his eyes sleepily. Suddenly, he sat bolt upright, eyes shining with clear delight.

"Emi!" he exclaimed, "We're going to Jerusalem!"

"Yes, Son, I know," Mary replied, laughing. "Get up now, and go help your father while I get breakfast on the table."

Quickly, Jesus dressed in his brown linen traveling tunic and heavy sandals.

"Jesus, you will need your cloak. It's still cold outside," Mary directed.

"Yes, Emi," Jesus replied, reluctantly putting on his plain woolen cloak.

How *long will it be before he stops calling me "Emi?"* Mary wondered to herself. *He is growing up so quickly. Too quickly.*

The little family breakfasted on fresh-baked wheaten bread, goat cheese and bowls of curd. Ample bread was packed for their journey, along with dried salted fish, some boiled chicken, goat cheese, dried figs and nuts. A leather bottle of wine, jars of water, and skins of goat's milk completed the provisions for the trip.

Joseph, Mary and Jesus set out as the early morning sunlight pushed aside the gray eyes of dawn. The sweet, soft wind of early spring caressed the eager faces set toward Jerusalem and the Temple.

Gloriel, Sariel and Samuel were their unseen companions as they set out on the long-awaited pilgrimage.

Jesus could hardly contain the excitement rising within him. He was eager to see the holy Temple, and participate in the wonderful Passover celebrations. Cousin Elizabeth, Zechariah, and their young son, John, would be there also. He had never seen John, and looked forward excitedly to meeting him. Jesus recollected Mary's stories about the beautiful home on the hillside in Ein Karem, where she visited Cousin Elizabeth before he was born.

Mary and Joseph made the trip to Jerusalem for Passover celebration every year since their return to Nazareth from Egypt. Anna and Joachim, growing old now, stayed home to care for their grandchildren, Jesus among them, so that the rest of their family could make the journey.

This year, Jesus was allowed to accompany his parents, as he approached spiritual adulthood.

The extended families of Mary and Joseph formed a caravan as they left the gates of Nazareth behind. Jesus spent the time visiting with his cousins as the day progressed. The boys hiked briskly along the muddy, rock-strewn road, stumbling occasionally.

Toward evening, a short, cold rainstorm dampened their spirits, and the caravan halted in the dull dusk. Lean-tos popped up along the roadside, and campfires soon warmed the tired sojourners. Joseph kindled a fire with dry sticks from the bundle on Eli's weary back.

The clouds soon whisked away on a gentle breeze, as pink light seeped across the sky. After a supper of boiled chicken and flat bread, Joseph, Mary and Jesus bedded down beside the crackling fire. Its warm light flickered against the gathering darkness.

Gloriel and her companions stood watch as the family fell quickly into the deep sleep of tired bodies.

Next day, the sun rose on a bright spring morning. All signs of the dreary clouds and rainfall of yesterday had disappeared.

"The Lord washed Earth's face," Mary said to Jesus as he opened his great dark eyes to the morning light. All around them, families prepared breakfast in the fresh morning air.

Soon, they were packed up and ready to resume their journey. As they walked, more pilgrims joined them on the muddy road, and excitement was growing.

Many boys being presented at the Temple this year were already wearing their velvet caps. Jesus kept his carefully folded in his knapsack, wanting to wait until his eyes fell on the Holy City before he put it on.

"He is so beautiful," Gloriel whispered to Sariel as they watched their little family begin the day's journey. "in heart as well as face and form."

Sariel smiled and nodded, her eyes fixed on her sweet Mary.

"I think he is beginning to realize who he is," Gloriel continued.

Samuel went on ahead to search the road for any hazards which might bring harm to the precious family. Children raced about, laughing with excitement and enthusiasm. As day wore on, the exuberance muted. Most of the children grew weary, and walked quietly beside their parents.

The leader of the caravan, Ahaziah, a cousin of Joseph's, urged the people onward, trying to make up for the early stop the day before. He kept close watch on the sojourners for signs of exhaustion. A small man, wiry and well-muscled at 39, he was getting along in years, and was well-respected by the community of Nazareth.

Samuel whispered in Joseph's ear. Soon afterward, Joseph approached Ahaziah.

"Cousin Ahaziah, some of our older relatives are growing fatigued. Perhaps we should make camp now," he suggested, in a low voice.

Ahaziah halted and rubbed his eyes.

"Yes, Joseph, I believe you are right," he replied, looking back over the caravan.

"Let's make camp for the night!" He called out to nearby family members.

Word quickly passed among the caravan from Nazareth. People moved off the road and began unloading their pack animals and making preparations for the evening meal.

Jesus started the camp fire for his mother while Joseph unloaded Ezra and Eli and fed them. Mary busied herself preparing supper for her men-folk. She set out some of the dried salted fish and the bread and cheese, along with foaming cups of goat's milk.

Joseph blessed the food and recited the evening prayers. A ravenous Jesus quickly disposed of his portions.

"Not so fast, Son," his mother admonished with a smile. "You need to chew your food before you swallow it."

*He has the appetite of a young lion*, Gloriel reflected, grinning.

The three chatted for a while around the fire, as the spring air cooled and the last glimmer of twilight left the sky. Night folded its cloak quietly around them.

An owl flew low overhead with an almost silent flapping of wings, calling his soft "Who-oo? Who-oo?" into the shadows.

Gloriel kept an eye on Jesus as he curled up on a blanket next to the glowing embers of the camp fire. His eyes grew heavy-lidded, drooping until the lashes lay on his cheeks like the faintest shadow.

"Father," he breathed as he drifted off to sleep.

Gloriel smiled, and nodded at Sariel and Samuel, who were standing their own watches.

#

It was noon on the fifth day of their journey. The little caravan from Nazareth was electric with excitement. Soon they would arrive at the foothills around the Holy City. The pathway was rockier now, strewn with dung. The hills of soft, chalky limestone shimmered in the mid-day sun. The road teemed with people, jostling one another in their eagerness to reach the Holy City. Jesus and the other boys could scarcely contain themselves, running back and forth between their families, shouting with exhilaration.

The three guardian angels stood alert for any danger which might threaten the Holy Family. Gloriel listened approvingly as Mary explained to her young son that Jerusalem was not all beautiful. She tried to prepare him for its stench, and the odors of the East that rode on the wind. She warned him about the hovels, and the frantic din of the market places. He would hear curses for the first time; and see the hated Roman soldiers swaggering through the narrow streets teeming with humanity.

But, she reassured her son, none of this would dim the magnificence of the holy Temple in all its incomparable splendor. Although it had been desecrated three times, it was restored, ironically, by the hated tyrant Herod. Still, after forty years of labor, the enormous complex remained incomplete, Mary told Jesus. Jesus nodded, eager to return to his companions as they approached the final hill.

The afternoon wore on slowly, and the sky softened to a delicate azure. Suddenly, as they started up the hill, a voice rang out in the twilight stillness. Clear and strong, it rose above the crowd, piercing the air with golden tones.

Jesus stood stock-still in amazement. A short man with chubby cheeks and a tumble of black curling hair, perched on a rock across the road. He lifted up his arms to Heaven as his joyful song poured forth. Never in all his life, had Jesus heard such glorious music. Even though they were some distance from the man, he could make out the glowing face and sparkling eyes. The crowd stood silent as the ancient Psalm filled the air, lifting each heart.

Mary recalled Joseph's song as they had approached Jerusalem on their way to Bethlehem. But this was even more joyful.

*I was glad when they said to me 'Let us go to the house of the Lord.' And now we are standing here inside your gates, O Jerusalem. Jerusalem is a well-built city, knit together as a single unit. All the people of Israel—the Lord's people—make their pilgrimage here. They come to give thanks to the Lord as the law requires. Here stand the thrones where judgment is given, the thrones of the dynasty of David.* Psalm 122: 1-5 NLT

The clear tones echoed off the nearby hills. As Jesus listened, awestruck, Gloriel placed her hand on his shoulder and whispered in his ear. Slowly, he lifted his arms and closed his eyes. All sound faded from his awareness, and he felt as if he were being lifted up into absolute silence. He became aware of vivid light surrounding him, but did not open his eyes. An exquisite face, delicate features framed with amber curls, materialized behind his closed eyelids. Great golden eyes gazed at him adoringly. Slowly, the face faded away, and he was enveloped with an almost unendurable bliss, a shining solitude, a deep assurance of love. Jesus was overcome, and collapsed in a heap on the ground.

"Jeshua! Jeshua!"

His mother's frantic voice penetrated his consciousness. Opening his eyes slowly, he smiled at Mary.

"My Father loves me," he sighed dreamily, smiling.

"Yes, Jeshua, I do," Joseph knelt by his side, looking bewildered.

"Yes, son, of course your father loves you. Are you all right? Do you want a drink of water? Do you feel faint?" Mary questioned anxiously, smoothing back the thick hair from her son's pale forehead.

Jesus sat up, still smiling. "No, Mother, thank you. I have had a drink," he replied, patting Mary's hand. She gazed at her boy, a mystified expression on her pale face.

"But . . ." Mary's voice trailed off into silence as Jesus stood up and gazed across the road. The man with the glorious voice had vanished.

# Chapter Fifteen

The little caravan from Nazareth camped outside the gates of the great city the night before the Passover celebration. Jesus rose before daybreak to get dressed in preparation for the Temple ceremonies. His dark eyes sparkled and his face shone with anticipation as he strained his eyes to see in the predawn darkness.

Gloriel examined her charge thoroughly as he prepared himself for the wonderful day ahead. Carefully, he removed the bright red velvet cap from his knapsack.

*I remember how Mary worked far into the night by the dim flickering light of the oil lamp. She wanted it to be perfect for her Jeshua,* Gloriel mused as she watched.

Jesus smoothed the cap between his fingers, admiring the tiny stitches and the softness of the fabric. He knew his parents had saved for a long time to buy the expensive ruby-red cloth. His heart swelled with love for them, as he placed the beautiful cap on his head with trembling fingers. He smoothed his soft white linen robe with its silken tassels. The garment was a gift from his grandparents, Joaquin and Anna. He thought of their bright faces, beaming with pride as he had opened the package.

*Oh, it will be so wonderful to be a part of the Passover Celebration at last!* Jesus thought to himself. Soon, he would meet his cousins, Elizabeth, Zechariah, and their son, John. Emi talked about them so much that he could scarcely wait to see them. They were to meet at the Temple gate after the day's ceremonies.

Faint streaks of pink suffused the horizon as Mary emerged from the lean-to which Joseph had erected for her privacy. She, too, was dressed in her best. A mantle of pale blue edged in white covered her soft brown hair. Her gown was a darker blue linen, with a soft leather belt circling her still-slender waist.

Joseph waited, standing outside the lean-to, smiling and resplendent in a robe of red and tan stripes with brown tassels.

After feeding and tethering Ezra and Eli, the little family left the caravan camp and entered the great city gates. Pilgrims crowded in on all sides. The streets were filled with shrieking women and shouting men; with beggars, the blind and the halt, lining the walls.

Jesus felt his heart thudding in his chest. The sights and sounds were overwhelming to the boy.

The early morning dew still lay sparkling on the narrow cobbled streets, strewn with the offal of both man and animals. The stench of the city assailed his nostrils. Jerusalem was already crowded with people shouting, shoving, laughing and cursing. Roman soldiers swaggered through the streets, shouting, quarreling, and pushing each other. Their curses and taunts filled the air with blasphemies. Mary covered her young son's ears.

But Jesus, speechless with excitement, seemed not to hear. His eyes grew huge in his young face.

Joseph pushed his way through the mass of humanity, clearing the way for his wife and son. Their relatives from the caravan were soon lost to sight in the crowds. Enthralled, the boy craned his neck to see, as they passed by Herod's royal palace with its golden dome gleaming in the morning light.

Returning his gaze to the road, he stared in wonder, his chin dropping. Directly in their path, a Roman legionnaire, face all hollows and angles in the shadow of a red-plumed helmet, sat astride a huge, shining black stallion, surveying the crowd with a practiced eye.

Horses were rare in Nazareth, and the powerful beast captivated Jesus. *All the noblemen we have seen, dressed up in their finery, have no coats as beautiful as that stallion's,* the boy thought. He longed to reach out and touch the gleaming ebony creature.

Finally, they arrived at the Gate of Copernicus. It was massive, set in an immense white stone wall, and beautifully decorated with a huge golden eagle.

The town stank of latrines and the offal of animals as they entered the gate. Jesus wrinkled his nose and thought of the fragrant morning aroma from the orchards of Nazareth.

The Temple itself, dressed in gold and pale marble, hung against the sapphire sky. It had just recently been rebuilt by Herod. He had paid ten thousand workmen for its repair, and for rebuilding the walls of Jerusalem. The magnificent marble spires of the Temple glinted rosy pink in the morning sun. Encompassing about 35 acres, it stood surrounded by double colonnades of white marble.

Jesus gasped at the beauty and majesty of the structure. The roofs were adorned with graven cedar.

"Each colonnade is 30 cubits in breadth," Joseph told the boy, "and altogether they cover six furlongs, along with the tower of Antonia." Speechless with amazement, Jesus nodded.

Everyone was allowed to enter the great outer portico around the Temple, and so it was called the "Court of the Gentiles," the swarming center of community activity.

The Temple itself was surrounded by a balustrade, an elevated stone railing about 4 and a half feet high. Non-believers were allowed no farther than this, on penalty of death.

The day bloomed lovely and warm as the small family entered the gate surrounding the Court of Women, a large space nearly 200 feet square.

"The four corners of this chamber serve various purposes," Joseph informed Jesus, putting an arm across the boy's shoulders. "The western chambers are used for storage, and those people who make special vows prepare their sacrifices in the eastern chambers. The western chambers are also used for the private ritual baths for the cleansing of lepers. Your mother will remain here with the other women."

"Why can't she stay with us, Father?" Jesus asked, looking up at Joseph in puzzlement.

"This is the way the Most High wants it to be, for now, Son. This is the Law."

A slight frown furrowed the boy's brow, but he did not question Joseph further.

Gloriel was filled with excitement for the holy child, as he beheld his Father's House for the first time. Porticoes surrounded the Temple, and here great crowds congregated, listening to the teachers and rabbis. Chests for charitable contributions lined the walls inside the porticoes. On the left side stood the money changers' booths, where animals and birds were being sold for sacrifices.

Jesus covered his ears, averting his eyes from the Place of Slaughtering, as goats, bulls, sheep and doves raised their voices in a cacophony of fear.

On the right, the towers of the Fortress Antonia rose high above the Temple walls, before Jesus' wondering gaze.

Gloriel and Samuel smiled at his wide-eyed amazement

Joseph and the boy then entered the Court of Men. Fifteen curved steps led to the Court of Priests, and inside of it, was the Temple itself. Only priests and Temple officers were allowed to enter the two huge chambers. The outer was called the Holy; the inner, the Holy of Holies.

Jesus sparkling eyes followed the priests in their billowing, flowing mantles. All mingled in a profusion of colors; glistening red, emerald green, deep yellow, rich brown with purple stripes and tiny silver threads between. He glimpsed the High Priest, arrayed in his embroidered blue robes, turban and sash. Twelve gems, representing the 12 tribes of Israel gleamed and sparkled on his breastplate.

A thick, heavy veil hung in front of the Holy of Holies. It was embroidered in rich, vibrant colors, with all the known flowers of the earth, and many different varieties of fruit.

Candlelit shadows flickered across the ceiling, as warm gold lamplight gleamed on the columns of varicolored marble.

Awestricken, Jesus knew that only the High Priest was allowed to enter this chamber where the Presence of God dwelled, and then only once a year. Joseph felt Jesus' shoulders begin to tremble.

Waiting in the Court of Women, Mary's heart thrilled for her son on his first visit to the Temple. She closed her eyes and remembered that day, so long ago, when the angel Gabriel appeared to her in the olive grove. Sometimes, in the routine of everyday life, it all seemed like a dream, and she forgot that this beloved son of hers also belonged to the Most High.

At this moment, the thought pierced her soul, and she bowed her head in prayer.

#

Elizabeth and Zechariah stood waiting eagerly outside the Beautiful Gate. John, their tall, strapping teenage son, paced back and forth, searching the crowd with his piercing black eyes.

"Where can they be, Father?" He questioned Zechariah impatiently. "They should have been here by now."

Placing a hand on his arm, Elizabeth smiled at her son.

"John, they will be here soon, just be patient!"

"Look, there they are!" Zechariah exclaimed, waving his wiry arms in the air.

As soon as they saw them, Joseph and Mary approached them quickly, hands outstretched to greet their relatives.

Jesus, suddenly feeling shy, hung back as the four adults exchanged warm embraces. He flushed as his gaze met the penetrating eyes of his cousin John.

"Hello, Cousin Jesus." John's voice was as deep as a grown man's, though he was still a few months shy of fourteen years.

Jesus felt small and weak beside the well-muscled youth, who appeared on the threshold of full manhood.

"Greetings, John," he said quietly.

Cousin Elizabeth enveloped Jesus in her ample arms, hugging him tightly. She held him at arm's length, suddenly solemn, searching his face with her warm brown gaze.

"Do you remember me, Jeshua?" she asked softly.

The two families had not seen one another since the two boys were small, when Elizabeth and Zechariah had come to Nazareth to visit their relatives.

"No, ma'am, I'm sorry, I don't," Jesus replied shyly, lowering his eyes to the ground.

Zechariah placed an arm around Jesus' slender shoulders. "Hello, Son. It's good to see you," he said warmly.

"Yes, sir, I'm glad to see all of you, too." Jesus replied politely.

His gaze returned to John, who was watching him intently, a strange expression on his sunburned young face. One dark eyebrow was raised in a questioning slant. John's head was a tumble of black curling hair, and already a dark shadow of promised beard lay on his cheeks

Elizabeth's plump face was wreathed in a beaming smile, and framed with a mantle of rose-pink, matching her cheeks. A deep dimple twinkled beside her mouth.

*Zechariah has hardly changed at all*, Mary thought, *only a little more silver in his beard.*

"Come, let's go to our camp and talk," she invited her elderly kin. She took Elizabeth's aged hand in her own, patting it warmly.

The little group soon arrived at the Nazareth caravan's noisy camp. Elizabeth and Mary busied themselves preparing the evening meal. Joseph and Jesus soon had a roaring fire going, as the last strand of red sky faded to dark, and the newborn evening star appeared.

Zechariah's knapsack yielded a feast of Passover lamb, honeycomb, fresh wheaten unleavened bread, and herbs. A leather bottle of sweet wine added to their merry conversation as they ate heartily and reminisced.

John and Jesus were soon exchanging tales of school and friends. Laughter and song rose from their campsite and neighboring ones.

Gloriel and her companions remained close-by, enjoying the pleasure of their charges.

"These two boys-their destinies are woven together," Gloriel confided to Sariel and Samuel. "Though I'm not sure how, yet."

Samuel and Sariel both nodded in agreement.

Soon, Elizabeth, Zechariah and John bid their kinsmen goodnight and farewell as they left for their lodgings inside the city gates. They planned to leave early in the morning for their home in Ein Karem.

Elizabeth and Mary shed quiet tears at the parting, for who could say when or if they would meet again?

John and Jesus embraced wordlessly. As they walked away, John turned and looked intently once more at Jesus, his eyes like dark stars in the firelight. Jesus raised his hand in farewell, puzzled at the strange expression on John's young face.

Three days later, it was time for Joseph's family to leave the great city, and head home for Nazareth. Early in the morning, a ragged veil of thin high clouds hung in the sky. Jesus helped Mary and Joseph pack up their belongings and load the two donkeys. Then he was off, running and rough-housing with the other boys in the caravan. Mary and Joseph walked silently for a while, each lost in thought, storing memories of the past few days.

After a while, Mary started walking with the other women of the group from Nazareth, and Joseph joined the men. Children scampered back and forth between the adults, laughing and playing, hiding from one another.

Other caravans surrounded them, and the road was congested with pilgrims returning to their homes in various communities. The Nazareth caravan headed for Jericho, planning to cross the river there, and head north. Mary saw no sign of Jesus throughout the day, and assumed he was with Joseph and the men, or playing with the other boys.

As the day drew to an end, the air cooled, and the last glimmer of twilight left the sky.

Joseph returned to Mary's side, leading Ezra and Eli. As he started unloading the donkeys, preparing to make camp for the night, Mary asked "Where is Jesus, my husband?"

"I thought he was with you," Joseph replied, rubbing Ezra's long ears.

Mary looked up at Joseph, her puzzled brown eyes searching his. "No, I haven't seen him since this morning. I assumed he was with you and the other men."

"Oh, he's probably with his cousins. I will go look for him while you prepare supper, my love." He smiled at his wife reassuringly.

A small frown puckered Mary's smooth brow. "He should have told us where he was going to be," she murmured irritably.

Joseph left while Mary set out a light supper of dried fish and rice. She fed Ezra and Eli, and spread out the sleeping mats. Joseph was gone longer than she expected. *Where can that boy be?* She wondered silently. Sariel stood close by, watching her Mary.

Footsteps approached the campfire, and Joseph appeared in the circle of light, alone. Alarm rose up in Mary's breast, and her brows knitted with sudden anxiousness.

Joseph's face colored with annoyance and some anxiety. "I cannot find him anyplace, Mary, and no one has seen him since we broke camp this morning." He rubbed a hand absently over his bearded chin.

Fear began to insinuate itself into Mary's heart with thin icy fingers. Her face grew pale and drawn in the firelight. She drew a shuddering breath, leaning her head on Joseph's shoulder.

"We will leave at sunrise and head back to Jerusalem. He can't be ahead of us, and we will check with every caravan on the way back. Let's get some rest now, Mary." Joseph's voice was sharp with worry.

"Lord God, have mercy. Be with our boy, wherever he is." Mary whispered. Neither she nor Joseph could eat a bite. They settled down for a restless night, tossing and turning.

Mary woke with a start. For a few moments, she forgot where they were. Then she remembered. Their boy was gone. She sat up quickly, looking around and rubbing tired eyes. The pre-dawn sky was a soft, pale blue-orange. *Maybe during the night . . . No, his sleeping mat is empty.* Mary thought.

A queasy sensation snaked through her bowels. *Where can he be?* Unseen, Sariel placed a small hand on Mary's head, and glanced at Samuel, standing over Joseph. A faint frown creased the little angel's brow. Gloriel was nowhere to be seen.

#

Gloriel followed closely as the boy threaded his way through the swarming streets of Jerusalem. Vendors hawked their wares over the shrieking voices of the market rabble. Even though the early morning was mild in temperature, the stench and noise and press of bodies assaulted her nostrils and ears. She wasn't sure why she suddenly felt the urge to assume her bodily form. She seldom did so. But today, as she trailed behind her young charge through the city streets, their frantic din ringing in her ears, she absorbed the excitement, and trembled with anticipation. Jesus was hurrying back to the House of his Father. Her red-gold curls clung to Gloriel's flushed face as she pushed her way through the narrow streets teeming with carts, donkeys, camels, and mobs of shoving, shouting people. Her unaccustomed senses were assaulted. The simple white muslin gown and mantle she wore was soon stained around the hem and wrinkled from the press of the crowd around her. Keeping her eyes fixed on the boy ahead of her, she prayed silently. *Father, help me keep him safe, for he is still just a boy.*

There it was, the jewel of Jerusalem, soaring skyward in all its glory and splendor, the Temple.

Jesus stopped short, drawing in a sharp breath involuntarily. It was as if he were seeing it for the first time. A thrill of wonder and promise raced through his young body. "My Father's House," he whispered to himself. "It truly is my Father's House!" He wiped the perspiration from his upper lip with a shaking hand.

Gloriel was behind him, then. He turned suddenly, as if someone had tapped him on the shoulder. He gazed full into Gloriel's small face with a startled expression. Those golden eyes, where had he seen them before? There was a tenderness in them, a knowing, a searching. Who was this lovely girl? Confused and vaguely embarrassed, Jesus turned back toward the Temple. He started forward again, straining to see the gate through the crush of bodies around him. Glancing back over his shoulder, he was surprised to see that the girl-woman had disappeared in the crowd.

Meanwhile, Mary and Joseph hurried along the crowded road in the early morning light. Yellow dust, illumined by the rising sun, glittered around them.

Mary prayed silently, *O Most High, be merciful to us, and to our boy.* She felt devoured by anxiety, and stumbled over a rock in her haste.

"Mary, you must calm down. We will find the boy. Watch your step." Joseph admonished, taking her arm and steadying her. He struggled not to let his wife see that fear was gnawing at his heart like a rat.

As they walked, pulling the two small donkeys, they anxiously searched each face on the road. Mary's heart skipped a beat every time she saw a young boy come into view. *Where, oh where can he be? How could I have been so irresponsible? God has given his son into my care and I have lost him!* Her thoughts raced.

Sometimes she forgot, in the mundane events of everyday life, that this Child did not really belong to them, to simple peasant parents. Right now, she was sharply aware of it. *Will the Most High forgive our negligence?*

In the afternoon, they had to stop to eat. Though appetite was gone, the weakness of their bodies told them they had taken no food since yesterday. They drank deeply of the tepid water in the jug. Chunks of goat cheese and oaten bread soon refreshed their tired dusty bodies. Mary's feet were swollen and aching, and her head felt light. *Where is he? Where is our precious boy?* She worried, silently.

Imaginings fought with one another for foremost position in her mind. *Perhaps he has been waylaid by robbers. No, they would know a young boy possessed nothing of value to them. But there are those evil men who stalk the dark streets, those who prey on young boys. Our lovely young boy . . .*

"No!" Mary jumped, startled by her own voice, not realizing she cried aloud.

"Mary, what is it, my love?" Joseph was instantly at her side.

"Oh, Joseph, I am so frightened for our boy!"

Joseph took his wife in his arms, smoothing back the soft brown hair from her furrowed brow.

Mary raised her head from Joseph's shoulder and gazed down the road toward Jerusalem. They should reach the gates soon. The road was still teeming with pilgrims, and the late afternoon sun hung low in a milky blue sky.

A short distance away, a child stood, her back turned as she looked toward the great city. Long golden curls glinted in the light. Suddenly, she turned and looked full into Mary's face. Her peaceful blue eyes smiled, and dimples flickered by her mouth. Mary stared at the beautiful child. Long ago memories stirred in her mind. *That lovely child! I have seen her before! But how can that be? So many years ago, and she has not changed!* Mary looked up at Joseph.

"Joseph, look! That young girl! I have seen her before!" She turned and pointed down the road. The child had vanished in the crowd.

Confused, Mary stammered, "She-she was just there!" She sighed deeply, and a sense of peace came over her troubled spirit. "Come, my husband, let's go on now."

Joseph smiled at her, his brown eyes heavy-lidded with fatigue.

Sariel and Samuel, unseen, cleared the path before them as Mary and Joseph once more entered the great city gates. Wandering the streets, searching, searching, questioning, the two parents' hearts ached with sorrow. The sense of peace was fading now from Mary's spirit as night fell on Jerusalem.

A strengthening wind descended with the failing light.

Fear awakened a sick feeling in the pit of Joseph's stomach. *I must be strong for Mary's sake, but oh, dear God, where is our boy?* He prayed silently. His mind raced, imagining all sorts of scenarios. *So much evil in this wicked world today; So many things that could happen to a young boy. Oh God, oh God!*

The streets were dark and mostly empty when Mary and Joseph returned to their small camp outside the gates. Dizzying, bone-weary fatigue drained and disoriented the two distraught parents. Too weary to fix a meal, they ate small pieces of bread, washed down with goat's milk. Despite the deep current of fear running through their minds, they slept soundly, as their angels stood guard.

They could hear the city stirring when the opalescent early morning light wakened the sleeping couple. Joseph sat up and rubbed his eyes sleepily.

Beside him, Mary yawned and stretched her arms toward the brightening sky. For a moment, she forgot that Jesus was lost, and smiled up at her husband. Then she gave a dry little gasp as realization flooded in.

"Oh, Joseph! Our boy!" A lump, thick with tears rose in her throat.

Joseph embraced her with a blind and desperate tenderness. "Come my dear, we must begin our search again," He croaked, his throat dry with sleep.

They fed Ezra and Eli, and breakfasted quickly on oaten bread and goat cheese, choking the food down throats pinched with anxiety.

Together they bowed their heads in prayer, asking the Most High's guidance and protection for their young son.

The spring sunshine washed the walls of the city with pure light as they entered the enormous gate once more. This was the third day that Jesus had been missing.

#

Gloriel stood unseen behind Jesus as he sat amid the elders, engaging some of the greatest scholars in Israel in a battle of wits. His face glowed, and his huge dark eyes gleamed with intelligence.

Her heart swelled with love, as the chief priests and elders surrounding him in the Men's Court sat questioning the boy, with expressions ranging from amazement to consternation. The rabbis and doctors of the Law listened, sometimes with jaws agape to the words of wisdom coming from the mouth of her young charge.

For three days, the boy had sat among them, a bit shy at first, asking tentative but probing questions. The authority with which he spoke was astounding to the wise and learned men seated around him.

Joseph of Arimathea, a tall, pleasant-featured young man of great wealth, sat next to Jesus, scrutinizing him intently. *There is something intriguing about this boy*, Joseph thought to himself. *He has wisdom far beyond his years, and the questions he asks; the passion with which he speaks; this is unheard of in such a young boy.*

Gloriel touched the young man's shoulder lightly. Suddenly, as Joseph leaned forward, listening in fascination to the boy's words, a twinge of distress struck him. A strange sadness, a longing, a faint hint of fear for the child snaked through his gut. His already pale skin blanched, and he felt slightly nauseated. Perspiration popped out on his thin upper lip and broad forehead. Tears dimmed his eyes as he reached out and laid a trembling hand on the boy's arm.

Jesus turned his head and gazed into Joseph's eyes, a puzzled expression crossing his young face. He smiled at Joseph tentatively.

"JESUS!" A strong voice rang throughout the court.

"JESUS!" All eyes turned toward the intrusive sound.

The boy rose quickly to his feet at the familiar voice.

"Father!" He cried out. "Avi! I'm here!"

Rushing down the steps, Jesus flew into Joseph's outstretched arms.

"Oh, my boy," Joseph murmured into Jesus' soft brown hair. "Come, your mother is waiting. We have been worried sick." Joseph's voice grew gruff and thick with tears.

"Avi, I must say goodbye." Jesus turned toward the group of elders watching the reunion.

"No, Son, we are leaving now." Joseph said, with a firm grip on Jesus' arm.

The group of men watched curiously as father and son left the court, the boy lifting his hand in farewell.

Outside the Temple, Mary shifted her weight from foot to foot, anxiously watching the entrance. Her pretty face looked haggard, with gray circles surrounded the beautiful eyes, now dull with fatigue and fear. Sariel stood beside her, keeping watch.

There! There was her boy, walking briskly toward her, Joseph's arm firmly around his shoulders.

"Emi!" The boy cried, running now, with Joseph close behind. Mary opened her arms wide, tears streaming down her face.

"Oh, Jeshua, my son, my son! We thought you were lost forever!" She clasped the boy close to her breast, sobbing raggedly.

Jesus hugged her tightly, eyes gleaming with tears. Ariel and Gloriel joined them as Joseph took both mother and son in his long arms. The crowd milling about them in the bright sunlight seemed oblivious to the small drama in their midst.

Mary took her son by the shoulders and held him at arm's length. "Son, how could you do this to your father and me? We have been frantic, looking for you everywhere! We thought we would never see you again!" She shook him gently as she spoke, her voice breaking, tears wearing pathways down her dusty cheeks.

Jesus looked at his mother, an expression of surprise spread over his young features. "But Mother, why have you looked for me? Didn't you know I would be in my Father's house, taking care of His affairs?" The young voice cracked slightly, incongruous with the rather formal words.

Mary gazed at Jesus in astonishment. Suddenly her mind fled back to that wondrous day in the olive grove. The angel's words echoed down the halls of her memory. *"He will be very great and will be called the Son of the Most High."*

She drew her breath in sharply, pulling the boy close once more. "Oh, my son," she whispered, "my sweet boy."

## Chapter Sixteen

Jesus threw back his head, laughing with delight. It was a glorious early autumn day in Nazareth. The air was crisp and bright, and the sun felt warm on his skin, despite the slight nip in the air.

Wheat fields, chest high now, nodded their seed heads, ripe, heavy, and ready for harvest. Golden waves billowed on the nearby slopes.

Jacob, never a graceful boy, was imitating the waddle of a fat white duck beside the path. He slipped on some wet straw lying on the edge of the pathway and rolled down the slope, coming to an abrupt and undignified stop at the bottom. Several pieces of straw stuck out at all angles from his mop of glossy black curls. The duck fled squawking down the path.

"Hey, that was really a great imitation, Jacob! Do it again, will you?" Jesus called to him, still laughing. Jacob grinned sheepishly, plucking the straw from his hair.

The two boys were now 15 and 16-years-old, and still best friends. Jesus had caught up with Jacob in height, though still slightly thinner. His light brown hair was now darkened to a rich, deep brown, thick and slightly wavy.

Their friendship had deepened throughout the years, and they loved each other like brothers. They still roamed the fields and hills of Nazareth together, whenever time from school and chores allowed.

Jacob's heavy black curls framed a sharp-featured but kindly face. At fifteen, a dark beard shadowed the still boyish cheeks and chin. His eyes were large and black as the night, shining with mischief and humor.

Jesus thought of all the wonderful times he had shared with Jacob and his family. He was always greeted with warmth and affection when he entered their home.

Suzanne, especially, made him feel welcome, dimples twinkling in her pink cheeks whenever she greeted him at the door. At 13, her once plump figure was now slender and graceful. The raven's-wing hair lay about her like a cloak, long and curling. Her clear gray eyes glowed, passionate and pensive.

"Hey, Jesus!" Jacob's deep voice disturbed his reverie. "Where did you wander? I've been talking to you, but you left me for thoughts more interesting than my conversation. Care to share?" He smiled at Jesus, arching one dark brow.

"Sorry, my friend," Jesus murmured sheepishly, his handsome young face flushing beneath the tanned skin.

"Well, I said, why don't we climb to the top of Job's Hill tonight? The moon will be full, and we'll be able to see for miles." Jacob's eyes gleamed with his love of adventure.

"Uh . . . I don't know, Jacob. I should study tonight. Rabbi Abner has asked me to read from the scroll of Isaiah at the Sabbath celebration."

"Oh, come on, Jesus, don't be so serious all the time! Let's have some fun for a change!"

Jesus looked at his companion's eager young face, eyes brimming with vitality and youthful exuberance.

"All-right, Jacob. Job's Hill it is," he replied, grinning. "I'll meet you here right after supper."

"Do you want me to bring Suzanne, Jesus?" Jacob asked, watching his friend with a sly cut of his smiling eyes.

Jesus gave Jacob's shoulder a rough shove, laughing.

Tackling his friend at the knees, Jacob brought Jesus down to the still damp grass. A tangle of long arms and legs soon brought uproarious laughter as the two boys wrestled, panting.

"Okay, okay, I give up!" Jesus said breathlessly.

"You know who will make it to the top of Job's Hill first tonight, right my friend?" Jacob said teasingly, punching Jesus' arm lightly.

"Hmmm . . . we'll see, we'll see," Jesus grinned.

Gloriel and Jacob's angel, Esdrel, smiled at one another, enjoying the boys' antics.

#

The night was clear, except for a few silver-gray clouds drifting across the rising yellow harvest moon. A handful of stars glimmered low in the darkening skies above hills of Nazareth.

The two boys began their ascent of Job's Hill, laughing and shouting insults at one another, their spirits high.

As the moon rose, its golden face turned a brilliant silver, leaving a luminous path on the grain fields below. A few more gray clouds appeared in the eastern sky as a faint breeze began to stir. The pungent scent of autumn pervaded the air.

A short time later, the moon was a huge orb gazing down on the two boys as they reached the half-way point in their climb.

More clouds skittered across the sky as the zephyr freshened into a stiff breeze.

Watching the boys closely, Gloriel felt a momentary pang of concern.

"Esdrel," she said to the tall young angel beside her. "I think perhaps a storm is coming. Don't you think we should warn the boys?"

Intense silver-blue eyes gazed back at her from under fine straight golden blonde brows. His fine-featured face, visible only to Gloriel, was silhouetted against the bright moonlit sky.

"Let's wait a bit, Gloriel. They are enjoying the climb so much," he replied reassuringly.

As he clambered up the increasingly steep hillside, Jesus remembered the conversation at the supper table. His mother had been doubtful about the wisdom of climbing Job's Hill at night.

"Jeshua, maybe it would be better to wait until daytime." Mary had said, concern underlying her soft voice.

"Mother, we'll be fine. The moon will make it as bright as daytime on the hill."

Mary placed her hand on her tall young son's shoulder. "I don't know, Son. I really don't think . . ."

"Mary, don't worry. The boys are skilled at climbing," Joseph interjected in his usual calm manner.

Jesus' sandal slipped on some loose pebbles, interrupting his thoughts. Startled, he drew in his breath sharply.

A pang of anxiety stuck in Gloriel's throat, and she reached out an arm toward Jesus.

"Jesus! Are you all right?" Jacob called from several yards away.

"Yes, yes, I'm fine." Jesus replied, breathless from the exertion of the climb.

Gloriel sighed, a small frown puckering her smooth brow.

A large dark purple cloud momentarily obscured the moon's glowing face.

"Esdrel, I really think we should warn the boys now," Gloriel whispered breathlessly.

The terrain was very steep and rocky now, as the two friends approached the top of Job's Hill. They chose their hand and footholds carefully.

Pausing, they turned to look at the valley below. The moon flowed over the landscape like a flood of silvery water. Warm yellow lamplight flickered in windows of the small homes of Nazareth.

"Look, Jesus! I can see our house!" Jacob pointed a long arm toward his home far below.

There was a profound silence, as if the autumn night was holding its breath. The boys, too, were silent, engrossed in the beauty spread out before their wondering eyes, and listening to the small voices within.

"Jesu, you must go home now," Gloriel whispered into the boy's consciousness. A small frown creased Jesus' forehead.

Esdrel laid an unseen hand on Jacob's shoulder. The boy looked around quickly. There was no one there. *Is my mind playing tricks on me?* He wondered silently.

"*Jacob, return home.*" The words seemed emblazoned on his minds eye. He shook his head, dazedly. *What's happening? Am I letting fear get the better of me? Well, we can't let that happen!* he scolded himself.

"Come on, Jesus! It's just a little farther. We can do it!"

"All right, Jacob. But it looks like a storm is brewing," Jesus replied hesitantly.

As they approached the summit, the moon was suddenly darkened by thick, black rolling clouds. Thunder rumbled in the distance.

At last they reached the top, breathing heavily, legs shaking. At that moment, the heavens opened, and rain poured down in blinding sheets on the hapless pair. As Jesus strained his eyes in the darkness, Jacob's streaming white face stood out stark against the black sky. His black hair was plastered tight to his skull. Lightning lit the black, streaming, chaotic storm.

"Jacob!" Jesus cried out against the wailing of the wind. "Jacob! We must find shelter!" Thunder answered him, stirring a response in his gut.

"There, Jesus! That big rock!" Jacob's deep voice was thin in the screaming storm, an anguished shout of fright.

Water poured down the hill in streams, washing the soil away from beneath their feet. Slipping and sliding in the rocky mud, the two boys struggled toward the huge rock.

Gloriel and Esdrel stayed behind their charges, ready to reach out and catch them if necessary. As they moved slowly around the rock, a brilliant flash of lightning suddenly revealed the edge of a steep and dangerous bluff. It fell sharply away and down some 200 feet, to a tiny, narrow valley filled with stones and scrub. The edges of the bluff gushed with mud, crumbling from the downpour.

Jacob was in the lead, his back pressed to the rock, arms outspread against its cold, slippery surface.

Unseen, Esdrel was on the far side of the boy now, Gloriel still close behind Jesus.

"Jacob! Jesus cried out loudly. "Jacob! We have to turn back! Give me your hand!" As Jesus reached out to his friend, a strange white look of terror swept across Jacob's blanched face as the earth gave away beneath his feet. Terror struck Jesus like a rock in the pit of his stomach, horror crowding into his chest.

He watched in terror as his friend fell screaming into the black void. Out of the corner of his eye, as another bolt of lighting split the air, Jesus saw a young man standing next to where Jacob had been, arms outstretched. Another flash, and the young man was gone. Jesus stared down into the dark pit below, stunned and bewildered. Jacob . . . Jacob was gone.

"JACOB! JACOB!" Jesus screamed into the angry face of the storm.

Suddenly, he was enfolded in warmth. He felt soft arms holding him in the darkness. He closed his eyes against the pain in his breast; his insides feeling like putty.

It seemed to the boy that Time was standing still. He wanted to shut the past few minutes into a dark inner room. And then the door to that room seemed too terrifying and painful even to consider opening.

Jesus opened his eyes slowly. He stood at the base of Job's Hill. A cold fist took hold of his heart and began squeezing.

The thunder and lightning ceased, and the rain fell softly and gently on his upturned white face. He shook his head slowly. *Wait, how did I get here? The storm . . . Jacob . . . JACOB!* A wordless cry of smothered agony and despair sprang from his ashen lips. He felt lost and drowning, overwhelmed with a sensation of profound loss and sorrow.

"Oh, Father, help me, help me!"

Gloriel reached out to the boy, but found her hand stopped.

The Father's soothing voice echoed inside her head. "Let him be, my child. He must be acquainted with grief now."

"But Lord, to the young, death is impossible," she whispered, gleaming tears flowing down her cheeks.

"He has to feel the emotions all humans have, Gloriel." The Lord's tone was firm, but gentle.

The rain stopped, abruptly. The clouds sped away on invisible wings, and the serene face of the moon once more revealed itself.

Jesus turned his stricken face toward home. His arms and legs felt leaden, as he tried to run. Stumbling and staggering, he struggled down the muddy path to his home.

Twin hot tides of pain and sorrow surged through his trembling body.

Suddenly, Joseph's strong arms enfolded him as he collapsed, spent and exhausted. Lifting his young son, Joseph carried him gently and tenderly the short distance to their doorway. Shouldering aside the heavy curtain, he set the boy down.

Jesus buckled into his mother's arms. Long, heaving, retching sobs wracked his young body. Mary stood frozen, clutching her son tightly. Her mind was blank as a babe's as Jesus clung to her like a toddler.

The three guardian angels each stood close to their charges, mourning the loss of Jacob's young, vibrant life. Gloriel wept with her Jesu, along with Sariel and Samuel.

#

Jesus stood outside the tomb of his friend. It was three weeks since that terrible night when he had met grief face to face. Yes, he had experienced death before. Both of his grandfathers had died in the past two years. But both were aged men, who had lived long and productive lives, passing quietly and peacefully into the arms of God. But Jacob, Jacob, who had plunged screaming to his death . . . *Oh, Jacob, how I miss you!*

Tears welled up in the dark eyes. Burying his face in his hands, he rocked back and forth in the ancient movement of mourning. His heart felt like one of the withered leaves still clinging to the sycamore tree growing beside the entrance to Jacob's family tomb. The tomb was a cave, dark, cool and dank. It was not yet sealed, as Jacob's parents could not yet bring themselves to shut the final door between themselves and their beloved son.

A few birds sang a disconsolate song to the approach of winter. The dawn was gray-eyed and somber, heavy with clouds. Gloriel stood beside her young charge. She had watched and waited, longing to comfort him. "Not yet, not yet, my child," the Father's warm voice echoed within her.

"Jesus," the soft young voice was hesitant.

Startled, Jesus turned abruptly, dropping his hands to his side. Suzanne stood small and pale before him, clutching her cloak close about her against the morning chill.

"Jesus, I . . ." Grief was a hard lump in her throat, swelling within her. She could not understand the pain, except that it was enormous. She struggled for words, and burst into tears.

Jesus didn't know what to do. Suzanne's slender shoulders were heaving, as heavy sobs racked her body. He looked down on her bent head, and compassion flooded his heart. His own grief was forgotten in his desire to comfort his friend's lovely young sister.

"Suzanne," he said, reaching out and touching her for the first time. He laid a trembling hand on her shoulder. He wanted to comfort, console, and protect her from this pain. He reached out and drew her into his arms. She grew quiet, tears still streaming down her white cheeks. Pressing her face into his shoulder, she raised trembling arms and wrapped them around his neck.

Jesus held her gently. The hood on her cloak fell back, revealing a midnight mass of curls. Lifting her head, she gazed at him with those amazing silver-gray eyes, brimming with gleaming tears. The sobs had ceased A strange warmth spread tingling fingers over Jesus' face and neck as he stared into the sweet face so close to his own. A great tenderness came over him, and he smiled tentatively, for the first time since Jacob's death. Suzanne's white face was slowly suffusing with a rosy-pink tinge. Shyly, she dropped her arms, and stepped back from the circle of Jesus' arms.

"Suzanne, I . . ." Jesus' voice was husky and his dark eyes shone with unshed tears. "Suzanne." He could find no words.

The rising sun broke through the clouds then, and her dark hair was struck with copper. Jesus drew in his breath raggedly. *She's so beautiful.* He thought to himself.

"Jesus." Suddenly, she turned and fled, her brown cloak billowing behind her, and the black curls bouncing.

Jesus watched the fleeing girl, stunned and confused at the unfamiliar feelings arising within him. Once more, the tentative smile appeared. Then he sighed heavily as sorrow flooded him once more, not for Jacob this time, but for Suzanne.

Gloriel stood nearby, watching with mixed emotions. *Can the eternal Son of God fall in love with one of his own creatures?* She wondered. *But he is fully human, as well as divine.* She reasoned. "Father, how am I to help him through this?" she whispered. No answer came.

#

That evening, as Mary, Joseph, and Jesus sat around the supper table, Jesus asked his mother,

"Emi, how old were you when you became engaged to Avi?"

Mary and Joseph exchanged glances, and both smiled. Was their grief-stricken son beginning to recover from the gray cloud of sorrow which had darkened his face the past few weeks?

"I was 13, Son, and I thought your father was the handsomest man in all of Nazareth." Mary looked lovingly at her Joseph, remembering. Joseph smiled at his wife, remembering also.

Jesus dipped a chunk of fresh-baked bread into the gravy bowl, deep in thought now. Gloriel listened closely. Was he going to ask questions about his birth? She could not discern his thoughts at the moment.

Mary watched her son's face. He was lost in his thoughts, his expression one of bewilderment, and yet a slight smile quirked the corners of his mouth. *What on earth is going on in his head?* Mary wondered. Lifting her cup, she drank the last of her supper wine, watching Jesus over the rim of the cup. It was good to see him thinking of something besides the tragic death of his friend.

"Son, tomorrow we'll be delivering the new yoke to Museph ben Josiah's farm. We'll need to get an early start. I'm going to bed now. You should do the same," Joseph said, rising from the table and stretching his long arms overhead.

"Yes, Father, I will," Jesus replied. "But I'd like to talk with Mother for a few minutes."

"All right, Jeshua, but get to bed soon," Joseph said, yawning.

Gloriel glanced around. Samuel was nowhere to be seen. *That's odd, he didn't tell me he was going Home for a visit.* She mused. Sariel was kneeling beside Mary.

Jesus got up and walked around the table, then sat down close beside his mother. Mary reached out and patted his shoulder gently.

"So, my son. How are you feeling?" *We really haven't talked much about Jacob's death.* She thought. *Perhaps he is ready now.*

"I'm fine. Mother, tell me about when I was born," he said quietly, fixing his gaze on the flickering lamp on the table. The light reflected in his dark eyes, warming the handsome young features.

Mary clasped her hands in her lap, examining them closely, as if she had just discovered them. *Oh, dear God. I knew this day would come. What do I say to him? How much should I tell him? What does he need to know now?* The questions arose quickly in her mind. Her eyes searched her young son's face. *He's almost a man, now.* She thought. *This terrible grief has tested him like fire.*

Memories flooded her mind, then. The appearance of Gabriel, the long visit with Elizabeth, the quiet marriage, the arduous journey to Bethlehem, the pain and the glory of his birth; then the flight to Egypt and the return to Nazareth; the wonders and joys of his infancy and young childhood; these were treasures laid up in her mother's heart. What lay ahead for this strong young man seated next to her, expectancy and curiosity gleaming in the great dark orbs of his eyes? Intelligence was like a glow on his face. The sweet baby, the dimpled, laughing young child, were gone now. Mary sighed deeply as she looked into those eyes and remembered.

The Son of God was awaiting her answers to his question. It was hard to remember, sometimes, that he was not just her little boy. *Do I really have the answers?* She asked herself.

Sariel leaned over, then, and whispered in Mary's ear. Gloriel looked on, breathing a prayer for Mary.

"My son," Mary began, "there are things that are not mine to tell." She reached out and laid her hand tenderly on Jesus' arm. "You are special, and most blessed by God. You have a mission which it is not given to me to know or understand."

Jesus looked intently into his mother's soft brown eyes, and nodded. She told him, then, of his birth in a stable in Bethlehem, of the magnificent star, the three wise men, and the flight to Egypt.

Sariel continued to whisper in her ear. Tears brimmed in Mary's eyes as she told her son of their return home to Nazareth. But she said nothing of Gabriel's announcement, or the visit to Elizabeth's and Zechariah's house.

"This is all I can tell you, Jeshua. God will reveal his Plan and his will to you. He will give you answers to your heart's questions. Seek his face, and study his word, my son, as you always have." She squeezed his arm gently.

Still gazing intently into his mother's eyes, Jesus whispered "My Father..." His own eyes grew glittering and passionate, radiant with the thought of God. Mary looked in awe at Jesus' shining face, which seemed to radiate a light of its own. Jesus felt a bursting in himself, his soul rising, soaring, floating.

He jumped to his feet, tears streaming, and looking down at his mother, he said tenderly, "Thank you, Emi." He turned then, and walked out the door into the chill of the night, Gloriel close behind.

# Chapter Seventeen

Mary paced back and forth in front of the doorway. It was late, and Jesus wasn't home yet. More and more, lately, he had gone off by himself after his day's work with Joseph in the carpenter shop.

It was dead winter now, the month of Shebat, the coldest month of the year. As she stood outside the doorway, a cold wind prowled about, and the bare trees responded, creaking and lashing. The dusky light of a dying day surrounded her, and night loomed heavily. She strained her eyes, peering up the pathway expectantly, drawing her plain woolen cloak close around her shivering body.

"Mary," Joseph's deep voice summoned her from within the small house. "Come in now, my dear. It's getting very cold. Jesus will be home soon."

Reluctantly, Mary passed back through the doorway, closing the heavy brown curtain behind her.

Joseph sat at the low table, the evening meal spread out before him. A bowl of lentils, some goat cheese, and a loaf of Mary's fresh flat bread awaited the family.

"We'll go ahead and eat without him, Mary," Joseph said firmly. "He is a man, now, and he knows when mealtime is."

Mary sighed, removed her cloak, and sat down opposite her husband.

After blessing the food, Joseph dipped a piece of bread in the bowl of steaming lentils, while Mary poured wine from a jar into his cup.

He watched his wife from under heavy black brows, now threaded with silver.

*She's still the most beautiful woman in Nazareth.* He thought to himself. Mary's skin was still smooth and unlined, although a few crinkles lay around the clear brown eyes and the soft mouth.

*Even after all these years,* Sariel thought, *Joseph still loves to watch his wife.* The little angel glanced at Samuel, and looked around for Gloriel, who was nowhere to be seen.

"Gloriel keeps such close watch over Jesus," Sariel murmured to her companion. "She's most likely with him"

"Indeed she does," Samuel responded. "But it has been a long time since her last visit Home. Perhaps she was summoned."

Suddenly, the door curtain swept aside, and Jesus stepped in, slightly breathless. Gloriel was close on his heels.

"I'm sorry, Mother, the darkness comes so early and swiftly now. I didn't realize how late it was getting," he apologized, a bit sheepishly.

"Where have you been, Son?" Joseph queried. "Your mother was getting worried."

"I was visiting Jacob's family, Father," Jesus replied, flushing slightly, and lowering his eyes.

Joseph smiled, covering his mouth with his hand.

Samuel's black eyes twinkled, as he listened to the exchange.

Three months had passed since Jacob's tragic death, and it seemed to his parents that Jesus was spending more and more time with the bereaved family.

"How is the family, Son?" Mary asked quietly, fixing him with her bright, alert eyes.

"They are doing fairly well, Mother, although Jacob's mother still weeps a lot. I have been helping his father with the chores."

"And Suzanne, how is Suzanne?" Mary eyed her son's face closely.

Jesus sat down and looked at his parents, his clean-cut features coloring. Flustered, he busied himself breaking off chunks of bread and cheese.

"Suzanne? Oh, she's fine, Emi. Her mother is teaching her to cook." He smiled at his mother, teeth flashing white in his handsome young face.

Gloriel and Sariel beamed at one another. Samuel watched Joseph carefully, studying his face.

*Jeshua's beard is beginning to grow*, Mary thought, *and he's so tall! Where has my little boy gone? It's so easy to forget who he is, now. So many years have gone by since Gabriel's visit. It seems unreal, almost like a dream . . .*

"Mary, May I please have some more wine?" Joseph's voice penetrated her reverie.

"Yes, of course, Joseph." She leaned over to refill his cup.

His father placed a work-worn hand on Jesus' arm.

"Jeshua, I will be fitting a door for Ephraim ben Jethro's house tomorrow. I need you to work on the table we started today. Please take Eli and deliver it when it's finished."

"Yes, Father," Jesus responded quickly, grateful for the change of subject.

Gloriel fell into deep thought as the little family finished their meal. *"Most High,"* she prayed silently, *"I need direction soon. How am I to guide your son through this awakening of his human desires? Is he to marry? How can this be, if so? Please help me to know, Father."*

#

In a flash of light, she found herself standing in front of the glittering throne of the Father. The figure seated before her sat shrouded in the golden light. But she still could discern no features. She sank to her knees before the Lord, and waited.

#

Early the next morning, Jesus set out for the carpenter shop, leading Eli. A bleak wind rushed howling around the corners of the house. It pierced through paper-thin layers of mist that hung in the chill air. He shivered and drew his heavy woolen cloak close about him. Joseph had already left for Ephraim ben Jethro's house.

Mary watched from the doorway as her son led the little donkey up the pathway, his shoulders hunched against the biting wind. She raised her eyes as the glow of sunrise touched upon the ordered ranks of cloud on cloud, all coldly beautiful in the morning sky.

"Goodbye, Son!" She called out to the tall young man as he trudged up the pathway.

He turned and lifted his hand. "Goodbye, Mother!" The wind swept away his voice.

Mary stepped back inside the house and dropped the rough curtain across the doorway. The household oven beckoned her with its warmth as she began preparing the three Sabbath meals for the next day.

Her thoughts dwelled on her son as she worked. *He has changed since Jacob's tragic death. He's now more man than boy. He will soon be 17 years old. How swiftly the years are flying! If he were an ordinary young man, he would have thoughts of marriage now.*

She thought of Suzanne, now hauntingly beautiful, and matured by her grief. *She's as lovely in her heart and spirit as she is in her body. Does marriage fit into God's plan for His Son?* Mary wondered, as she shaped the loaves of barley bread with practiced hands. She slipped them into the hot oven, enjoying the warmth radiating from it. *I know he loves her.* She paused thoughtfully "Father, Most High, how do we counsel him in this?" she breathed a prayer. His being different worried her, yet how could he be anything but different?

Sariel stood by, listening closely. "I don't have answers for you, dear heart. This is beyond my knowledge," she whispered, unheard by Mary.

#

Jesus tied the table securely to Eli's strong back. It was early afternoon, and the pale winter sun shone bleakly through a break in the heavy gray clouds. The wind ceased abruptly. The hills rose purple and somber against the shadowed sky, and there arose an all-pervading scent of earth. A flock of ravens flew overhead, their raucous chorus renting the air.

He breathed deeply, content with his morning's work well done. After he delivered the table, he and Eli would head home to help his mother with the chores as she prepared for the Sabbath. He would not be visiting Jacob's family today.

Jesus smiled to himself. *This will be an especially joyful Sabbath*, he thought. Jacob's father had invited him to share Sabbath supper with the family. He hadn't told his mother yet. This would be the first time he would not be eating the Sabbath supper with his parents. Would they object? His heart jumped in his chest at the thought. No, surely . . .

He knew that Emi sometimes still thought of him as her little boy. But he no longer felt like a young boy. The past few months brought with them a new seriousness to his thoughts and plans. He spent more time alone. He walked the fields and hills, observing, and listening to the multitudinous voices of creation. He felt constantly overwhelmed by the beauty of the world. There grew inside him a sharp awareness of purpose, lying just beneath his conscious thought. Try as he might, he could not discern this purpose. He only knew it was the answer to his existence.

His heavenly Father's presence was a delight to him, and he spent his solitary time praying and listening. Sometimes, he was conscious of another voice, speaking to him deep in his spirit. It was a familiar voice, long known to him, but he could not put a name to it. He only knew that this voice was a gift from his Father.

He and Eli soon arrived at their destination. Jesus unloaded the table from the donkey's back, and they started down the road toward home. A faint mingling of pale lavender and crimson glimmered on the horizon as the sun prepared to end its day's journey.

Jesus' thoughts turned to Suzanne. A slow warmth crept over his face and neck. *She's so beautiful, and so sweet. Her spirit is beautiful, too.*

He recalled his visit the day before. Suzanne was busy with her chores when Jesus arrived. Her cheeks bloomed pink from the crisp air, and satiny stray curls were lying feathery across her lovely face. She was feeding the chickens, scattering grain from a pocket in her blue apron.

Jesus stood a short distance away, watching her as she clucked softly to the flock. He noticed one hen in particular. Fat and shiny black, she stood surrounded by a cloud of fluffy yellow chicks. They followed close behind her, some trying to sit under her wings as she scratched the soil. A few of the chicks wandered away from their mother, but came scampering, tiny wings flapping, when she clucked at them nervously.

*They know her voice*, Jesus had mused, his attention momentarily diverted from Suzanne.

Gloriel had whispered to his spirit then. "There are several hens and chickens, here, Jesu. But see how they each know their own. The hen can't count, nor can her chicks, and there are many of them. But if one is lost, even the smallest, or the dirtiest, or the feeblest, she will search for him until she finds him. Even though he may seem worthless and insignificant, his mother cares for him, always. Love never abandons, Jesu."

Jesus stood deep in thought, oblivious to his surroundings. *The hen has all those chicks; how can she know where her lost one is, or know that he needs her attention?* He wondered. The answer had come clearly and swiftly: *For Love, nothing is worthless, or too much, or too little, or too many, or too hard.*

"Erev tov. Good evening, Jesus," Suzanne's soft voice startled him from his reverie.

"Hello, Suzanne." He flushed slightly.

She moistened her full pink lips, smiling. Her silver eyes shimmered in the sunlight, and Jesus was mesmerized. Suzanne had dropped her gaze then, shyly lowering her eyes behind dark, lush lashes.

In an instant of awareness, Jesus knew. A rushing tide of love flooded through him, and his heart fluttered. He loved Suzanne now, as a man, with power and intensity and his whole soul's longing.

Acutely aware of Jesu's feelings, Gloriel had thought *It is not strange that he admires a beautiful girl, and wants a wife, just as other men do. He is made of flesh and blood, the same as all men.*

Suddenly, Jesus' reverie was rudely interrupted as he stumbled over a rock in the pathway. He had been so deep in thought, that it took a moment for him to orient himself to his surroundings. He and Eli had reached their destination.

#

The Sabbath day dawned in a dazzling, bleak incandescence. The sky burned clear, the air chilly. Joseph, Mary and Jesus sat at the table, enjoying the breakfast Mary had prepared the day before.

Gloriel found herself suddenly standing next to her young charge as he broke off a piece of bread and bit into it hungrily. Her visit to her heavenly home had ended a bit abruptly, and she felt momentarily disoriented.

"Jesus," Mary was saying, "You should wear your white linen tunic this evening."

Jesus had told his parents about the invitation to Sabbath supper the evening before, as they sat around the supper table.

"Yes, Emi," Jesus grinned at his mother. He washed down the bread with a swallow of wine.

"I would like to go visit Benjamin this morning, I think," Jesus said quietly. "I haven't seen him since Jacob . . ." his voice trailed off.

"All-right, Son," Mary replied. She laid her hand on Jesus' shoulder.

"It's still hard for him," Gloriel murmured to Sariel and Samuel.

"Yes," Sariel replied, "it is; and welcome back, my friend"

Samuel nodded in agreement as he stood behind Joseph. He looked preoccupied, watching his charge closely.

"Is everything all-right, Samuel?" Gloriel asked.

A small frown appeared momentarily between Samuel's bushy brows. The usually merry black eyes held a somber light.

"I don't know, Gloriel. I really don't know."

Jesus put on his heavy brown cloak, embraced his mother, and promised both parents he would return in plenty of time to prepare for his Sabbath visit with Jacob's family.

As he walked up the pathway, he side-stepped the puddles left from yesterday's rainstorm. He breathed deeply of the clean, crisp air, pungent with the smell of wet earth. The fields on either side of the path were stubbled, after the harvest, awaiting the summons to new growth in the spring.

Leaving the beaten path, Jesus cut across a desolate field, heading for Benjamin's camp. He was acutely conscious of the sights and sounds of nature around him. A flock of chirping sparrows pecked greedily around in the sparse vegetation, as they searched for their breakfast. He stopped to watch them, suddenly keenly aware of their vulnerability. He squatted down and listened to their noisy chatter. The sun's pale watery light lay in patches on the cold ground.

Gloriel stood beside him. His thoughts were revealed to her with such clarity that at first she felt they were her own.

*My Father sees these little ones. He loves and cares for them, just as the mother hen cares for her chicks,* Jesus thought. Tenderness swelled in his breast as he thought of Suzanne's gentle ways with her flock of chickens.

Silently, Gloriel directed his gaze to a spot in the shadow of a rock a few inches from him. One of the small brown sparrows lay on its back on the damp earth, eyes closed. Its little twig-like legs stuck in the air with claws furled.

Slowly, Jesus knelt down from his squatting position. He was careful not to startle the little flock of birds. He reached out slowly and picked up the little fallen sparrow. He cupped its still-warm body against his chest. Tears stung his eyelids.

Gloriel's heart melted as she watched the tender compassion move over the young face of her charge.

Jesus lifted his cupped hands to the sky, cradling the small creature.

"Father," he whispered, almost inaudibly. "Father . . . I know you love all your creatures, great and small. Please let this little one live, to your Glory." Silver tears glistened in the corners of his closed eyes.

Gloriel held her breath, mesmerized, as the small drama unfolded before her.

Jesus lowered his long arms and held the little bird close against his chest once more. Then he remained utterly still, eyes still closed. Even the flock of sparrows grew suddenly silent.

*Creation is standing still,* Gloriel thought, in awe.

An almost imperceptible movement came from the bit of feathers in Jesus' hands. Bright beady eyes opened slowly and gazed into the young man's face.

Jesus' eyes flew open as he felt the tiny heart beat against his skin. The sparrow fluttered its wings and cocked its small brown head, still eyeing Jesus.

Joy spread across Jesus' face as an incredible assurance of love flooded over him. Slowly, he held out his hands once again to the heavens. The sparrow fluttered away, chirping, to join his brothers.

Gloriel felt a strange mixture of sadness, joy, and wonder. This tall, handsome lad, whom she had nurtured and protected from his infancy, in one small moment had awakened to his identity as the Son of God. *What happens now, O Lord Most High?* She breathed the silent question in her heart.

Jesus murmured low in his throat. "Thank you, Father." He rose from the ground and watched the flock of sparrows still pecking greedily. Feeling a little dazed, he swayed slightly as he closed his eyes and tried to fully comprehend the miracle that had just occurred.

Gloriel stared at her young charge. She wanted so much in that moment to reveal herself to him, to share this revelation in the physical realm. However, *this is not the time*, she realized. *Perhaps, one day . . .*

Jesus shook his head, as if to clear away any shadows of doubt. Pacing slowly, he returned to the path and headed toward Benjamin's pasture once more.

Gloriel placed her hand on his shoulder. A bewildered frown appeared between his dark brows. He stepped off the pathway again, and started toward a nearby hill. His pace increased as he walked, until his stride was strong and purposeful. He was smiling broadly, now.

#

Suzanne's silver eyes sparkled in the flickering lamplight as she slipped the soft blue linen tunic over her dark head. "Mother, may I borrow your silver belt?" Her soft voice was trembling slightly.

"Yes, my child, of course you may. Here, let me brush your hair for you." Ophrah replied, gathering the mass of black curls together.

Her daughter's dimpled cheeks shone pink with excitement as she awaited their Sabbath guest's arrival.

Ophrah suspected that perhaps tonight Jesus would ask permission to begin courting Suzanne.

*Jared and Joseph will need to consult together before permission is granted,* Ophrah mused, smiling to herself. She brushed her daughter's hair back from her shining face. Taking a blue ribbon from her apron pocket, she tied it around the ebony cascade. *What a beautiful bride she will be!* She thought, already making wedding plans in her head.

"How do I look, Mother?" Suzanne questioned, as she fastened the narrow silver chain around her slender waist.

"Lovely, Suzanne, you are lovely, my daughter."

"Mother do you think that Jesus will . . ." her sweet voice trailed off as she heard footsteps approaching the doorway.

The curtain was thrust aside, as her grinning father entered, followed by Jesus, also smiling.

"Look who I found on the path, Suzanne!" Jared exclaimed. He winked at his flustered daughter.

"Good evening, Jesus." Suzanne said, blushing deeply.

"Good evening, Suzanne. Ma'am," Jesus replied, nodding to the disconcerted girl, and bowing slightly to her mother.

Ophrah's plump face wreathed in a smile of welcome. Her dark hair, streaked with silver, framed a sweet, animated face.

"Welcome, Jesus ben Joseph, to our home. Peace be with you."

"And also with you," the young man replied, gazing at Suzanne.

Gloriel stood close beside Jesus, with a sense of disquietude. She watched the play of emotions on Suzanne's young face. *She truly loves him,* the angel marveled, moved by the intensity of the girl's feelings. *She has a beautiful soul, brilliant and quick. This is going to be a painful time for both these young people.*

As they gathered around the supper table, Jared asked Jesus to recite the Sabbath meal blessing.

The strong young voice joyfully invoking the ancient prayers struck music in Suzanne's young heart.

Jesus sat among them, enjoying the conversation and drinking the Sabbath wine. Occasionally he smiled and glanced furtively at the exquisite young face sitting across from him.

*Jeshua, you must remember who you are,* Gloriel breathed.

As the evening wore on, Jesus' face took on a more serious expression; and he occasionally appeared to lapse momentarily into deep thought.

Suzanne studied him from under the dark screen of black silken lashes which shadowed her silver eyes. He seemed curiously apprehensive or bewildered. *Isn't he going to speak with Father tonight?* She wondered anxiously to herself. *What's wrong?* She clenched a soft pink lip between her teeth.

After supper was ended, as they rose from the table, Jared turned to Ophrah and took her by the arm. "My dear, let us get a breath of fresh air." He draped her shawl about his wife's shoulders, and they stepped through the curtain, leaving the two young people alone.

Jesus turned to Suzanne, his eyes glowing like topazes. Abruptly, a shadow darkened his young face. He took her hand, trembling slightly.

Suzanne sat motionless, as if suddenly turned to stone. He gazed into her eyes for what seemed an eternity to the young girl.

*Jesu,* Gloriel urged silently.

"Suzanne, I love you," he blurted out finally, his voice cracking with deep emotion.

*Then why is there sorrow in your eyes?* Suzanne wondered to herself.

"I will love you forever" His breath grew raspy in his throat.

Suzanne caught her breath and stared at him stunned at his expression. Fullness rose up in her throat, a silent cry. Her eyes grew moist with dreams and love.

Brilliant tears glistened in Jesus' eyes. He wanted desperately to love her openly, without fear, to fold her in his arms, and rejoice in their love.

"But I cannot ask you to marry me." He choked on the words.

"Oh, Jesu, you must have courage, now." Gloriel whispered in his ear.

"But Jesus, I love you, too!" Suzanne protested. Two large, shining tears rolled down her ivory pale cheeks. "Please, tell me why . . ." she whispered through lips stiff with pain. "What's wrong? Have I done something to displease you? Are you sick?"

Jesus lifted her small hand to his lips and kissed it tenderly. "Oh, Suzanne, I am so sorry. I-I know now that my life is not to be as other men's. I think I have known this in my heart for a long time now. The Most High has revealed this to me the past few days." His voice broke, and he hesitated.

"I was born for His purposes, and I cannot take a wife."

He reached out then, and took her sweet face between his hands. He longed to touch the soft lips with his own, but knew he must not. A wildly tender pang of compassion struck his heart, and he drew in his breath raggedly.

"Suzanne, my dearest, you will always be a part of who I am as a man," he said, the tears brimmed over now. "I am made of flesh and blood as all other men are. I feel everything they do—grief, pain, desire. But I have to be about my Father's work. I must be ready when He calls."

Gloriel felt the sharp stab of her Jesu's pain, and wanted desperately to comfort his breaking heart. But for now, she could not.

Suzanne was sobbing now. Jesus took her in his arms, softly kissed the top of her dark head, and smoothed back the curls from her forehead.

"Why did you make me love you, Jesus?" she cried brokenly.

"Forgive me, my darling, please forgive me," he pleaded.

He enfolded both of her hands in his. "We must face your parents now. They must find someone else for you." He took a deep breath and led her through the curtained door and out into the night.

## Chapter Eighteen

Jesus reveled in the Passover celebration. Gloriel struggled to keep the enemy Pride from entering her heart as she stood close by the young man's side. *How wonderful he is! How strong and handsome and perfect in thought, word and deed!* His rich brown hair lay in shining waves around his glowing face as he tried to take in all the marvelous sights and sounds of the Temple.

Although still under construction, the Temple plazas with their massive walls and exquisite decorations delighted his eyes. The elegant beauty of the Portico of Solomon shone in the mid-day sun, and reflected off the white marble steps. The day felt lovely and warm after the chill of the night before.

Rabbis sat in the shade of the blue and white Greek columns.

Jesus watched intently as Temple aides dressed in short white tunics followed a solemn procession of priests as they ascended the 13 curved steps to the Court of Men.

Trumpet blasts pierced the air, summoning the faithful to prayer, bringing forth an ecstatic response from the hundreds of pilgrims crowding around the entrance to the Temple.

He turned a radiant face from side to side, trying to assimilate all the sights and sounds which bombarded his senses. Ceremony, brilliant color, ancient tradition, odors and aromas—some pleasant, some nauseating-vied for prominence among his senses. The Temple was overflowing with the smoke of sacrifices, and the pungent scent of incense filled his nostrils.

The High Priest slowly ascended the steps at the head of the procession. His richly embroidered royal blue robes, turban and sash of fine linen shimmered, luminous in the bright sunlight.

Next came the priests of lower rank, dressed in bright white linen tunics and turbans, with silk sashes embroidered in deep purple, crimson, and peacock blue.

Finally, the Levites and Temple officials filed up the steps, strumming their lyres. The ancient melodies filled the Temple with vibrant song.

For Jesus, everything was thrilling, bursting with the palpable life of the Temple.

"Jesu," Gloriel whispered into his consciousness, "Jesu, look at the young man in front of you."

Jesus turned his attention from the procession, and his eyes came to rest on a tall, thin young man standing directly ahead of him.

He was obviously well-to-do. His bright white silk robe embroidered with gold threads gleamed in the light. The young man turned his head and gazed full into Jesus' face. His pale skin seemed luminous and paper thin, revealing the underlying delicate purple veins. Lack-luster brown hair framed a very thin and fragile-looking face. A sparse brown beard covered his chin and cheeks.

Clear, bright green eyes peered from beneath thin brows, shining with a clear delight in living.

"Good morning, sheli, my friend." Despite his apparent frailty, his voice was lilting, deep and strong.

"Good morning. Shalom alechem, peace be with you." Jesus greeted him with a bright smile.

"Have you journeyed far for Passover?" The young man leaned forward slightly, an earnest expression on his sharp-featured face.

"I live in Nazareth with my parents. It's been two years since we were last able to make the trip. Where is your home?"

"Oh, it's only a short jaunt for my sisters and me. We live in Bethany. My name is Lazarus," the young man commented, bowing. "Are your parents here?"

"They are visiting cousins in Ein Karem who are too far along in years to make the trip to the Temple for Passover. They will be here tomorrow. My name is Jesus." Grinning widely, he returned the bow.

A puzzled expression spread over Lazarus' angular face, and a small crease appeared between the green eyes.

"Have we met before, Jesus?"

"I don't think so, Lazarus. I'm sure I would remember if we had. Perhaps we've seen one another before, here at the Temple."

"Perhaps so. Where are you staying tonight?" Lazarus inquired, placing his hand on Jesus' arm.

"Oh, I'm with a small caravan from Nazareth. My cousin, James, my mother's brother Jacob, and their families made the trip with us."

"You know, Jesus, I would really like to get to know you better. Since your parents won't be here, will you come and spend the night as our guest? I'm sure my sisters, Mary and Martha, would love to have some company. How about it, my friend?" Lazarus smiled, his pale face suffused with warmth.

"Well, Lazarus," Jesus hesitated, a bit bewildered. "I am honored by your invitation, but . . ."

Gloriel interrupted his answer with a mental nudge. *It's all right, Jesu, the Father wishes this.*

Doubt fled on the heels of caution, and Jesus graciously accepted the invitation, though feeling puzzled as to why.

The two young men walked up the steps together as the clear tones of the High Priest's voice rang out.

"Sh'ma! Hear, O Israel!"

Jesus heart responded with joy, and he grinned at his new-found friend.

#

The small, sleepy town of Bethany lay about two miles from Jerusalem, on the eastern slope of the beautiful Mount of Olives. Silver-leaved fig trees dotted the hillside as the small group of young people approached their destination.

Lazarus, Mary, Martha and Jesus chatted amiably, pausing to pluck plump ripe figs from the trees along the roadside.

In contrast to their brother, Mary and Martha glowed with good health, Gloriel noticed. She followed the young people, enjoying their banter.

Mary, the youngest of the three siblings, had her brother's clear green eyes, though lighter in shade. Smooth, honey-colored hair hung far down her small back, swinging from side to side as she bounced along the path, chattering animatedly.

*She must be about my age*, Jesus reflected, *and very pretty*.

Her golden skin glowed in the late afternoon sunshine. A pink mouth, full and sensual, revealed shining white teeth as she tossed back her head and laughed at her brother's witty remarks.

Her sister, Martha, walked primly, with precise and delicate steps. She shook her head at Mary's lively chatter. Thin, angular and rather plain, she had yet to have a marriage proposal at 20 years of age. Light brown hair framed her bony face. Her mouth was rather colorless, carved and still. A small frown furrowed her narrow forehead.

*She is jealous of her sister, poor thing*, Gloriel sighed, *Jesu perceives that*.

They walked up a smooth red-gravel pathway to the entrance of the large and sumptuous home of Lazarus, Mary and Martha.

Jesus paused to breathe in the fragrant aroma of the surrounding gardens. The scent of jasmine rose, and the sweet effluvium of roses filled his nostrils. To the left of the doorway, a large fig tree provided cool, dark shade over a stone bench.

The sun was setting now, drawn in bold strokes of gold, dusky pink, and lavender. Jesus' heart lifted in thanksgiving to his Father for these gifts to his senses, and momentarily, his new friends were forgotten.

"Jesus!" Lazarus stood in front of an intricately carved teakwood door, beckoning. "Welcome to our home! Come in!"

Jesus smiled sheepishly and replied, "Peace be to this home, my friends."

The heavy door opened then, and a full-muscled manservant greeted them politely. The delicious aroma of roasting garlic and lamb permeated the air in the entranceway.

"Ephraim," Lazarus instructed the servant, "We have an honored guest for supper. He will be staying the night. Prepare a suitable room for him."

Martha stepped forward, moistening her thin lips and clearing her throat. "If you will excuse me, I will see to our dinner." She did not look directly at Jesus, but at a spot on the wall behind him. Her narrow sallow cheeks were lightly tinged with pink.

Jesus' eyes twinkled as he bowed slightly to the young woman standing stiffly before him. "Of course, Martha, thank you."

"Mary, come with me, please." Martha turned to her younger sister and murmured, rather curtly, Gloriel thought.

Mary's animated face clouded. "Oh, Martha, why don't you let the servants take care of dinner? Let's visit with our guest!" She turned a beaming smile toward Jesus.

Gloriel chuckled to herself. *How different these two girls are! Like bubbles and starch!"*

However, Martha prevailed over her younger sister, and the two hurried toward the kitchen. The angel stifled a full-blown laugh as she watched Mary stick out an impudent tongue at the back of Martha's head.

Still smiling, Jesus looked around curiously at the lavish but comfortable room where his host had led him.

Lazarus apologized for his sister's behavior, and bid Jesus sit down on one of the richly colored velvet cushions next to a low oak table.

Jesus ran his hand over the smooth and gleaming surface, admiring the finish with a perceptive and appreciative eye.

"So, my friend, tell me about yourself." Lazarus fixed him with his large, child-like green gaze. "What kind of work do you do?"

Jesus looked at his host, his heart touched. Lazarus' face was a macabre landscape of bony prominences, and yet aristocratic. *Something gnaws at him.* Jesus mused, as he settled into the soft cushion.

"I am a simple carpenter, like my father Joseph. My family has lived in Nazareth for many generations now." He fixed Lazarus with a gentle gaze.

"And you, my friend, you are not well, I think." He leaned over and placed a callused hand on the young man's arm.

Lazarus drew in his breath sharply at Jesus' touch. He gazed at his new-found friend with a vaguely dazed expression. "Oh, it's nothing, really, a cough that has hung on for a while. Just a nuisance, actually. Don't concern yourself, Jesus." He patted the hand on his arm, and smiled weakly.

Jesus removed his hand, and sat back with a nod. He regarded Lazarus silently from under lowered lashes.

Gloriel sat behind the two young men, watching and listening thoughtfully. *Lazarus is very ill,* she mused, *and yet he will be an important part of Jesu's life. How is this to be, Father?*

She realized her abiding curiosity was seldom fully satisfied, but this did not deter her from questioning the Lord.

"In due time, my child, you will know." The answer came clearly.

Jesus and Lazarus chatted amiably, while Mary and Martha busied themselves in the kitchen. Soon, Ephraim appeared, bearing a silver platter. Steaming roast lamb, browned to a succulent richness, and chopped into cubes delighted their senses.

A servant girl followed closely on his heels. She carried a basin of water, with clean white towels draped over her arm. She set the alabaster basin before Jesus.

"Miriam, bring our guest another cushion." Lazarus sat upright, pale face gleaming in the lamplight.

"Oh, thank you, Lazarus, but I'm very comfortable." He glanced at Miriam and smiled. The girl lowered her dark eyes and bowed, blushing slightly.

Jesus washed his hands and dried them on the soft towel Miriam extended to him.

Mary and Martha, pink-cheeked from the heat of the kitchen, appeared and took their places at the low table.

Other servants followed Ephraim and Miriam, bearing plates of opalescent grapes, olives swimming in delicate oil, cheeses and sweetmeats.

Lazarus asked their guest to recite the blessing prayers over the food.

Gloriel enjoyed watching the young people feasting. Laughter and gaiety filled the warm atmosphere as the evening wore on. "These young ones," she prayed, "There are special plans for them in Jeshua's life, are there not, Father?"

"Special plans, my angel, yes. Very special plans." The answer came instantly, whispering into her spirit.

The evening resonated with prayers and wine and song, as shadows danced in the lamp light. It was a joyful time.

## Chapter Nineteen

Gloriel looked on appreciatively as Jesus ran his fingers over the smooth surface of the finished yoke. "He is so meticulous," she said to Samuel. "His work is always flawless."

"Yes, Joseph is very pleased that his son has become such a fine carpenter," Samuel replied. He stood behind Joseph, who was sitting on a low stool, observing Jesus' work.

"It's always been so important to Jesu that he has his father's approval." Gloriel moved close to Jesus' side.

Samuel's broad forehead creased with a slight frown as he looked down at his charge. *Joseph is leaving more and more of the work in the shop to his son now,* he mused.

Gloriel scrutinized Joseph's aging face. It was pale and deeply lined, his complexion slightly gray. He passed a shaking hand across his eyes, rubbing them wearily. A sigh escaped his pinched lips.

Jesus looked up from his work. "Father, you seem tired. Please take Eli and go on home. I'll finish up here. It's getting late, and Mother will have supper waiting. I'll be along shortly." He laid his hand on Joseph's shoulder. *He's getting so thin,* he thought, surprised at the feel of sharp bones under his fingers.

"Yes, Son, I believe I will go home now. It's been a long day," Joseph said, heaving a deep sigh.

"Are you feeling well enough to go by yourself, Avi?" Jesus asked, a note of anxiety in his voice.

"I'm fine, Son, I'm fine." Joseph rose slowly to his feet, swaying slightly. Jesus reached out a steadying hand, concern etching his face.

The late afternoon sun slanted its rays through the trees, scarlet and gold and bronze from the first frost, as Joseph moved slowly along the rocky pathway to his home. Samuel followed closely, watching each step Joseph took. *He's getting old now, and obviously weaker,* he thought. The sun suddenly dimmed as a cloud passed before its pale face.

#

Inside the warm house, Mary busied herself preparing the evening meal. Sariel hovered nearby, watching her charge bustle about, humming to herself.

*She's almost 41 years old now,* Sariel thought, *yet she is still lovely, even with the silver threads in her hair.*

Mary's beautiful face glowed like a young girl's. She was preparing a hearty soup, rich with meat juices, vegetables and barley. Garlic and basil from her small garden lent their heavy fragrances to the delicious aroma.

Joseph pushed the light curtain aside as he entered the welcoming room. *I must hang the heavy curtain soon,* he reflected, as he greeted his wife.

"Mary, peace be with you." He put his arms around her, as the warm woman scent of her flesh, and the fresh fragrance of her hair filled his nostrils. He kissed her forehead softly.

"Joseph, you are home early. Is everything alright?"

Mary's brown eyes, still clear as in her youth, gazed into Joseph's.

Lines of weariness were driven into his forehead, cheeks and mouth. She felt a swift pang of uneasiness as she caressed his cheek.

"I'm just tired, my dear. Your soup smells wonderful."

"Sit down, my husband, and rest. Supper is almost ready. Is Jesus on his way home?"

He eased himself down on the mat with a small groan and wiped his sweating face with his sleeve.

Sariel and Samuel exchanged worried glances. Joseph looked old, and stricken, and sick.

"He'll be along shortly, my dear. He was just finishing up a yoke for Reuben ben Joash," Joseph replied, wearily. His usually hearty voice sounded weak and tremulous to Mary's ears.

#

Jesus finished tidying up the small shop, gathering the wood chips for his mother, putting away the tools. He carefully wrapped the just-completed yoke in some burlap, and glanced around to make sure everything was ready for tomorrow's work. As he laid new straw on the floor, the room filled with the scent of the fields. Shouldering the yoke, he walked out into the golden light of late autumn. Leaves fell whispering from the trees around the market place.

His thoughts raced as he stepped carefully along the familiar path. Memories came rushing, jostling one another for status. His head whirled with them. His mother . . . childhood memories of her constant and loving devotion, her tender caresses, rose up before his eyes. Stumbling slightly, he repositioned the yoke across his shoulders.

Gloriel followed him closely, acutely aware of his nostalgic mood. Images of his childhood flashed through her own consciousness. Once more, the desire to reveal herself to him clamored inside her. "Father, help me to quench this desire until the time is right," she breathed. "He's 27 years old now, Lord, a man grown. Grant me the wisdom to help him accept and recognize the mission which lies ahead. Strengthen him to stand strong against the pressures of his friends and family to follow all the ancient customs for marriage." A lump rose in the throat of the diminutive angel as she watched the fleeting emotions flicker across the chiseled features of her Jesu.

*John, John, why am I thinking of him?* Jesus wondered as he neared his home. *I haven't seen him in several years.*

News of Zechariah's death had arrived with a caravan from Jerusalem several months earlier. Elizabeth was being cared for by a young neighbor who moved in with her after Zechariah died. Rumors were that John had disappeared into the desert, living in a cave and subsisting on locusts and wild honey. People gossiped among themselves about the strange, wild-looking young man who refused to follow his father into the priesthood as his heir.

*John, has my Father called you, too?* Jesus' throat tightened, and unexplained tears filled his eyes. His mind whirled tumultuously.

Warm light from the window of his childhood home beckoned down the pathway. He was breathing heavily now, from the burden on his shoulders. Outside the curtained doorway, he lowered the yoke carefully to the ground.

Eli stood by the doorway, unattended. *Strange,* Jesus thought.

Rubbing his shoulder, he paused to catch his breath before entering. Nostalgia filled his breast as he gazed around at the familiar surroundings.

Gloriel whispered in his ear, "Jesu, treasure your mother and father, always."

Tears brimmed up again to fill the brown eyes. Brushing them aside with the back of one hand, he opened the linen curtain, and entered the warm room. A low red fire rustled on the hearth.

Mary and Joseph looked up at their son as he walked in. Mary's eyes, dark with anxiety, shone with unshed tears. She rose quickly and embraced her son.

"Your father is sick, son. I want you to go get the doctor." Her voice quavered as she looked down at her husband.

Even in the warm glow of the fire, Joseph's face was gaunt and gray. Sweat gleamed on his forehead.

Jesus knelt down on one knee beside Joseph, taking his gnarled hand in his own. His father's skin felt icy and clammy to Jesus' touch. "Avi, are you in pain?"

"Yes, Son," Joseph's voice was ragged and gasping. "But—it's—probably just—indigestion."

Samuel stood close-by with Gloriel and Sariel, his usually jolly round face somber.

Gloriel laid her hand on his arm. "Samuel, what's happening to Joseph?"

Samuel's black eyes grew shadowed and dark with compassion. "He is very sick, Gloriel, perhaps unto death. I have heard nothing from the Father yet." He sighed deeply, drawing closer to his suffering charge.

Sariel's round eyes grew huge in her small face as she moved quickly to Mary's side.

"I'm going for the doctor. Mother, let me help you get him on his pallet," Jesus rasped, his voice hoarse with fear.

He reached down and gathered his father into his arms, lifting him easily, surprised at the fragility of the once strong body.

Mary quickly prepared Joseph's bed, bringing one of the cushions from beside the low table.

Laying his father down gently, Jesus cradled Joseph's head and shoulders as Mary quickly positioned the pillow for him.

Jesus bit back tears, and hugged his mother. "I'll be back with the doctor as soon as I can, Emi."

"Go with God, my son," Mary breathed, stifling her fear and anxiety.

Outside, the light was fragile and tenuous, as if refusing to give way to night. Jesus raced down the path, stumbling in his haste, and praying out loud. "Abba, Father, hear my prayer. Please help your servant, my Avi." His breath came in ragged gasps as he ran.

Dusk crept in softly now as the desperate young man approached the house of Jeremiah ben Elias. Panting and breathless, Jesus stood at the doorway of Nazareth's only physician. He lurched, stumbling a little, as he paused to catch his breath.

Gloriel pressed her forehead against his shoulder, transmitting the warm love of God to her charge, and encouraging him.

"Jeremiah!" Jesus' voice was raspy as he knocked on the wooden portal of the physician's house.

Gloriel felt a catch in her heart as she stood beside him once again, she experienced a strong desire to reveal herself to him in her human form, wanting to cover him, to shield him from this pain. But she knew this was not in the Father's plan for the moment, and so she remained unseen. *The Father loves you, Jesu . . .*

Again, Jesus called out "Jeremiah ben Elias!"

The door opened slightly, and a sharp-featured face appeared, shadowed in the twilight. The doctor's deep-set eyes widened at the sight of the disheveled and distraught young man on his doorstep.

"Jesus, what's wrong?" He asked, opening the door wide.

"It's my father! He's terribly sick! Please come quickly!" Jesus pleaded, grabbing the doctor's arm.

#

Samuel tried to comfort Joseph, placing his hand on the frail thin skin of his brow as the old man struggled for breath.

Sariel knelt beside Mary, murmuring softly in her ear as she placed her arms around the trembling woman's shoulders.

*Even when I walk through the dark valley of death, I will not be afraid, for you are close beside me; your rod and your staff protect and comfort me.* Psalm 23:4 NLT

*God will lead you faithfully, Mary, even through this frightening time.* Sariel's hand lay lightly on the back of Mary's bowed head.

Joseph moaned softly, his gaunt face ashen. Great beads of sweat stood out on his brow.

Mary drew the blanket up under Joseph's chin, crooning softly. "Don't worry, my love, Jesus will be here soon with the doctor. Rest, my dear husband, rest."

A large tear rolled slowly down one cheek as she leaned over her suffering spouse. Tenderly, she soothed him, wiping his forehead with a soft towel.

Footsteps sounded outside the door, and a breathless Jesus held the curtain aside for Jeremiah ben Elias.

"Peace be to this house," the doctor greeted the white-faced Mary.

"And also with you, Jeremiah." Mary drew in a ragged breath.

Jeremiah ben Elias knelt down beside Joseph. "Joseph, can you hear me?" He laid his palm against his patient's cold and clammy forehead. "Are you in pain?"

Joseph's lips trembled, his face had turned a sickly gray. He raised a shaking hand and clutched his chest. "Can't—breathe. Pain—here" His breath came in rapid, short gasps, his voice nearly inaudible.

"Jesus, bring my bag here." Jeremiah motioned to the anxious young man. "Mary, get me a cup."

Jesus, pale and distraught, handed the doctor's bag to him.

Jeremiah rummaged through the sack, and brought out a small flask. Mary handed him Joseph's cup with shaking fingers.

"I will need some water, too, Jesus." The doctor's voice was brusque with concern.

Mary placed her hand against Joseph's face, and he turned his cheek as if to nuzzle her palm. "Joseph, my husband,—Joseph" she murmured, sobbing softly.

The physician poured a small amount of liquid from the little flask into the cup, and added some water. "Jesus, raise his head so he can drink," he ordered.

Jesus quickly positioned himself at Joseph's head, raising him gently to rest against his own chest.

Gloriel moved to kneel at Jesus' side, and Samuel stood watching at Joseph's feet. Sariel eyed Mary's blanched face anxiously.

Jeremiah pushed the rim of the cup against Joseph's parched lips. "Drink, Joseph, this will ease your pain," he said gently. Joseph swallowed weakly as Jesus supported his head from behind. The once bright eyes opened slowly, revealing a dull and lusterless gaze, filled with pain and exhaustion.

Samuel moved to the head of the pallet, knelt down and placed an unseen hand on Joseph's head.

The doctor laid his ear against Joseph's chest. The room was silent except for the patient's labored, shallow breathing. Jeremiah raised his head and looked at Mary. Closing his eyes briefly, he shook his head.

"It's his heart, Mary. It is very tired and weak. He probably will not live through the night. I'm sorry. There is nothing we can do except make him as comfortable as possible."

Mary stared at the doctor blankly.

Jesus turned a stricken face toward his mother. She didn't seem to comprehend the doctor's words. He looked down at his father, lying quietly in his arms, eyes half-opened, dull and unseeing.

"Avi—Avi," he whispered hoarsely, placing one hand on Joseph's thin chest. He bowed his head and kissed his father's cold, sweaty forehead.

A glimmer of light touched Joseph's eyes then, and his cracked lips moved slightly. A ragged whisper slipped through them. "Son, S-son, Ma-ry . . ." He struggled to speak, lifting one bony hand a few inches. It dropped back to his side, and his eyes closed once more.

"Father, Avi, it's all right. I will take care of Mother. Rest, now," Jesus whispered tenderly into his father's ear.

"Jesus!" Mary's voice, sharp with anxiety, shattered the quiet. "Jesus, help him! You can help him! The bird, remember the bird?"

Startled, Jesus stared at his frantic mother. Gloriel placed a hand on each of his shoulders.

For a moment, Jesus was bewildered. What did his mother want him to do? Suddenly, he realized. Mary wanted him to heal his father. He closed his eyes, praying silently, *Abba, Abba, help us.*

Gloriel whispered in his ear, then. "Not yet, Jesu, not yet."

Jesus' eyes flew open, and he looked around the shadowed room. It was empty, save for his frantic mother, and the helpless doctor.

Confused, Jesus sighed deeply. He gently lifted Joseph's limp head and chest from his lap, and laid him back on the cushion. He stood up and walked to the foot of the pallet. Picking up a blanket, he turned to his mother, placed it on her shoulders, and wrapped it around her tenderly.

Gathering her in his arms, he held her tight, whispering in her ear.

"Emi, Emi, I cannot. It is not time yet. It is not time." His breath caught in a sob.

"Son, please!' Mary breathed raggedly. "You must try!"

Jesus bent his head and softly kissed his mother's forehead. He dropped his arms and returned to his father's side. The doctor looked at him with compassion in his eyes, slowly shaking his head.

Once more, Jesus took Joseph's frail body into his arms. Closing his eyes, he bent his head until it touched his father's cold, wet forehead.

Joseph's breath came in intermittent ragged gasps. Gloriel thought each one might be his last.

Samuel stood at the head of the pallet, eyes closed and head bowed.

Sariel kept her hands on Mary's trembling shoulders.

"Father, Abba . . ." The words were almost inaudible as Jesus' lips moved against Joseph's skin. "Hear my prayer for your servant, my Avi. Spare him to us. Let him remain with us a little longer." A gleaming tear slid from beneath his eyelid and dropped on Joseph's forehead, mingling with the beads of sweat. "And yet, not my will, but only yours be done, O Most High."

A strange pang struck Gloriel's heart as she heard those words.

Jesus laid his father's head down on the pillow once more. Mary knelt on the other side of the pallet. Sobbing, she laid her head on Joseph's chest and slid her arms around him.

Sariel stroked Mary's hair with a trembling hand.

"Oh, Joseph, my love, my dear love, p-please d-don't leave us." Mary's words were broken and muffled. Gradually, her sobs quieted.

Silence filled the little room, interrupted only by an occasional rattling gasp from Joseph's throat.

Samuel moved closer to Joseph's side, his black eyes gleaming in the fluttering lamplight. Reaching down, he took Joseph's limp hand in his own. "Joseph," he whispered. "Joseph, it's time to go rest now."

Jesus drew in his breath sharply as his father's eyes opened slowly.

Mary lifted her head from Joseph's chest, startled. Joseph looked into her eyes, a shadow of light wavered over his eyelids, and his lips moved. He raised his gaze to Jesus, and a small smile touched the corners of his parched mouth. A great heaving sigh lifted his breast, and his spirit rose into Samuel's arms.

And so, Joseph ben Jacob, faithful servant of the living God, loving husband and father, entered Paradise accompanied by a joyful band of angels, one of whom seemed very familiar to him.

## Chapter Twenty

Gloriel sat quietly at a table toward the back of the long, gaily decorated room. The rich aroma of roasting lamb filled the air. Tables laden with cheeses, sweetmeats, pastries and breads stood around the perimeter of the room. A wedding celebration was in full swing. The bride stood radiant in the midst of the celebrants, smiling up at the bridegroom.

"Isn't she lovely?"

Gloriel turned to look at the middle-aged woman seated next to her.

"Especially for a bride of her age," the woman continued, whispering conspiratorially. "Twenty-two years old! Can you imagine getting married that late in life?"

Gloriel smiled, a twinkle sparkling in the amber eyes.

"She is indeed beautiful, for any age. And such a kind and gentle person, don't you think?"

She looked deeply into the woman's pale, shadowed eyes. The eyelids were papery and blue-veined. Envy peered back at the angel from their watery, red-rimmed depths.

Plump and neck-less, the woman shrugged her fat shoulders. "Why, yes, yes, Suzanne is very kind," she replied, raising her voice. "I have known her since she was small, you know. Such a nice family, and so much tragedy in their lives. Her brother, Jacob, was killed in a fall on Job's Hill several years ago. Then her mother died of a fever just last year."

Whispering again, the woman leaned toward Gloriel. "Suzanne's first love wasn't Joash." She inclined her head toward the bridegroom. "It was that man standing by the door, the tall, handsome one talking to Suzanne's father."

Laying her hand on Gloriel's arm, she leaned closer. "His name is Jesus. They say he rejected her before a marriage could be arranged. He's a local carpenter. Do you know him?" Her plump cheeks grew pink as she chattered on, not waiting for Gloriel's reply.

The angel raised her gaze to Jesus. He stood silhouetted against the bright sunlight in the doorway. She drew her mantel close around her head and shoulders, the soft blue linen shadowing her face. Seldom did she take on her bodily form where Jesus could see her easily. However, this day it seemed important that she become part of Suzanne's wedding celebration.

The crowd was large and noisy, and no one seemed to take much notice of the comely young amber-haired girl in their midst. Mingling among the guests, she took care to stay out of Jesus' line of vision.

*He seems to be enjoying himself*, she thought.

But she knew his face did not mirror his feelings. Occasionally, he lifted his eyes to watch the joyful bride and groom. He smiled and applauded when they danced, and chatted amiably with the other guests. *His spirit is sad, I know. This is a hard thing for him. Father, must he bear this hurt forever?* Gloriel prayed silently.

"When they happen at the same time, deep love and great pain enrich a soul in a way that nothing else can, my child," the answer came swiftly.

Suddenly, Gloriel froze, hardly able to trust her eyes, as a dark form took shape in the corner of the room, not far from where Jesus stood. The figure stood shrouded in dark gray, face hidden in the shadows. An icy chill swept over the angel. Many years had passed since she last recognized one of Satan's minions.

The woman beside her was still prattling, pointing out and commenting on various people in the crowd. ". . . and that old woman over there, standing by Joash, she . . ." Turning toward Gloriel, she stopped in mid-sentence.

Confused, she searched the crowd with her pale eyes, bewildered. "Where . . . ?Gloriel had disappeared.

Swiftly, and unseen, the angel positioned herself between Jesus and the dark figure in the corner. A predatory malevolence emanated from the ominous form as it advanced slowly toward her. She stared at him and shuddered with a sudden awareness.

Behind her, Jesus turned slowly and watched the advance of the figure. His eyes narrowed, and his breath grew shallow. "Father," he whispered.

Gloriel took a deep breath, stepped forward and raised both arms. "Be gone! In God's Name, I command you to return to the Evil One who sent you!!"

Arms stretched wide open, she advanced another step. Her amber eyes glowed with an inner light, riveted on the demon's dark face.

He shuddered, turned, and faded away into the dark corner.

"Thank you, Father," Jesus sighed deeply. Still unseen, Gloriel took her place by his side.

"Jesus!" A familiar voice called out from the doorway.

"Lazarus! Mary! Martha! How good to see you!" Jesus strode toward his friends, who greeted him warmly.

"It's been far too long since we last saw you, my dear friend." Lazarus' green eyes shone with pleasure.

Mary hugged Jesus, but Martha hung back shyly.

"Where is your mother, Jesus?" Mary's pretty face was wreathed in a dimpled smile as she searched the crowd with her sparkling eyes.

"She wasn't feeling well, Mary," Jesus replied. His features grew serious. "She is still grieving for my father, even though it has been almost three years since his death."

Mary placed a small, warm hand on Jesus' arm. "And you, dear friend, how are you?"

Jesus smiled down at the lovely woman. "I am doing well, thank you, Mary. My father's carpentry business has grown, and it takes me on frequent trips. In fact, I will be going to Bethany in a few days, to make some deliveries."

"You must stay with us, old friend!" Lazarus tossed a thin arm around Jesus' shoulders, grinning broadly with pleasure.

"Thank you, Lazarus, I shall be honored," Jesus replied, returning the grin. "Martha, are you well?" He turned his smile on the anxious-looking woman beside him.

"I am quite well. Thank you for inquiring," Martha replied, a little stiffly. She blinked rapidly and lowered her eyes, clenching and unclenching her thin fists.

Gloriel stood by, keeping a wary eye out for any more unwelcome visitors. Relaxing her vigilance for a moment, she searched Martha's sharp features. *Such a worried one, she is. Her heart is so anxious, and her spirit restless*, she mused.

"I believe I'll just sit down for a while, and sample some of the wedding delicacies." Lazarus' voice interrupted Gloriel's thoughts.

His bony face looked haggard, despite the brightness of the room. Dark circles framed his eyes, and his usually strong voice sounded thin. "But you young ones go join in the dancing," he said, gently pushing Jesus and Mary toward the merry-making. "Go on, Martha, relax and enjoy yourself. I'll try not to eat all the refreshments" He pinched Martha's cheek and smiled.

"No, no, Lazarus. I shall stay with you," she protested, her voice nervous and high-pitched. Anxiety traced lines beside her mouth.

Jesus reached out and took her hand. "Martha, come, join us. Leave your brother to stuff his face," he laughed, winking at Lazarus.

"Yes, Sister, come!" Mary cried gaily, grasping Martha's other hand.

Reluctantly Martha agreed. Her thin features were flushed and blotchy.

As the trio joined the laughing crowd, Jesus turned and looked intently at Lazarus sitting on a red cushion by a well-laden table. His friend returned his gaze, nodding, and smiling gently.

#

Mary stood in the doorway of their cozy home, watching her son with mixed emotions as he led Eli and their new donkey, Roshan, down the path.

"He's doing so well in his business, Mary Elizabeth," she said, turning to her sister. "But he works too hard. This trip to Bethany, and then on to Jerusalem for Hanukkah; I really should be going with him," she sighed, brushing back a loose strand of dark, silver-streaked hair from her forehead.

"Mary, you need to rest. Come, sit down," her sister cajoled as she removed a fresh loaf of bread from the oven. "Here, have some bread, and I'll get you a cup of goat's milk."

Sighing again, Mary sat down on a low stool by the table. Her face was etched with fine lines of grief, the once bright eyes shadowed and heavy-lidded.

Sariel moved closer to her charge, ever watchful. *The past three years have take their toll on my sweet girl*, she mused. *No, she is no longer a girl, or even young. And yet she grows more tender and gentle day by day.*

"Yes, she does, Sariel."

"Gloriel! I thought you were with Jesus!" Sariel exclaimed, startled.

"I'm going to join him in a few minutes, my friend." Gloriel reached out and touched Sariel's round cheek. "But he is anxious about his mother, and I wanted to speak with you about her. How is she, Sariel?"

The little golden-haired angel grasped her friend's hand tightly. "Oh, Gloriel, she is so fragile, like a full-blown rose ready to drop its petals"

Gloriel smiled as a memory crept into her mind.

"Sariel, once long ago, while I was sitting at his feet, the Father told me a story about a rose and a stone"

"A rose and a stone?" Sariel echoed, looking puzzled.

"Yes," Gloriel replied, smiling. "He talked about how both the rose and the stone were surrounded by the rich natural environment, and the earth, free to both. The rose grew vivid and deep in color, velvety and fragrant, stirring in the breeze. But the stone lay gray and cold and hard, showing no signs of life.

The Father said that this is true of any two men, or women, also. The same people and culture, perhaps even the same family; and the same beauty in life surrounds them, at no cost to both, like the rose and the stone. Yet one man or woman grows kinder, more gentle and sensitive; while the other becomes harder, crueler, more uncaring each day. One grows a hard, impenetrable shell, and the other opens his or her heart like the rose, to the Holy Spirit."

Gloriel paused and gazed at Mary, smiling. "She is truly one of God's most precious roses, Sariel. His dew will refresh her, soon." She kissed Sariel's satin cheek, and vanished.

Sariel placed her arms around Mary, and whispered in her ear. "God is with you, blessed one. Lift up your heart." Mary's brown eyes opened wide, and light flickered somewhere in their depths. One corner of her mouth curled up slightly as she reached for a chunk of her sister's fresh baked bread.

#

As Jesus and his donkey companions trudged down the dusty road to Bethany, he fell into a deep reverie. Oblivious to his surroundings, he plodded along with the two donkeys, his spirit soaring, at one with his Father.

Gloriel remained beside him, sharply aware of his communion with the Father. She watched, listened, and rejoiced in his increasing realization of who he was.

The day wore on, and still Jesus walked on tirelessly, unaware of hunger, thirst or weariness. Eli and Roshan, too, seemed content to pace along steadily, feeling no need for rest.

Dusk fell, and soft mauve shadows lay across the road until all colors blended together in the dim twilight. Campfires flickered along the sides of the road, as weary travelers settled down for the night.

Jesus and the donkeys walked on, unaware of time and place.

Deep into the night, Jesus halted suddenly, shaking his head dazedly. Leading Eli and Roshan off the road, he unloaded their burdens. He stretched out on the bare ground and fell asleep, instantly and deeply.

Assuming her bodily form, Gloriel quietly fed and watered the two donkeys. Her heart felt light and peaceful as she covered Jesus with his cloak. He was sleeping so deeply that his breathing was barely perceptible. Tenderly, she touched his weary head. "Jesu, dear Jesu," she breathed, smiling tenderly. "Sleep well."

Suddenly, she was caught up in a blinding flash. Breathless, she found herself standing before the Father's great Throne. Its brilliance blinded her momentarily, and she covered her eyes with trembling hands.

"Gloriel, my child."

The familiar voice sent a thrill through her body. Still keeping her eyes closed, she clasped her hands together in a prayerful gesture.

"Father," she whispered, almost inaudibly.

"You have done well in your service to my Son, Gloriel. But now you must prepare him, and yourself, for the fulfillment of his mission. He will be starting soon on a journey which will lead to the most important events in the Plan of salvation for my people. His awareness of this mission is growing more clear each day. You must help him, for his human nature is reaching its most perfect proportions. Everything in nature and the universe has its own hour of perfection. My beloved Son approaches his. He has grown in grace and wisdom and stature, with your help. Continue your guidance and protection, Gloriel. Keep him from the Evil One until the hour he must face him alone. I give to you now, all the wisdom, the power, the grace, and the knowledge you will need to fulfill your own mission."

The Father's voice rose and filled the heavens with its powerful tones. "Receive these now, my child!"

The little angel felt as if she were being lifted off her feet, surrounded by a force of indescribable power. Seized with an uncontrollable rapture, she gasped as Jesus' days were laid out before her like a vividly colored river, full of pain and promise, bliss and sorrow. The Father's Plan opened clearly to her wondering gaze. Knowledge and perception flooded her spirit. Her body shook with the awesome vision of her responsibility.

"Go now, my child. Return to my Son, and stay close by his side, until you are summoned once more." The voice was gentle and soft now.

A deep, slow warmth flooded Gloriel's being as she closed her eyes once again.

"Father . . ." she basked in the warm glow of the Lord's love.

Opening her eyes slowly, she was startled to find herself kneeling by her charge's side. She gazed down at his peaceful face, soft with sleep. Her deepened awareness brought forth a strange mixture of sadness and joy. Heaving a great sigh, she placed a hand gently on his sleep-smoothed brow.

"Jesu, dear Jesu," she breathed quietly. Her human form began to fade as dawn opened its gray eyes in the eastern sky. "Sleep sweetly a bit longer."

Morning unfolded slowly over the landscape. It was the month of Tishri, and the fresh air of autumn was clear as molten glass.

Jesus slept on, oblivious to the sounds of life surrounding him. Eli and Roshan grazed quietly on a few tufts of grass by the roadside.

A small but noisy caravan on its way to Jerusalem passed slowly by. The beasts of burden were laden with rich and colorful rugs from Persia.

Still Jesus slept.

The pale sun was high in the sky when he finally awoke. Eli and Roshan stood quietly by, ears and tails flicking.

Jesus sat up slowly, stretching his corded arms overhead and yawning loudly.

"Well, my friends, did you rest well?" He scratched Eli's long ears and patted Roshan's broad back. "It's time we delivered our wares, don't you think? Lazarus and his sisters will be wondering what's delaying us. But first, some breakfast."

Rummaging through his supplies, Jesus fed the donkeys some oats, although they didn't seem to be very hungry. *That's odd,* he thought to himself. *I'm starving, and they act like their bellies are full.*

He found some dried fish and one of his mother's flat barley cakes, which he washed down with the tepid fluid from the water jug. Sharing the water with Eli and Roshan, he gazed around at the stark landscape.

"I think we should reach Bethany by sundown, Sheli'." He patted Eli's scruffy neck. The little ass bobbed his graying head with pleasure.

Gloriel looked on as Jesus arranged the packs on their backs, giving the heavier share to the young and strong Roshan.

He raised his arms in prayer then, reciting the familiar words with fervor and warmth. The donkeys stood very still, ears alert, as if listening intently.

#

The sun, large and lowdown, beamed its orange-yellow light through the date palms along the road leading into Bethany as Jesus and his trusty helpers approached.

"Not much further now," Jesus reassured the two little donkeys. "A good dinner and a night's sleep, and we'll be ready to deliver our goods."

Soon they reached the road leading to the home of Lazarus, Mary and Martha. Jesus paused to wash his travel-stained face and hands before knocking on the familiar teakwood door. Gloriel heard him humming softly under his breath. The door swung open, and a beaming Ephraim greeted Jesus.

"How wonderful to see you, sir! Enter, Enter!"

"Peace be with you, Ephraim." Jesus clapped the husky servant on the shoulder. "I need to unburden Eli and Roshan, Ephraim. They are tired and hungry."

"Oh, no, sir. We will take care of them. Do come in. Please be seated, and I will call my master," the servant replied, still beaming.

"No need, Ephraim. Welcome, welcome, my dear friend!" Lazarus' large child-like green eyes shone with pleasure as he greeted Jesus.

"We were wondering when you would arrive." He placed a skeletal arm around Jesus' shoulder.

"Yes, we thought perhaps you had lost your way!" Mary's dulcet tones greeted their guest. She stood in the archway of the entry hall, her hair circled like a golden moon about her pretty face.

Jesus grinned broadly at his friends. "It is good to see you again so soon, Mary, and your brother, too, of course. But where is . . ."

"Mary, did you offer our guest water for his feet after his long journey?" Martha's sharp voice cut the air.

*Poor woman, she's disgruntled as usual.* Gloriel thought.

"No, not yet, sister." Mary answered softly, lowering her sparkling eyes.

"Hello, Martha. How are you?" Jesus smiled affectionately and bowed to the thin, taut figure.

Martha's pale cheeks suffused with a faint dusting of color. "I am well, thank you. You must be starving. I shall see to dinner." She turned abruptly and fled the room.

Mary curtseyed slightly and bestowed a warm dimpled smile on her guest. "I should go help her. Lazarus, please show Jesus to his room, so he can refresh himself. Ephraim, you may go see to the donkeys now."

As the evening wore on, laughter filled the dining room with camaraderie and warmth. The four friends bantered back and forth as they had that first evening together long ago. Even Martha relaxed and joined in the lively conversation.

Gloriel watched, listening with interest to the subtle changes as they talked.

The conversation grew serious, and the angel noted the rather bewildered expression on Mary's sweet face. *She feels there is something different about her friend,* Gloriel thought. *She's beginning to see him with new eyes.*

Mary bowed her shining head and closed her eyes.

"Sister, are you feeling ill?" Lazarus' deep voice held an anxious edge.

"No, no, Lazarus, I'm just fine," Mary replied, lifting her head and smiling reassuringly.

"You look a little pale, Mary," Martha interjected, leaning toward her sister and frowning.

"Perhaps I am a bit tired." She turned to Jesus. "Will you excuse me, please?" She asked, voice trembling slightly.

Jesus rose hastily to his feet and extended his hand to help her up. She slipped her small hand into his work-callused one, and rose to her feet. Little spots of light swarmed before her eyes as she lifted them and gazed full into his face. A soft blush spread from her neck into her white cheeks. Her lips parted, and she exhaled softly, whispering. "My Lord . . ."

Silence descended like a sudden fog. Lazarus and Martha stared at her, dumfounded. Had they heard what she said correctly?

Jesus looked deeply into the green eyes now glimmering with tears. A shadow fell across his own eyes as he enveloped Mary's hand in both of his own. A slow, pent-up breath escaped his lips, and he smiled down at the shaken young woman.

## Chapter Twenty-One

Jesus' eyes moved slowly around the walls of the little carpentry shop. He picked up a hammer and hefted it in one hand, swinging it in an arc through the air. Laying it down on the workbench, he turned and paced back and forth across the sawdust-strewn floor.

"My heart is restless, Father," he whispered, closing his eyes, and rubbing exhaustion from them. Lines of fatigue crinkled in their corners.

Gloriel stood by the doorway, watching and listening. She and her charge had just returned from Bethany, and he was dusty and weary from the journey. He breathed in the familiar scents of sawdust, cedar, pine and oak. His heart was torn with memories, sweet and sad, clamoring through his mind.

Joseph, his beloved Avi, bending over the workbench, absorbed in his craft. He saw himself as a young boy, sitting at Joseph's feet, listening raptly to his father's instructions as he carefully chiseled a block of sweet-smelling cedar.

"Fine work, Son!" Joseph's familiar voice rang down through the years, wrenching Jesus' heart. The silence trickled into his soul.

Gloriel's eyes filled with tears as she watched him tenderly wrap up the tools of his trade in soft cloths, running his fingers lightly over each one as he placed them carefully in the large wooden chest crafted by Joseph.

His hand brushed against an unwrapped piece of wood. Curious, he withdrew it from the chest. Sweet memories crowded his mind as he ran his fingers over the beloved ball Avi had fashioned for him so many years ago. He carefully wrapped it in one of the cloths and placed it in his knapsack.

*This chapter of his life is coming to a close*, Gloriel reflected. *His heart is yearning for his boyhood days.* She sighed and laid a hand on Jesus' shoulder.

"Oh, Father, I know it is time to take the first steps of the journey you have laid out before me." His brow creased as he closed his tired eyes once more. "I am so reluctant to leave this shop, my family, this town. I know the path ahead of me leads to pain and sacrifice. Nevertheless, I was born for this purpose." Tears glimmered brightly under his dark lashes.

A chill sweat broke out on his forehead, as in his humanity, he hesitated.

*Ah, but his divinity grows eager, Father.* An enigmatic little smile crossed Gloriel's face.

A slender thread of golden sunlight lay gleaming on the hard-packed dirt floor. Light from the door created a nimbus around his bowed head.

Jesus' face was emptied out now, utterly still. A soft breeze wafted through the open door, stirring the curtain. A shadow of a smile touched his lips, and he sighed deeply.

"Lead me, Abba, I am ready."

The moment he had been preparing for throughout his childhood and youth had finally arrived.

Gloriel's thoughts raced back to the moment of Jesus' birth. The same joy and gratitude she felt then filled her breast now, tempered with a sense of the sorrow and the suffering yet to come.

Jesus finished tidying the shop, savoring his last moments in the small community of Nazareth. Here, he was simply Jesus, son of Joseph the carpenter, member of a large family, friend to all.

Ahead lay a pilgrimage fraught with joy and sorrow, laughter and tears; a journey bordered in darkness, yet full of light and service. He walked hesitantly toward the door, exhaling slowly as his gaze moved around the room once more. His dark eyes glistened with unshed tears. The ray of sunlight disappeared as a cloud passed across the small window.

Gloriel stood behind him, sensitive to both his sorrow and his expectancy. Once more, she felt the familiar lure to reveal herself to him. *No, this isn't the time,* she whispered to herself.

Jesus lifted his chin, straightened his shoulders as Emi had taught him, then turned and walked out the door.

#

The little room flooded with bright afternoon sunlight as Jesus took his mother in his arms. Mary stood in the circle of her son's embrace, an overwhelming sense of dread draping her like a shroud.

"Son, must you go now? Can't you wait until the spring rains are over?" Her cheeks were blanched, and her fine eyelashes fluttered like moths. Worn and delicate hands held his face tenderly.

"Emi, it's the month of Adar, and I must begin my journey now." He smiled down at the beloved face with the brimming brown eyes. "Aunt Mary Elizabeth will stay with you while I am gone, and our family will see to your needs." Gently, he took both her small hands in his, and kissed the trembling fingers.

*She is so good, so innocent, Father. Give her the strength of your presence. All of my life she has nurtured and cared for me. I know that her heart will be pierced by Sorrow's sharp sword one day. Stay near her, dear Abba,* he prayed silently.

Gloriel's eyes welled and darkened with compassion as Jesus lifted his heart in prayer for his mother.

Mary nodded. "Yes, Son, I understand." Her voice trembled for a moment as she flew back over the years in memory. "But I shall miss you so much. When will you return?"

*Ah, so the first seeds of sorrow begin to take root*, Gloriel thought.

"I'm not sure yet, Mother. I only know I must go first to the River Jordan." Ridden by a sad compassion, Jesus looked down tenderly at the fine-featured face he had loved for thirty years.

"Your Aunt Mary Elizabeth and I have prepared provisions for your journey, Son." Mary smiled tremulously, reaching up and smoothing back his shining brown hair. A stab of nostalgia brought up the vision of a tousled head of short gold ringlets.

"Thank you, Emi, I will be happy to have some of your good food to enjoy along the way." He patted her soft cheek gently.

Mary walked slowly across the room, and picked up Jesus' knapsack. "There is flat bread, dried fish, goat cheese and fig cakes, Son. We filled a wineskin and water bag, also."

Jesus took the knapsack from his mother's hands." I must leave now, Emi."

He hugged her once more, enfolding her slight form in his sinewy arms.

"Farewell, my son. God go with you," Mary breathed, her voice ragged. She patted his shoulder, strong and supple under the rough brown linen.

"Goodbye, Mother. I love you."

He released her from his embrace, glanced around the familiar spaces of his childhood home, and walked out the door.

Mary leaned against the doorpost, her still lovely face pale and drawn, quiet as marble. Bright silver tears trembled on her eyelids as she watched her beloved son striding resolutely toward the Unknown.

Jesus paused, turned, and waved at the small figure standing in the doorway. Heaving a sigh, he set forth on a journey leading toward his final destiny. His mind swirled with myriad memories.

He prayed silently as he walked through the familiar dusty streets of Nazareth. *Father, since my birth, you have drawn me close to your heart, and filled me with your boundless love. I turn to you now, as the Journey begins, for sustenance and strength for whatever lies ahead. I commit myself to love and serve you all the days of my life. The earth is filled with your awesome deeds, Abba. Help me to make your Glory known to the world.*

Gloriel walked beside her charge, listening closely to his thoughts. She felt an almost childlike delight. *Jesu, my Jesu, it begins*, she whispered into his subconscious.

They passed silently through the village gate as sunbeams sparkled through the ancient alder trees surrounding the sleepy town. Jesus walked resolutely, with long, purposeful strides toward a distant horizon edged with silver clouds.

#

To the north, Mt. Hermon, the "Ancient of Days", reared its lofty white head. The deep purple hills of Moab edged the southern view. A heavy mist hung over the waters of the lower reaches of the Jordan River, and the pungent odor of sulfur permeated the atmosphere. A few rest houses and an inn nestled along the river's edges at Bethebara. There, a ford and a bridge offered safe crossing to travelers.

A small clearing at the river's edge provided a place for the people who gathered to listen to the first visionary voice to be heard in over 500 years. *But this prophet's proclamations aren't what they expect*, Gloriel thought.

John's message, like no other they had ever heard, stirred something deep within their hearts. The inner turmoil that followed this self-examination exposed many of them to the teaching of the Holy Spirit, and so, they believed.

The lost and lonely, the cowardly and wicked, were finally hearing not only that the Most High was a righteous God, but that He truly loved them.

These were people drowning in desperation, on fire with the need for repentance; and many who heard the Lord's word through John abandoned their evil ways and turned to the Most High.

The crowd grew more and more excited as they listened to John, murmuring among themselves, yearning for solace and encouragement.

"It seems as though God has been silent for so long." An elderly man with a long curly white beard and cornflower blue eyes turned to a young man standing at the water's edge. "I had almost given up hope, until I heard rumors of a true prophet here at Bethebara. It appears that the rumors have truth to them. Have you traveled far, my son?"

"I come from Jerusalem," the youth replied, smiling at the old man. "But see! Not only have our people come, but also Arabs, Abyssinians, and Babylonians! Look over there! Those men with skin like ebony; they come from the Sudan. I heard that some of them have actually left their caravans to become John's followers," he exclaimed breathlessly.

"Ah, so his name is John?"

"Yes, sir. They call him 'John the Baptist'."

Both men regarded with wonderment the sinewy figure standing on a rock next to the fast-flowing waters. Very tall and lean, his skin nut-brown and weathered; he exhorted the crowds to turn to the Most High, repent of their sins, and be baptized.

John—Johannan, "Gift of Jehovah," clad only in a short camel's hair garment and a leather belt, loudly proclaimed the approaching Kingdom. His persuasive voice carried deep assurance to his listeners. The very air vibrated with his presence. Awe-inspiring power sprang from him, and many grew uncomfortable under his gaze. This caused numerous people to begin to believe that he was the Messiah, come at last.

John climbed down from the rock, his long, tangled dark curls blowing in the breeze. Wading out into the water, he raised his wiry arms toward heaven, and summoned the penitents.

"Repent! Repent, lest the final judgment come upon you, sinners! The Kingdom of Heaven is in sight! Turn away from evil thoughts and ways!" The powerful voice echoed off a circle of reddish hills.

His gaze settled on a group of Pharisees standing at the rear of the crowd. "Come, you den of snakes! Wash away your sins; be cleansed from all your filth! Prepare for the coming of the Messiah!" He shouted vehemently.

A gasp rippled through the crowd. The Messiah? The long-awaited Savior who was to free the people from their oppressors, and destroy their enemies with his rod of iron?

Within moments, large numbers of the people left the shore, wading through the swirling eddies and pressing around John, waiting to be immersed in the cleansing waters.

"I have come to prepare the way of the Lord! My purpose is to tell people about the One who will follow me." John's eyes burned bright with fervor, as if a fire crackled behind them.

Directed by the Spirit, his gaze swept over the milling crowd. "You generation of vipers! You snakes! Who warned you of the dreadful fury that is to come?" he cried hoarsely, glaring at those still reluctant ones standing on the shore. "You are all sinners, and Herod Antipas is among the worst of you!"

He pointed a long bony finger at a hapless, undecided transgressor standing ankle-deep in the waters. "You! Both you and Herod—adulterers! Repent, and throw yourselves on God's mercy!"

Stunned, the elderly man whispered to his young companion, "How does he know these things?" He turned toward John, visibly shaken, and asked apprehensively "Are you the Messiah?"

"I am not the Christ," John replied, pinning the stricken old man with a piercing stare.

The offender withered under the icy glare. "Then wh-who are y-you, sir? Are you Elijah?"

His gaze softening somewhat, John replied in the powerful words of the prophet Isaiah, *"I am a voice shouting in the wilderness. Prepare a straight pathway for the Lord's coming!"* Isaiah 40:3 NLT

Scattered among the crowd, messengers sent by the Pharisees to investigate John, questioned him further. "So, if you aren't the Messiah, and you aren't Elijah, who gives you the right to baptize?" one inquired boldly. "That sort of talk can get you arrested and jailed," he added smugly.

John replied, pinning the interrogator with the intensity of his stare. "Simply being descendants of Abraham doesn't make the Sadducees and Pharisees any better than everyone else. Although I baptize with water, there is among you, One who will soon begin his ministry, One whose sandals I am not worthy to untie. He is much greater than I, and he existed long before I was born. He will baptize you with fire, and the Holy Spirit." John's voice cracked with passion.

The messengers glanced around nervously at the people standing around them, and asked no more questions of John.

#

The following day, the spring sun danced through the trees along the banks, as John baptized the penitents one by one in the purifying muddy waters of the Jordan.

Standing among the throng on the shore, a tall figure in a brown linen tunic and woolen cloak watched silently. He began advancing toward John.

The Baptizer glanced up, paused, and looked intently at the man, then drew back abruptly. This was no sinner who approached him.

Jesus smiled warmly at him. "Hello, John. Peace be with you. I have need of baptism."

John demurred in a choked voice, "It is I who need to be baptized by you. Why do you come to me?"

He took another step backward, and shouted to the crowd, "Behold! This is the Lamb of God who takes away the sins of the world!"

A ripple of excitement passed through the throng

"He is the one of whom I spoke."

The people gasped and murmured among themselves.

At that moment, Jesus stepped forward and laid his hand on John's bony shoulder. Gloriel stood unseen at his side.

"This is most appropriate and fitting, and as it should be for now, John. It is best for us to fulfill all the requirements of the Most High's holiness."

Jesus stood waist deep in the waters, head bowed. Reluctantly, John lowered him into the water slowly. As he came up out of the river, the muddy water spume rustled like silk, and the Holy Spirit came down upon Jesus, in the form of a white dove.

A thrill passed through her as Gloriel recalled her first glimpse of the Lord who is Spirit. The dove descended gently on Jesus' bowed and streaming head. The angel gasped at the glory and majesty of the moment, as God the Father's powerful voice filled the heavens.

"This is my beloved Son. I am well-pleased with him." All the angels leaned down from Heaven and rejoiced.

Jesus raised his head as the Holy Spirit returned to the Heavens on swift and glorious wings.

A veil was lifted from John's vision then, and he recognized his cousin. Long-ago memories of family flooded his mind. The years in the wilderness, fasting and praying, subsisting on locusts and wild honey; these had stripped away his association with family and friends. The passionate fire within his soul had seared away connections to any except the Most High.

But here, standing before him, dripping wet and smiling broadly,—his cousin, Jesus—the Messiah? Johannen the Baptizer was speechless.

Among the people gathered along the shore, stood two of John's disciples. Stunned, the sons of Zebedee watched the astounding scene unfolding before them. They looked at one another open-mouthed with bewilderment and perplexity. Was this not their kinsman Jesus, from their hometown of Nazareth? Weren't his mother and theirs sisters? They hadn't seen him in years, not since Salome and Zebedee moved their family to Bethany. Yet they recognized him.

Immediately after his baptism by John, Jesus made his way through the thick undergrowth of bushes, reeds, and ferns edging the river. Heedless of thorns and branches snatching at his flesh, he withdrew by himself to spend some time in prayer.

Gloriel accompanied him, still rejoicing in the instigation of her charge's ministry.

Shadows and shafts of fading light lay across the healing vastness of the quiet desert as Jesus walked. Colors began to blend together as a dim twilight fell. He stopped and sat down on a rock, which still held the warmth of the sun.

Bowing his head, still damp from the baptismal waters, he prayed, "Father, Abba, I praise you for the Glory that fills my soul," he whispered.

Suddenly, he lifted his head, and a startled expression crossed his strong features. Gloriel watched, listening closely.

A faint tinkling of pure melody whispered into his consciousness. The music was vaguely familiar, but barely discernible, just brushing the edge of his awareness.

Gloriel smiled to herself. *"He's listening to the music of Heaven. He needs time alone to draw near to the Father and absorb the strength he needs."*

All at once, the whirring of powerful wings drowned out the soft song. Startled, Jesus searched the air around him. The sound of music still lingered entrancingly in his ear, and a sweet, familiar fragrance enveloped him. He closed his eyes, spellbound.

"My Son! Hear me now. You are to go into the desert for a time of testing and preparation. You will be utterly alone. Your angel guardian will withdraw. Go now, with my blessing, into the wilderness."

Jesus' eyes flew open, and he searched the surrounding twilight eagerly. Gloriel placed a trembling hand on his head. He appeared dazed and confused.

"Father, are you speaking to me? Angel guardian?" Jesus rubbed his eyes with shaking hands.

"You must go, Jesu, and do the Father's bidding. Farewell for now, until we can be together again," Gloriel whispered soothingly into his soul.

#

In a blinding flash of light, Gloriel found herself at the foot of the Throne, the familiar golden mist enveloping her.

"Well done, Gloriel. You have served my Son with wisdom and devotion. Now come and be with your companions for a time. You will need to get ready for the mission that lies ahead of you and my Son."

The dearly loved voice caressed her ears as the Throne faded slowly back into the mist.

"Welcome Home, Gloriel!"

"Gabriel! How wonderful it is to see you again!" A soaring joy filled her breast as Gabriel's warm voice greeted her.

The two angels embraced, while on a tiny, desolate speck of earth below, their Creator closed his weary eyes and slept.

# Chapter Twenty-Two

An horizon tinted with orange and gold shimmered in the first light of morning when Jesus awoke the following day. He breakfasted on the last of the goat cheese and dried figs which his mother had packed.

The smell of sulfur lay heavy in the warm air as he began his solitary trek. He had no idea where he was going, or how long he would be alone, and yet his heart grew light as he walked toward the unknown.

Ahead lay the source of the pungent odor. The Salt Sea, a gleaming silver strip on the horizon, was fed by springs from the surrounding hills. Beyond that, mountains rose like menacing giants, sleeping in the sun.

A clear azure sky embraced the bright sun overhead as he skirted the sea and left it behind.

"Father, lead me. Show me the way." Sweat beaded his forehead, and he paused to drink a few swallows from the water bag. Overhead, a white dove glided gracefully across the brilliant sky. Shading his eyes with his hands, Jesus followed its silent flight until it disappeared in the distance.

"Thank you, Father." The sound of his voice piercing the silence of the huge solitary desert felt comforting and peaceful.

At that point, he turned his footsteps in the same direction as the flight of the dove. He passed a few wizened trees bent by winds of the past, spreading out their knotted, lifeless branches like scrawny arms reaching to the heavens.

Incongruously, some wild crocuses, purple and gold, pushed their radiant royal heads through the rocky soil beneath the trees. Jesus bent down on one knee to admire the burst of color in the dreary vista.

The surrounding hills with their play of subtle colors trembled with radiance in the heat.

As the afternoon wore on, he found himself feeling renewed and invigorated, though he had eaten nothing since his meager breakfast.

The hills drew near as twilight approached. He came upon a weedy path meandering gently upwards, and began following it. Soon the ground reared steeply, and loose pebbles skittered away beneath his sandals. A snake slithered silently across the pathway ahead.

Breathing heavily, Jesus approached the rim of the hill. He skinned one knee as he scrabbled over the crest and stood erect on the wide craggy ridge of the summit.

Shading his eyes, he surveyed the landscape below.

An oasis of lush growth spread its verdant green a short distance away. A small grove of olive trees turned their silver faces to the setting sun, reflecting a tint of gold.

Jesus descended the rocky hillside, slipping and sliding. His skinned knee smarted and throbbed sharply.

He entered the oasis and relished the cool shade of the flourishing vegetation of palm trees, bougainvillea, and other colorful plants and trees. Patches of green grass surrounded him, tempting his weary body to lie down.

A small brook wandered aimlessly from side to side of the oasis. Through the trees, Jesus glimpsed the surrounding yellowish hills, dotted with numerous grottoes.

"Thank you, Father," he murmured aloud.

Squatting down by the stream, he washed his stinging knee in the brook. He dipped his fingers into the small blue eddies, cupped the clear water in his hands and splashed his grimy face with it.

He drank deeply of the sweet cool water, and then filled the water bag. All of the provisions were gone now, but he decided to carry the empty knapsack with him, anyway.

Yawning and stretching his weary limbs, he resolved to spend the night at the oasis. He spread out his robe on a patch of grass and lay down on his back, gazing up at the mingled purple and crimson of sunset tinting the sky overhead.

The next thing he knew, the following day dawned with the birth of a blustery north wind. It swept through the oasis, swirling a stinging cloud of dust with it. Jesus woke with a start, scrambling to his feet. His stomach rumbled and his mouth felt as dry as the Chalk Mountains beyond Jericho.

He crouched down, sat back on his heels and closed his eyes.

"I praise you, Father, Lord of Heaven and earth. Thank you for this day." The blustery wind blew his words away. "Where do I go from here, Abba? Guide my footsteps."

A sudden pang of homesickness snaked through his heart. *Emi, I miss you, and your cooking,* he thought, and smiled.

The wind continued moaning and howling through the treetops as Jesus knelt down on his uninjured knee and drank his fill of the clear stream water. After washing up, he hung the water bag from his belt. Standing up slowly in the stinging wind, he stretched his arms and winced as sore muscles protested.

Gloriel saw that he was tempted to remain in the oasis, which afforded some protection from the howling wind. He could hear it racing across the mountains with a banshee shriek.

The ochre half-light of the dust storm provided little help as Jesus left the oasis and blindly stumbled through the desert countryside.

"He can't even see where he is going!" Gloriel exclaimed to Gabriel as the two angels watched the scene below. "I want so much to help him," she sighed, rubbing her amber eyes as if she could feel the grit of the sandstorm.

"Yes, I know, Gloriel. So do I. But we must not interfere with the Father's plan," Gabriel reminded her, taking her hand.

Jesus shielded his eyes from the hot desert glare. "Father, I have no idea where I am going. I can't see the road ahead of me. Where am I now?" His throat felt parched and swollen, and his tongue clung to the roof of his mouth. His mouth and ears were full of grit.

Suddenly, he recalled the stories he had heard at his mother's knee. A vision of the Chosen People roaming the cruel and desolate desert wilderness searching for the Promised Land appeared before him in his mind's eye.

"Am I going to wander for forty years too, Father?" He laughed at himself then, and wiped his eyes with the hem of his tunic. "This is only the third day," he chided himself, shaking his head.

Gloriel grinned at Gabriel. "His sense of humor never fails him when he needs it."

Gradually, as the day wore on, the raw wind abated and a bright turquoise sky appeared overhead. Jesus could clearly see the Chalk Mountains now. Their gray slopes were cut by a dark gorge rushing headlong into the Jordan River. Reflected shards of sunlight gleamed from its undulating surface as the river wound like a serpent across the shining sands.

His strength renewed as he directed his steps toward the river's shores in the distance.

Two magnificent eagles swooped overhead, gliding on silent wings, their shadows rolling blackly over the wasteland.

Jesus arrived at the shores of the Jordan just as a soft mauve twilight crept over the waters. He knelt on one knee, cupped the cool water in his hands, and bathed his burning face.

On the shore across from him, three jackals slaked their thirst, their sharp, shifty eyes watching his every move.

His empty stomach protested noisily as he gulped the muddy water. Nearby, a fox stuck his curious black nose out of a hole in the riverbank. A hawk swooped down and skimmed over the rushing water, surveying her domain with a piercing eye.

"Go find your nest, sister bird; and may you sleep well in your cozy bed brother fox."

Jesus searched up and down the shoreline for a place to lie down and rest for the night. Brambles and bushes yielded no comfortable bed for the Son of God.

Gloriel kept a silent and powerless watch as her charge folded his robe to cushion a flat rock for a pillow.

The weary sojourner closed heavy eyelids over his stinging eyes as the third day in the wilderness drew quietly to a close.

#

Jesus opened his dark and sunken eyes slowly. At first, he couldn't recall where he was. His body ached. A chill ran over him as his eyes searched the dim, shadowy surroundings. It smelled musty and dank.

*Oh, yes . . . the cave.* He rose up on one elbow and shook his swimming head. Bright pinpoints of pain shot out from his joints.

"Oh, Gabriel, it's his 40th day of wandering. When will it end? He has had nothing to eat in all this time." Gloriel's golden eyes brimmed over with tears as she watched Jesus helplessly. "He's so hungry and exhausted. See how thin he is! I know this is part of the Father's Plan, but it's so hard to see him suffering!"

She yearned to caress the gaunt features, gnawed thin and sharp by hunger, and hardened by sun and searing air.

"Yes, it is, my friend. But see how keen and strong his mind and spirit have grown in these forty days," Gabriel replied, putting his arm around Gloriel's shoulders.

"Yes, yes, that's true. I see that clearly, Gabriel. It's just that I long so to comfort him." She smiled through her tears.

Jesus stumbled to his feet and staggered out the entrance of the cave, high on a barren hillside. He stood silent and tall and thin, his body laden with immense fatigue and gnawing hunger. Slowly, he lifted his face to the bleak gray sky, raising his arms toward Heaven.

The words of a beloved Psalm of King David burst from his cracked lips, *"Do not abandon me O Lord. Do not stand at a distance O God. Come, O Lord my Savior."* Psalm 28:21-22 NLT

Jesus' prayer evoked no reply within his spirit, no tide of love or reassurance.

Abruptly, he remembered the virtually sleepless night. Even the short periods of sleep were fitful and ridden by terrifying nightmares.

*The dream, the awful dream . . .* He was staggering up a narrow, boulder-strewn road that climbed around a lofty mountain. The summit blew with dark clouds. No trees, no grass graced its slopes, only rocks and yellowish-white cliffs. On and on he climbed, higher and higher, panting desperately for breath. A heavy weight crushed his shoulders. They screamed with the pain of the awful burden. He struggled to awaken, through a mist of pain, feeling as though he was stretched out on a bed of fire. The darkness seemed suffocating.

His eyes had flown open, then. Sweat gleamed on his moist and clammy skin. But his mind was lucid and clear.

The memory of the nightmare overpowered him briefly, and a sob caught in his throat.

He took a deep breath, and swept the panorama spread before him with drowsy eyes. A cool and pearly dawn began to suffuse the horizon with gold and rose. The desert lay at his feet, blending into distant hills the color of plums in the pre-dawn light. The air shone iridescent, and perfectly silent.

The sun slowly appeared, blazing on the rim of the hills. It lit up the wretched piece of land filled with rocks and thorn bushes at the base of the mountain.

Jesus' stomach rumbled and growled. He was hungry beyond any hunger he had ever imagined.

"Father, Abba, how long must I wander? What would you have me do? I am hungry and lonely." His humanity hesitated. "But whatever Your will may be, I accept it. Only help me to know what it is." His voice cracked and his throat felt gritty.

He had spoken to no one, nor seen another soul, for 40 days and nights. Pressing his hands over his face, he rocked back and forth. Silence lay deep on the sloping hillside.

"Jesus." The voice, smooth and well-modulated, seemed suspended close by his ear, soft and warm in his head.

Jesus dropped his hands, and his eyes flew open. "Who . . . ?"

"Peace be with you, Jesus."

He spun around, startled and puzzled. A vaguely familiar figure stood before him, tall and powerful. Large, expressionless sapphire blue eyes gazed back at him.

The figure lifted his eyebrows and reached out toward Jesus. "So, it's been a long time, my friend." His voice was mesmerizing. A faint smile curved his lips.

Clear memories flooded in, then. "Lucifer . . . Satan," Jesus whispered. "What are you doing here? What have you to do with me?" He stepped back involuntarily.

The faint smile became beguiling, wreathing Satan's aristocratic face.

Jesus remembered the imperious features of his old enemy.

#

From her heavenly vantage point, Gloriel watched anxiously as the drama continued below. Gabriel walked beside her, intrigued and baffled.

"Gabriel, do you know what Satan is doing there? I haven't seen him since the Fall, have you?"

"No, I don't know what he's doing there, and I haven't seen him either," he remarked in a perplexed tone. "But I do know he wants to test and tempt, always hoping to get God's people to sin. That's his mission and purpose now."

"Oh, Gabriel, Jesus is so tired and lonely and hungry," Gloriel said as they came into view of the Father's great Throne. "I need to be with him." Her voice shook as gleaming tears ran down her soft cheeks.

"Not yet, Gloriel, not yet!" The Father's voice was stern. "You must let him deal with Satan on his own. Just watch and wait."

The two angels bowed low before the Lord.

#

"Well, well, Jesus. So you think you have finally figured out Who you are?" Satan cleared his throat. "But it looks to me that you are faint with hunger. Here, let me help you . . ." He reached out again, stretching out his long fingers toward Jesus.

Stepping back again, Jesus replied firmly. "Don't touch me." He felt his skin crawl.

Satan's vacant blue eyes took on a hint of offense. "Sorry, I just want to help you, my friend. I know how hungry you are." He sidled a few inches closer to Jesus. "Tell you what. Since you are, or if you are, the Son of God, why don't you turn some of these stones into bread? That should be easy for you." He pointed to a few pebbles lying around the entrance to the cave.

Jesus hesitated. Just the thought of warm, fresh bread made his dry mouth water. He swallowed and cleared his throat. Looking Satan squarely in the eyes, he croaked

"No! The scriptures tell us that God's children need much more than bread to keep them alive. They must feed on His Word!"

"Oh, oh, I see. Sorry." Satan turned and gazed out over the desert, toward the purple mountains in the distance. "Well then, let's take a little tour, since you've been stuck here in this desert place for so long. Maybe you would enjoy a change of scenery." The voice was very soft.

Suddenly, Jesus was caught up in a whirlwind. Almost instantly, he found himself perched high on a pinnacle of the Temple in Jerusalem. The ancient city lay stretched out before his startled eyes. He gasped as the myriad odors of the city assaulted his nostrils. He could hear the faint voices of vendors hawking their wares, and the dim clatter of horses' hooves on the cobblestone streets. The vista was breathtaking. Dizzied, he leaned back and clung to the pinnacle with both hands, pressing back against its warm surface.

"Amazing, isn't it?" Satan's breath was in his ear again.

Distressed, Jesus drew back and felt one foot slip on the smooth golden surface of the Temple dome.

Satan reached out and grasped his arm. The sharp fingers burned fiery hot on his flesh. Jesus shook off his grip, shuddering.

"Don't be afraid, Jesus, after all, you ARE the Son of God, right? I would think you could even cast yourself down from here, and God's angels would immediately be here to save you." The soft voice hesitated. "Why don't you try it?" Satan's smiled sweetly. "Surely you have enough faith for that? For the scriptures say: *'For He orders his angels to protect you wherever you go. They will hold you with their hands to keep you from striking your foot against a stone.'* Psalm 91: 11-12 NLT

"Or perhaps you don't really believe that." Satan's gaze narrowed and he stared accusingly at Jesus, his eyes like blue stones.

Jesus returned Satan's stare steadily. "The scriptures also tell us that we must not put the Lord our God to the test." His voice was stronger now. He lifted his chin and straightened his shoulders, remembering his parents' teaching. *Emi . . . Avi . . .*

Gloriel's attention riveted on her charge. As if to lend him her own strength, she lifted her chin and straightened her shoulders. "Oh, Jesu, stay strong," she breathed, knowing full well he was prevented from hearing her now.

Without a word, Satan extended his long arm toward a distant mountain top. Instantaneously, Jesus found himself standing on the crest of that mountain, the breeze catching his hair and robe in its swirling grasp.

He stood breathless with awe at the amazing panorama at his feet. He could see what seemed like all the great cities and nations of the world, gleaming and glittering in the bright sunlight. He turned slowly around, caught up in the grandeur displayed before his startled eyes. Some of the cities were so magnificent; they seem almost alive in their splendor.

"Wonderful, is it not, my friend?"

The beguiling voice was soft and silky-smooth in his ear again. He could see Satan's tall figure out of the corner of his eye. He did not turn his head to look. The marvelous scene was gripping and thrilling, and he could not tear his gaze away from it.

"So, Jesus, wouldn't you like to have all these wondrous cities and nations, in all their glory, for your very own?" The voice flowed like golden honey, dripping in sweetness and soft as velvet.

Jesus made no reply.

"Sheli, I will give all of this to you, every powerful nation and every beautiful city. Wouldn't you love that?"

He breathed quietly, a mere whisper now. "All you have to do is bow down now and worship me—such a little thing for such a wonderful reward . . ."

Jesus turned slowly and looked full into the face of the Enemy. His brown eyes shone clear and bright with a light glowing like a lamp in their depths.

"Get out of here, Satan," he snapped. "Leave me alone! For it is written in my Father's Word: *'You must worship the Lord your God; serve only him.'*" Deuteronomy 6:13 NLT

Satan's expression altered then, darkening, and slipping into shadow. Gradually, without another word, he faded away in silence and defeat.

Jesus closed his eyes, unutterable weary, and faint with exhaustion. He shook his head painfully.

"Abba, my Abba, thank you."

He slowly opened his eyes, and gasped. Glancing around, he realized that he was back at the entrance of the cave. Abruptly, his knees folded under him, and he sank to the ground with a groan.

#

"Gloriel! The Father is calling for us. Come quickly!" Gabriel's tone was urgent. He and Michael each took hold of one of her arms, and whisked her over the glittering sea of glass, the golden mist parting before them. In but a moment, the three angels bowed low before the presence of the Lord God on the great shining Throne.

"My angels, lift up your heads and your hearts." The Father's voice was music in their ears; comforting, encouraging. "My Son needs you now, Gloriel. The moment has finally come for you to reveal yourself to him."

It seemed to Gloriel that the voice had a smile in it, and her heart took wings.

"My Son has triumphed over the Enemy's wiles and temptations. But he is exhausted and weak with hunger. Go to him now, all three of you, and minister to all his needs; physical, mental and spiritual."

Gloriel felt as though she was going to burst with joy. So many long years, waiting to reveal herself to her beloved charge, and now the moment had finally arrived.

#

In the blink of an eye, the three angels found themselves standing next to Jesus' prostrate form.

"He's unconscious," Gloriel cried, sitting down on the ground and lifting his limp head into the crook of her arm.

Gabriel and Michael knelt down beside Jesus and Gloriel. Michael noticed a knapsack lying next to Jesus on the hard-packed dirt of the cave entrance. He reached over, dragged it closer, and opened it.

The warm fragrance of fresh-baked bread drifted out of the sack, followed by the distinctive aromas of roast lamb, braised fish, cheese, figs, and honeycomb.

Michael spread the fragrant victuals out on a cloth buried beneath them in the knapsack. "This bag seems to be bottomless," he remarked with a grin.

Gabriel spotted a leather flask lying nearby and opened it. Goat's milk, frothing and cool, bubbled from its mouth.

"Jesu, Jesu, wake up . . ." Gloriel murmured softly to her charge. She bathed his grubby forehead and face with a cloth soaked in cool water from another flask lying by her side.

Jesus' brow and cheeks were cut with deep lines of pain and weakness, his lips swollen and cracked. He moaned, eyelids fluttering against his haggard cheeks.

Gloriel raised his head higher, placing the water bag to his mouth. The cool water flowed over his lips, and ran down his neck. He opened his mouth and swallowed painfully. His eyes flickered open, and he blinked in the bright sunlight.

Gloriel smiled at him, her amber eyes shining with love. "Hello, Jesu. Try to drink slowly."

Her soft voice trembled slightly. Amber hair curled around her face in a brilliant aureole.

"Who-who are you?" Jesus whispered hoarsely, his eyes widening at the vision holding him in her arms.

She helped him sit up. "Jesu, I am Gloriel, your guardian angel. I have been with you since you were born," she replied, bestowing her bright smile on him. "And I will be with you until you return to the Father."

"Gloriel, I . . ." his voice failed him, and he closed his eyes briefly.

He looked up again, and saw Gabriel and Michael sitting quietly nearby, their magnificent wings furled. A faint recollection stirred in his mind, but he could not quite remember . . . All three angels seemed familiar to him.

"Jesus, I am Michael. We are here to care for your needs, and to help you recover your strength." Michael reached out and laid his hand on Jesus' thin shoulder. "We have food and drink prepared for you," he said, pointing to the hearty meal laid out on the cloth.

Jesus smiled weakly and look inquiringly at Gabriel, who sat by Michael's side, beaming. The angel's hazel eyes sparkled in the sunlight. "My name is Gabriel," he said, handing a plate of roast lamb to Jesus. "You should eat now, and then rest, Jesus. Michael and I will remain with you and Gloriel until you are ready to begin your ministry."

#

Misty gold shafts of morning light pierced through the trees as Gloriel, Michael and Gabriel stood watch. A lone bird twittered in the branches overhead as Jesus lay sleeping on the grass of the oasis. His exhaustion had taken its toll outside the entrance to the cave. He fell into a deep sleep as soon as he had devoured the plate of lamb and a few figs. The three angels then whisked him away to the oasis where he had rested before on his desert journey.

"He looks so vulnerable," Gloriel whispered, smoothing back the lank, disheveled hair from his forehead.

"But we know he has tremendous strength and courage, Gloriel," Michael commented, "as well as great faith."

"He's ready to begin his ministry now," Gabriel said, taking Gloriel's hand.

"Yes, yes he is. He needs just a little more food and rest." She smiled at her two dear companions.

A pack of jackals voiced their sharp cries nearby, penetrating the calm of the oasis and awakening the sleeping Jesus. He sighed deeply and rubbed his eyes, blinking in the pale light. Rising up on one elbow, he smiled at the angels gathered around him. "I remember now. I am ready," he whispered huskily.

"Just a little more rest, Jesu," Gloriel replied gently. "Only a little while . . ."

*He was out among the wild animals, and angels took care of him.* Mark 1:12-13 NLT

## Chapter Twenty-Three

The sun etched a pale blue sky with streaks of light early the next morning as Jesus and Gloriel bid farewell to Gabriel and Michael in the oasis. The two angels made certain that there were enough supplies to get Jesus to his destination. They embraced him and Gloriel warmly as they prepared to leave.

"Stay strong, Jesus," Gabriel said, his eyes sparkling cheerfully. "We will be watching and praying, along with the rest of the Heavenly Host." He placed a hand on Jesus' shoulder.

"Shalom, Jesus." Michael clasped both Jesus' hands in his own. "The Most High is with you always," he said, in a slightly choked voice.

Gloriel reminded Jesus she would be with him until his homecoming to Heaven. "I will remain unseen, unless it becomes necessary to take on my bodily form, Jesu," she said, smiling gently at her charge. *He looks well-rested and ready to take on this world*, she thought contentedly.

Jesus looked around slowly at the three angels-those beings afire with love. "My dear companions, I am so reluctant to leave you. I will always be grateful for your devoted care, and I shall miss you sorely." His large dark eye shimmered bright with tears, as he was enveloped by a powerful sense of love and protection.

His seamless robe, lovingly fashioned by his mother, was once more unstained, and freshly laundered. The knapsack overflowed with fresh provisions, and a water skin filled with cool water hung from his belt.

"I am well-prepared to begin the mission my Father has planned for me. Thank you, my friends."

As he stood smiling at them, Michael and Gabriel vanished, leaving no trace of their splendid presence.

Gloriel sighed and smiled affectionately at Jesus. "I will miss them, too. Jesu, but we should be going now. The journey begins."

"Yes, Gloriel, it begins. But first, I must see John again. We should go back to Bethebara to see if he is still there."

"I am with you, Jesus, wherever you go." Gloriel stood radiantly beautiful in the brilliant sunshine, her golden eyes like autumn leaves, gleaming.

Jesus turned and gazed toward the distant desert horizon, vast and lonely with its palette of muted colors. He felt invigorated and eager to start his mission. Closing his eyes briefly, he breathed deeply of the warm, fragrant air. Birdsong filled the oasis and touched his soul with joy.

He turned back toward the angel. "Gloriel, you . . ." he blinked in surprise. His angel companion had disappeared.

#

Jesus approached Bethebara with a spring in his step and a light heart. He slipped in among the crowd lining the shore of the Jordan River. John had many followers, and several disciples who were hanging on his words.

*The throng has grown considerably in the past weeks,* Gloriel noted, standing unseen at Jesus' side.

The sweet, wild blue breeze of an early spring afternoon swept the shoreline and the river's deep emerald surface. The sparkling sun seemed to dance through the trees along the banks.

Jesus edged closer to the water, mingling with the people. He looked neither to right nor left now, but kept his gaze fixed on John.

The Baptist stood waist deep in the swirling waters of the river. Passionate and uncompromising, he exhorted the crowd with his powerful voice. "You must repent! Turn from your wicked ways, and embrace the truth!" His face shone eager with zeal. "The Kingdom of Heaven is very near! Repent, and prepare for the Passover Feast!"

His smoldering eyes settled on the Pharisees and Sadducees among the people. "Beware, you snakes!" he thundered, pointing a bony finger at the hapless group. His voice broke with emotion.

He had been speaking for hours, with no apparent need for rest or nourishment. His knife-like stare swept the assemblage slowly. He lowered his voice, and some listeners had to strain to hear him then.

"All who repent, I will baptize in these waters." He indicated the river surrounding him, with a sweep of his long arm. "But there is One who is to follow me, who will baptize with the Holy Spirit, and with fire!" His voice rose again to a crescendo as his fire and passion held the audience spellbound.

A few people in the crowd murmured among themselves. "Who is he talking about?" one of the Pharisees said to his companions. "What does he mean, 'baptize with fire'?"

A fisherman named Andrew, a tall, husky man deeply browned by his days in the sun, stood on the shore with his friend and business partner, John.

Andrew called out to the Baptist. "Tell us when we will see this man, Teacher. Where is he now? Are you talking about the Messiah?"

John regarded him calmly, shading his eyes with his hands. "He will come soon, Andrew. But many of you will not recognize him," he said, again turning his black stare on the Sadducees and Pharisees.

The crowd parted as Jesus drew nearer the shore. He stopped at the edge of the water, smiling brightly at John.

The people grew silent as John unexpectedly ceased speaking and looked intently at the striking tall figure in the light brown seamless robe.

He reacted as though a vision had suddenly materialized before his eyes. He shook his shaggy head as if to clear it.

"Behold!" he cried out in his fiery style, "the Lamb of God, who will bear the sins of the whole world!"

An excited murmur coursed through the gathering. John quieted them with an outstretched arm.

Andrew and his friend John glanced at one another in surprise, as the Baptist waded through the murky green water, approaching Jesus.

His cousin reached out and embraced John warmly. "John, it is good to see you again." His deep voice was music to John's ears. Although the Baptist was the taller of the two, Jesus seemed to tower over him.

A shiver surged down Andrew's spine, a chill finger tracing from neck to base. "He truly must be the Messiah," he whispered to John, his voice quavering.

"I must decrease as you increase. For it is you who brings salvation to the people," the Baptist murmured. He turned to the crowd. "Hear me! I am not the Messiah, but only a messenger sent before him to open the way! Behold, both the son of man, and his Savior!" He exclaimed joyfully, placing a sinewy hand on his cousin's shoulder. A hush fell on the enthralled crowd.

Consternation and anger swept over the Sadducees and Pharisees. Darting murderous looks at John, they turned and left the riverside, quarrelling fiercely among themselves.

Jesus' eyes roamed over the assembly and settled on Andrew and his partner. Andrew's alert green eyes, bright in the dark frame of his weathered face, returned Jesus' gaze, looking confused and dazed. His partner stood at his side, equally bewildered and confused.

With his hand resting on John's lean shoulder, Jesus turned and looked lovingly at the Baptist.

"John, I must set the Most High's Plan in motion now. Shalom, peace be with you. We shall not meet again in this world." Jesus' voice was shaded with sorrow, and his eyes shone bright with tears.

Abruptly, he turned and strode away from the shore. Gloriel followed, unseen.

Andrew and John, both followers of the Baptist, hesitated momentarily, then trailed close behind. Andrew's curly auburn hair and beard shone in the sunlight as he stretched his long legs to overtake Jesus. John scurried along behind him, his shorter legs pumping.

Andrew was eager to spend time with Jesus so that he could confirm in his own mind what the Baptist had declared.

*I don't know what to call him*, Andrew thought, as he hurried to catch up with Jesus.

"Master!" The name sprang naturally to his lips, startling him for a moment. "Master, wait!"

Jesus halted and turned around. "What are you looking for, my friends?" he inquired, warmly.

*He already knows the hearts of both these men, and what they seek*, Gloriel realized.

"Master, can we talk to you?" Andrew asked, breathlessly.

"Of course. Come with me. We will stay in Capernaum tonight, and talk as much as you like." Jesus smiled amenably.

"This man, Andrew, seeks Truth with a passion," Gloriel whispered into Jesus' consciousness. "He's thoughtful, meditative, and will lead many people to you, Jesu. He will serve you in countless small ways. But it is John who will be especially dear to you; for Truth is his true love. Although, in his zeal, he can be a bit of an extremist."

One corner of Jesus' mouth curved up in a covert smile.

By then it was late afternoon, and rays of golden sunlight slanted low over the sandy road. The three men were silent on their walk to Capernaum, the largest town on the northern shore of the Sea of Galilee.

When they arrived, they soon found lodging at a local inn. Gloriel listened and watched as Jesus talked far into the night, responding to eager questioning from the two excited and enthralled men. He spoke of John's teaching, and confirmed everything the Baptist had said. He revealed a depth and power to John's words that Andrew and John had never really grasped until now.

The two were convinced by Jesus' manner, his words, and his very presence. They heard enough to be persuaded that this charismatic man was indeed worth following.

*And so Andrew and John become Jesu's first disciples*, Gloriel mused.

Early the next morning, after a brief sleep, Andrew and John set out for the nearby shores of the Sea of Galilee. Convinced they had found the Messiah, Andrew's face radiated excitement. His heart was eager to share the good news with his brother, Simon.

Andrew and Simon were partners with John and his brother James, in a thriving fishing business. Years ago, the four had moved with their families from their birthplace in Bethsaida to the thriving town of Capernaum.

Andrew was breathless with excitement as he approached Simon, who was sitting on the sand along the shore, busily mending their fishing nets. His hair, a deep rich red, hung loose, framing a red-bearded face and deep-set green eyes. He was so absorbed in his work, that he didn't notice Andrew and John approaching.

James, John's brother, sat in a boat a short distance offshore, busily hauling in a net, his shoulders gleaming with sweat. The sun shone warmly, and the smell of the drying nets filled the damp air. A lazy flock of seagulls circled overhead.

"Simon! Simon!" Andrew, breathless with excitement, collapsed in a heap on the sand beside his brother.

John followed close behind, panting in his struggle to keep up with Andrew.

"Simon, we have found the Christ! Come, you must come and see him now! Leave the nets!" Andrew gasped, pulling impatiently on Simon's muscular arm.

"James, James, you must come, too!" John called out excitedly to his brother, motioning him to row into shore.

#

As James, John, Simon and Andrew approached, Jesus gazed fixedly at Simon.

"Jesu," Gloriel whispered, "this is the man appointed by the Father to lead your disciples. He is impetuous and brash, quick-tempered, and sometimes undependable. But he is destined to be an unforgettable shepherd."

Jesus greeted the four men, smiling, and grasping their hands one by one. When he came to Simon, he looked deeply into the clear green eyes under bushy red brows. He laid his hands on both of Simon's broad shoulders.

"Simon, son of John," he said in a husky voice, "we have a long and stony road ahead of us."

A puzzled expression moved over Simon's broad face. A simple man, he was totally without guile. He looked at Jesus curiously, raising his eyebrows questioningly.

"I will follow you anywhere, Rabbi," he replied quickly, to his own amazement. A wisp of a smile curled the corners of his mouth. Jesus nodded and patted Simon's back.

After this first encounter with Jesus, Peter and Andrew, James and John, returned to Capernaum, and continued working with their fishing boats while they waited for his summons.

## Chapter Twenty-Four

Mary glanced around the crowded room expectantly. This was the third day of the wedding festivities at Cana, a small hill town in Galilee, not too far from Nazareth. The celebration was at its peak.

*Will he be here today?* She wondered to herself. *It's been so long since I've seen him. I can hardly wait.* A small crease crinkled her brow as she clasped her hands together.

Sariel stood nearby, ever-watchful of her charge, and acutely aware of Mary's anxiety.

Turning to her companion, Mary murmured. "I know Jesus would not miss Seth's wedding, Salome, and he was invited." Her brown eyes glowed bright with anticipation. "Jesus and Seth were such good friends after we moved to Egypt. We were so delighted when he and his parents moved to Cana from Alexandria five years ago."

Salome smiled and patted Mary's hand. "Yes, Mary, I know." she replied. "Seth's bride is so lovely, isn't she? Her father has arranged a really beautiful wedding. Everyone is having a wonderful time. By the way, James and John should be here, also. Zebedee and I just heard from them a few days ago. They sent a message from Capernaum with a caravan passing through Nazareth," she confided.

"Oh, Sister, there they are," Mary whispered, breathless with excitement. "Over there, by the door, see them?" She grasped Salome's shoulders and turned her toward the group of men just entering the wedding tent. "Come on, Salome," she said.

"I see James and John, too," Salome cried eagerly.

The two women threaded their way through the guests, eager to greet their sons. The men stood in the doorway, framed against the dazzling morning sunlight streaming into the tent.

"Jesus! Jesus!" Mary called out as they approached the small group of men, abandoning her usual quiet public demeanor.

Jesus turned his head quickly at the sound of the familiar voice. His face lit up when his eyes fell on his mother's sweet features.

"Mother!" he cried out joyfully, clasping her slight form in his long arms and lifting her off the floor.

Mary felt his shoulders strong and supple under the coarse brown muslin of his robe.

"Oh, my son, my son," Mary whispered against his chest. Tears smarted her eyelids as she hugged him tightly.

Gloriel and Sariel, unseen, greeted one another with delight.

"Sariel, it is so good to see you."

"Oh, Gloriel, it seems forever since we were together last."

"Yes, and this will be a very special day, long remembered, my friend," Gloriel replied.

"How so, Gloriel? Are the bride and groom special in the Most High's eyes?"

"All are special to Him, don't you agree, Sariel? But just watch closely. God's glory will be shown in a clear way today," Gloriel replied, grinning surreptitiously.

Four other disciples accompanied Jesus as he approached the bridegroom and bride. Holding Mary's arm, he kept her close by his side, guiding her through the revelers.

"Jesus!" the bridegroom cried out happily, when he saw his friend's sun-browned face approaching through the crowd. "Jesus! Welcome! I was afraid you weren't going to make it." He seized Jesus in a bear-hug, his shining black eyes mirroring his pleasure.

"How could I miss my old friend's wedding, Seth?" Jesus laughed, returning the hug. "Now, introduce us to your lovely bride." Jesus disengaged from his friend's embrace and smiled down at the vision standing before them.

Radiant in her traditional bridal garment, Seth's bride returned Jesus' smile. The white silk gown flowed in soft folds over her slight, delicately formed figure. A band of blue, denoting her purity, edged the hem of the garment.

"She is Egyptian, Sariel," Gloriel confided to the little angel. "She and Seth were betrothed before his family moved here. But her family didn't arrive until two years ago."

"She's so beautiful, Gloriel. Her hair is black as a raven's wing." Sariel responded.

Both angels were suddenly reminded of another ebony-haired and beautiful bride.

"Jamila, this is my childhood friend, Jesus ben Joseph. Jesus, may I present my bride," Seth said, flushing with pleasure.

Jamila's wide-set almond-shaped eyes sparkled brightly beneath winged black brows. Her features were serene and clear, her mouth full and sensual.

An Egyptian necklace, fringed with gold and small amber jewels circled her slender neck.

Jesus inclined his head and grinned. "Shalom, Jamila. May you find much happiness and peace in your marriage."

"Thank you, Jesus. I'm very pleased to meet you. Seth has told me so much about you. Even about your little wooden ball," she replied mischievously, beaming up at her bridegroom.

Jesus smiled affectionately at his old friend. "So, you have a long memory indeed, Seth."

There was an ivory flash of teeth behind Seth's black beard. "How could I ever forget your eager willingness to share your treasure?" he replied, teasingly.

Jesus clapped Seth on the shoulder, laughing out loud.

Calling his disciples over, Jesus introduced them to the bride and groom.

Seth and Jamila urged them all to help themselves to the banquet table and to join in the festivities.

Mary led Jesus over to greet Seth's mother, Leah, who welcomed him warmly, patting his shoulder.

"Jesus, it is wonderful to see you again. Seth still talks about his happy memories of your friendship. Please, enjoy yourself, join in the dancing," she sang out cheerfully.

Festivities were in full swing. Music and laughter filled the large tent as the wedding celebration continued. Wedding garments in a variety of hues and materials added bright spots of color to the surroundings.

The pungent fragrance of roast lamb permeated the air, along with the lively music and merriment. Tables stood laden with rich cheeses, bowls of curds, breads and honeycomb. Peaches showed off their creamy cheeks among rich purple clusters of grapes, sweet melons, and nuts in silver bowls displayed on ivory silk tablecloths.

The guests drank copiously of the chilled wine, as if it were water.

Mary and Leah took leave of Jesus to help Jamila's mother in the kitchen.

Sariel and Gloriel, enjoying their reunion, looked on with delight.

As evening drew near, the merriment continued, the guests taking great pleasure in the abundance of food and wine.

Outside, the sun sank swiftly into the horizon, flinging long fingers of shadow across the landscape.

Servants began lighting the oil lamps inside the wedding tent as deepening purple shadows gathered in the corners.

Mary approached her son and drew him aside from the crowd. Gloriel and Sariel accompanied them.

"Son," Mary said quietly, "they have no wine." Her eyes were clear and warm. Jesus looked deep into their depths. A small frown appeared between his brows. Mary's gaze did not waver.

"It's a great embarrassment for the family to fall short of this responsibility," Gloriel murmured to Sariel. "It's their duty to make sure there's plenty of wine."

"Why is Mary telling Jesus this, I wonder?" Sariel commented. "It's obvious she wants him to take care of the problem. But I cannot sense her reasoning right now, Gloriel. Do you know what's happening?"

"I think Mary expects him to do something, Sariel." Gloriel replied, absorbed in the scene unfolding. "She's simply bringing the problem to her son."

A few moments passed before Jesus responded. "Woman, how does this concern you and me? It's not my time yet," he said in low tones.

"Hmm . . . He's using the formal "woman" address, instead of 'Mother'. Interesting . . ." Gloriel mused to her companion.

"Ah, Mary is thinking that his ministry is beginning, that he has already been revealed as the Lamb of God. I see that now," Sariel replied.

"But he will respond to Mary's request in a way that doesn't draw attention to himself, Sariel. No one will know the miracle stems from him, except the servants and Jesu's disciples," Gloriel said, smiling. "However, most servants are prone to gossip at times, don't you think?"

"Miracle?" Sariel questioned, a puzzled expression crossing her sweet features.

Mary turned and beckoned to six servants standing nearby. With quiet conviction, she directed them. "No matter what he tells you, do it," she said, placing a hand on Jesus' arm and smiling gently up at him.

Gloriel whispered in Jesus' ear. He paused thoughtfully, and then turned to the servants.

Lined up against the side of the tent, in the dim light, stood six large stone water jugs, each capable of holding 20 or 30 gallons of water. The supply was running low after three days of celebration.

"This water is for the guests' purification before they eat," Gloriel commented to Sariel.

"Yes, I remember, at Suzanne's wedding they had eight jars."

Jesus closed his eyes momentarily, and sighed deeply. He opened them and nodded to his mother. Turning to the servants, he said in a low voice, "Fill the jars to the brim with water," pointing to the nearly empty water pots.

The servants shouldered the jars and bore them outside to a nearby well, where they filled them all to the brim with clear, cold water. When they returned and placed their burdens on the ground before Jesus and Mary, Jesus instructed them further.

"Dip some out now, and take it to the master of the wedding feast."

A tall young servant with bright blue eyes and hair the color of honey stepped forward, wearing a bewildered expression. He dipped a cup into one of the jars and took it to the master steward. The man tasted the sparkling liquid and blinked in surprise.

The master sought out the bridegroom and called him aside from the guests. Looking very mystified, the steward questioned Seth.

"Always, the family sets out the finest wine at the beginning of the wedding celebration. Then after the guests have had plenty to drink, they bring out the poorer quality wine, when the people won't notice its inferiority. But you have kept the best wine until now!" he exclaimed. "I don't understand."

Sariel and Gloriel smiled at one another.

"Sariel, isn't it wonderful that Jesu cares enough about the hosts of the feast to save them from embarrassment? He cares enough about the guests that he made the very finest wine, and he cares enough about his mother's concern that he heeded her. How loving and thoughtful our Jesu is!" Gloriel exclaimed with delight.

The two angels watched curiously as Seth gazed at the master of the feast, his brow knitted in bafflement.

"I don't know what you're talking about, Caleb. I only know the wine supply was getting low, and I was concerned that we might run out. But there was no more wine!" The two men stared at one another in consternation.

The music and the merriment continued uninterrupted, the guests oblivious to the miracle which had occurred in their midst.

However, Jesus' disciples, never far from his side, had witnessed the whole scene unfold. Only they, his mother and the servants knew that it was Jesus who had turned the water into wine. So, for the first time, James and John and the four other disciples beheld a manifestation of Jesus' power.

This miraculous sign at Cana in Galilee was Jesus' first manifestation of his glory. And his disciples believed in him.

When the wedding celebration was over, at his invitation, Mary accompanied Jesus and his disciples back to Capernaum.

As they left on their journey, the young golden-haired servant gazed after them, blue eyes glistening in the morning light.

## Chapter Twenty-Five

Gloriel and Sariel accompanied their charges to Capernaum, where Jesus had decided to settle. They felt that this was a wise choice on Jesus' part, since Capernaum was located on the Damascus highway, where his teaching would be likely to spread more quickly than in the isolated country community of Nazareth.

When they arrived in town, Gloriel whispered to Jesus, "Jesu, this is the best place to settle. You will be able to preach your message and teach, without drawing the attention of the religious leaders and politicians in Jerusalem. People from so many different walks of life live here," she added.

Jesus was eager to begin his ministry. At Andrew's and Peter's invitation, he and his mother settled into the brothers' house.

It was a large house with several rooms surrounding a spacious courtyard. The garden in the courtyard was drenched in sunlight when Jesus and Mary arrived. The bright, insistent twittering of birds filled the fragrant air with cheeps and trills. Bees hummed lazily among the roses. Jesus and Mary paused to breathe in the heady fragrances of the garden before entering the house.

Three families lived in the house; Peter's, Andrew's and Peter's mother-in-law's.

When he and Mary had settled into the busy household, Jesus began teaching in the local synagogue every Sabbath. When he first entered the building, he attracted little attention.

"He looks just like any other ordinary Galilean, Sariel. There's nothing about his appearance to indicate any special powers or authority." Gloriel whispered to her small angel companion the first time Jesus spoke in the small synagogue.

But then he began to teach with authority, with conviction, and his words pierced the hearts of the local people. More and more of the populace of Capernaum gathered to listen in astonishment to this amazing man who spoke with such great power and confidence. His fame began to spread throughout the countryside surrounding the town.

Early one morning as he was starting up the steps of the synagogue, a middle-aged man in dirty, tattered clothing approached him and began shouting loudly in a hoarse voice.

"Get out of here! Get out of here!" The man's eyes glittered wildly.

Jesus stopped and turned toward the gaunt-faced creature.

"He is possessed by one of Satan's demons, Jesu!" Gloriel's warning came swiftly.

The man lunged forward menacingly, his face distorted with rage. A dark beard hung tangled and filthy on his bony chest. His mouth twisted scornfully, spittle dribbling from one corner.

"Why do you come here to annoy us? Do you mean to destroy us? We know who you are!" His voice dripped with contempt. "You are the Holy One—God sent you here!"

The man's eyes burned black and empty in a face glimmering with sweat as Jesus' gaze probed deeply into them.

Then Jesus raised both hands. "Be quiet!" He commanded the demon loudly, his voice hard, resounding off the synagogue walls and echoing down the street. "Come out of him now!"

The creature fell headlong onto the synagogue steps, thrashing wildly, screaming, and foaming at the mouth. Abruptly, the demon fled with a disembodied shriek. The exhausted man lay quietly at the feet of Jesus. The early morning sun reflected off his pale but peaceful features.

The crowd surrounding the steps of the synagogue gasped, whispering among themselves in hushed voices. "Who is this man? His power and authority are so great that even the demons obey him!"

Jesus reached down, grasped the man's hand, and helped him to his feet. "Go home in peace, Jared, and stay close to the Most High. His mercy has brought you back whole and healthy to your family," he said, placing his hand on the man's matted, mangy hair, which hung in ragged clumps about his stunned face.

"The story of this deed will spread like a wild fire throughout Galilee, I think, my friend." Gloriel whispered to Sariel. She beamed at the little angel.

"Oh yes, Gloriel, indeed it will!"

From then on, Jesus began to preach "Turn from your sins and turn to God, because the Kingdom of Heaven is near."

#

"Mother," Jesus said as he escorted Mary to the synagogue the next morning. "I'm going to Jerusalem for the Feast of Passover. I'll be leaving tomorrow."

Mary stumbled slightly, and he grasped her arm. She stopped, turning to face her son. Her questioning expression emphasized the fine lines creasing her skin.

*She's beginning to look older,* Jesus thought to himself as he smiled down at the beloved face. *Her hair has quite a bit of silver in it now.*

"I think you should return to Nazareth now," he continued in a gentle voice. "You should be with our family while I am traveling, Emi." The childhood endearment slipped out easily.

Mary's brown eyes flooded with emotion as her cheeks paled. "Oh, Son, I want to be with you."

"I know, Mother, I know. I want to be with you, too," he said, touching her face. "But I will be there soon to see you, I promise. Please do this for me. A friend of Andrew's is leaving for Nazareth in two days. He has agreed to escort you home."

Mary's usually placid expression struggled with tears.

"All right, Son, if this is what you want," she replied, sighing deeply.

"Yes, Mother, it is. Thank you." He cupped her chin in his hands and kissed her soft cheek.

#

Gloriel and Sariel bid one another goodbye two days later, as Mary reluctantly left Capernaum with Andrew's friend Arach, and his family.

The air was heavy with the scent of drying grass as the sun stared down from a brilliant blue sky. Jesus stood on the dusty road, waving and smiling at his mother. He remained watching until the small caravan disappeared from sight.

He looked down then at the package wrapped in rough muslin which his mother had placed in his hands when she kissed him goodbye. Curious, he opened it slowly. Inside, lay the soft folds of a finely woven, seamless robe, the color of heavy cream. It felt silky and soft to his touch as he smoothed it with his fingertips.

"Oh, Emi," he whispered, "how many long hours did you work at the spinning wheel to make this for me?" An enormous tenderness filled his breast, and tears clogged his throat.

Gloriel looked on with compassion for her charge. Memories of the young toddler clinging to his mother's knees flooded her mind, and tears trembled on her eyelashes as she flew back in remembrance over the years.

Jesus turned and walked slowly back into Peter's house, lost in thought. "Goodbye, Mother. I must be about my Father's business now," he said quietly under his breath.

"So, Jesu, your first journey as the Anointed One begins. Change is part of the Father's plan for you, but you will also discover great joy, and contentment beyond your hopes and dreams," Gloriel whispered into his consciousness.

He smiled and inhaled deeply of the velvety spring air.

Early the next morning, pink light seeped across the sky as Jesus, Peter, James and John, along with Andrew and a growing number of disciples set out for the Feast of Passover in Jerusalem. Among the disciples, the tall young golden-haired servant from Cana followed closely behind Jesus.

The atmosphere already held the warmth of a late spring day. The group of men was light-hearted as they strode briskly down the sandy road to Jerusalem. A sense of adventure and purpose surrounded them, and their laughter filled the soft air.

#

As the golden dome of the Temple came into view three days later, a cacophony of sound rose from the teeming courtyard. Jesus frowned and increased his pace.

The group entered the gate to the courtyard and stopped abruptly, amazed at the scene in front of them.

Cattle and sheep, awaiting their fate, milled about, lowing and bleating among piles of dung and sheep droppings. Some even stood on the steps of the Temple. The stench and press of animal bodies drenched the air. Cages of doves fluttered their wings frantically. Money-changers shouted, standing behind their counters, vying for attention.

Gloriel watched as Jesus stood stock-still, a slow flush rising to cover his face. A pure, hot anger seized him with sudden ferocity, and his brows drew together in a dark bar of outrage. His dark eyes flashed fire. The fury forced his lips into a tight line.

He strode over to a nearby wall where a length of rope lay coiled against its foundation. Quickly, he fashioned a whip from the rope. Wielding it right and left, shouting, he drove the cattle and sheep out of the Temple.

The crowd gaped in amazement, chattering angrily among themselves.

"Who is this wild young man?"

"Can't someone stop him? He has no right . . . !"

But no one had the courage to confront the furious young man.

Turning then to the money-changers, Jesus hurled their tables upside down, scattering coins all over the floor. The money-changers gaped in astonishment and fled, as Jesus flailed out at them with the knotted rope.

He spun around, breathing hard, and glared at the people selling doves. "Get out of here, and take these birds with you! You shall not turn my Father's house into a market place!" he shouted, his voice cracking with outrage.

The young servant from Cana turned to another disciple and commented breathlessly, "Do you remember the scripture passage which says *'Passion for God's House burns within me'*"? John 2:17 NLT

The disciple nodded, speechless with shock.

By then, the Jewish leaders had heard the commotion, and hurried out from inside the Temple itself. They arrived just in time to hear Jesus shouting at the sellers of the doves. The courtyard was now almost empty

One of the Temple officials approached Jesus and grasped him roughly by the arm. "What gives you the right to do these things? Who are you?" The man paused and gazed scornfully at Jesus. "If you have any authority from God, prove it by showing us a miracle," he snapped irritably.

Jesus shook off the official's hand, still angry and glowering. "All right, since you demand a sign—Destroy this Temple—and I shall raise it up in three days," he replied, gasping for breath.

At this, the Jewish leaders began to laugh and snicker among themselves.

"What are you talking about!?" Another leader stepped forward and confronted Jesus, standing almost nose to nose with him, glaring. "Forty-six years it took to build this Temple and you say you can do it in three days?" he scoffed, his lip curling in a sneer.

Still breathless, Jesus simply returned the stare. Making no reply, he turned abruptly and left the Temple.

Gloriel knew that Jesus meant his body, when he spoke of "this Temple."

Afterward, many people who witnessed this scene, or heard about it from others, were convinced that this stranger might indeed be the long-awaited Messiah. But the Temple officials began to plot how to rid themselves of this pesky rabble-rouser.

#

One dark night during the Passover celebration, one of the Jewish leaders came to talk to Jesus under cover of darkness. His name was Nicodemus, and he wore the striped blue shawl of a Pharisee.

*He comes to Jesus at night, because he's afraid the other religious leaders might find out that he's speaking with this 'radical' preacher.* Gloriel thought to herself, with a sad smile.

Nervously, Nicodemus questioned Jesus, glancing furtively around as he spoke, eyes wide with fear.

"Rabbi, he said, voice quivering, "everybody thinks that God has sent you. I know you are here to teach us His truths. The miracles you do prove that He is with you, indeed."

Jesus looked at Nicodemus' kindly face, and gazed deep into the gentle gray eyes. "Nicodemus, I tell you now," he said compassionately, "unless you are born again, you will never enter God's Kingdom," he said, laying his hand on the man's shoulder.

Nicodemus gaped in astonishment. "What do you mean? How can a grown man go back inside his mother's womb to be born over again? That's impossible!" he exclaimed. A frown clouded his face, darkening his kindly features.

Jesus' dark eyes glistened with zeal. "My friend, what I am telling you is the truth," he said fiercely. "There is no person, not even one, who will be able to become part of my Father's Kingdom, unless he is born over again of water and the Holy Spirit."

Gloriel murmured in Jesus' ear. "Jesu, he is willing to learn, but his mind is clouded with fear and his lifelong devotion to tradition."

Jesus paused and nodded, then continued, still speaking with authority and gazing intensely into the religious leader's eyes. "Nicodemus, as human beings, men and women are only capable of having children of their own kind,—more human beings." He cleared his throat and lifted his eyes toward Heaven. "But the Holy Spirit, who gives Life, imparts that new life from Heaven. You shouldn't be amazed, or shocked, when I say you must be born again. God gives you everything you need to participate fully in his life. The only thing He asks is that you plant the seed He gives you into the rich soil of a strong faith, my friend. You must open your heart to the Holy Spirit, so that the seed of His life can ripen into the fruit of the Spirit. This is the new beginning, the new birth, in the Spirit."

Nicodemus stared speechlessly at Jesus, astonished.

Jesus paused and held up one hand. "Listen to the wind, Nicodemus. Do you have any idea where it's coming from, or where it's going? In the same way, one can't explain new birth in the Spirit. It has to be experienced."

"I-I still don't know what you mean," Nicodemus replied hesitantly, a baffled look spreading over his face.

A small wrinkle appeared between Jesus' brows, and his strong piercing eyes penetrated Nicodemus to the heart.

"Are you not an honored and admired guide of the Jewish people? Yet you still don't understand what I am saying to you?" His tone was incredulous.

Nicodemus shook his head and bowed his head in shame.

Jesus closed his eyes momentarily, and sighed deeply, rubbing them with one hand.

"I'm telling you what I know to be the truth, what I have seen, and yet you don't believe me. If you can't understand and believe about earthly things, how can you possibly understand the things of Heaven? Only I, the Son of Man, have come to earth and will return to Heaven again. And as Moses lifted up the bronze snake in the wilderness, so I, the Son of Man, must be lifted up on a pole, so everyone that believes in me will have eternal life."

Nicodemus looked up then and stared open-mouthed at the tall figure standing before him. Amazement spread over his startled features.

Gloriel's heart thrilled as Jesus continued, his voice vibrant and strong.

*"For God so loved the world that he gave his only Son, so that everyone who believes in him will not perish but have eternal life. God did not send his Son into the world to condemn it, but to save it."* John 3:16 NLT

Nicodemus shook his head sadly, turned and walked slowly and silently into the darkness.

*This man wants so much to believe,* Gloriel mused, *but he is afraid and uncertain. He will have many sleepless nights ahead,* she sighed.

#

Jesus remained in Judea for about six months, preaching and teaching. Then word came that his cousin, John the Baptist had been imprisoned by Herod in Mashacruz. Cautious because of John's incarceration, Jesus and his disciples set out for Galilee by way of Samaria, skirting the larger communities, and traveling side roads.

## Chapter Twenty Six

Weary from the journey, Jesus stood a short distance from Jacob's Well. He was talking with Anthony, the young servant from Cana, and two new disciples. His other followers had gone on ahead into the town to seek lodging for the night. It was noon, and the air shimmered hot and still, the sun intense.

The countryside surrounding Sychar was sparsely populated, but a well-worn path led from the town to the well on the outskirts. The well had been dedicated to his son Joseph by the patriarch Jacob.

"Anthony, have you been to Samaria before this?" Jesus smiled at the blue-eyed young man.

"No, Teacher. My parents would not travel through this territory. They said that no loyal Jew would ever abide here overnight, nor drink from that well," he said hesitantly, gesturing in the general direction of the well.

As Anthony was speaking, a woman approached the well, balancing a water jug on one shoulder. Jesus placed his hand on the boy's arm.

"Wait here, Anthony," he said, nodding to the other two disciples. "You, too, my friends."

He walked purposefully toward the woman as she lowered a bucket down into the depths of the well. Her face was pinched and thin, with sallow, narrow cheeks. Fine lines creased the corners of her eyes. A thin muslin robe of crimson and blue hung from her slender shoulders.

"Shalom, my daughter," Jesus said quietly, as he approached the woman.

Startled, she turned toward him, almost dropping the rope. Quickly, she began drawing the bucket back up.

Gloriel watched with interest, standing unseen at Jesus' side.

"Who are you, Sir?" the woman asked, as the bucket appeared at the lip of the well. She lifted it onto the edge.

"I thirst, Photina." He spoke almost in a whisper, gazing deep into the woman's shadowed emerald eyes.

The eyes widened in amazement. "How do you know my name? I have never seen you."

"I know you well, Photina." A smile flickered around Jesus' lips.

The woman's face took on a distressed look, as she pushed back lusterless fine black hair from her eyes.

"Give me a drink, Photina," Jesus said, still looking deep into her sad eyes.

"Jesu," Gloriel whispered in his ear, "she is afraid."

"I don't understand, Sir. You are from Judea, I can tell by your accent." Her voice quivered. "I'm a Samaritan. You think I am unclean. Everyone knows our peoples are feuding." She raised her chin as a puzzled frown lined her forehead. "Why are you asking me for water?"

Jesus knew the woman was getting water at this time of day because of her shame. In order to avoid the taunting and gossip of the people in the town, she came to the well in the heat of the day, rather than in the morning when the other women would be there.

"You Samaritans worship that which you do not know. We know what we worship, for salvation is of the Jews. But all are children of the Father, Photina, and all are called to drink of the Living Water," Jesus said firmly. "Whoever drinks this water which you give me, will thirst again, but if he drinks of the Water which I will give him, he will never be thirsty again." His eyes glistened in the bright sunlight.

Fearfully, the woman held out a dipper of the cool water to Jesus. "Sir, will you give me some of this Water, so that I won't have to come to the well anymore?" Her hand was shaking as Jesus took the cup from her.

"She doesn't understand what you mean by 'living water', Jesu" Gloriel whispered.

"If you are able to get water without drawing it from the well, you are greater than Jacob," Photina continued timidly.

Taking the cup from her, Jesus looked at her speculatively.

"Go get your husband and bring him to me."

The woman looked down at the ground, a pinkish flush slowly rising from her neck and suffusing her face.

"I-I do n-not have a husband, Sir," she stammered.

Jesus was silent for a moment. The woman raised her eyes, the blush still staining her skin.

"Yes, you have had five husbands, Photina. And the man you are living with now is not your husband."

The woman's jaw dropped, and she covered her mouth with one hand. Jesus' dark eyes bore deeply into the depths of the Samaritan woman's frightened ones. She quickly averted them.

"If you knew who it is who is speaking to you, you would ask me for a drink of this Living Water. I am the Messiah who was foretold."

More frightened than ever, Photina set down her water pot, gathered her skirts together, and fled into the town to tell everyone about the wonders she had experienced.

"Hurry!" She shouted to the people in the street, forgetting their disdain for her. "Hurry! You must come and see the man at the Well. He told me everything I have ever done! I think he may be the Messiah!" She was breathless with excitement and exertion.

More people came out of their houses to listen to what the woman had to say about the mysterious stranger at Jacob's Well. Keyed up by her enthusiasm, and curious, some of the people followed Photina back to the well.

Meanwhile, Anthony and the other two disciples approached Jesus with some flat bread and cheese, and a bottle of wine.

"Teacher, you must eat something. You haven't eaten since yesterday. Please sit down and refresh yourself," Anthony pleaded, concern knitting his smooth brow. Pale hair curled moistly on his forehead and shoulders.

"Anthony, don't worry. I have food that you don't know about," Jesus answered gently, smiling at the lad.

One of the two disciples whispered to the other. "Who brought food to him?"

Jesus' eyes moved from Anthony to the other disciples. "I am nourished by doing the bidding of my Father, my friends. He sent me. I am fully fed by doing his work. The harvest is four months from now, when summer ends. Do you really think it will not begin until then?" Jesus gestured toward the crowd of people approaching. "Look around! The fields are ripe and ready to gather. Great joy waits for all those people, and for you who gather them in. You've heard the proverb 'One person plants and someone else reaps'? This is very true." Jesus clapped his hand on Anthony's shoulder. "I am going to send all of you to reap in places you never planted. Someone else has gotten the crop for you. You will bring them in."

The disciples looked at one another in wonderment. As the people of the city gathered around with eager faces, many of them already believed in Jesus, because of what Photina told them.

Gloriel whispered to Jesus. "Jesu, one day this woman will be martyred for you. She will travel to faraway places, carrying your Word to many peoples."

Jesus bowed his head and closed his eyes in silent prayer for the Samaritan woman called Photina.

The people of Sychar implored Jesus to come into the town and stay for awhile. So he and his ever-increasing group of disciples remained in the town for three days, preaching, teaching, and healing the sick. Many of the people were convinced that Jesus was indeed the Messiah whom they were looking for, when they witnessed the miracles he performed in their midst.

Early one morning, Jesus called his followers together. "We need to resume our journey to Galilee, my friends. Let's be on our way." Within an hour, all were ready to leave Sychar. Jesus was eager to return to his hometown, and looking forward to seeing his mother and the rest of his family.

Gloriel was thrilled, also, at the prospect of reuniting with her small friend, Sariel. It seemed so long since the two angels had been together.

## Chapter Twenty-Seven

Jesus and his disciples entered Nazareth late on a cloudy afternoon. After finding lodging for his followers, Jesus hurried down the pathway from the town to his boyhood home. Looking up as he walked along, tears stung when his eyes fell on Job's Hill, where his young heart first experienced grief.

His small home soon came into view. The blue summer curtain was hanging over the doorway. Jesus paused a few feet from the entrance, as sweet memories of his childhood flooded his mind.

"Avi, dear Avi, I miss you," he whispered, wiping his moist eyes with the back of his hand. There was a huge lump in his throat.

Gloriel stood by Jesus' side, absorbed in her own recollections of her charge's boyhood.

*"Jesu, my sweet Jesu, we have come a long way together,"* she reminisced.

"Emi!" Jesus called out eagerly, "Emi! Are you home?" Unable to wait, he pushed the curtain aside and stepped into the warm cozy room.

Mary stood by the household oven. The delicious fragrance of fresh-baked bread filled the room. Her cheeks were flushed and rosy from the oven's heat. At the sight of her beloved Jeshua standing in the doorway, her eyes widened in disbelief.

"Son! Oh, Jeshua, is it really you?"

At 43, Mary's once golden brown hair was heavy with silver, and the crinkles around her eyes and mouth had deepened.

*Her smile stills lights up her face*, Gloriel mused.

"Yes, Mother, it's me."

Jesus took a step toward Mary, holding out his arms. She flew into them and buried her face in his chest, her slight form trembling with delight . . .

"Oh, Jeshua, my son, my son, I have missed you so much!" Her words were muffled by his tunic.

Jesus kissed the top of her head. "Emi, I am so happy to be home. How are you? Where is Aunt Salome?"

Mary threw back her head and gazed into his face. "She just left for home, Son. She's been here all day, and she needs to be with her family. Are you home to stay?"

"No, Emi. I still must finish my Father's business. I have come only to visit you and the family. I will be reading the scriptures at Synagogue on Sabbath Day, also." He smiled down at her and hugged her tightly. "Now, how about a chunk of that fresh-baked bread?"

Gloriel and Sariel greeted one another joyfully while mother and son were talking. "Sariel, I am so happy to see you! Has everything gone well here in Nazareth while we were gone?"

Sariel beamed at her friend, delight written on her childish features. "Oh, Gloriel, Mary has missed Jesus so much. But the family has seen to her needs, and Salome is here everyday.

The two angels looked on with shining faces as mother and son shared the evening meal of lentils and goat cheese, along with Mary's fresh flatbread. A pitcher of cool goat's milk, completed their meal. After eating, they drank some of Joseph's red wine from earthen-ware cups, in celebration of Jesus' return. Mary still had several skins of the slightly sweet wine, now well aged.

Mary and Jesus talked far into the night, as he shared the exciting story of his journey.

Finally, exhausted, Jesus blew out the sputtering fat yellow candle in the niche on the wall. He lay down on his old pallet, stretched out his long legs, and closed his weary eyes with contentment.

Mary slept soundly, a small smile curving the corners of her mouth.

The two angels kept watch, chatting and rejoicing in one another's company.

The next day, Jesus and Mary visited their family members and friends. A few of Jesus' disciples accompanied them, and Gloriel and Sariel remained close by.

When they entered the house of Jesus' grandmother, a bent and aged Anna gathered her grandson into her plump wrinkled arms and blessed him. Her black eyes were dimmed by the years, but still sparked with joy in Jesus' embrace, fixing him with their alert gaze.

Her beloved Joaquin had passed away a few years earlier; his blue eyes sightless, and his tall frame bent and twisted with years.

Gloriel thought of Joseph's aged parents then. They had moved to Cana after their dearly loved son's death. There they dwelled with relatives who cared for them until the years claimed their toll; and they died peacefully within a few weeks of one another.

The Sabbath Day commenced as the sun sank into the western sky amid a sea of scarlet and gold. A few thunderheads glowered as Jesus, Mary, and his disciples entered the small synagogue.

The shadows around the entrance were pointed, dark blue, and sharp against the building's walls. Nostalgia struck Jesus' heart as they walked through the door.

"He's remembering his school days, Sariel;" Gloriel said to her friend, "especially the first day, when Joseph brought him here." Sariel nodded and smiled

Inside, the benches were already crowded in the women's section. A low murmur of voices swept over the gathering as Jesus and his followers entered.

"Naomi, Isn't that Joseph ben Jacob's son, Jesus?" A slender, middle-aged woman whispered to her companion, inclining her head toward Jesus.

"I believe it is, Miriam. I'd forgotten how tall he is," commented the elderly woman beside her.

Jesus seated his mother in the women's section and moved into the main room of the synagogue, where the men of the village were gathered.

Sariel remained standing behind Mary, while Gloriel accompanied Jesus.

As soon as he and his disciples were seated, Jesus' old schoolmaster, Rabbi Abner ben Abijah, shuffled up to him, his back now bent with age. Smiling, he placed the scroll of the prophet Isaiah into Jesus' hands.

"Jesus ben Joseph, welcome. Please stand up and read the Holy Scriptures," he said, his voice cracking and trembling.

Jesus took the scroll from the Rabbi's twisted fingers. His gaze was gentle as he smiled at the old man. Unrolling the ancient parchment carefully, he found the portion where it says:

*"The Spirit of the Lord is upon me, for he has appointed me to preach Good News to the poor. He has sent me to proclaim that captives will be released, that the blind will see, that the downtrodden will be freed from their oppressors, and that the time of the Lord's favor has come." Luke 4:18-19 NLT*

Jesus stopped reading. Looking around the room at the gathering of men, he rolled up the scroll and handed it to an attendant. The synagogue was silent, and everyone looked intently at the tall figure still standing before them.

Gloriel knew they were amazed at the power he displayed in a simple reading of the Scripture. His eyes seemed to look into every person's heart.

"Before your eyes, today this prophecy has come true!" Jesus' voice echoed throughout the synagogue as he raised both arms toward Heaven. "The Most High has sent me to declare His Kingdom, and His plan for your redemption! He has sent me to heal your sicknesses of body, mind, and spirit, and to turn your hearts back to Him."

Gloriel's heart thrilled with joy at the love of the Father shining in Jesu's face.

After a moment of shocked silence, a rising murmur of voices swept through the assemblage.

"This is the prophet who will free us from Roman rule?" An elderly man in the back of the room whispered to himself.

"This man will lift us up out of poverty and oppression?" A sad-faced middle-aged man commented loudly.

"This cannot be. Isn't he the carpenter, Joseph ben Jacob's son? How is this possible?" A loud comment from an old woman in the women's section floated in the tense atmosphere. "Come, now. We knew him as a young boy growing up in our midst, and now he's claiming to be the anointed one! We know him too well to believe that!" She continued

"No, wait a minute; just listen to how he speaks with such authority. This is amazing!" A younger woman seated next to her replied excitedly.

"He's got to be a prophet of God. His words are so powerful!" A young man with a newly sprouted beard shouted.

The old Rabbi's face was white and still, his rheumy eyes large and moist.

Jesus waited until the tide of voices died down. Every eye was fixed on him. Again he looked around into each face. He lowered his arms then, and stood silent before them.

Gloriel held her breath. *He has two choices*, she thought. *He can try to explain to the people how what he is saying is scriptural, and that all their years of hope and expectation are not what the Most High has really planned for them; or he can state the plain truth that they really don't want to hear,* she mused.

Jesus continued gazing at the people. *They are waiting for me to confirm their mistaken ideas,* he thought. He raised his voice once again.

"I know you remember the proverb 'Physician, heal thyself.' You are wondering why no miracles are happening here in my hometown, since you have heard of the ones occurring in Capernaum."

The murmur of voices began again. Jesus raised both arms to quiet the people, then began pacing back and forth.

"If you recall, there were many widows during Elijah's time in Israel. For 3 1/2 years Yahweh sent no rain, and people were starving. But God didn't send Elijah to any of them. He sent him to a foreign widow living in Sidon. Why do you suppose he wasn't sent to the widows in Israel?"

Jesus paused, and stopped speaking. There was absolute silence in the synagogue, as everyone waiting with bated breath for Jesus to finish the ancient story.

"Remember how the prophet Elisha did not heal the lepers in Israel who were helpless; God sent him instead to Naaman, a Syrian leper. And it was this foreigner whom Elisha healed. Why do you think this happened?"

The people remained totally silent. The atmosphere in the synagogue seemed electric with resentment.

Jesus' powerful voice resounded throughout the building.

"Elijah and Elisha weren't able to heal people in their own country because the people didn't believe they could! A prophet is without honor in his own land, in his own home town!" Jesus' eyes brimmed with tears as he looked out once more over the people.

Suddenly, a voice in the back of the synagogue shouted angrily. "How does this man dare speak to us like this!?"

A fleshy, red-faced man near Jesus jumped to his feet, shouting "Let's throw him over the cliff! Then we'll see what kind of prophet he really is!"

The people jumped to their feet, and many rushed forward, seizing Jesus roughly and dragging him outside to the brow of the hill on which the town of Nazareth was built.

Gloriel stayed by Jesus' side, unseen, as the people pushed and shoved and dragged him to the cliff's edge. It was dark now, except for the warm gold light of a harvest moon. Still unseen, the angel quickly removed the mantle she was wearing and threw it over and around her charge.

Suddenly, he disappeared from the angry mob's view. The people were stunned and mystified.

"What happened to him?"

"Where did he go? I just had hold of him!"

"Does anyone see him anywhere?"

Gloriel guided Jesus quickly through the crowd, and he found himself outside the town. He felt a little dazed and hurt by what had just happened in his hometown. Turning around in a circle, he noticed a small group of people approaching. When they got closer, he realized it was his mother, and those disciples who had accompanied him to Nazareth.

Sariel looked questioningly at Gloriel, puzzled over what had just occurred in the synagogue.

"Sariel, we have to leave Nazareth for now," Gloriel said sadly, hugging the little angel. "It isn't safe for Jesu."

"Yes, I know, Gloriel. I shall miss you, for I don't think Jesus will be taking Mary with him now." Sariel's round eyes brimmed with tears.

"No, she's not strong enough to travel extensively now, I know." Gloriel replied, patting Sariel's dimpled arm.

Sariel threw her arms around her friend. "I don't know when we will see one another again, Gloriel."

"Neither do I," Gloriel said dejectedly, returning Sariel's hug. "Farewell, my dear friend. Peace be with you."

# Chapter Twenty-Eight

Jesus and the little band of disciples, including Anthony, the servant from Cana, arrived in Capernaum at dusk a few days later. As he walked, Jesus thought about how difficult it had been to leave his mother. Mary seemed so sad and fragile, smiling through her tears as she told him goodbye. *I know the family will take good care of her,* he told himself. He breathed a short prayer as they approached Simon's house, his brow knit in concentration.

"Abba, please set the angels guard over Emi. Keep her well and safe while I fulfill the task you have set before me."

Gloriel drew close and whispered in his ear. "Jesu, a very dear angel guards your sweet mother. You must not worry."

Jesus sighed deeply and smiled as the door to Simon's and Andrew's house opened wide. Simon's rugged features glowed with delight as he greeted them.

Soon after his return to Capernaum, Jesus began teaching in the local synagogue every Sabbath day. His reputation spread far throughout the region, just as Gloriel had envisioned. People who heard him speak were amazed by the things that he said, as he spoke with great strength and authority. He healed everyone who came to him, no matter what sort of diseases afflicted them.

Gloriel remained always by his side, ever alert and on guard to protect, counsel, and guide her precious charge.

It was a crisp, bright autumn morning when Jesus left the synagogue and strolled down to the Sea of Galilee, Gloriel following close behind. The earth and heavens seemed incandescent around him. The shining waters of the sea sparkled like blue sapphires in the sunlight.

Some raspberry bushes along the pathway were scarlet with tempting berries. Stooping, he plucked a few and popped them into his mouth, savoring the slightly tart juices.

As he walked along the shore, he came upon some fishing boats a short distance from the shore. Simon and his brother Andrew were casting out their nets, their muscles rippling under skins browned from years in the sun. Their red beards gleamed in the bright light.

Jesus stood watching them for a few minutes, his face quiet and still.

"Jesu," Gloriel whispered. "Jesu, it's time to call them. The Father knows that you are reluctant to take them from their families. But it is time, and it must be done."

There was a flash of bright color on Jesus' cheek bones, and his dark eyes shimmered in the sun like two pools. He took a deep breath and called out in a strong voice. "Simon! Andrew! Come with me now, and I will show you how to be fishers of men!"

Simon and Andrew stood stock-still for a moment, consternation flooding their tanned faces. They looked at one another, and wordlessly dropped their nets. Jumping over the side of their boat, they waded ashore and joined Jesus, who was already walking ahead along the water's edge.

He turned and smiled encouragingly. "It's all right, my friends. It was for this reason God gave you life. Don't be afraid."

The two brothers looked at one another, non-plussed and puzzled. Neither one said a word.

A short distance down the beach the three men came across another boat. James and John were sitting in the boat with their father, Zebedee, and some hired men. All were busily mending their nets. They didn't notice the three men standing on the shore.

"James! John! Leave your nets and follow me now!" Jesus' voice echoed clear and compelling through the air.

The brothers shaded their eyes and squinted in the brilliant sunlight, staring in amazement at the tall figure beckoning to them on the shore. Uncertainty clouded their faces.

Zebedee sat open-mouthed in the stern of the boat, stunned and speechless. The hired men stared at Jesus curiously.

"Come now, it is time!" Jesus called again.

The two men looked blankly at their father. Without further hesitation, they stood up and jumped out of the boat into the water. Dripping wet, they joined the three men on the shore.

"My friends," Jesus said to the bewildered little group of men, "you are going to begin to serve and love your fellow men now. Always remember, that to Love, nothing is useless, nothing is too much, or too unimportant. You will leave your former lives behind soon, but I promise, you will find something far beyond your greatest dreams. Come, let's get started."

He placed a hand lightly on Simon's shoulder and beckoned the others. The little cluster of brothers looked at one another, slack-jawed in bewilderment, but turned and followed Jesus, never looking back.

Gloriel watched closely, feeling the anxiety of the men. "Jesu, you have chosen well, and the Father will be pleased," she whispered. "Simon is passionate and impetuous. He loves deeply and he feels deeply. He will have a vigorous faith, and yet he will always be plagued with indecision and doubt. God intends him to be chief among your followers. Andrew is loyal and trustworthy. Many people will believe in you because of him, Jesu. James and John, God has chosen to be closest to you, along with Simon. Their personalities are fiery, and their impassioned devotion to you will lead them to act impetuously sometimes, but they will be steadfast until the end."

Jesus stopped abruptly and looked around slowly at each man, dark eyes narrowed and squinting in the bright sunlight. "Now is the time to leave, my friends, if you have any misgivings in your hearts," he said, quietly and gently.

Simon folded his arms nervously, shifting from one foot to the other. Andrew ran his fingers through his curly mass of red hair as James and John exchanged disconcerted glances. No one spoke.

Jesus nodded his head, smiled, and continued walking.

From that moment on, Simon, Andrew, James and John followed Jesus everywhere throughout Capernaum, constantly at his side.

#

One morning after synagogue services, Jesus and the disciples returned to Simon's home. As they entered the house, a servant approached them, anxiety etching her pretty young face.

"Master," she said to Jesus, her voice soft and diffident. "My master Simon's mother-in-law is very ill with a high fever. Please come to her." The girl's full, wide-set hazel eyes were sparkling with tears. She looked at Simon, and then lowered her gaze. A single gleaming tear rolled slowly down her pink cheek.

"Don't worry, Tabitha, only believe." Jesus said reassuringly to the girl. He turned and walked slowly to Simon's mother-in-law's room. Entering the bedchamber along with Simon and Andrew, James and John, he stood at the elderly woman's bedside. Simon's wife, Esther, was sitting on the bed, her palms pressing together in a convulsive gesture. She stood up quickly, trembling, and greeted the group of men.

Jesus nodded reassuringly to Esther, as he reached down and took hold of her mother's wrinkled hand. The parched skin felt fiery hot to his touch. The old woman's temples were knotted with swollen veins, and her breath came in quick gasps. A cobweb of fine silver hair surrounded her prim, flushed visage.

"She's feeling very anxious and frightened, Jesu." Gloriel spoke softly at his side, unheard by all except Jesus.

Still holding her hand, Jesus put his arm around the old woman's shoulders and helped her up into a sitting position.

"It's all right, Hannah, God loves and cares for you," he whispered in her ear.

Then he spoke to the fever, his voice quiet, firm, and commanding.

"Be gone from Hannah's body now."

Bewildered, Hannah looked into the brightly shining dark eyes and the smiling face so close to her own.

"Stand up now," Jesus said to her reassuringly.

Trembling slightly, she rose slowly to her feet. The flush left her soft old features, leaving only a trace of rosy pink on her plump cheeks. Her hand grew cool in Jesus' grasp.

A slow smile spread across her features, revealing a deep dimple. She drew in a quavering breath, straightened her shoulders, and brushed the mist of silver hair back from her face.

"Thank you," she murmured, bowing her head in deference to Jesus. "Well, is anybody hungry?" Hannah's voice rang strong and clear. "Excuse me while I go prepare a good meal for everyone. Some of you look like you need one," she said pertly, smoothing her wrinkled skirts.

Esther plopped back down on the bed, open-mouthed with astonishment as her mother flounced out of the room.

Gloriel smiled and placed her hand lightly on Jesus' shoulder. He closed his eyes and breathed a prayer of thanks to his Father.

At dusk, the sun set over the smooth waters of the Sea of Galilee, sketching bold streaks of gold, pink, and dusty lavender against the sky. The story of Hannah's healing spread quickly throughout the town, and many people brought the sick members of their families to Jesus that evening.

Gloriel looked on with delight and thanksgiving as with a word, or a simple touch of his hand, he healed every ailing person. Many demons fled shrieking at that same touch, and a stern command.

#

A few weeks later, Jesus and his disciples still remained in Capernaum, as the people pleaded with them not to leave. This warm, bright day, golden sunshine dappled the Sea of Galilee. Jesus stood on the beach with his followers. A flock of seagulls screeched overhead, and then circled silently, white wings flashing pink in the sunlight.

A great number people crowded around him to listen to his preaching, and the press of bodies grew very uncomfortable. Jesus glanced around. He noticed two empty boats along the shore. One of them belonged to Simon, who sat on the beach next to it, washing his nets. Jesus approached him, leaned over and questioned him in a low voice. He then stepped into the boat and asked Simon to push it out into the water. Jesus continued teaching the people who were standing on shore for a little while. Everyone hung on his words, astonished by the wisdom and love displayed in them.

Climbing out of the boat, Jesus turned to Simon and grinned broadly. "Simon, my friend, why don't you go out into deeper water and cast your nets? You will surely catch lots of fish there." His dark eyes twinkled with suppressed glee.

"But, Master," Simon protested, "we have fished all night long, and didn't catch even one fish. But if you say so, I will try again," he sighed, scratching his curly red beard.

The blue waters swirled around his legs as Simon moved his boat out into deeper water, climbed in, and cast his nets out upon the flat blue silk of the sea. The waters were calm as a soft breeze arose.

"Pull your nets in now, Simon!" Jesus called out loudly from the shore.

Simon shrugged his shoulders and began to haul in one of the nets, his muscles bulging and straining. Disbelief spread slowly across his features, and he looked up open-mouthed with amazement. He could not budge the nets.

Gloriel grinned, watching Simon's powerful arms strain in vain. *So you're having a bit of fun along with the lesson, Jesu,* she thought to herself.

The nets were so loaded with struggling fish that they began to tear. Frantically, Simon looked around for his brother. "Andrew! Come and help me! The nets are full to overflowing! James! John! Come and help! Hurry!" He called, gasping for breath, to the two brothers in the other boat.

The soft breeze grew stronger suddenly, moaning and sighing down the shore. The four men struggled and strained, finally hauling the nets into the two boats. Both vessels were so over laden that they were at the point of sinking, gunwales barely clearing the water.

When they reached shore, Simon jumped clumsily out of his boat and fell to his knees at the feet of Jesus, burying his face in his hands. "Lord, leave me, for I am a truly sinful man," he cried in a muffled voice.

Jesus leaned down and placed both hands on Simon's trembling wet shoulders. His expression grew serious.

"Simon, don't be frightened. You know it is people that you will fish for from now on; you and Andrew, James and John. Come, it's time to begin our journey to Jerusalem. We will leave in the morning." Jesus helped the shaking man to his feet and put his arm around his shoulders.

The following day dawned chill and gray. The sea turned a beautiful, flashing pewter, all swirling motion and coldness, as Jesus and the disciples strolled along the shore. As they walked, they came across a tax collector's booth. The disciples, except for Anthony, made a wide berth around it, averting their eyes.

*Tax collectors are certainly a detested lot, being allied with the hated Roman subjugators. I see that the disciples consider this man to be a cheat, and a betrayer of his own people,* Gloriel mused to herself.

She whispered in Jesus' ear "This man collects fees from people passing over the Sea of Galilee, Jesu. But, part of the money goes into his own pocket, at the expense of his own countrymen. They really detest him."

Gloriel stood unseen by the booth, waiting to see what Jesus would do. He stopped in front of the booth and stood silently for a few minutes, looking intently at the man seated in the booth.

The tax collector grew uncomfortable under Jesus' searching gaze. His close-set green eyes shifted from one person to another. His face was pinched and narrow, despite his pudgy build. Growing even more uneasy, he brushed back his scraggly brown hair, and nervously fingered his sparse beard.

"Levi, son of Alphaeus, come, be my disciple." Jesus' voice was quiet but firm. His gaze did not leave the apprehensive man's face.

Levi's jaw dropped in astonishment. He hesitated momentarily, and then rose and stumbled awkwardly out of the booth. He followed Jesus, who was already walking briskly toward town. Increasing his pace, Levi caught up with Jesus, his features reflecting his pleasure at the honor just bestowed on him.

"Teacher, I want to invite you and your disciples to dinner at my house tonight," he blurted out eagerly.

"Of course, Matthew, I accept your invitation," Jesus replied heartily, clapping the excited man on the back.

The tax collector stopped dead in his tracks, a bewildered expression sweeping over his flushed features. He pursed his thin lips. Had Jesus mistaken him for another? Maybe he hadn't really meant to call him. Levi's face fell, disappointment replacing the puzzled look.

"Matthew? My name is Levi, Teacher, not Matthew." he replied reluctantly.

Jesus leaned forward and looked directly into the bewildered man's eyes. "Oh, but from this day on, you will be known as 'Matthew,'" he said resolutely." For you are a 'Gift from God,' truly."

"Well chosen, Jesu. This man's recorded words about you will be immortal. He will preach in far away lands, and in the end, sacrifice his life for your name," Gloriel murmured.

Jesus closed his eyes momentarily, and nodded.

Later that evening, the moon pushed over the horizon and painted a silver path over the countryside. Jesus and his disciples stood outside Matthew's beautiful home on the outskirts of Capernaum.

Matthew was eager to please his guest of honor, who had thrilled him with his call. He had invited some other publicans, and a few people of dubious reputations, including two harlots.

Some Pharisees passing by as Jesus and the disciples prepared to enter the house, stopped and stared, outraged.

"Teacher! Why is it you eat with tax collectors and other disreputable people? They are scum, the dregs of society!" One of the Pharisees shouted angrily.

Jesus turned slowly and directed a probing look at the questioner. "Why do you question my motives, Josiah? Didn't God give life to tax collectors and sinners, as well as Pharisees and teachers of the Law? He sighed and rubbed his eyes. "However, to answer your question, it's those who are sick who need the doctor's help, isn't it? I am here to set the sinful free, not those who think they are already holy enough."

Jesus' scrutiny penetrated Josiah's haughty façade. The Pharisee turned and swished away abruptly. The nostrils of his beaked nose flared, and the fringe of his robe fluttered behind him.

"All of you Pharisees! You need to learn the meaning of the scripture which tells us that God wants us to be merciful. He doesn't want your sacrifices!" Jesus called after the retreating group.

Gloriel looked on with concern, reflecting to herself. *The Pharisees will not accept Jesu, ever. They want him to be as they are, and he will never be like that. They don't have the wisdom to see that Jesu sees all people as beloved by his Father, that they are creatures of great worth in His eyes.*

Jesus shook his head, and entered Matthew's house. Although it wasn't large, it was luxuriously furnished. The floors were a fine marble, with Persian rugs like woven jewels scattered about on the gleaming surface. The long dining table was a satiny lemon-wood, surrounded by silken cushions in bright hues of red, blue, gold and purple. The table groaned under the burden of many costly delicacies. The sweet fragrance of roast lamb permeated the air. Golden clusters of dates lay here and there on the table, along with gleaming silver dishes of locust cakes fried in olive oil.

Gloriel stood by Jesus' side, watching as her charge reclined with the disreputable people gathered around Matthew's banquet table.

"Jesu, you do well to see all people as valuable in the Father's eyes. How could you tell them your Good News if you avoided them?" she whispered quietly.

Jesus carefully regarded all the people gathered around the table, smiling as he greeted them, looking deeply and lovingly into each curious pair of eyes fixed on him; and studying every face with quiet intensity.

#

## Chapter Twenty-Nine

The rising sun drew bold strokes of gold, pink and lavender on the horizon as Jesus and his growing group of disciples left Capernaum and began the journey to Jerusalem to celebrate the Feast of Pentecost.

For several days, as they traveled, Jesus taught and counseled both men and women along the roadsides and in the small towns. His healing touch brought health and wholeness to all the sick among the throng of people following him.

One particularly warm afternoon, as they approached Jerusalem, Jesus strolled off to the side of the dusty yellow road, his disciples following closely. A group of herdsmen squatted in the shade of a scraggly terebinth tree nearby, watching curiously.

"Jesu, you need to rest," Gloriel whispered. Concern about his exhaustion filled her heart.

Anthony approached him, a worried frown creasing his broad forehead. "Teacher, please sit down and rest. Let me bring you something to eat and drink."

Hot yellow dust surged over the desert as the noonday sun beat down overhead, free of the clustering clouds on the horizon. Anthony peered up into the sky, his azure blue eyes squinting in the glare.

"Let me fix a lean-to where you can rest and take some refreshment, Master," he continued, anxiously.

Jesus smiled affectionately, putting his arm around the boy's shoulders. "Anthony, my friend, don't worry about me. Remember, I told you before. I have food and drink you don't know about," he replied huskily.

The young man looked at Jesus, then cast down his remarkable blue eyes, and nodded.

Jesus lowered his voice and murmured, "My Father provides the sustenance I need, always, Anthony. Come now! Join the others and relax a while!" He gave the boy a playful push and grinned widely at him.

*Anthony still doesn't understand that Jesu is talking about food and drink for his spirit,* Gloriel thought.

The herdsmen seemed fascinated with Jesus and his followers as they sat watching curiously. One of them, a man in his mid-forties, lounged on his elbow and gazed intently at Jesus from under shaggy brows. His eyes took on a faraway look, as vague memories stirred within him. *Many years ago, in Bethlehem? Or was it Nazareth? Where . . . ?*

Gloriel recognized the man, though most of his face was hidden by a grizzled gray beard. *Ah, Benjamin, your path crosses once again with my Jesu's. And it will not be the last time.*

The sun began its flaming golden descent down the western sky as Jesus and his followers stopped to camp for the night.

After a light supper, all was quiet. A copper moon hovered low on a horizon heavy with a crimson mist. Gloriel kept silent watch and dreamed of her heavenly Home.

#

A few days later, when they finally approached Jerusalem, the pilgrims spotted the dome of the Temple glinting like a golden shield in the dazzling light of the sun bursting into the clear from behind a scudding line of clouds.

They entered the Sheep Gate, which opened close to the pool of Bethesda. People were being healed every day under the five covered porches of the pool. Gloriel looked around at the crowds of sick; the blind, lame, paralyzed, lying beneath the porches, waiting for an angel to stir up the waters. Accordingly, the first person to step into the pool after the stirring of the waters emerged healed.

"Jesu, look over by the pool under the nearest porch. The man lying there has been sick for 38 years," Gloriel whispered to Jesus.

The man lay on a sleeping mat a few feet from the pool, his haggard face shadowed and gray. His eyelids rested half-open, despair hidden in his eyes dark depths. A tangled mass of gray hair fanned out around his head like a halo.

Jesus quietly approached the emaciated figure and knelt down on one knee.

"Isaac," he murmured softly, leaning down close to the man's ear. The sunken eyes remained half-closed, and there was no response.

"Isaac," Jesus repeated, placing one hand on the man's forehead. Suddenly, the dull eyes opened wide and stared into the kind face bending over him.

"Wha . . . H-how do—you know—my name?" he croaked, his words raspy and hesitant. He cleared his throat.

Some of the disciples gathered around, watching expectantly with shining eyes.

Jesus smiled at Isaac, whispering, "Do you really want to get well?"
Gloriel moved closer to Jesus' side.

Isaac shook his head slowly and painfully. "S-sir, I can't. No one will help me into the pool after the angel stirs the waters." He moistened his cracked lips and his voice grew a little stronger. He raised one wasted arm feebly. "I have to crawl, and someone always crowds me out and gets there ahead of me."

Jesus rose to his feet, leaned down and took hold of Isaac's hand. "Stand up, Isaac! Pick up your mat and walk!" His tone was firm and commanding as he pulled the amazed man to his feet. The healing was instantaneous, and people all around gasped in astonishment.

*Some of them have seen this man lying here every day for years,* Gloriel thought. *Yet none has ever bothered to help him.*

"Take your mat and go home, Isaac," Jesus said, patting the man on his back.

Isaac rolled up his mat and carried it away, with a spring in his step, praising God in a loud voice. A gentle rain settled the dust of the city streets as he approached the Temple.

Some of the Jewish leaders pressed around him, halting his joyful dance. "Don't you know it is illegal to carry anything on the Sabbath? You must do no work on the Sabbath Day," one of them said indignantly, scowling under the broad phylactery on his forehead. He shook his finger in Isaac's startled face.

Isaac looked the Pharisee straight in the eyes and replied clearly. "The man who healed me told me to pick up my mat and walk! And so I did, praise be to God."

"Who is this man who told you that?" another Jewish leader demanded crossly in a harsh voice.

"I don't know who he is!" Isaac replied, his voice rising. I only know that he healed me, and I am able to walk after 38 years lying on a mat!" His gray eyes shone clear and bright with gratitude.

"Where is he now? Show him to us!" The first Pharisee commanded roughly, jabbing his finger into Isaac's thin chest.

Isaac turned around and searched the crowd with reluctant eyes. "He's gone. I don't know where he went."

"If you see him, you must come and tell us who he is," the Pharisee continued, shaking his long fat finger in Isaac's face.

Intimidated, Isaac nodded fearfully in reply and entered the Temple, as the rain slicked down the sides of the great dome. Standing on the wet cobblestones in the courtyard, still praising God for his healing, he felt a touch on his shoulder. Startled, he spun around abruptly. Jesus stood by him, gazing at him solemnly with his piercing dark eyes.

"Isaac, you are well now. You must stop sinning, or something even worse may happen to you." Jesus spoke in a firm, low voice. His eyes never left Isaac's face.

The astonished man's jaw dropped in surprise. A raindrop dripped off the end of his aquiline nose. *How does he know?* He wondered to himself. No one knew that for years he had been picking the packs and pouches of anyone who sat down near enough to him at the pool. Despite his illness, his fingers were very deft. *But how can this man know that?* He felt a little indignant and defensive at Jesus' stern attitude.

Jesus turned and walked away. Isaac stood staring after him, dumbfounded, as he disappeared into the crowd.

Turning then to a man standing nearby, Isaac asked, "Do you know who that man is that was just talking to me?"

"His name is Jesus," the man replied breathlessly, excitement glowing in his eyes. "His fame is spreading throughout the countryside. He heals people wherever he goes, I hear."

Abruptly, Isaac turned and headed back to where the Pharisees had stopped him. Several of them still stood in the courtyard, ignoring the increasing size of falling raindrops.

Isaac approached them diffidently.

"I saw him in the Temple," he said excitedly to one of the Jewish leaders." His name is Jesus." He glanced over his shoulder nervously, as if he were afraid that Jesus might be standing behind him.

The Pharisees quickly decided among themselves to attempt to bring charges against Jesus for violating the Sabbath. They scurried into the Temple, the long tassels on their prayer shawls trailing behind them.

But Jesus was not to be found. From that time on, they conspired to discredit Jesus.

A few days later, mid-morning of the Shavuot, the day of the Feast of Pentecost, long lines formed outside the city as people waited for the formal procession into the city to begin.

Colored awnings fluttered in a sharp breeze as the people processed in, and the beautiful harvest festival celebration began in the Temple.

The barley crops were harvested; the earliest fruits had been picked. People brought the finest of these to the Temple as an offering.

Jesus and his disciples carried several choice loaves of bread in the procession.

The atmosphere was heavy with the fragrance of incense as each participant offered honor to the Torah.

Jesus and the disciples remained in the Temple all night, reading the sacred books.

At dawn on the following day Jesus and his followers began their journey back to Capernaum. The air was cloudless and warm as they left the holy city behind. Their hearts were rejoicing, for many people had been healed during their stay in Jerusalem, and the number of disciples was mounting rapidly.

Several more women had joined their group, a few of them of wealthy means. *Ah*, Gloriel mused, *these women will serve Jesu well, and love him deeply; along with Susannah, Sapphira, and Joanna.*

That evening, Gloriel looked on happily as Jesus and the disciples sat around a campfire next to a small stream a few yards off the side of the road. Laughter filled the air as they joked among themselves, enjoying a bit of horseplay. Simon's boisterous voice could be heard above all the others. James and John began wrestling with one another, each trying to toss the other into the stream. The women busied themselves preparing supper for Jesus and his most devoted disciples: Peter, and Andrew, James and John.

*They needed this*, Gloriel mused. *Much hard work and sorrow lie ahead for all of them. It's so good to see Jesu laugh and relax.*

The dazzling stars overhead sparked huge in the solitary desert. Light from the silver evening sky rippled across the stream.

After supper, Jesus rose quietly to his feet and walked slowly off into the shadows alone. Gloriel followed closely behind him. Some distance from the campfire, he paused and contemplated the midnight blue sky. Raising his arms toward the heavens, he prayed softly.

"Father, I thank you for all these you have given me. Strengthen them for the long, hard journey that lies ahead for each and every one of them. Set the angels guard over them until their missions are completed. Grant them vigor and passion of body, mind and spirit. Thank you for hearing my prayer. May it be so."

Gloriel moved in close beside her charge, her heart brimming with love for him. "Oh, Jesu, the Father loves you so," she whispered into his consciousness. Jesus smiled, bowed his head and lowered his arms.

As he approached the campfire, the exuberance of his companions was beginning to wane. Everyone was heavy-eyed and weary. James and John scratched their beards and yawned in unison.

"My friends," Jesus looked around at the ring of tired faces, "let's get some rest now. We still have a long journey ahead of us." He yawned and stretched his sinewy arms overhead.

The stars stood watch brightly, as the band of disciples settled down for the night, some pitching small tents, others spreading a blanket or pallet on the sandy ground. Silence fell quickly over the camp.

#

As he and his followers approached the familiar outlines of Capernaum a few days later, Jesus felt a thrill of excitement.

*He knows that he will perform scores of miracles here, and draw many souls to God,* Gloriel reflected happily.

They went immediately to Simon's house. Simon's wife, Esther, greeted them at the door, smiling broadly, her pink cheeks demure and dimpled. Simon, with a roguish twinkle in his eyes, lifted her off her feet in an exuberant bear-hug.

"Simon! What will our guests think!" she cried, flushing.

Simon laughed uproariously. "My dear, we need to find places for our guests to sleep!" He pinched her cheek, his green eyes crinkling with mirth.

"Some may lodge at our house," James suggested.

"There is room in the courtyard for many pallets," Andrew interjected. "And perhaps the rest can find lodging at the Inn"

So the weary travelers were accommodated at several different locations. Jesus waited until all his followers were taken care of, and then retired to the room which had been his since the beginning of his journeys.

Gloriel's spirit filled with an acuteness of love as Jesus finally closed his shadowed eyes and fell immediately into a deep sleep.

"Jesu, rest well, for many await your healing of their bodies, minds and spirits," she whispered deep into his subconscious.

The following morning, Jesus went to the synagogue to teach, as it was the Sabbath day. Jesus' eyes swept over the worshipers gathered.

There were many people there in need of healing, Gloriel noted.

The Pharisees and the teachers of the Law watched him closely and listened carefully, hoping to catch him in some violation of the Sabbath Law.

Gloriel knew that the Pharisees, who believed in a literal interpretation of the scriptures, were "separated" from the people. Most of them were tax collectors, and sinners, hated by the populace. They did not believe in resurrection, and could not associate with the Sadducees, who were mainly priests and aristocrats, and interpreted the scriptures literally.

The teachers of the Law, the scribes, were primarily trades people, craftsmen, and day laborers. Their great influence came from their knowledge of the Law. They were highly respected as experts, and people referred to them as "Rabbi."

Gloriel spotted a tall, middle-aged man, unkempt and ragged, standing off to one side of the synagogue. His body slumped to one side, and his demeanor seemed diffident and fearful. One hand lay concealed beneath the folds of a tattered dark blue robe. His eyes were downcast. Jesus' keen gaze swept past him, and then returned to focus on the dejected figure.

"Obidiah ben Hezekiah! Come forward." Jesus smiled and beckoned to the shabby figure.

Obidiah raised dull black eyes without sparkle or interest. Then he blinked in surprise. *How does this man know my name?* He wondered silently.

*Hmm . . . The Pharisees are interested in this,* Gloriel thought to herself. *They are waiting for any chance they can get to arrest Jesu.*

She quickly moved closer to Jesus' side. "Jesu, be careful," she whispered in his ear.

"Come, Obidiah, don't be afraid. It's all right," Jesus said reassuringly.

The crowd parted to make way for the tall man as he approached Jesus at a snail's pace, until he stood before him. His eyes remained downcast.

"Obidiah, look at me." Jesus' voice was gentle, but firm.

Trembling now, Obidiah raised his hooded black eyes and looked full into Jesus' face.

"Stretch forth your hand now. Uncover it, and hold it out to me."

Tears filling his eyes, Obidiah slowly withdrew his right hand from its hiding place. The people standing nearby gasped at the sight of the grotesquely withered and wasted member held out to Jesus.

Jesus smiled, briefly placing a supportive hand on Obidiah's thin shoulder. Then, gently, he took the misshapen hand in both of his.

Obidiah sobbed, and the tears spilled over as Jesus opened his hands to reveal Obidiah's, whole, well-shaped, and totally normal. Wonder and joy spread slowly over his gaunt features as Obidiah flexed his fingers and held them up to the amazed congregation.

The Pharisees, confounded, put their heads together, muttering among themselves.

"Jonathan!" Jesus voice resonated throughout the synagogue.

"Tell me, Jonathan," he said to a short, balding Pharisee standing a few yards away. "Is it against God's Law to do good deeds on the Sabbath?" Jesus' clear eyes widened and fixed on the annoyed Pharisee.

Jonathan plucked at his graying beard and turned his back without answering.

"Josiah? Zarius? Do you have an answer?" Jesus questioned, turning to other Pharisees.

The group glowered at Jesus, turned on their heels and roughly pushed their way through the crowd to the exit of the synagogue.

Jesus grinned and called out to the congregation, "The Son of Man has come to save that which was lost."

People turned to one another, bewildered, whispering.

*Hmm . . . None of them have any idea that Jesu is talking about the understanding which they have lost; the realization of what they are meant to be and do. How sad!* Gloriel thought, her eyes following as Jesus moved slowly through the assembly.

# Chapter Thirty

The warm molten gold sunlight of a beautiful early summer day cast its music before them on the path as Jesus and his disciples approached the glistening blue-green Sea of Galilee.

Following closely, a mounting multitude of people overflowed the pathway. Jesus' fame by this time had spread far beyond the borders of Galilee and Judea.

Gloriel noticed that many among the throng had traveled from as far away as Tyre and Sidon. Most of the people sought healing; the blind, the crippled, the deaf and mute, the paralyzed, the lepers and those with all kinds of diseases.

The crowd began pressing in upon Jesus, pushing him closer and closer to the water. Gloriel remained by his side.

Jesus turned his back to the sea; and standing on the shore, called the people to himself, one by one. He restored them to health, whatever their illness, laying his hands on them tenderly. His compassion for those afflicted with illnesses of spirit, body and mind touched the hearts of all his followers.

Watching, Gloriel recalled the prophetic words of Isaiah:

*"The Spirit of the Sovereign Lord is upon me, because the Lord has appointed me to bring good news to the poor. He has sent me to comfort the broken-hearted and to announce that captives will be released and prisoners will be freed. He has sent me to tell those who mourn that the time of the Lord's favor has come . . ."*
Matthew 6:44-47 NLT

"This prophecy is being fulfilled at this very moment," she whispered to herself, filled with awe and gratitude.

#

Very early the next morning, while darkness still lay like a blue velvet cloak upon the landscape, Jesus trudged up a nearby hillside. Several of his disciples accompanied him, following closely in his footsteps, sleepy-eyed and silent.

After a while, noticing that the men were growing weary from the climb, Jesus stopped and sat down on a smooth gray rock. His followers immediately followed suit, perching on rocks, or sitting on the ground. Jesus yawned and stretched his sinewy arms overhead.

A soft, silent breeze arose, and a fragrant morning aroma from blossoming orchards of olives and figs floated gently up from the valley below. Jesus breathed deeply of its freshness, closing his eyes briefly.

Glancing down into the valley, Gloriel could see a large multitude heading toward them. "Jesu, many people are approaching," she whispered.

The horizon infused with a faint rose and gold as Jesus stood up and stretched his arms toward the lightening sky.

"Rest, my friends," he said to his disciples, "and watch God's glory displayed in the rising of the sun."

He withdrew by himself to pray. Gloriel stood close by, watching and listening as her Jesu implored his Father for guidance and discernment. After a few minutes of fervent prayer, Jesus returned to his disciples just as the sun trembled on the horizon, etching the sky with veins of gold. A faint chill descended with the light, carpeting the ground with glistening dew.

The crowd of devotees looked up at him expectantly, many of them rising to their feet. Silence lay deep on the sloping hillside.

"My friends, gather around." Jesus' voice was crisp and clear. The disciples drew nearer, looking eagerly into the Teacher's face. His profile flooded with the golden light of the dawn.

Gloriel looked over the crowd, knowing full well that Jesus was about to summon those who would remain by his side for the rest of his life. A thrill of excitement quivered in her heart.

"Simon, Andrew, James and John, come forward and stand by me." Jesus said, beckoning. The crowd parted to let the four men through.

Gloriel could see the auburn heads of Simon and Andrew move quickly to Jesus' side, followed closely by the young faces of James and John.

*John is just a lad*, she commented to herself, gazing at the smooth, almost beardless innocence of the 19-year-old face.

Quickly, Jesus called eight others. "Phillip, Bartholomew, Matthew, Thomas, James ben Alphaeus, Simon the Zealot, Jude ben James" . . . Jesus paused momentarily. A slight sigh, audible only to Gloriel, escaped his lips. "Judas Iscariot," he breathed.

As the men came forward out of the crowd and gathered around him, Jesus looked closely into each man's face.

Phillip, a fellow townsman of Simon and Andrew, stood quietly, returning Jesus' gaze. Wise and discerning deep-set brown eyes shone from a thin, sharp-chinned face. His light brown hair and beard glinted in the light of the rising sun.

"Jesu," Gloriel whispered in Jesus' ear. "Phillip is practical and sensible. He will serve you well."

Jesus' eyes moved on to Bartholomew, sometimes known as Nathaniel. A small older man with weathered skin and deep wrinkles around intelligent hazel eyes, he drew himself up to his full stature as Jesus looked at him. His eyes and mouth were lined with the marks of laughter. Jesus smiled at him.

"One day Bartholomew will be martyred by the knife, in a terrible way, all for love of you, Jesu." Gloriel commented sadly. "He will travel into many different countries preaching the Good News."

Jesus' eyes filled with bright tears, and then moved on to Matthew, the ex-tax-collector once known as 'Levi'. He smiled, recalling the day when Matthew abandoned his tax collector's booth to follow Jesus eagerly and without question.

"Matthew, also, will be martyred in a foreign land, Jesu," Gloriel said with a sigh.

Jesus patted Matthew's back as he turned to face the tall, middle-aged man called Thomas. He looked into the man's puzzled dark gray eyes. Thomas returned the gaze with a furrowed brow, his thin lips down turned at the corners. Black hair streaked with gray, hung neatly around his narrow shoulders.

"Ah yes, Thomas." Gloriel mused, "He's introspective and scholarly by nature, often lost in thought. A man of logic and deep reasoning, he is not easily persuaded, Jesu. He believes you have come to deliver the people from Roman bondage. Never-the-less, he will serve you well, though sometimes reluctantly."

Jesus nodded his head, and his eyes fell on James, son of Alphaeus.

"James, my kinsman, it has been a long time since we have been home, hasn't it?" Jesus said, clasping the young man's blunt-fingered hand in both of his. James' angular features, weathered and hawkish, creased into a smile as he nodded in response. Hair the color of polished oak curled around a broad forehead and along his sharp jaw-line.

"Someday, Jesu, James will give up his life for his faith in you. It's his nature to be forbearing, and he will serve as a beautiful example of forgiveness to others," Gloriel declared.

Next Jesus turned to Simon, whose plump jolly face dimpled in a bright smile. A sparse black beard shadowed his round chin. Large black eyes glistened with a polished and clear light as he looked into Jesu's face.

"Simon, come, follow me as one of my chosen twelve. I know you are brave and zealous, and I will need you." Jesus said cheerfully.

"Simon is also one who believes, like Thomas, that you will free the Jews from Roman rule," Gloriel murmured in Jesus' ear.

*He reminds me of Samuel,* she thought nostalgically. *It seems so long since I have seen him, and Sariel. He must have a new assignment by now.*

Jesus closed his eyes briefly, and nodded to Simon. Silently, he moved on to Jude ben Alphaeus, brother to James. "So, Jude, I am happy to have you numbered among my apostles," he said warmly, laying his hand briefly on Jude's arm. Jude fixed Jesus with his tawny eyes, shining serene, bright, and alert in his handsome oval face.

"Jude has a great gift of discernment, Jesu. There's an aura of thoughtfulness and integrity about him," Gloriel said quietly. "He will protect your followers from false teachers and heresies. Though he is a family man, he will travel to distant nations carrying the Good News. Sometimes he is called 'Thaddeus,' Jesu."

A shadow moved over Jesus' features as he turned to the next disciple standing before him. Small deep-set black eyes gleaming restlessly, Judas Iscariot looked eagerly into Jesus' face. "And you, also, Judas, you are to be a part of God's plan," Jesus said softly.

Judas' unruly eyebrows flared, and a curious glimmer touched his eyes. Thick black, oiled locks hung loosely around his taciturn face.

"Thank you, Teacher," he replied excitedly. "I have much to offer you. You will find my accounting skills of great value, I am sure."

A chill crept over Gloriel as she listened to the exchange between Jesus and Judas. "Judas is adept in the handling of money, so much so that maybe he has a lust for it. Also, he has a weakness for overindulgence in wine. Be careful, Jesu," Gloriel murmured.

*There is a certain arrogance in the way Judas carries himself,* she reflected.

Jesus looked down at the ground thoughtfully, and sighed deeply. Then, raising his head, he smiled broadly, a glint of pleasure sparkling in his eyes.

"James and John, you Sons of Thunder! Simon and Andrew! All of you, come stand by me."

The four men moved quickly to Jesus side. Clapping Andrew on the shoulder, Jesus looked into his kind face, with its rich red beard reflecting the morning sunlight.

"Andrew, my friend, you have been with me since the beginning. You will be with me at the end too," Jesus said, grinning.

"Yes, Master, I will stay with you, always," Andrew replied eagerly.

"Simon." Jesus beckoned to Andrew's brother. The burly fisherman stepped forward to Jesus' side, his square ruddy face alight with eagerness. Jesus placed both hands on Simon's broad shoulders and raised his voice.

"Simon, my impetuous one, from this point on, you shall be called 'Peter', 'Petros', and on this solid 'Rock' I will develop my Church. The doorway to Hell shall never overcome it. Whatever you hold to be true on earth, shall be held true in Heaven. Whatever you require on earth, will be required in Heaven. I will give you the Keys to the Kingdom of Heaven, Peter."

Jesus voice reverberated, resounding across the sands, down among the multitude, and echoing out onto the restless waters of the Sea of Galilee.

Peter sank slowly to his knees before Jesus, trembling, his head bowed. His flushed face paled as he whispered hoarsely," My Lord, I-I am so unworthy."

Jesus placed a hand on Peter's coppery curls. "Come, my friend, we have much work to do," he said quietly. He grasped both the fisherman's large, work-worn hands, and pulled the dazed man to his feet.

Glancing around, Gloriel spotted Anthony, never far from Jesu's side, standing motionless and silent to one side of the group. She could see his cornflower blue eyes were downcast, his fine features crestfallen. The morning sun haloed his bright flaxen hair, curling at the nape of his neck and around his cheeks. She gasped in surprise as a poisonous look passed briefly over his ashen face.

*He's thinking that he has been devoted to Jesu since the day of the first miracle, in Cana. I know he's feeling deeply hurt, and aches to be chosen as one of the Twelve. I can't make out his attitude right now, but I sense that it is changing quickly*, Gloriel reflected, scrutinizing the young man closely.

By now, the multitude had swollen to huge numbers, covering the slopes of the hill. Many people tried to get close enough to touch Jesus, as great healing power emanated from him. Gloriel and the apostles looked on as he granted healing to all who sought it.

Jesus climbed laboriously to the top of the tall hill. The mid-day sun hung high and warm in the cloudless sky. A hush fell over the people as he began to speak, his powerful voice again echoing and resounding down the side of the mountain.

"You who are poor," he said, looking around at those in the crowd clad in shabby and tattered clothing, "God is blessing you. He is giving you His Kingdom."

He lifted one arm and gestured from side to side. "You who are hungry, God is blessing you, and you will be filled. Happy are the persecuted, who are cast out and hated for following me; yours is the Kingdom of Heaven. Be joyful! A wonderful reward will be yours in Heaven!"

Pausing for a moment, Jesus cleared his throat. "You who are sorrowing, God is truly blessing you; though you are miserable right now, you will one day laugh with joy."

He stopped and looked around at his apostles standing close by. His dark eyes shone softly in the sunshine, and his voice rose to a crescendo. "And you, all of you who will be abused and persecuted because of me; when they speak all kinds of evil against you for my sake, rejoice! Remember that most hostility comes from fear of change, and people may resent anything new. Rejoice, and be thankful, for your reward will be greater than you can possibly imagine, because this is how they treated all the great prophets of the past!"

Again Jesus paused, bowing his head as if in prayer. Finally, he raised his eyes and looked out over the great multitude. Slowly, he walked a few paces down the hill. Momentarily, he shaded his eyes with his hands against the brilliance of the sun. Then he stretched out his arms, palms up.

"But for you who are rich, much grief waits for you! Because you prosper now, and are satisfied while ignoring the needs of the poor among you, a terrible hunger will come upon you."

Sorrow tainted his tone, and his face became strangely gaunt and still. "You who laugh carelessly now, while misery intensifies all around you, one day this laughter will die in your throats, and turn into grieving and tears. And you, you who seek the praise of others," Jesus lowered his arms and sighing deeply, gazed at a Pharisee with a fierce dark face, standing a short distance away. "You will be utterly crushed by sorrow, for in the same manner, your ancestors praised the false prophets!"

He paused for a moment, eyes radiating an amber light, and then continued.

"Listen to me, you who are willing. I'm going to tell you a huge secret—one of the keys to Heaven." The crowd grew totally silent, straining to hear every word.

"Love your enemies!" A gasp of astonishment arose from the people. "Return love for their hatred. If someone curses you, ask God to make them happy. Avoid displaying a pitiless attitude, or acting with cruelty."

Jesus paused, turned and clambered up on a large flat black rock. Gloriel moved to stand beside him, unseen.

"Suppose someone hits you on one cheek. Do not try to strike him back. Turn your other cheek to him. Don't try to get even."

Gloriel could hear a faint murmur arising from the huge gathering. *To these people, this is a totally unfamiliar way of speaking. Jesu knows that this teaching will always be very difficult for human beings to understand,* she mused to herself.

Jesus continued, raising his voice until once again, its powerful tones rang out over the hillside and the valley below.

"If someone should demand that you give him your shirt, give him your cloak also. If anyone asks you for anything-don't hesitate to give it to them! And if someone borrows from you, don't look for a return."

His piercing eyes searched among those standing closest to him, his gaze alighting on a white-haired elderly man. Guilt moved stealthily over the grizzled, life-toughened old face.

"Here is a rule that will bring you great blessings." Jesus paused, and his eyes, bright with fervor, moved on and swept over those gathered a few yards down the hill. "Whatever it is that you want someone to do for you, do the same for him. Be considerate in everything that you do. Always be loving, kind, and thoughtful. This will result in people treating you the same. Do these things and you will please your Father in Heaven. You must love just as He loves. You ought to mirror Him to the world. Base all your actions on love for others, not on what you think they deserve."

Jesus continued speaking to the crowd for a long time, pacing back and forth on the huge rock; teaching, admonishing, loving.

Gloriel's heart melted with adoration as she witnessed his reflection of his Father to the masses of people starving for God's Word.

She noticed Anthony standing at the foot of the rock, a dark look clouding his features. *Anthony is growing more and more discontent, Father*, she prayed silently. *I'm getting concerned about him.*

The multitude of people settled down for the night as Gloriel watched over the group of apostles sleeping at the base of the mountain. Her eyes moved across the slumbering men. Suddenly, she noticed that Anthony was not among them.

"Anthony, where are you?" she whispered into the cool fresh darkness. A chill quivered through her as she realized the once-devoted young man had disappeared.

#

*Jesu and the apostles are bone tired. They have completed four journeys now, and they need rest badly,* Gloriel thought.

It was early on a pleasant morning in the month of Nisan, and Jesus invited the apostles to rest awhile apart from the pressing crowd. "Let's go across the sea and find a place of solitude, where we can rest and refresh ourselves before we begin the next journey," he suggested.

Crossing the northern part of the Sea of Galilee in a sturdy boat borrowed from a follower, Jesus and the apostles disembarked on the shores of an isolated area. Pebbles crunched underfoot as they began walking along the shore. A low murmur of voices reached their ears. Looking up, they saw a great multitude of people coming toward them, some running in their eagerness.

"Apparently these people found out where you were going, and got here before you," Gloriel whispered to Jesus.

He sighed, smiled, and welcomed the people. He climbed up an incline and sat down on a boulder, where all the followers could see and hear him. Peter, Andrew, James and John seated themselves on the ground around him.

The crowd hung on all of Jesus' words. He taught them throughout the day, and they were entranced by his wisdom and drawn by his love. Many came to realize that this was not an ordinary preacher. This was a great healer and teacher.

Here and there among the people, listeners were whispering.

"Do you think this could be the Messiah?"

"But he has said nothing about freeing us from the Roman oppressors, so how could that be?"

"Surely the Most High has sent him!"

Late in the afternoon, towards evening, Jesus grew concerned about the people. They had gone all day without eating, and he knew they were hungry.

Just then, Peter approached him. "Master, these people are hungry. Send them away now, so they can find food at the nearby farms, or in town. And they will need someplace to stay for the night. There is nothing to eat around here." He gestured around at the countryside, his green eyes heavy with weariness.

Still seated on the rock, Jesus looked up at Peter. He smiled, and his dark eyes sparkled, despite his fatigue.

"No, Peter, you feed them."

Peter's eyes widened in surprise, and his jaw dropped. "Master, that's not possible!" he said incredulously. A slight frown wrinkled his forehead.

Andrew stepped up to his brother's side. "We have only two fish and five loaves of bread, Master. Are we supposed to buy enough food for 5,000 people?" He asked, his voice cracking with incredulity.

At the foot of the rock, Judas' dour face darkened. He scowled and turned away.

Jesus rose to his feet then, rubbing his eyes and yawning widely. His face showed no concern.

"All right, my friends. Tell the people to sit down on the grass in groups of 50 or so." He stretched his back and yawned again.

Shaking their heads, the apostles moved among the crowd and gave them Jesus' instructions.

When the people were all seated, Jesus asked John to bring him the 5 loaves and the two fish. John gathered up the food and brought it to the Lord, his young face puzzled. Jesus watched John's eyes as he took the loaves and fish from the young man.

He looked up into the deepening blue of the sky, toward Heaven. "Father, we ask your blessing on this food, for the sustenance of these people, and for your Glory!" he said with a piercing resonance in his voice that seemed to vibrate the very bones of the listeners.

He began breaking the bread and fish into pieces. He handed them to the apostles, who distributed them to the crowd and then returned to find him still breaking the fish and bread.

Stunned, they continued dispersing the food, each time returning to find the supply unexhausted.

Everybody ate until they were satisfied. The meager supplies had contented the huge multitude, including the apostles.

"Gather up what remains of the fish and bread," Jesus told the dumbfounded apostles.

They followed his instructions, ending up with 12 baskets full of leftovers. The men were taken-aback and silent as they brought the baskets to the Lord.

*They seem awe-stricken, even after all the miracles they have seen Jesu do,"* Gloriel reflected.

After Jesus sent the apostles back to their boat, Gloriel helped him pass through the crowds, shielding him from their sight. He went off into the mountains, where he prayed far into the night.

#

As time passed, Jesus and the apostles traveled great distances, healing all kinds of diseases and afflictions, bringing peace and recovery to those sick in mind and body.

Seven journeys had been completed as he brought freedom to the spiritually wounded, and even raised the dead. People loved to listen to him, because he taught them in parables, stories they could understand, taken from their everyday lives.

One cloudy day, Jesus and the apostles got into Peter's boat and started across the Sea of Galilee. Suddenly, as was common on the sea, a violent storm arose. Thunder roared like the wheels of chariots, and lightning lit the sky in flashes of shattering brilliance.

The waters began breaking over the boat until it appeared ready to sink. The men were all wide-eyed with terror.

Gloriel watched to see what Jesus would do. However, he lay sleeping peacefully in the stern of the boat, his head on a pillow, totally undisturbed by the wild elements raging around them.

Peter clambered over Andrew and John, half-blinded by the pelting rain and screaming wind. He grasped Jesus' shoulder and shook him awake, shouting above the shriek of the tumult.

"Master! We are about to die!" He screamed into the wind, as a huge wave washed over the boat, tearing at the hapless crew. We're going to drown! Don't you care?!"

Jesus opened his eyes and gazed questioningly at Peter. Sitting up and yawning, he replied calmly, "What are you so frightened about? Why is your faith so small?"

He staggered to his feet in the pitching vessel and extended his arms out over the violently tossing sea. Water streamed down his face and plastered his hair to his skull.

"Peace, be still!" he commanded in a thunderous voice. The sound was ripped away by the raging winds. Instantly, the storm died, and the waters grew silky smooth and calm once more.

The apostles, awestricken and dripping wet, stared at Jesus, openmouthed with astonishment.

For a long moment, no one spoke. Then Andrew whispered to the others in a husky and trembling voice.

"Who can this be, that even the winds and the sea submit to him?"

#

Several days later, the disciples were visiting the region of Magdala, on the western shore of the Sea of Galilee, where they had stayed a few weeks earlier.

A Pharisee named Simon, curious, and secretly hoping to catch Jesus breaking the Law, invited him to dinner.

Peter accompanied him as he entered the courtyard of Simon's home. The meal was being served outside, because the weather had turned very warm. The guests were reclining on Roman couches around a low table

While they were eating, a woman approached Jesus from behind, carrying a beautiful alabaster jar filled with expensive perfume.

Gloriel watched with curiosity to see what Jesus would do. The Father had given her no inkling of what was to occur.

The woman was very beautiful, with shining golden hair, and eyes the color of the sky on a cloudless summer day.

Gloriel watched the woman kneel at Jesu's feet, tears flowing unchecked down her ivory cheeks.

He glanced down at her, and smiled gently. The gleaming tears fell on Jesus' feet, and she wiped them off with her long thick golden curls. She kept kissing his feet over and over as she anointed them with the fragrant perfume from the alabaster jar.

The guests were aghast at her audacity, and murmuring among themselves.

Simon thought to himself, *this proves that Jesus is not a prophet. If he were, he would know this woman putting her hands on him is a sinner. She's a loathsome creature. He can't be sent from God and allow her to do this.* He stroked his grizzled beard in self-satisfaction, and watched to see what Jesus would do next.

Jesus turned to Simon, searching his face with probing dark eyes. "Simon, listen to me," he said quietly. "There is a story I want to tell you."

"Yes, go ahead, Teacher." Simon replied uneasily, shifting his gaze anxiously around the courtyard.

Jesus cleared his throat and raised his voice, still looking directly at Simon.

"Once there was a man who loaned money to two different men. To the first one, he loaned 500 pieces of silver; to the other he loaned 50 pieces. Time went by, and it became obvious that neither one of these men would ever be able to repay him. So, this kindly man cancelled the debts of both men, forgiving them freely."

Jesus turned and slowly paced a few steps, folding his arms. He stopped and faced Simon again. "Now, Simon, which of the two men would you say loved him more after the debts were forgiven? Would it be the one who borrowed 500 pieces of silver," Jesus paused for a moment, looking down at the woman, "or the one to whom 50 pieces were loaned?" His dark eyes widened and glowed as they returned to Simon's face, waiting for a reply.

Simon glanced quickly around at the guests, then back at Jesus. "Well, I would think that the one with the larger debt was most grateful." He peered at Jesus from under shaggy dark brows.

"You are correct, Simon." Jesus smiled and turned toward the woman, who was still kneeling on the ground. Her back was to him now, her head bowed.

"Look at her," he said, gesturing. "When I first came to your home this afternoon, you were very rude. You never offered me any water to wash the dust from the road off my feet. But she has been washing them with her tears, and drying them with her hair. You never gave me a greeting kiss, but she has never stopped kissing my feet since she entered this courtyard. You did not even have the courtesy to anoint my head with olive oil. But see, this woman has anointed my feet with a rare and costly perfume. Breathe in its fragrance, Simon."

Slowly, Jesus reached down and placed one hand gently on the woman's bowed head. "I say to you that her sins, and they are great in number, have already been forgiven. Therefore, she has demonstrated great love for me by her actions. Remember then, Simon, that someone who has little to be forgiven will show only a small bit of love in return. But those for whom many sins are forgiven will reveal great love."

Jesus placed his hand under the woman's chin and lifted her face. The blue eyes still streamed with tears. "Your sins have been forgiven, my daughter," he said clearly.

Murmuring among the guests grew louder, and someone said indignantly "Who is this, who thinks he can forgive sins?"

Ignoring the comment, Jesus smiled, held out his hand, and helped the woman to her feet.

"Come, follow me, Susannah. Faith has brought you freedom."

#

# Chapter Thirty-One

Gloriel stood invisible among Jesus and his disciples, who were sitting around a campfire alongside the road to Bethany

The late fall evening grew chilly as a lonely mournful breeze filled the dusk.

Susannah and the woman called Mary Magdalene huddled close to the fire, wrapped in blankets.

The mood was happy, and laughter and singing resounded around the campsite.

The angel felt a delicious sense of delight in her heart over the always-increasing number of followers of Jesu. Almost three years had passed, and nearly eight separate journeys completed.

*How fruitful the years and the journeys have been for the disciples and apostles. The preaching and teaching, the healing of psyches, bodies and spirits; it has all been so wonderful,* she reflected.

Gazing into their faces as they talked among themselves, Gloriel's breast swelled with love for all of them.

She bowed her head. *Father,* she prayed, *they have come so far from the little band of followers with whom Jesu began his journey, to the huge crowds who follow him now. They are well seasoned, and deeply devoted. Are we nearing the end of Jesu's mission?*

#

"Gloriel."

Startled, her eyes flew open, and she gasped in delight. In her bodily form, she stood at the foot the Father's shining Throne! The familiar sparkling golden atmosphere glittered around her.

"Gloriel, my child, welcome Home." The Father's powerful voice warmed her heart. She sank to her knees and bowed her head. The amber curls glowed in the golden ambiance.

"I want you to rest here with your fellow angels for just a little while, Gloriel. The final stages of my Son's mission will begin when you return to his side. Go now, refresh your sprit and rejoice with your friends, for Man's redemption draws near."

Gloriel raised her golden eyes to the glittering Throne. Will I ever see your face, Father?"

"One day, my child, one day your eyes will truly open and you will distinguish my face. Be off now, Gloriel. Michael and Gabriel await you in the City." There was a smile in the Father's voice.

She rose slowly to her feet and bowed low before the Father's Throne. Straightening, she smiled and turned toward the great City, shimmering across the glassy surface, beyond the colorful fields of asphodel.

Sweet scents pervaded the atmosphere. The familiar golden mist swirled around her feet. As she walked, she reflected on the past few years.

A particular scene rose up in her memory, as she recalled a woman mingling with the crowd surrounding Jesus in a small town in Galilee. The day was cloudy and gray. The narrow, winding street clamored with voices. People were pressing in on Jesus, each one eager to touch him. Noisy and demanding, they jostled one another. The apostles tried to give Jesus breathing space, with little success. She remembered standing next to Jesus and watching a middle-aged woman in a well-worn pale blue linen robe, who was struggling to get close to Jesu. A strand of ash gold hair with streaks of silver had escaped from under her shabby blue veil.

The Father gave Gloriel insight into the woman's condition. Her name was Ruth, and she had at one time been very wealthy. Twelve years of hemorrhaging had left her penniless, as she spent all of her money on doctors, to no avail. Her face was haggard, and lined with pain.

Pushing weakly but steadily, she came up behind Jesu, bent down, and tentatively touched the hem of his robe. The bleeding stopped instantaneously. She felt it to the depths of her being, the ubiquitous heavy pressure in her pelvis had disappeared. Breathless and slightly apprehensive, the woman thought, *Can it really be true? Is my suffering at an end?* But deep in her heart, she knew it was over. *I always thought that miracles happened to someone else at some other time and place,* she reflected.

Jesu raised his lean arms and extended them out over the people standing nearby.

"Who touched me?" he inquired loudly.

Startled, the people in his vicinity vehemently denied it.

"I-I didn't do it."

"It wasn't I!"

"Not me! I wasn't anywhere near him!"

Peter, standing close by, had appeared disconcerted. "But Master," he said in a perplexed voice. "all of these people are pressing on and around you. Why do you ask who touched you?"

"No, Peter, that's not what I mean, Jesus had replied patiently. "Someone touched me deliberately. I felt healing go out to them from me."

He had looked around with a sharp, probing glance into the faces surrounding him. His eyes stopped searching and gazed into Ruth's thin, pointed countenance.

Badly frightened, the woman had realized that Jesu knew exactly what had happened. Pallid and stunned, she fell to her knees in the dust in front of him.

"My Lord, it-it was I." Her voice had been a mere whisper. "I touched you, and healing has come to me after twelve years of seeking." Her heart beat like a trapped bird in her chest. Huge tears of joy began rolling down her cheeks in a steady stream.

All the people crowding around were amazed that Ruth had been healed by simply touching the hem of Jesu's robe. Many witnesses to this healing, some of whom had known Ruth for years, began to follow Jesu then.

Gloriel remembered his words to Ruth, as he raised her to her feet and placed his hands on her bowed head. "My daughter, your faith has healed you. Go now in peace," he said gently, smiling.

High color had flooded Ruth's milk-pale cheeks, and her blue-gray eyes shone vibrantly.

Gloriel beamed at the memory of Ruth's great joy and gratitude to Jesu for her healing.

The little angel was coming closer to the great city now. The glassy surface yielded to a meadow, full and green. She leaned down and touched the bright head of a lovely blossom crouching in the grass at her feet. Bright hued butterflies fluttered and dipped above the fragrant flowers.

She was reminded then of the beautiful gardens surrounding the luxurious home of Lazarus and his sisters. The last time Jesu had visited his good friends, he spent a long time talking, and teaching them. The relationship had changed between them by then, Gloriel realized. Oh, they were still great friends, but the three recognized the fact, by this time, that their long-time friend was truly the Messiah, the Chosen One for whom they had longed those many years. Awe and reverence had become the central part of their love for Jesu.

In her minds eye, she could see Mary sitting enthralled at Jesu's feet. She had hung on his every word, and gazed up with rapture into his face, green eyes sparkling. Her golden skin glowed, and her honeyed curls were swept back and held in place by a pale blue ribbon.

Gloriel smiled, recalling Martha bustling about; toiling and worrying over meeting the needs of their guest, preparing a sumptuous meal for him, while keeping track of every detail. It had been apparent that she was growing more and more impatient and frustrated with her sister, who was oblivious to Martha's glares. Finally, unable stand it any longer, her anger had become overwhelming

"Lord, won't you please tell my sister to come and help me in the kitchen?" she had complained in a choked, exasperated tone. "Pitchers need to be filled, plates brought to the table, and pillows fluffed. Don't you care that she has left me alone to do all the work?" Tears brimmed in Martha's pale brown eyes. Her lank and mousy brown hair had escaped her veil, and hung about her flushed features in loose strands.

Jesu looked up into the frantic woman's face, and love and compassion had softened his features.

"Martha, Martha, you worry too much, and are burdening yourself with so many things that are really not that important, things you can leave to your servants," he replied. "Mary has chosen the most valuable part. I will not take that away from her," he had chided gently.

One lone tear glistened down Martha's thin cheek as she bowed her head in deference to the Lord, and returned to the kitchen, chastened. Gloriel knew that in her heart, Martha had realized that Jesus loved her, even after his rebuke.

Still more memories kept bursting into her mind. She recollected how the people in his hometown of Nazareth had rejected Jesu, for a second time. His Mother, with her sweet quiet spirit, had stood by his side, head held high, comforting and reassuring him in his sorrow for his home town.

Oh, and the children! How he loved the little ones! Gloriel laughed aloud at the sweet memory. Jesus and his disciples had visited a small town by the Sea of Galilee on their way to Jerusalem. Everyone there had been talking about Jesus, and the astounding things he had done. The people were very excited, wanting to see these miracles for themselves, and to hear his parables.

A large group of parents had decided to bring their babies and small children with them, wanting Jesu to touch and bless their little ones.

However, when they arrived at the place where he was, the crowd was so dense that the parents had been unable to get anywhere near Jesu. After a struggle, they had finally been able to push through the throng with their children.

James, Judas, and Matthew had blocked their way then, not wanting Jesu to be bothered with children.

"You must leave now," Judas said, pointing over the heads of the people, toward the entrance of the street and glowering darkly.

"The Master doesn't have time for children. Can't you see he's very busy?" Matthew had inquired indignantly, frowning at a mother who held a crying baby in her arms.

"But-but I just want him to touch my baby girl. She cries all the time, and I know she is in pain. The doctors can't seem to help her at all. Please, please let me take her to him," the woman had pleaded, tears spilling down her pallid cheeks.

"Bring the children here!" Jesu's voice, clear and demanding, pierced through the crowd. "Don't tell them they can't come to me!"

A pathway had cleared through the throng quickly, then. The little ones had surrounded Jesu, eager to touch him. Their parents followed behind. He held out his arms to the children, and they clambered up onto his lap, and clung to his broad shoulders. He had hugged and kissed them, tossing a small, gleefully squealing boy into the air and catching him.

Grinning in pleasure and gently touching each small head in blessing, he had looked around at his disciples then. "Everyone should be like these little ones. I tell you that the Kingdom of my Father belongs to such as them," he said firmly and loudly. "You must become as they are, if you want to be part of that Kingdom. Always treat the children with care and love, for their hearts are pure and honest."

Jesu then penetrated his followers with his strong, piercing eyes. "If anyone should offend one of these little children who believe in me, it would be better for him if someone hung a huge stone around his neck and threw him into the sea!" he said indignantly.

The crowd, including the disciples, had been shocked and amazed at his words. Everyone knew that children just had to be fed and clothed until they were old enough to help their parents.

The mother with the weeping baby came to stand before Jesu. She did not speak a word, but her eyes, blinded by tears, had pleaded with him.

"Give her to me," Jesu told her, in a soft, low voice.

The mother had placed her child trustingly in Jesu's strong hands. He clasped the little one to his chest, bending his head to kiss her gently on her curly brown hair. Instantly, the child stopped crying and peered up into his face. Jesu had smiled, and taken her small pale face between his hands.

"I bless you, sweet Anna. You shall grow up to be my witness to many people," he whispered in her tiny ear.

The baby had gazed up into Jesu's face with large, sweet brown eyes. Suddenly, she smiled, clapping her tiny hands together. Color flooded her face, and two deep dimples appeared in her little cheeks.

Jesu had laughed his warm, rich laugh, throwing back his head with pleasure. He handed little Anna back to her delighted mother.

"What a joyful time that was! Jesu always seems to find time for the children" Gloriel said, aloud.

Her thoughts then turned to a time of grieving for Jesu. The imprisonment and beheading of John the Baptist at the hands of the despot betrayer, Herod, had affected Jesu deeply. John's outspokenness and criticism of Herodias, Herod's adulteress wife had landed him in prison months before. The Jewish leaders wanted John's indignant voice silenced forever.

*If he had only remained silent about Herodias, and not criticized her adulterous marriage to Herod . . .* Gloriel mused.

White-faced with silent grief, Jesu had fled to the hills by himself, when he received the wrenching news. He loved his cousin deeply, and had needed prayer and solitude to sustain him then.

Gloriel recalled his saying to his disciples that among all the prophets, there was none greater than John the Baptist, nor would there ever be.

The angel paused and sat down on the soft grass. She remembered the feeding of the five thousand, and how the next morning, the crowds had found Jesus, and followed him across the Sea of Galilee to the synagogue in Capernaum.

Knowing that they followed him because he had fed them, Jesu had told them that they should not be so worried about perishable things like food. He was concerned that they should be seeking the eternal life that he was able to give them, and not be so occupied with material needs.

The people had kept asking for a sign, reminding him that Moses had given them bread from heaven to eat. Jesu had assured them that it was his Father who had given them the bread, not Moses. He explained to them that the real, true bread of his Father was the One who had come down from Heaven to give life to the world.

Then, the people had said "Master, we want that bread. Give it to us, too."

Gloriel felt a thrill of excitement as she recalled Jesu's reply to their request.

"I am the Bread of life! Your ancestors ate manna in the wilderness, yet they all died. However, the Bread from Heaven gives eternal life to everyone who eats it. I am the living Bread that came down out of heaven. Anyone who eats this Bread will live forever; this Bread is my flesh, offered so that the world may live."

The crowd had begun arguing among themselves about what he meant by these strange words. They couldn't understand how he could possibly give them his flesh to eat. Jesu had continued with his discourse then.

"I assure you, unless you eat the flesh of the Son of Man and drink his blood, you cannot have eternal life within you. But those who eat my flesh and drink my blood have eternal life, and I will raise them at the last day. For my flesh is the true food, and my blood is the true drink. All who eat my flesh and drink my blood remain in me and I in them. I live by the power of the living Father who sent me; in the same way, those who partake of me, will live because of me. I am the true Bread from Heaven. Anyone who eats this Bread will live forever and not die as your ancestors did, even though they ate the manna."

The people, even his disciples, had found this doctrine exceedingly difficult to understand. Some felt repulsed by his words.

Many of his followers had deserted him then, unable to accept this bizarre teaching. Jesu had let them go, not looking to dissuade them from leaving. Only his disciples remained with him then.

*It will always be very hard for people to comprehend this teaching, even down through the ages to come,* Gloriel thought.

She was now drawing very close to the gates of the City. She paused, caught up in remembrance of all Jesu's wonderful deeds.

Her thoughts wandered back to a rainy day on their last visit to Magdala. They had been in town for several days, preaching, teaching and healing. Many of the townspeople had become followers of Jesu.

This day, they were walking down a side street with shuttered windows fronting it in the small seaside town. A woman who had been standing next to a wall approached them, hastily pulling a shawl over her blue-black hair. Gloriel watched closely as the woman drew near, her movements nervous and fidgety. Her head was bowed and her hands trembled. She had stopped a few feet from Jesu, and her face had suddenly changed, and turned dark and inscrutable. Raising her head, wide, glassy deep violet eyes locked onto Jesus, but there was nothing in the contact. Her face contorted, and she had shifted her gaze.

Some in the crowd had looked at her contemptuously, disdain shadowing their eyes. Others had appeared to be terrified of the woman.

She was possessed by demons, Gloriel had realized. *She feels filthy, hopeless and evil*, she had thought sadly.

Jesu had stopped walking, turned and looked at the woman. He waited, his eyes never leaving her exquisite face as she drew near. Her slight figure had begun shaking violently. The violet eyes darkened and filled with despair. She fell to her knees at his feet, burying her wild white face in her hands. Her slender body was racked with sobs. Jesus had bent and placed his hands firmly on her head.

"Mary." His voice was gentle.

The woman's body jerked wildly, and she shrieked in a low, guttural voice, "No! Get away from us! Obscenities had streamed from a mouth contorted with rage and terror.

She stared at him, her face twisted in sudden and uncontrollable panic. She had begun scrabbling along the ground, eyes wild, screaming in terror.

"Come out of her!" Jesu had commanded in a loud, stern voice, "Go back to your father, Satan, and never return! Leave her now!"

The woman's figure had stiffened, and an unearthly moan issued from her lips. Suddenly, she screeched shrilly, over and over, then shuddered and relaxed. She lay motionless and exhausted at Jesu's feet.

"Mary." His voice had been mellow and tender.

The woman slowly raised her head and looked up into his face. How did he know her name?

"Mary, it's all right." His eyes seemed like diamonds in their fire and brilliance, radiating pure love and goodness. "You are free now."

Mary had drawn in her breath sharply. Her body felt flooded with light, and almost weightless. Relief rushed through her being as she had begun to comprehend that the evil spirits had been expelled with just a few words from Jesu. Her liberated body now trembled with adoration.

Great joy had illumined her lovely features, and she cried aloud in ecstasy, "Oh, my Lord! My Lord! Thank you!" She exulted in a rapture of relief, and an agony of loving.

"Be at peace now, Mary of Magdala, and come, follow me." Jesu had spoken in a clear positive voice.

He had always treated women with great compassion and gentleness, Gloriel recalled.

And so, Mary Magdalene had become one of Jesu's most devoted disciples. From that day forward, she had followed him, caring for his needs wherever he went. Her extraordinary devotion to him was unlimited and consuming.

Then, there was the Transfiguration! How breathtaking that miracle had been. Images of the spectacular day rose up behind her eyelids as she closed her eyes.

Jesu had taken Peter, James, and John high up on a mountain top to pray together. Exhausted, Peter, James and John had dropped to the ground and fallen asleep immediately, after the steep ascent up the mountain.

Unseen, Gloriel had knelt beside Jesu. Suddenly, while she was watching him, his face altered before her wondering eyes. It was as if it were lit from within, by a refulgent light so bright that he was surrounded by its aura. Even his clothing had shone a luminous, dazzling white.

At that moment, without warning, Moses and Elijah suddenly appeared and began talking with Jesu. They had discussed his strategy to fulfill his Father's Plan by going to Jerusalem to die.

The three disciples had wakened then. Startled, but exuberant, they beheld Jesu's glory, and Moses and Elijah standing beside him. The radiance was so bright that the disciples had shielded their eyes from its brilliance. The faces and clothing of the three men were a glorious, but terrifying sight to Peter, James and John.

Jesu touched them then, and told them not to be afraid.

Moses and Elijah were preparing to leave.

Peter, dazed with excitement, in his usual impulsive manner had stepped forward and blurted out,

"L-lord, this is s-so wonderful! We w-will b-build three shelters, one for each of you!" he had stammered in his enthusiasm.

He had no sooner said this when a boundless cloud of light, filled with drifting flickers of white fire appeared overhead and covered them.

The three disciples had been filled with terror when a thunderous voice came from within the cloud.

"This is my beloved Son, my Chosen One. Listen closely to him."

"There have been so many astounding restorations and healings of bodies, and minds, and spirits," Gloriel whispered to herself. "And a multitude of lives changed forever by Jesu's healing power."

Her heart expanded with a soaring joy as she walked through the softly glowing gates of the magnificent City of God. She looked around eagerly for Michael and Gabriel among the multitudes of the Heavenly Host engulfing her. The sweet familiar music of Heaven, barely discernible, caressed her ears.

"Oh, it's so wonderful to be Home, even for just a little while," she breathed, her heart at ease, and gratified for now.

## Chapter Thirty-Two

Gloriel found Jesus and the disciples still sitting by the road to Bethany when she returned to his side.

*It feels as if no time has passed since I left them. That must be because there really is no time as earth knows it in our Heavenly Home*, she thought to herself.

Jesus was deep in conversation with his disciples. Gloriel realized that he was speaking to them once more about his imminent death.

*It's like they close their ears whenever he tries to talk to them about the sacrifice and suffering that lie ahead*, she thought sadly. *They just don't seem able to comprehend, when he says that he will be raised up again, and that they also will be raised to eternal life because of his sacrifice.*

"I will be alone at the last. No matter how much you want to stay with me, you will not be able to do this," Jesus said softly, looking around at the circle of well-loved faces surrounding him. Some looked bewildered, some lost, some sad.

Peter piped up "Master, I will stay with you always! Nothing will ever drive me away!" He boasted, a little resentfully. He rubbed his eyes with a sun-bronzed hand.

Jesus looked full into Peter's reproachful face. He was about to answer when a disheveled young man in a dusty white tunic pushed his way impatiently through the crowd and approached him.

*Oh, it's one of Lazarus' servants*, Gloriel thought to herself.

"Master!" The young man cried breathlessly, "Please, you must—come at—once. Lazarus, your—dear friend, is gravely ill,—and about to die." He panted. "Please—come and—save him," he implored, sinking to his knees in exhaustion.

Jesus put out his hand and touched the messenger on his arm. "Jason, it's all right. This sickness will not end in death. It's only happening to bring glory and honor to my Father."

Jason looked at Jesus in bewilderment. "But—Teacher—it's two days journey—" he paused, still laboring to regain his breath. "from here to—Bethany. My master is truly—sick unto death. Please—come now," he pleaded, wringing his hands in distress.

Jesus turned to one of the women standing nearby. "Susannah, please get Jason something to eat and drink, and enough supplies to sustain him on his journey back to Bethany."

With this request, Jesus resumed his conversation with the disciples. "Lazarus is already dead, and for your sakes I am very glad I was not there; so that you may truly believe that the Father sent me. But we shall go to him soon," he said reassuringly, nodding his head and smiling.

#

Two days later, early on a frosty morning in the month of Kislev, Jesus stood up by the campfire, rubbing his hands together. Everyone had breakfasted, and the women were cleaning up the campsite. He clapped his hands to call the apostles attention.

"Well, my friends," he said cheerfully, "it is time. Let's go on to Judea now."

Thomas shook his head and whispered to James and John. "All right, if the Master is so determined, let's follow him, even though we will most surely be killed along with him." His melancholy face was drawn, and his mouth tight-lipped with disapproval.

*Thomas, ever the pessimist*, Gloriel smiled to herself.

James and John both leapt to their feet, always ready and eager for adventure. "Let's go! James sang out cheerfully, his ruddy face aglow.

Judas walked around behind the Lord, glowering fiercely. *We should be heading for Jerusalem, not stopping to help someone who is already dead!* He thought angrily. *It's time we made plans to take our land back from the Roman invaders. After all, that is why the Messiah was to come. It makes me wonder if Jesus really is the Messiah.*

After packing up, Jesus and his followers began the journey to Bethany. Gloriel, as always, walked close beside her charge.

These past few days, the disciples had questioned among themselves as to why the Lord was delaying the journey, when one of his dearest friends lay at death's door, and was probably already dead. None of them was able to understand. Yet they knew that the closer they got to Jerusalem, the more danger threatened them all.

Within the walls of the great city, lay the center of the Master's opposition. The apostles and disciples were growing deeply apprehensive and fearful, for themselves as well as for Jesus. There had been rumors that some of Jesus' enemies were even threatening to stone him.

Bethany is awfully close to Jerusalem," Thomas said to his companions quietly.

*None of them has the courage to question Jesu*, Gloriel thought, shaking her head. She already knew what lay ahead in Bethany. The Father had informed her of the events about to occur.

#

It was a cool, sun-kissed afternoon, and the air was laden with the scent of the flowers crowding the colorful gardens surrounding the house of Lazarus, Martha and Mary two days later. The sky overhead was the color of the delphiniums tossing their heads in the soft breeze. Wisteria tumbled gaily over the veranda. The trilling of birds, and bees humming lazily in the roses fell on Jesus' ears. The large crowd was standing about quietly.

Jesus looked around at the beautiful surroundings, and the great gathering of people standing about. Many of them were his enemies, as well as those who had come to comfort the sisters in their loss.

His eyes fell on the familiar heavy oak door to the house. He thought then of the years since he had first met these dear friends. None of them had married, so the two sisters still lived with their brother.

Someone stepped into the house to announce the Lord's arrival. Lazarus had been in his grave for four days.

Suddenly, Martha came rushing out of the door, her face pale and tear-streaked.

"Master!" she said, her voice quavering. "Our brother is dead. If you had only been here, he wouldn't have died." Resentment colored her words. She began to weep, harsh, racking sobs that shook her shoulders as tears streamed down her haggard cheeks.

"Martha, Martha, sshhhh," Jesus replied gently, putting his arm around her trembling shoulders and making soft shushing sounds. "Your brother will rise again."

"Yes, yes, I know he will rise up again on the last day," she replied, a bit impatiently. "But he need not have died now."

"I think she's feeling a little betrayed, Jesu." Gloriel whispered in Jesus' ear.

He took the weeping woman's ravaged face between his hands. "Martha, don't you know by now that I am the Resurrection and the Life? Do you not trust that whoever believes in me will never die?" He questioned her in a clear voice.

"Yes, Lord, I do know and believe that you are the Christ, the Messiah. The world has been waiting a long time for your coming," Martha sniffled, her voice choked.

At that moment, Mary came hurrying out of the house, sobbing, pursued closely by a large following of wailing friends. When Jesus saw her, he became deeply distressed. He started weeping, shining tears tracing their way down his cheeks.

Mary collapsed at Jesus' feet, gazing up into his face with red-rimmed eyes. Anger, hurt, and grief etched their marks into her lovely features.

*If he really loves me and my family, why didn't he come when we called him—Why?* her mind raced, and she sobbed in anguish.

Some of those standing around watching the poignant scene commented,

"Look how much he loved Lazarus!"

"But if he had come sooner, couldn't he have prevented the death of his friend?"

"Yes, why didn't he do that? Then nobody would be weeping now."

Jesus ignored their taunts, wiping the tears from his face with his sleeve.

*They don't realize that he is only crying out of compassion for the mourners. He knows what is going to happen,* Gloriel commented to herself.

Jesus reached down and raised Mary to her feet. She sagged weakly against his chest. "Mary," he whispered through his tears.

Taking the two grieving sisters by their hands, he walked with them to the grave of their beloved brother. They quickly arrived at the tomb, a cave hewn out of rock, with a huge stone laid across the entrance.

The birds in the trees around the tomb suddenly ceased their chirping. All conversation in the crowd stopped, and an unearthly quiet descended, as if all nature waited in breathless anticipation.

Jesus looked slowly around at the people. Every eye was riveted on him. He let go of the sisters' hands.

"Remove the stone," he said quietly to some servants standing nearby.

"But Lord," Martha's voice was thin and querulous, her face taut. "By now our brother's body will stink. He's been dead for four days!"

Jesus looked down at the ground and sighed deeply.

Mary and the other people standing nearby nodded their heads in agreement, not daring to speak.

Jesus raised his head and looked solemnly into Martha's face. "Martha, didn't I tell you that you only have to believe, and you will see my Father's Glory?"

Martha bowed her head in silent acquiescence.

Jesus nodded to the servants, and they slowly rolled the huge stone to one side of the entrance, grunting and straining.

Gloriel stood close the Jesus. She lifted her heart up to the Father as Jesus stretched both arms toward the heavens. The sharp planes of his golden brown face seemed etched in the light of the mid-day sun.

"Father, he prayed in a clear, strong voice. "Thank you for always hearing me." He paused and inhaled deeply. "For the sake of all these people watching, I thank you for hearing me. I am saying this so that they may believe that you have sent me." He lowered his arms, bowed his head and closed his eyes.

Suddenly, a long-ago memory arose in his mind; another dear friend, another death, when he had not been able to help. A lone tear crept out from under an eyelid, glistening in the sun.

*Abba—please let it be*, he pleaded in silence.

Gloriel stood breathless in anticipation of the Father's Glory to be shone.

The stillness was profound as everyone waited with bated breath to see what Jesus would do next. Not a breath of air stirred. Birds and insects were silent and motionless.

Suddenly, Jesus raised his head, opened his eyes, and cried out in a deep, resonant voice.

"LAZARUS! COME OUT!"

The sound echoed clearly around the neighboring countryside.

Everyone assembled stood mesmerized by the drama unfolding. No one spoke or moved a muscle. Again, there was utter silence, and all eyes fixed on the entrance to the tomb.

There was an almost imperceptible movement inside the darkness of the cave. All the people gasped in unison as Lazarus, still wrapped in his grave clothes, shuffled slowly out into the pale sunshine and cool clear air. He stopped right outside the mouth of the tomb, the head covering still shrouding his face.

A few moments of stunned silence passed, and then a soft murmur started moving through the crowd. The trees and the birds awoke then, and their songs filled the air with joyful sweet music.

Mary covered her mouth with both hands, the pupils in her green eyes huge with shock. Martha sank to her knees, her face drained of all color.

"Remove the grave clothes and set him free," Jesus instructed the servants, grinning.

Gloriel took on her bodily form and stood quietly to one side of the crowd, watching the jubilant scene, and the celebration that followed. In the midst of the excitement, no one except Jesus noticed the beautiful young amber-haired girl in a lovely blue gown, standing silently in the shade of an olive tree.

A kind of bitter sweetness filled Gloriel's heart. *The Jewish leaders will be even more determined to destroy Jesu now, and perhaps even Lazarus, too,* she mused. *But the Father's Plan is nearing fulfillment.*

Her sweet face wreathed in a brilliant smile and Jesus fixed his eyes on her, nodded and smiled.

Still, no one noticed her form fade away, and she walked unseen through the crowd.

The Jews who had been commissioned by their leaders were walking around questioning many of the people, and conducting a whispered colloquy among themselves.

*They are looking for reasons to arrest Jesu as a seditionist. They're worried that his raising Lazarus from the dead will draw even more people to follow him,* Gloriel reflected.

Two of the Jewish leaders strolled casually over to stand by Jesus.

"Gideon, Asher, what can I do for you?" Jesus inquired, smiling broadly.

Asher, a tall, heavy-set gray haired man, fixed Jesus with a haughty stare. "Teacher, is it your intention to declare yourself King of the Jews? This is the rumor we are hearing." He drew his robe about himself, as if he were afraid he would be contaminated. A sudden breezed lifted the phylacteries on his narrow forehead.

Jesus fixed the man with his clear, steady gaze. "My Father's Kingdom is not of this world, Asher."

"Your father! I understand your father has been dead for some time, Jesus ben Joseph," Gideon interjected, his pale brown eyes flashing with indignation.

A few other Pharisees were gathering around, curiosity creeping over their features.

Gloriel remained unseen behind them, listening closely.

"Gideon," Jesus replied calmly and resolutely, "I speak of my Heavenly Father."

"The Most High? Do you speak of the Most High as your Father?!" Asher was apoplectic with rage, his stout florid face turning sour, his pinched nose stuck high in the air. Veins bulged in his wrinkled neck.

"I do. He is. I am come to do his will." Jesus turned his back and walked away, striding over and placing his arms around a beaming Lazarus.

"Are you hungry, old friend?" He asked jokingly.

The religious leaders were left standing open-mouthed, some sputtering with rage.

"Jesu, Jesu, it begins now. The hour is coming," Gloriel whispered in Jesus' ear.

# Chapter Thirty-Three

Jesus and the disciples remained at the home of Lazarus, Martha and Mary for several days. News of the miracle of Lazarus' rising from the dead spread like a wildfire, and the ranks of the Master's followers increased daily.

Meanwhile, the anxiety of the chief priests and Pharisees grew to the point of desperation, so they called for an emergency council in Jerusalem.

"What are we to do? This man is drawing more and more followers with his miracles. If we keep letting him have a free hand, soon all the people will believe in him," Asher said petulantly. He rose to his feet, dark eyes moving like a cobra's over the gathering. "Soon the people will accept him as their King, and this will antagonize the Romans."

Gideon stood up beside Asher, glowering darkly. "We must find a way to rid our country of this pain-in-the-neck permanently."

Caiaphas, the high priest, a very crafty and devious man, stood up abruptly. His headdress was of purest white silk, sewn with various hues of sparkling gems, with wisps of silvery white hair standing out like dandelion fuzz around it. His long silver beard and colorful robes, commanded the respect of the men gathered before him.

"None of you have a scrap of discernment or insight," he interjected disdainfully in a thin, querulous voice. Pacing slowly back and forth, he shook his gnarled fist in the air. "For the people's sake, to save our nation, it is better for one man to be put to death." A fierce cold flash darted from under his hooded lids. "We must concentrate our efforts to stop this renegade from captivating all the people."

A murmur of assent swept over the assemblage.

It was then, and from that day onward, that the Jews conspired together, plotting to bring about Jesus' death.

#

One mild winter evening, Jesus and the apostles gathered around the dinner table with Lazarus and his sisters. Jesus grew quiet, his face pale and stern. Conversation ceased, and all eyes fixed on him.

The flickering light of fat yellow candles warmed the rich wood of the table. Peter and John looked at the Lord expectantly, for they realized that he was troubled about something.

Gloriel stood nearby, listening closely.

Jesus cleared his throat and looked around the table into each face, his dark eyes filled with mysterious liquid lights.

"My dear friends," he paused and closed his eyes momentarily. "The Son of Man must suffer grievously, and be put to death. But, he will rise again on the third day." His voice cracked, and he heaved a great sigh.

Stunned and disheartened, Peter rose from the table and stared at Jesus. "No, Master, this cannot be. You shall not die," he said raggedly.

Jesus shook his head. "Peter, you don't understand. Unless a seed falls to the ground and is buried, it cannot bear fruit. My Father's Plan must be carried out. Don't be afraid, my friends. You trust my Father, now I need you to trust me, also."

The candle light gleamed like a yellow halo around his head. He rose to his feet and put an arm around Peter's shoulders.

"My Father's house has many rooms. I am going to prepare a place for all of you there." He looked into each face once more. "When it is ready, I will return to get you, so that you may be with me forever. You already know where I'm going, and also how to get there."

Thomas raised his voice, trembling in indignation.

"No, we haven't the slightest idea where you are going, Master." His sharp features colored with annoyance. "So how on earth can we possibly know how to get there?" His gray eyes flashed in the candlelight.

"Thomas, my dear cynical friend, I am the Way, the Truth and the Life. There is no one who can get to the Father except they go through me. If you really knew who I am, then you would know my Father, also. I tell you, from this moment onward, you have seen Him; you have known Him."

Jesus' voice was gentle but firm and his gaze riveted Thomas, who swallowed nervously, and lowered his eyes, unable to reply.

Everyone was silent once again, a shadow clouding each face.

"Come, let's get some rest. We'll leave early in the morning for Ephrem, and then on to Peraea, Jericho and Capernaum. At Passover, we will return to Jerusalem. There is still much to do." Jesus finished quietly.

Early the following morning, as the pale winter sun rose above a faded lavender horizon, Jesus and his followers packed for the journey and gathered together.

Lazarus, Martha and Mary busied themselves making certain that their guests were well supplied for their journey.

Gloriel whispered in Jesus' ear "Jesu, you must send for your mother now. It is time; she needs to be with you." Jesus closed his eyes and nodded.

"Mary," he called out to Mary Magdalene. "Mary, will you and Susannah please come here?"

The two women hurried to his side. "I want you to take two or three of the disciples and go to Nazareth. It is time for my mother to be with us. Bring her to Capernaum, and we will meet you there. Take care on your journey, and be sure you have enough supplies." He smiled at them.

"Yes, Lord." Susannah replied, her blue eyes sparkling. "We are almost finished packing now."

Mary Magdalene looked sharply at Jesus, her brows as black as a raven. "Master, will your mother be going with us when we return to Jerusalem?" Her lovely brow furrowed with concern. The silky blackness of her hair escaped from the confines of the veil along her temple.

"Yes, Mary. She will remain with me until the end. This is my Father's wish," he said, laying a hand on her shoulder.

"The end, Lord?" Her deep violet eyes filled with tears as she gazed at her beloved Master.

Jesus smiled at her gently, and replied "Let's get ready now, Mary." He turned and strode away to speak with Peter, Andrew, James and John.

Mary Magdalene's eyes followed him adoringly, and she was lost in thought.

"Mary, let's finish packing, and get started on the journey to Nazareth. Whom shall we ask to go with us?" Susannah inquired, jarring Mary Magdalene out of her reverie.

"I think probably Philip and Thomas, Susannah. I'll go ask them now." Her eyes were already searching the crowd for the two apostles.

#

Several days later, Jesus and his disciples were still a day's journey from Capernaum. As they traveled, many healings and other miracles occurred among the crowds of people following them, and their numbers continued to expand.

After a night's rest, the apostles bustled about getting ready to resume the journey. Across the dusty road, a few unkempt shepherds were finishing their breakfast and preparing to herd their sheep into Jerusalem.

Gloriel noticed a familiar figure among them. His gray beard obscured most of his nut-brown face, but she recognized him. "Ah, Benjamin, so we meet again. You were there at the beginning. The Father wants you there for the finish. Do you recognize our Jesu yet?" She whispered under her breath.

The shepherds stood close together, deep in conversation, and not paying any attention to the large throng starting to move down the road in the opposite direction. The people parted to let Jesus walk at the front of the crowd.

As he started through the rising dust of the road, staff in hand, he stopped abruptly, and looked curiously at the little band of shepherds. Benjamin turned his head at that moment, and his eyes locked with Jesus' intense gaze. A strange expression moved over the shepherd's weathered features, and his brows knit together in a puzzled look.

Jesus smiled and nodded. Benjamin politely returned the nod.

*Who.? I know him, I know him . . . but where . . . ?* Benjamin searched his memory for an answer, but none came. He watched curiously as Jesus walked on down the road followed closely by the vast crowd accompanying him.

"Hey! Benjamin! The gruff voice of one of his companions brought the shepherd out of his reverie. "I asked if you were ready to get started. Were you off in the land of dreams? Come on, let's go, you lazy son of a barkeep!"

"Just a minute, Abijah, just a minute. Don't be in such a big hurry." Benjamin replied, scrambling to his feet.

He walked over to one of the men following Jesus and clutched his sleeve. "Friend, who is that man you're traveling with?" he inquired.

The man paused and stared in disbelief at Benjamin. "Where have you been, living in a cave? Everyone knows that's Jesus of Nazareth. He's a great teacher and healer. He has worked many scores of miracles. A lot of people believe he is the Messiah." Impatiently, he shook off Benjamin's restraining hand and rejoined the throng.

*Jesus of Nazareth? Jesus! Can it really be the Jesus who was my friend when he was a child? I remember he and another young boy used to come and play with the lambs. He is about the right age. No, it cannot be. He was only a simple carpenter's son,* Benjamin said to himself. Memories stirred in the dimmest corner of his mind.

"Come on, Benjamin, we need to get going!" Abijah's rasping voice interrupted his thoughts.

Benjamin turned and looked at the other shepherds, shook his head, and started walking toward the flocks bleating and milling about in the field beside the road.

#

During the days that followed, the multitudes were amazed by the wonders worked throughout the journey at the hands of this charismatic man called Jesus. The blind received their sight; the deaf regained their hearing; the mute spoke; the lame walked; and even lepers were cleansed by just a word from the lips of Jesus.

Many more began to realize that indeed this was the Messiah they had awaited for so many centuries. Others, particularly the scribes and Pharisees sent by Caiaphas to spy on him, grew more and more concerned that soon all of the people would be disciples of this itinerant upstart. Their influence and power were at stake. Escalating feelings of outrage and fury spread throughout their group.

Gloriel, mingling unseen among them, grew increasingly anxious for the safety of her charge.

#

Jesus placed his arms around his mother's slight form. Kissing the top of her head, he whispered, "Emi, I am so glad you have been with me these past few months."

It was the beginning of the month of Nisan, and the weather was growing warmer as the time for the Passover celebration drew near. Jesus, his disciples and apostles had just left a small town east of the river Jordan, and were now southbound, heading for Jerusalem.

Gloriel and Sariel stood close by, smiling at the exchange of affection between their charges. They were both feeling anxious, as they knew what lay ahead for Jesus, and for his mother, in the great city.

Suddenly, there was a commotion among the crowd, and a disheveled young man appeared, pushing his way through the people.

"He is so handsome! Almost beautiful," Gloriel whispered to Sariel.

He was wearing a tunic of the finest white linen, colorfully embroidered. A gold necklace hanging around his neck glinted brightly, reflecting the rays of the springtime sun. Sandals of the finest leather adorned his feet as he dropped to one knee, gasping, in front of Jesus and Mary. Chestnut colored waves of hair clung to his neck and perspiring face.

Mary disengaged herself from her son's embrace and moved to one side. Sariel stepped back with her.

"Teacher!" The young man gasped, breathless. "Teacher! I was afraid you had left already!" Continuing to wheeze and pant for breath, he reached out a sun-browned and muscular arm toward the Lord. A huge multi-faceted emerald ring displayed its deep heart on his forefinger.

"Abasalom, it's all right. Catch your breath. I will wait." Jesus said quietly. "You are well-named, son of David," he added, smiling.

*How does he know my name?* Absalom wondered, beginning to breathe easier.

"Teacher, I heard you speaking yesterday in town." Absalom paused, and took a deep breath." I need to ask you a question."

Jesus took hold of the young man's outstretched arm and helped him to his feet.

"Yes, my son. What is it?" Jesus asked encouragingly.

"What do I need to do to inherit the eternal life you talked about, Teacher?" Absalom gazed at the Master, fascinated by the depth in the dark eyes which seemed to probe his very soul.

Jesus returned his gaze, and his face softened. "Absalom, you know the commandments, of course. 'You shall not kill. You shall not commit adultery; you shall not covet your neighbor's wife.' You know them all, do you not? His intent look of love did not waver from Absalom's cool gray eyes.

The young man smiled, and his white teeth gleamed in the sunlight.

"Yes, Teacher! Yes! Ever since I was a child I have studied all these things. I have kept all of the commandments. But there is more I must do, I know. I felt it in my heart while you were speaking yesterday. Please tell me what else I must do, and I will do it!"

Jesus took the lad's hand in both of his own, his eyes never leaving Absalom's face. "Yes, yes there is something else you must do."

People standing nearby in the crowd strained to hear what Jesus would say to the young man.

"I think Absalom is holding his breath," Gloriel whispered to Sariel, smiling.

"Go home, Absalom, sell what you have, and share it with the poor." The Lord's tone was gentle, yet firm. "There is wisdom not available on easier pathways, my son."

Absalom' glittering gray eyes widened and his fine features fell, the smile fleeing. He dropped his gaze from Jesus' face, and sighed deeply, for he was immensely wealthy.

One gleaming tear slid slowly down the golden-brown skin of Absalom's cheek. He slowly withdrew his hand from Jesus' grasp. Without a word, he turned and walked slowly away, shoulders hunched and head down.

*He will not be coming back*, Gloriel thought sadly. *He thinks that he can comply with God's laws and still remain in control of his life.*

Jesus sighed deeply and shook his head. "It's so hard for those who are rich in this world's treasures to enter my Father's Kingdom. It is actually easier for a camel to pass through the eye of a needle than for a wealthy man to get in," he said loudly and clearly. "There is no beginning that isn't blemished with sorrow over some ending. You must remember that everyone who is not with me aligns himself against me, and everyone who doesn't harvest with me, causes a rift."

He lowered his head and whispered, "Oh, Absalom, it was your heart I wanted, not your conformity to the Law."

"Then who on earth can ever be saved?" A surly voice from the crowd boomed out.

*That's one of the high priest's Pharisee spies*, Gloriel thought.

Jesus' reply was loud and clear. "It may be impossible for you, and everyone else. But it is not impossible for my Father. With Him, nothing is impossible," he said firmly.

Mary returned to his side, smiling up at his dear face, her still lovely features softly creased. She felt in the depths of her soul that the end of his mission was growing near.

Sariel looked gravely at her precious charge, her childish face somber.

*Oh, my sweet Mary, your time of pain and sorrow approaches also,* she thought to herself.

## Chapter Thirty-Four

Jerusalem! The holy city stood starkly outlined against a multi-colored sunset. Red, gold, pink, lavender, purple, orange, yellow and mauve contended for prominence, gleaming behind the black silhouette of the city.

Jesus stood in the midst of the throng accompanying him, staring at the shapes etched in the darkening sky. Gloriel, standing beside him, felt the tension in his body and spirit. He was frowning, and his neck was splotched with red.

She placed an unseen hand upon his shoulder and whispered in his ear.

"Jesu, dear Jesu, set your mind and heart upon the Glory that lies beyond the days ahead in the city. You will soon complete your mission."

Jesus closed his shadowed eyes briefly, and nodded his head.

He raised his voice, and his words resounded clearly through the gathering. "We shall spend the Sabbath in Bethany, and on the following day, go on into Jerusalem. Those of you who wish to go into the city for the Sabbath now, go in peace, and we shall join you there."

Reluctantly, most of the crowd then proceeded on into the city, for there was not room in Bethany for such a huge assembly. They were anxious to catch sight of Lazarus, for the city was buzzing with the story of his restoration to life.

Jesus, his apostles and a few disciples who were especially close to him, sought lodging with Lazarus and his sisters; who welcomed them with joyful greetings.

"Master, welcome! We are honored to have you in our home once more. Peace be with you!" Lazarus exclaimed. He embraced Jesus, a huge smile wreathing his thin features.

Mary and Martha greeted their guests cordially, and Martha immediately fled to the kitchen to prepare a sumptuous repast for their guests. Mary, as always, stayed close by Jesus' side, her face glowing.

Mary Magdalene and Susannah followed Martha into the kitchen, with offers of help.

Gloriel studied the little group, remembering the journey just completed. Jesu had told his followers many wonderful parables during this last journey. People everywhere were astounded by his marvelous deeds and wise teaching. From Ephrem, eastward along the border of Galilee, south through Peraea, west along Jordan and on into Jericho, to the delight of his followers, he worked many miracles, and multitudes gathered and followed.

Gloriel recalled in particular the healing of a blind beggar. The man had been sitting in the dirt along the edge of the road, just outside the city. His curiosity aroused by the noise of the passing crowd, he asked one of the people what was going on. The passerby paused long enough to inform the blind man

"It's Jesus of Nazareth going by. He has worked many marvelous miracles. I myself have seen several of them."

"Yes," the blind man replied eagerly, "I have heard the stories about him."

He struggled to his feet, tripping over his dirty tattered robe. He began shouting at the top of his lungs. "Jesus, Son of David! Jesus, Son of David! Stop!"

Jesu had turned his head quickly at the outcry, and saw the blind man waving his arms and yelling excitedly.

"Have mercy on me!" The man's shouts grew louder with his desperation.

Jesus approached the frantic man. "What do you want me to do for you, Tubal?" He inquired gently.

"Please, please, Lord. I want to see! I want to see!" Tubal responded, his voice cracked and quavering. His arms extended pitifully to Jesus, as tears cut a pathway down his dusty cheeks. "Oh, my Lord, please." He covered his filmed, opaque eyes, his voice but a hoarse whisper now.

"Very well, my son. You can see!" Jesu had commanded. "Your great faith has brought you healing."

Slowly, Tubal lowered his grimy hands. His eyes remained closed. Gradually, bit by bit, his papery, veined eyelids opened. Bright, piercing blue eyes gazed out at the long-forgotten countryside of Jericho. The ugly film had disappeared from his eyes. Great joy illuminated his features, and he fell at the feet of Jesus, praising God.

And all who witnessed the miracle had raised their voices in worship.

*There has been so many, many wonderful healings.* Gloriel thought, contentedly.

Her reverie was abruptly interrupted by Jesus' voice.

"My little children," he said quietly to the apostles and disciples gathered for the Sabbath meal in the warm lamplight of Lazarus' dining room. "Tomorrow we shall enter Jerusalem. Inside the city, all the words of the ancient prophets regarding the Son of Man will begin to come true. A traitor who is close to him will hand him over to the Romans. He will be beaten with whips and fists, mocked, spat upon, and tormented. He will be treated in an appalling way, and in the end, they will kill him." Jesus paused then, and swallowed. "But do not despair, for he will rise up again on the third day," he finished with a smile.

"No, no, Lord . . ." Simon Peter's strangled voice was a faint whisper in the silent room.

Over in a shadowed corner of the room, Judas Iscariot averted his dark predatory face and bit his lower lip.

Gloriel moved unseen to Jesu's side and placed her small hand upon his shoulder. His dark eyes shimmered brightly in the lamplight.

There was total silence. Sitting beside him, his mother moved closer to him and laid her head on his arm. No one else said a word.

Across the table, John's wide, expressive black eyes filled with tenderness as he gazed at his Master.

"They don't understand, Jesu. The meaning of your words is hidden from them, and they cannot grasp what you are saying," Gloriel whispered in his ear.

Jesus bowed his head and closed his eyes. He sat quietly for a moment, then opened his eyes, looked around at the circle of bewildered faces, and smiled at his mother.

"Well then, friends, let's finish our Sabbath meal. We need to get up early in the morning. Lazarus, you are looking very well, dear friend," he said with a grin.

Gloriel removed her hand from his shoulder and smiled at Sariel.

#

Early in the morning the next day, Jesus stood outside the home of Lazarus, Martha and Mary. The apostles situated themselves around him, talking quietly among themselves.

Gloriel and Sariel stood close by their charges.

"Sariel, this is the day Jesu will declare to the people that he is the promised Messiah, the King that was to come. It's no ordinary day, my friend," Gloriel whispered to her companion.

Sariel nodded her golden head in understanding.

Suddenly, thoughts of Anthony, of his beautiful face and golden hair, and his devotion to Jesu, crept into Gloriel's mind. *I wonder if we will see him in the city,* she mused. *Oh, there are thousands and thousands of people here today. There really is not much chance of that.*

Jesu's voice interrupted her daydream.

"Matthew, Philip, I want you to go into the city now. When you enter the Sheep Gate, you will find a white colt which has never been ridden, tethered just inside. Untie it and bring it to me. If anyone should question you, just tell them, "The Lord needs it."

Matthew and Philip looked at one another in puzzlement, but were afraid to question the Master's strange request.

"Yes, Lord," Matthew said, looking bewildered.

The two men scurried away toward the great city, robes flapping around their legs.

As soon as they left, Jesus entered the house and went into the room which had always been his in Lazarus' home. When he emerged from the house, he was wearing the fine cream-colored seamless robe which his mother had spun for him with such loving care.

Mary smiled up at him with tears in her eyes. Jesus placed an arm around her shoulders and hugged her tightly.

"It's all right, Emi, it's all right."

"Yes, I know, my son," she said with a ragged sigh.

Before long, Philip and Matthew returned with a small white donkey colt in tow.

"It was just as you said it would be, Master," Philip said, breathlessly. "The owner asked us why we were untying his colt, and when we told him that the Lord has need of it, he made no more objections."

Both Matthew and Philip threw their robes over the colt's back for Jesus to sit on. Then they began to descend the Mount of Olives down to the gates of Jerusalem. A huge multitude of Jesus' followers had re-joined the apostles by this time.

James, John, Peter and Andrew whispered among themselves.

"This great gathering of people is sure to attract the attention of the Roman patrols," Andrew said, mopping his forehead.

"Yes, the master could be arrested for disturbing the peace," James commented quietly.

As they drew close to the city, Jesus paused, and gazed ahead. The immense crowd waited with bated breath. Was Jesus going to announce his mission to cast out the Roman invaders?

"Oh, Jerusalem!" he cried out in a loud voice, "So many times, I have longed to gather your children under my wings like a mother hen does her chicks!" His voice fell, and glistening tears traced their way down his cheeks and into his beard. "I so hoped that you would find the way to Peace. But alas, it's too late now. The Way is hidden from your sight. Soon your enemies will surround you, crush you, and your families also. There will not be one single stone left in its former place. You have turned down God's offering. The opportunity is no more." He sighed deeply, and wiped his tears away. "Come now, my friends," he said to his disciples.

Those nearby in the crowd stood frozen in disbelief. Jesus had just thrown away their long awaited freedom, and they were stunned.

Everyone began hurrying down the hill, except those who had heard Jesus disavow his kingship. Their faces were downcast, reproachful. Some were in tears.

Mounting the little donkey, Jesus led the way into the city. Joyful followers who still saw him as Messiah spread their cloaks on the path before him, shouting and singing and praising God for all the wondrous miracles Jesus had done among the people. They laid palm branches and flowers along the way before him.

Soon a huge crowd from the city gathered along both sides of the road, eager to see the miracle-worker who had raised Lazarus from the dead. Surely, this was the Messiah who had come to free them from the hated Roman rule. Hosannas resounded through the streets.

Overhead, golden sunlight illuminated the joyful scene. A gentle breeze lifted the shining brown hair from Jesus' suntanned brow. His bronzed features and muscular arms accented the creamy ivory of his linen robe.

*He is so beautiful, my Jesu,* Gloriel thought lovingly.

A tight ring of space surrounded the slowly plodding little white donkey. Peter, Andrew, James and John encircled Jesus, trying to protect him from the surging masses of people pressing in upon him. The shouts of the crowd grew deafening.

Gloriel's heart rejoiced to see her Jesu so honored. But her joy was tinged with anticipation of the bitter trial which lay ahead for him. *Before, he would not accept praises from the people,* she thought to herself. *But now the time has come. The Pharisees are so angry now.* She watched the tight, furious faces of the little clusters of Pharisees, who gathered together listening jealously to the shouts of the people.

"Hosanna to the son of David!"

"Blessed is the King who has come in the name of the Lord!"

"They don't realize that he has not come to destroy, but to save," Gloriel whispered to herself, as she walked beside Jesus. "And so, the prophecy is fulfilled."

*"Rejoice greatly, O people of Zion! Shout in triumph, O people of Jerusalem! Look, your king is coming to you. He is righteous and victorious, yet he is humble, riding on a donkey—even on a donkey's colt.* Zechariah 9:9 NLT

"Prophecy is coming to pass before their very eyes, and they do not recognize it," Gloriel whispered in Jesu's ear.

He nodded and smiled. His luminous dark eyes, gleaming with a dark flame of sorrow, wandered over the enthusiastic multitude.

*Even those closest to him don't realize that his kingdom is not a political one,* Gloriel mused, sadly.

The people grew more and more energized and excited. So many of them had waited for years for this triumphant day. Most of them were thinking that he was indeed the Messiah, the long-awaited Savior who would deliver them from the iron Roman yoke. He would raise the twelve tribes of Israel up to be rulers of the whole world, the richest and most powerful nation ever!

"Hosanna! Save us, son of David!"

The people's voices rang through the air and reverberated clearly down the streets of Jerusalem.

The Pharisees looked on with increasing dread and fury. One of them bellowed out to Jesus as he rode slowly by.

"Teacher! Tell these people to stop this nonsense! This is a dishonor to God! Our city will be destroyed!"

Jesus paused and looked straight into the eyes of the Pharisee. His gaze was steely.

"No, Jacob. Even if I did that, the rocks at your feet would take up the cry."

The Pharisee looked stunned. Mostly because Jesus had called him by name, even though there was no way he could have known it. Jesus nodded and resumed riding down the street.

"We must do something now. We must not wait any longer," Jacob said quietly to his companions. "Soon the whole world will be chasing after this drifter, and we will lose control of the people."

## Chapter Thirty-Five

The disciples spent the night once more at the home of Lazarus, and early in the morning, Jesus was up and eager to return to the city.

"I want to go directly to the Temple this morning," he said to Peter, yawning and stretching his long arms, as they left the house and passed through the colorful garden. "It's been a long time since our last visit."

"Yes, Lord." Peter replied, leaping over a low garden wall.

"He's surprisingly graceful for a man with such a muscular, stocky frame," Gloriel whispered to her charge. Jesus grinned and nodded in agreement, increasing his pace.

"Jesu, rumors are spreading that the Messiah is not fulfilling the people's expectations of him. They want to know where the conquering hero is, the one who is to finally get them out from under the heels of the Roman oppressors," Gloriel continued, unheard by the others. "They are looking to you for fulfillment of their hopes and dreams, and a lot of people are questioning whether you really are the Messiah, in spite of your miracles."

Jesus paused, and his eyes narrowed speculatively. Resuming his steady pace, he began whistling a bright melody; his head lifted high, his shoulders back.

"Just as Mary taught him," Sariel whispered to Gloriel.

The gray-eyed dawn brought with it a heavy mist, which was permeating the air, even though it was the month of Nisan, when days were usually warm and sunny.

The group of disciples accompanying Jesus walked silently, each caught up in his or her own thoughts. Mary Magdalene, Susannah, and Jesus' mother walked quietly behind the other disciples, increasing their pace to keep up.

Gloriel remained close at hand, never far from her charge.

Pausing, Jesus called out in a loud clear voice. "We will go straight to the Temple this morning, to join the other pilgrims in honoring my Father's House."

As they ascended the Mount of Olives, overlooking the magnificence of the Temple Mount, the disciples paused in awe. The mist was clearing, and rays of pale yellow sunlight touched the streets of Jerusalem. Hundreds of thousands of sojourners jammed the city.

Jesus strode eagerly down the slope of the Mount of Olives. The crowd began to move with him, some of them slipping and sliding and scurrying to keep up.

Pacing purposefully, Jesus entered the Nicanor Gate, along with the trailing crowd. Hot bodies pressed around them and the acridness of sweat saturated the air. Jesus and his disciples pushed through and headed directly to the gates of the Temple.

The air in the city lay like a warm blanket on them now; all signs of the gray mist had dissipated.

"Sariel, so many of the pilgrims are weary and footsore. They've traveled such great distances to celebrate the Passover." Gloriel commented, watching the crowd.

"Yes, I see people from Mesopotamia, Parthians, Edomites, and even some Egyptians. Look, there are blacks from Abyssinia. A lot of the people are barefooted and ragged." Sariel replied, sighing.

The huge crush of humanity jam-packing the narrow cobblestone streets of the great city seemed to ebb and swell like the rolling tides of a vast sea.

The Temple itself sparkled with a shimmering golden brilliance, illuminated by a radiant shaft of sunlight.

By now, Jesus was almost running, elbowing his way through the mass of humanity. Pulling open the door of the Royal Portico, he paused, breathing heavily. His dark eyes swept swiftly around the courtyard. A milling assortment of sacrificial animals, bleating, bawling, and defecating, met his probing gaze. Cages of doves, their wings fluttering against the bars, and squawking in terror, were sitting on tables. The smell was sickening.

Tables of the money-changers were positioned around the edges of the portico. These self-serving and despised men extricated 5 percent from the people for converting the standard Greek and Roman money to Jewish and Tyrian money, the only coinage that was allowed to be used in the Temple.

Bargaining, prattling, and hawking their "wares" the sellers sat on high stools behind the tables.

Gloriel, standing close beside the Lord, watched in amazement as his features became distorted with fury. A pure, white-hot anger seized him with sudden ferocity. Never in his life had she seen such a ferocious, harsh expression on her Jesu's face. His eyes were flashing and filled with fiery zeal as he glared around this bargaining market in the House of God.

His followers watched open-mouthed. Knowing their corrupt hearts and minds, Jesus raised his staff high over his head and smashed it down on a money changer's slab, cracking the table into two pieces. Seizing them by the edges, one by one, he violently overturned all the heavy tables, as if they were kindling wood. Boxes of coins flew through the air onto the floor among the milling animals and their feces.

The money changers fled, robes flapping around their legs, as if in fear of their very lives.

Ferocious and scowling, Jesus roared in a voice filled with wrath and disgust, "My Father's Temple is to be a House of Prayer! You have turned it into a lair for robbers! Begone, all of you!! Get out, you priests, Levites, all of you Pharisees!!

He fashioned a whip out of some cords lying nearby, and drove all the animals out of the Temple, still shouting with rage.

*No one dares question him now, or raise a voice in protest,* Gloriel mused. *They are afraid, even the Pharisees. I remember when he cleared the Temple once before, at the beginning of his ministry. How quickly they forget.*

The outraged religious leaders whispered among themselves, fanning their anger to a fever pitch. They were afraid of the people's reaction if they tried to arrest Jesus now. Their fury rose to a white-hot level.

"We can accuse him of blasphemy," said one, sputtering in his impotence.

"Or arrest him secretly," another murmured, looking around furtively.

"Even if we do arrest him, only the Romans can pass a death sentence, and we must silence him permanently. After all, the Romans are counting on us to maintain order," replied the first Pharisee sarcastically, a sneer on his cold crafty face.

Later that evening, back in Bethany, Jesus, the apostles, and a few weary disciples once again gathered around Lazarus' table for supper.

After they had eaten, Lazarus' sister Mary left the room and returned carrying a beautiful alabaster jar of expensive nard. She loosened the golden cascade of her beautiful thick honey-colored hair, which hung about her slight figure like a shawl. Kneeling down, she poured the ointment over Jesus' feet, and wiped them with her hair. The aromatic oil brought with it a sense of peace, and those present in the room felt soothed and relaxed.

All save one. Burning with indignation, Judas Iscariot jumped to his feet, shouting. Anger lay in his eyes like a smoldering fire.

"Stop it! Master! Tell her to stop! That ointment should have been sold, and the proceeds given to the poor!"

*Hmm . . . As if you're really worried about the poor, Judas.* Gloriel said to herself.

"Judas! Leave her alone. She has been saving it to anoint me for my burial. She shall not be denied this," Jesus chided Judas. Tenderly, he placed his hand on Mary's bowed head. "Mary . . ." he whispered.

His face flaming with embarrassment and anger, Judas whirled around abruptly and stormed out of the house. As he hurried out the door, Satan came rushing into him, finding entrance through his anger at the Lord. He fled immediately into Jerusalem heading straight to the leading priests in the Temple. Now was the time to discuss how best he could betray his Lord to them.

*Judas, Judas, are you selling him out even at this moment? God have mercy on your soul. Your dream is dead and buried. But it was not the hope that God had for you. He gifts men with dreams to help them find the narrow gate to his dwelling place. You are slamming that gate shut now.* Although she knew the truth of what was happening, and going to happen, Gloriel's heart was leaden with sorrow for the betrayed, and for the betrayer.

A short time later, Judas stood silently in the Court of Priests, surrounded by the chief priests. Sweat beaded his forehead and ran down his face into his eyes. He had just handed over his Lord into their eager and evil hands. A nervous chill trickled down his spine.

"Hakhaverah sheli, my friend," said Caiaphas the high priest." You shall be justly and amply rewarded. Go now, and prepare your strategy. We have no further use for you. Erev tov, good evening." His crafty face wore a cold sneer, a sign of the immeasurable mercilessness which was an integral part of his nature. He stroked his forked gray beard and stared at Judas with piercing coldness.

Another high priest, Gamaliel, looked on in silence. His strong-boned face, framed by thinning white hair, bore a pensive expression. "Perhaps it is best for one man to die for the people, so that our entire nation does not perish," he interjected suddenly.

Judas, face fiery with anger and bitterness, nodded his dark oily head. "I will do it," he muttered. He slowly turned, and then fled the Temple quickly.

#

Next evening, as dusk drew near, crowded closely by night, Jesus and the disciples left the city to return to Lazarus' house. The sun was a red globe captured in banks of clouds, and peering down on them.

The day had proved to be disappointing and disturbing. The crowds were not so friendly now. So many were disenchanted because Jesus had proven not to be the conquering Messiah they had hoped he was. Their expectations that he was the One, sent to lead them to freedom from the hated Roman Empire, lay dead in the dust.

"Jesu, the people are feeling disillusioned and thwarted, and are murmuring against you," Gloriel whispered in the Lord's ear as they walked.

"Even though you have worked so many miracles among them, they realize now that you are not who they thought you were."

Jesus' pace slowed, and he nodded his head.

As they gathered together once again around the supper table, silence prevailed among the group of apostles and disciples. The fire burned low, and the corners of the room disappeared into darkness. The trembling flames of candles caused strange shadows to dance over the walls.

"No more enthusiasm or celebration, Sariel," Gloriel whispered to her angel companion. Sariel nodded, her small sweet face clouded by a stricken expression.

"So, dear companions," Jesus' quiet voice interrupted the silence. "The time draws very near when the Son of Man will be taken from you."

Peter shook his head vehemently in denial, and closed his eyes, pulling at his red beard pensively, as if he could somehow shut out the words he was hearing. He sighed, and slumped over heavily in his seat.

Lazarus' deep-set green eyes brimmed silvery with tears, and he bowed his head. An enigmatic fear, overwhelming and nameless, came over his spirit.

"He will be beaten and shamed, mocked and tormented, and finally, lifted up on a tree, so that he may entice all men to himself," Jesus continued. "You must build up and empower yourselves with prayer; for many ordeals and much suffering await all of you." He looked around at every face with quiet intensity. Compassion gleamed in his luminous dark eyes.

James and John jumped to their feet in unison. "Lord, do you want us to call down fire from Heaven on your enemies?" James burst out in his usual impulsive manner, shaking his fist in the air.

John nodded his head vigorously in agreement, eagerness shining in his innocent and vulnerable young face.

"Yes, Lord!"

"Master, we will surround you wherever you go, and defend you with our lives!" Peter's coarse voice resounded through the small room. The ruddy color in his cheeks deepened.

"Calm down, my impetuous friends. This is the time for prayer," Jesus said softly. "You should pray like this." Quietly, he rose to his feet and raised his arms to Heaven. Everyone in the room stood up, then, their eyes riveted on the Lord.

"Our Father, who dwells in Heaven, may your Name be always kept holy. Let your Kingdom come among us, and may your perfect will be forever done here on this earth, just as it is done in Heaven. Give us our bread every day, and pardon our sins and trespasses, just as we forgive all those who do evil to us. Let us not be tempted, but protect us from the evil one. For the Kingdom, all power, and all glory are yours this day and for all time to come. Amen."

Jesus' voice grew husky with the final words. "I want you to remember that the more surely you know that you are loved, the easier you will find it to love in return. You are loved, my dear friends. Make sure that your love is known to others, also." Jesus' eyes were gleaming like full, dark stars as they moved around the room from face to face.

All eyes remained fixed on the figure of the Lord. All faces reflected deep love for him. Some were clouded with sorrow, some with confusion, and others with shock.

"I'm so happy to have all of you here with me tonight. Where is Judas?" The Lord asked suddenly, glancing around the table and into the shadowed corners of the room.

"Master, Judas decided to stay in the city tonight. But he will be with us for Passover," Jude commented softly.

"Yes, yes, of course," Jesus smiled and nodded.

*There is no smile in his eyes,* Gloriel thought.

#

At dawn the following morning, Jesus and his followers gathered again in Lazarus' garden. The scent of jasmine floated softly in the spring air, along with a fragrant morning aroma from the surrounding orchards.

Jesus cleared his throat as his eyes swept around the gathering of disciples.

"Today, I want to walk among the people in the streets of Jerusalem once more, my friends. The end of my journey grows near, and my heart yearns to be with my Father's Chosen ones. Also, we must visit the Temple again to see if it remains undefiled today," Jesus said, smiling. He scuffed at a small stone lying on the ground at his feet. "I would like to leave as soon as we have breakfasted. I think we will stay only a short while today, as I am anxious to spend time with all of you this evening." He turned and placed an arm around John, clapping James on the shoulder with his other hand.

Mary Magdalene and Jesus' mother sat on a bench nearby in the garden, under the branches of a gnarled red cedar. The fruit trees were globed in green and golden fruit.

Both women breathed deeply of the fragrant blossoms surrounding them.

Mary's heart felt burdened this morning, and tears gathered close to the surface. *My son, my boy, what lies ahead for you now? I am frightened for you,* she thought. Suddenly, a memory long buried emerged clearly in her mind. *Simeon, the prophet in the Temple when our babe was newborn; what was it he said as he held Jeshua in his arms?* The words crept slowly into her consciousness. *A sword shall penetrate your own spirit, too. Was that it? I didn't know what he meant then. Is that sword awaiting me now?* She shuddered involuntarily, her brown eyes narrowed and thoughtful. A frown appeared on her pale brow.

Sariel, standing nearby, listened closely to her charge's thoughts. Gently, she laid a reassuring hand on Mary's arm.

"Sweet Mary, you will not have to face alone the fiery ordeal that is to come. The Father holds you in the palm of his hand. Do not be afraid."

A puzzled expression moved over Mary's still lovely features, but the worried frown slowly faded away.

A servant appeared at the door to the house. "Master," he said firmly, "breakfast is ready."

Jesus grinned at Ephraim, white haired now, remembering the first time he had seen him. *A lifetime ago, my old friend, a lifetime ago,* he reminisced. *Lazarus, Mary, Martha . . . we were so young then.* Sudden tears stung his eyes, and he swallowed a lump in his throat.

#

Later, as Jesus and the disciples entered Jerusalem, the air was warm and clear. The crowds had multiplied even more; the rich were packed tightly with the poor; and sojourners from faraway countries mingled with the local citizens.

"Come, let's go into the Temple and pray," Jesus called to his followers.

As they approached the Temple gate, Jesus' attention was drawn by a group of scribes and Pharisees standing to one side. They were richly dressed in fine robes and their faces reflected the disdain they felt for the dirty, sweating riff-raff packing the streets.

"Friends," Jesus said in his firm, clear voice, addressing his disciples. "Beware of those who seek ritual greetings, and the important seats in the synagogues. They always claim the places of honor at meals, and demand that all defer to them. Yet they devour what little money poor widows have, while they recite long prayers for attention. Believe me, they will pay one day." He turned and looked directly at the group of scribes and Pharisees, who were standing stock still, gaping at Jesus with shocked and furious faces.

"They heard every word he said, Sariel," Gloriel said with a grin.

"Yes, they did indeed," Sariel replied, dimpling. "I don't think they are too pleased with his words."

Jesus turned and entered the door, heading for the inner court.

"It's because he wants all of us to be together, and women cannot worship before the altar," Mary Magdalene whispered to Suzannah, smiling.

As Jesus entered the court, he looked around the room at the worshippers gathered there. An assortment of pilgrims sat or knelt upon the stone floor.

He walked over and sat down by the collection box for the poor, which stood against one wall.

Some rich Jews, tunics and robes shimmering in crimson, blue, white, and delicate jade, walked over to the box. A few wore ornate headpieces. One, attired in a robe fringed in the deep blue of a pious Pharisee, made a grand show of the gold coins he was placing ostentatiously in the treasury.

Others, from all walks of life, came by and placed their offerings in the box, as Jesus watched with interest. There were many well-to-do people who gave very generously, and without fanfare.

"They are not all as pretentious as our rich Pharisee," Gloriel whispered to Sariel, as they watched with curiosity, also.

"No, they aren't, my friend," the little angel replied, grinning. "Look, here comes a sweet little old lady. She is a beggar, so I wonder what she has to give."

"She's a widow, too, Sariel. So she has no means of support." Gloriel said sadly.

Jesus also was watching the bent and aged woman, who was dressed in a coarse brown muslin robe. Slowly, she shuffled toward the collection box. She bowed her head, and waited respectfully while the rich individuals finished their show of charity.

"Jesu is wondering how this poor woman came to be so poverty-stricken," Gloriel commented to Sariel. "Have the scribes convinced her to contribute what little she has to the Temple treasury?"

The poor widow now had access to the collection box, as the last of the wealthy people moved away. Jesus watched closely as she placed two small copper coins in the treasury. Her tiny face was crisscrossed with delicate, fine lines and wrinkles, like a little brown walnut.

Jesus' eyes glistened as he turned toward John and Matthew sitting next to him. "This poor widow has put more into the Temple treasury than all the others combined," he said sadly.

"But, Lord, the others have given generously, a great deal of money," Matthew said, puzzled. "She put in only two prutahs! That's merely a very small fraction of what the rich people gave." A perplexed frown knotted Matthew's forehead.

"Yes, Teacher, I don't understand what you mean, either. How can she give more, with only the two little coins?" John inquired, his sunburned cheeks shadowed in the dim light of the Temple.

Jesus smiled a little sadly at the two apostles. "My children, you need to look beyond outside appearances. This poor woman gave everything that she had in this world. She has no means of support; she has no one to take care of her. Yet she gives freely and with love for God in her heart. The wealthy gave from their surplus. She gave from her need. Do you understand now?" His expression was gentle and patient.

Matthew looked embarrassed, his open face flushed and perspiring.

"Yes, Lord," he answered sheepishly, "I do."

John nodded wordlessly, his eyes following the bent figure of the old woman as she left the Temple.

"Come on, now, friends," Jesus said, placing an arm around each of the two men. "Let's go back to Bethany. I am looking forward to dinner tonight, aren't you?"

#

The new day dawned warm, breathless and clear. In Lazarus' garden, the perfume of lilacs rose in clouds. The sweet incessant crooning of puffy-breasted doves greeted the rising sun.

Jesus' mother stood amongst the blossoms, breathing in their delicate scent. She bent and gently touched a rose which was spreading its fragrant petals to the newborn rays of sunshine.

Jesus quietly closed the heavy oak door, and joined Mary.

"Mother . . . Emi," he murmured in a low voice. "Creation is so beautiful this morning, isn't it?" He placed an arm around her slender shoulders, bent, and gently kissed her forehead.

"Good morning, my son." Mary replied, smiling up at him. "It is indeed lovely. Do you remember the little garden we had in Nazareth, Jeshua? When you were little, you called them 'fow-ders', and you would always bring me a crumpled blossom clutched in your little fist . . ." Tears welled in her eyes, and she choked on her last words.

"Yes, Emi, I do remember. Avi would sometimes bring you a bunch of wildflowers down from the hills, too." Jesus smiled tremulously. "I shall always remember that." Enfolding his mother's slight figure in his long arms, Jesus hugged her tenderly and released her. "Let's call the others, Emi. It's time to go into the city for Passover."

Gloriel and Sariel watched the tender scene and remembered, also.

## Chapter Thirty-Six

Jerusalem bustled under the pale warmth of the spring-time sun. The great city's streets swarmed with humanity, each person struggling to reach his own destination. The Temple tower soared in gleaming splendor, hanging against the sky, shining like a great golden shield overlooking the teeming masses.

Roman soldiers wearing short suits, and leather armor covered with gleaming bronze, stood guard in the watchtowers; their helmets bright with red plumes, an ever-present reminder to the people of their domination.

A frantic cacophony of shouting, haggling voices cut through the air. Merchants scurried noisily about, as heavily laden camels and donkeys pushed their way through the narrow cobblestone streets. The market places presented a rich mixture of delicate, colorful silks and cashmeres; along with jewels, spices, and all the desires and cravings of the wealthy people gathering around the booths.

The moment Jesus and his followers passed through the Beautiful Gate, their senses were assaulted by innumerable odors and aromas, vivid colors, and the frenzied clamor. As they entered the Temple courts, three blasts of silver trumpets split the air, signaling the Passover sacrifices.

After spending most of the day in worship, and reading the sacred scrolls inside the Temple, Jesus and the disciples emerged and gathered outside in the courtyard. A pale setting sun threw its frail rays over the city street.

The Lord stood between Peter and John, putting an arm around each man's shoulders. "I need you to go and prepare the Passover meal. We should eat it together. Please go and make arrangements now."

Perplexed, Peter questioned, "But Master, where should we go to do this?"

"When you go out into the street, you will notice a short, bald man carrying a jar of water. Follow him closely. When he goes into a big house, go and tell the owner, 'The Teacher needs a guest room where we can prepare the Passover meal.' He will take you to a spacious room upstairs that is already prepared. That's where we will go."

The Lord laid his hand on the back of John's head, and patted Peter's broad shoulder "My dear friends, I am anxious to eat this meal with all of you. I'm looking forward to it. Go now, and fix our supper there."

Gloriel and Sariel watched as the two apostles left on their errand. "They really have no idea of the significance of this Passover meal, Sariel" Gloriel remarked to her companion.

Jesus beckoned Mary Magdalene to his side. "Mary, I want you to find a place for my mother and the other disciples to eat the Passover meal. The Twelve and I will be eating it together."

"Yes, Lord," Mary Magdalene replied, nodding her head, a bemused expression moving over her lovely face.

"Take Susannah with you, Mary." Jesus smiled down at the woman who had served him with such devotion the past few years. "Hurry now, for it will soon be evening."

"We'll leave right now, Teacher," she replied, her deep violet eyes shining softly in the waning sunlight.

Jesus walked over to his mother and enfolded her in his arms. *She's getting so frail,* he thought to himself, noticing the gentle lines signifying a face accustomed to smiling. He kissed the top of her head.

"Mother, I want you to go with Mary Magdalene and Susannah now. They will find a place for you to stay tonight," he said quietly, cupping her chin in his hand. His eyes welled with sudden tears, as he swallowed a lump in his throat.

"Jesu . . ., Gloriel whispered into his ear. "Jesu, it's all right, she will be safe."

Jesus heaved a sigh and smiled tremulously at his mother. "I will see you later, Emi. I love you."

The beloved face gazed up at him solemnly. "Son, I want to stay with you." Her sweet brown eyes pleaded with him. She reached up to rest a small hand lightly on his shoulder.

"Emi, I'm sorry. That cannot be. My hour is here, and I want you to be safe," her son replied gently but firmly.

Sariel whispered into Mary's consciousness. "You must be brave now, Mary. The Father needs you to be strong for your son, as you have always been. Lift up your heart."

Mary sighed deeply and nodded. Placing a trembling hand on Jesus' cheek, she leaned her head back and gazed deeply into his eyes. "Jeshua, I love you so much, my son. May your Heavenly Father go with you." Her face held the clear translucence of a girl's, as her mouth curved into a sweet smile.

#

The upstairs room proved warm and cozy as Jesus and the twelve reclined on cushions around a large table, later that evening. Flickering candlelight softened the shadows in the welcoming atmosphere.

The men relaxed, talking among themselves as they finished up the Seder, the Passover meal. The air was fragrant with the aromas of the Passover food.

They had sung all the customary songs and psalms; they had eaten the hard-boiled eggs and the savory roasted shank bone of lamb garnished with parsley and celery; along with the traditional bitter herbs with rice and horseradish. They finished their meal with nuts, and crisp apples spiced with cinnamon.

Bellies were full, the men content and sleepy-eyed. Simon, called the Zealot, his iron gray eyes aglow, recited the traditional Exodus story in his rich deep voice, beginning with the years of slavery to the Egyptians; on through the plagues; the passing through the Red Sea; the giving of the Law by Moses; and finally, Yahweh's great gift of the Promised Land.

Quietly, Jesus rose to his feet, and walking over to a table standing against a far wall, he removed his outer garments. The room was cloaked in silence as the 12 men sat up and watched him curiously.

*I think Jesu is about to teach his apostles the meaning of humility*, Gloriel mused to herself. She stood to one side, watching the faces of the men.

Jesus filled a basin with water from a pitcher alongside a stack of towels on the table. He tied one of the towels around his waist, his bronzed skin darkening to amber brown in the soft light.

Silently, he carried the basin over to the dinner table and knelt before James, the son of Alpheus. Gently, he began washing the feet of the astounded apostle, drying them with the towel from around his waist.

The men sat in stunned silence as the Lord moved around the table, washing and drying the feet of the dumbfounded apostles, one by one.

When he came to Peter, the big fisherman objected vehemently, shaking his shaggy head in protest.

"Lord, why do you want to wash my feet? That's a servant's job!" he choked out.

"Peter, you can't understand right now why I'm doing this, but one day you will," Jesus replied quietly.

"No, Lord! Never! You shall not wash my feet! Peter answered in a strangled voice, his weathered face flushing a deep red.

"Simon, if I don't wash your feet, you cannot have any place with me." Jesus replied, his features softening in the candlelight as he looked up into Peter's face.

Peter heaved a shuddering sigh. "All right, Lord. Then please wash my hands and face as well, not only my feet," the apostle acquiesced, bowing his head and holding out two great gnarled fists to Jesus.

"Anyone who has taken a bath doesn't need to wash anything but his feet in order to be completely clean, Simon. You are clean, my friend. But, not everyone at this table is," he said sadly.

The apostles looked around at one another, bewildered, puzzled expressions moving over each countenance.

*Jesu knows who it is who is betraying him,* Gloriel thought. Her gaze moved to the dark, guarded features of Judas Iscariot.

Jesus finished washing the feet of the apostles, put his robe on, and returned to his place at the dinner table.

"Dear friends, let's finish our meal together," he said.

He looked slowly around into each face. There was Peter, bold, eager, brash and out-spoken; Andrew, eager and devoted; James, a strong leader; and his brother John, quiet, loving John, zealous and ambitious; these were those nearest and dearest to him. Philip, Bartholomew, Thomas and Matthew, significant among his apostles, returned his look with furrowed brows and questioning faces.

His gaze swept about the table to Thaddeus, and Simon the Zealot. Judas Iscariot, selfish, greedy, and full of worldly ambition, sat staring down at the table; and finally, pulling pensively at his graying beard, James son of Alphaeus.

*He has known them from the beginning of Time, and He loves them all, even the one who is about to betray him,* Gloriel thought.

Jesus gave thanks for the loaf of bread lying on the table in front of him, broke it into pieces and held one up so that all of those gathered around could see it clearly. The room grew utterly silent.

His dark eyes studied each face once more, and then he spoke. "This is my body," he said clearly in ringing tones. "It will be given up for you. Take and eat." He passed the pieces around, so that each of his disciples had one. "Do this to remember me, from this time forward."

Gloriel watched with tears in her eyes as her Jesu poured a cup of deep-red wine and held it up for all to see, as he had done with the bread.

"This is the cup of my blood, which will be shed for all of you, and poured out for many, even those not yet born. My blood seals the Father's covenant." His voice trembled. "Do this also, in my memory." The cup was passed around the table, and each man silently sipped from it.

Jesus heaved a great sigh, as an expression of deep sorrow passed over his face. "All of you will desert me. One will betray me. I will be subjected to humiliation, torture, and finally, hung on a tree."

John leaned over to rest his head on Jesus' chest, bright tears brimming in his eyes.

Judas Iscariot licked his lips nervously, his black eyes shifting from face to face.

No, Lord!" Peter's deep voice rang out in the stillness. "I will NEVER, EVER desert you, even if everyone else does!" he blustered. He looked around at the other apostles, glowering at them indignantly.

Jesus gazed sadly into Peter's flashing eyes. "Peter," the Lord sighed," I am telling you the truth. Every one of you will turn tail and run tonight. But you, my friend, before the rooster crows twice, you will swear you don't know me, three times over."

"No! I will never deny you. Even if I have to die with you, still I would never renounce you!" Peter was sobbing now, his voice ragged with grief and righteous anger.

"Who is it, Lord? Is it I? Andrew's quiet voice interjected.

"Is it I, Master?" Matthew queried timidly.

One by one, the disciples asked the same question, glancing sidelong at one another, suspiciously.

"It is the one to whom I give this piece of bread, dipped in the gravy," Jesus said clearly.

He turned and held it out to Judas Iscariot. Shocked and white-faced, Judas stumbled up from the table and fled the room without a word. Jesus' sad gaze followed him. The candles fluttered in the draught created by Judas' hasty exit.

"It won't be long now before I must leave you," the Lord continued, his voice like warm honey. "You won't be able to follow me now. But later on, you will. I am going get a place ready for you, where we can all be together, forever. But before we part, I am giving you a new commandment. You must always love and care for each other, as I have loved and cared for you, and will for all eternity." His dark eyes sparkled with tears in the candlelight. "Come, my friends, let us sing a hymn and go to the hilltop to pray together."

#

The night air lay very still and chilly on the surrounding countryside as the little band of disciples crossed the brook of Kidron, and trudged up the Mount of Olives.

*Jesu is thinking of what lies ahead for him tonight*, Gloriel thought, somberly. *Oh, Father, I wish I could help him now. But I know this must be. Strengthen him for the torment that he must undergo.*

They soon arrived at the garden of Gethsemane, in the midst of a stand of ancient olive trees. The garden was familiar ground, as Jesus and his disciples often came there together.

The night was dark as pitch, and ghostly quiet. Andrew held a small torch high above his head. Shadows shifted in the grove as Jesus stopped under a huge, gnarly olive tree. Its twisted branches seemed to reach out to shelter him as he turned to speak to his followers.

"Dear friends, we will stop here to rest together, and to pray. Please sit down." His voice was subdued, and sorrowful. "Peter, James, John, come with me."

The three men followed closely as Jesus moved farther into the garden, where the shadows were even deeper, and totally silent.

Turning to the bewildered men, the Lord said quietly, "Wait here, watch, and pray that you will not have to be tested."

Mystified, each man nodded in acquiescence. Jesus walked on for a short distance. Stumbling a little, he sank to his knees next to a massive rock, and began to pray.

Gloriel stood unseen beside him. *Oh Father, his heart is in anguish in anticipation of what is about to happen. Let me help him,* she prayed silently.

Jesus raised his arms to heaven, and whispered "Father, if it is possible, spare me from drinking this cup. Let it go by me!"

Great beads of sweat began to form on his forehead as his mental suffering deepened. "Even now, I know you can save me from this ordeal, if you will!" He cried out desperately, sobbing now. There was no comforting word from on high. Drawing in a ragged breath, he whispered "And yet, not my will, but yours must be done, Father." His fervent prayer only seemed to increase the anguish in his spirit.

Gloriel gasped as she realized that his sweat was now tinged with blood as it ran slowly down his face and dripped onto the ground. She longed to gather him in her arms and comfort him, as she had when he was a toddler. Her heart felt as though it was ripping in two.

And then, the Father's voice spoke gently in her mind.

"Gloriel, you may comfort my son now, in his hour of great need. But you will not be able to help him later."

Taking on her bodily form, the small angel knelt beside Jesus and placed her arms around him. Startled, he drew in a quick breath; and then relaxed as he recognized her lovely face, now shadowed with pain.

"Jesu, my Jesu. The Father loves you so much, and will be watching as you complete your mission here on earth. Soon he will greet you, rejoicing, at the gates of Heaven with the entire Heavenly Host, when you return Home in triumph."

She smoothed back the dark hair from his forehead, and wiped the bloody sweat from his features with the edge of her gown. Reaching up and taking his face in both of her small hands, she smiled at the beloved one she had treasured and protected for all these years.

Jesus looked deep into the familiar amber eyes now sparkling with tears, and returned her smile. Unable to speak, he swallowed and nodded slowly.

Gloriel rose to her feet. Jesus stood up with her, staggering a bit in his weariness.

"You will be strong now, Jesu, you will be strong." she whispered as her bodily form faded slowly away into the darkness.

Jesus straightened his shoulders and lifted his head, as Emi and Avi had taught him so long ago. Walking slowly back to where he had left Peter, James and John, he found them sleeping, exhausted from sorrow.

"My friends, could you not watch with me for even one hour? Get up now, and pray that you do not have to endure a trial," Jesus said in a firm, strong voice.

A short distance away, the gleam of many torches chased the darkness as scores of people, priests, and temple guards approached. Leading them into the grove, Judas Iscariot moved toward the Lord. His eyes were like black holes in his white face, and no light shone in them. Placing both hands on Jesus' shoulders, he leaned forward and kissed the Lord on his cheek. The shifting light of the torches splashed them with red.

"Oh, Judas, do you betray me with a kiss? And with such an overpowering force behind you!" Jesus' eyes flashed in the torchlight.

He spoke to the mob then, in a powerful, fearless voice. "Was I not among you often, preaching and teaching in the streets of Jerusalem, and in the Temple? Why do you come after me in the dead of night, with swords and torches? Am I a thief, whom you come to lay hold of now?"

Judas staggered back, almost losing his footing. Malchus, the chief Temple guard, stepped forward, attempting to grab Jesus by the arm.

Peter, bellowing in wordless rage, drew his sword and lunged forward, severing Malchus' ear in one swift stroke. It hung by a small shred of flesh, spurting blood down his neck and onto his toga. The wounded man shrieked in pain.

Jesus stepped forward quickly, and placing his hand gently on the wound, healed and restored Malchus' ear in an instant.

The Lord turned to Peter and rebuked him. "Put away your swords now, or you will die by them!" His voice softened as he looked around at the eleven. "Don't you realize that I only have to ask Him, and my Father will send twelve legions of angels to save me from this moment? But if I did that, how would I fulfill the mission that He has entrusted to me? Go now, all of you, and save yourselves. I must do this alone."

The twelve, including Judas, turned and fled, disappearing in the darkness and leaving the Lord to face the murderous crowd alone.

Jesus stretched both arms out over the mob, and instantly, the entire crowd fell to the ground as if struck by a thunder-bolt.

As they scrambled to their feet, both frightened and angry, Gloriel reflected, *He did this to show them that no one can take him by force, unless he permits it. He is going with them willingly.*

Jesus held out his hands, wrists together, to the Temple guard. He bowed his head, lips moving in silent prayer. The burly guard bound Jesus' hands together tightly with a long, heavy piece of rope.

Shoving him roughly and pulling him by the rope, the crowd began the trek through the dark, narrow, sloping streets of Jerusalem. They soon arrived at the residence of Annas, former High Priest, and now leader of the Jewish community.

Annas, however, quickly dismissed Jesus and the crowd, sending them on to the palace of Caiaphas, the High Priest.

Simon Peter and John followed along behind, keeping their distance, and staying in the shadows.

# Chapter Thirty-Seven

Gloriel positioned herself alongside her charge. The Lord stood quietly on the gleaming marble floor before Caiaphas, his head bowed, but shoulders erect.

The High Priest, seated behind a highly-polished marble table in the huge, ornate hall just inside the palace doors, glowered at the figure standing silently before him.

*Caiaphas thinks that he can't permit this 'nobody" to upset the order of things, and that he needs to get rid of him before he causes any more trouble,* the angel reflected.

"What evidence do you have against this man? There must be two witnesses. You people know that" the High Priest proclaimed self-righteously, a frown of annoyance crossing his sharp, thin-beaked face.

A raucous voice from the crowd in the background rang out. "He swore he would destroy the Temple! I heard him say it!"

"Yes! I heard him, too! Many of us did! He said he would rebuild it in three days!" A tall, gaunt man standing on the sidelines spoke up loudly.

*Oh, they don't understand that Jesu was speaking of the Temple of his body,* Gloriel thought.

"He says that he is the Messiah!" Another voice shouted indignantly from just outside the door.

"He must die!"

"He is guilty!"

"Silence!" Caiaphas shouted, scowling at the crowd and waving his hand dismissively. His stony gaze returned to Jesus.

"So, Jesus of Nazareth, what say you? How do you answer these accusers? Are they telling the truth?"

Jesus raised his head and looked full into the hardened, almost skeletal features of the high priest. His eyes did not waiver, but he spoke not a word.

"Oh, come now. You have the right to defend yourself. Are you a fool? Speak up, man!" Caiaphas prodded the prisoner.

*They fear change; they don't want to lose what privileges they still have under the boots of the Roman invaders. This is foremost in Caiaphas' mind. I think the religious leaders have already determined beforehand to rid themselves of Jesu. The sooner the better, since he is such a thorn in their sides,* Gloriel thought, as she moved closer to the Lord.

"What have you been teaching the people, and your followers? Have you told them that you are the Messiah?" Caiaphas lowered his voice and leaned forward in his chair, his black eyes squinting with suspicion.

Heaving a sigh, Jesus replied. "Everyone knows what I teach. Many times, and very often, I have preached in synagogues all over Galilee, and in the Temple. I have never taught anything in private that I have not said in the communities. People all over have heard my teachings," Jesus said, frowning. "Why do you ask me these questions? Ask those who have heard me speaking for the past three years. They know perfectly well what I have said." He turned and looked out over the assemblage as he spoke.

One of the Temple servants stepped forward suddenly, and struck Jesus brutally in the face with his fist. "Do not speak to the High Priest like that!" he snarled.

His lower lip split and bleeding, the Lord staggered under the blow, but did not fall.

Unseen and unheard, Gloriel placed both hands over her mouth and moaned. "*Father, O Father . . .*"

"What have I said that was wrong?" he asked, shaking his head and turning to face the guard. "What evidence do you have that anything I have spoken is not true? Why do you strike me for telling the truth?" He spoke quietly, fixing his eyes on the Temple guard's flushed face.

Gloriel stood helplessly behind her charge, yearning to go to his defense, but knowing she must not interfere.

Facing once more toward Caiaphas, Jesus continued firmly, a trickle of blood oozing down from the split in his lip.

"Yes, what you ask is true. I am the Messiah, and one day you will find me sitting at my Father's right hand, in the place of great power. Then I shall return to earth among the clouds, with all the angels, in absolute, glorious power." His eyes shone brightly as he spoke.

At this statement, Caiaphas jumped to his feet and ripped his costly robe, shrieking, "We need no other witnesses! All of you heard these blasphemous claims! What do you say?" His face stained red with fury, and his eyes glittered black and hard, like chips of jet under their grizzled brows.

The mob began milling about restlessly, murmuring among themselves.

Then a raspy voice screamed, "GUILTY!"

"He has to die!" Another voice cried out.

"Crucify him!

"Death to the blasphemer!"

The guards spat in Jesus face, slamming him with their fists, and slapping him repeatedly. Jeering, they bound his eyes with a cloth, spewing insults punctuated with obscene words.

Gloriel struggled to restrain herself from taking her bodily form and standing between her charge and his persecutors. She felt as if the cruel fists were smashing into her own face.

"Tell us who hit you, prophet! If you are the Messiah, then predict!"

A sturdy reed slashed across his face and forehead, leaving an angry red welt.

"Who hit you that time, your Highness?"

"Let's see you foretell who's gonna hit you next!"

"Hail, King of the Jews!"

Raucous laughter echoed around the room as Jesus reeled and fell under the rain of blows. The brutal soldiers jerked him roughly to his feet. His hair, dark and heavy with sweat, hung in wet strands over bruised and swelling features. One eye was beginning to puff shut, and dried blood encrusted his lips.

Gloriel stood to one side as the Lord endured the savage abuse of the guards for what seemed to her an interminable time. She felt faint, and her heart cried out in protest, but she made no move to help him.

Gradually, she became aware of Jesu's mother, Mary, Mary Magdalene, and Susannah standing huddled together off to one side. They were clinging to one another, looking on the terrible scene with frightened eyes and fading hopes. Sariel stood unseen behind Mary, her hand on the slender shoulder of her white-faced charge.

Gloriel's gaze returned to the shameful spectacle in front of her.

"I tire of this foolishness," Caiaphas snapped, "We have no authority to put him to death. Take him to the Roman governor, he can handle this." He turned his back abruptly and retreated into the ornate interior of his home.

#

Meanwhile, outside in the courtyard, guards huddled around a charcoal fire which they had kindled, trying to keep warm in the increasing chill of late night. An enormous glimmering moon was rising in the dark curtain of the eastern horizon.

Since John was acquainted with Caiaphas, he was allowed to enter the courtyard. He then persuaded a servant girl, called Rhoda, to let Peter inside the gate, also. As the men entered, Rhoda glanced at Peter.

"Oh, you were with that man they have inside, too, weren't ya?" she inquired, peering closely at Peter.

"No, no I wasn't," Peter replied quietly, his eyes downcast.

The two apostles settled themselves around the fire, glancing at the others gathered around it.

After a few minutes, Rhoda wandered over to the fire to warm herself. Peter lowered his head, so that the firelight didn't illumine it.

Bending down and peering into Peter's shadowed face, Rhoda remarked, "I could swear yer one of them people who was with that preacher man, Jesus."

"No, I am not," Peter replied in a muffled voice, turning his face away from the fire.

"Oh, I'll betcha are," the girl said, nodding her head emphatically, and forming her lips into a little pout.

"You mistake me for someone else, girl. I don't know what you're talking about." Peter's voice grew harsh.

Rhoda rolled her round eyes and shrugged her thin shoulders. "Hmmmph! I dunno who ya think yer foolin'," she sneered.

Gathering her thin muslin cloak around her, she moved back to the gate, swishing her hips saucily.

Peter looked around furtively at the other people gathered around the fire, but no one spoke, or appeared to take any notice of the exchange with the girl.

Dumbfounded, John stared at Peter, a confused and perplexed expression on his young face.

It wasn't long before Rhoda sidled casually up to the fire again. "I know yer one a' his buddies," she said with girlish petulance, hand on one hip, and pointing her finger at the frightened disciple.

"No, damn you to Hell! I am not! You filthy daughter of a goat herder. I don't know him, I swear to God! Now leave me be!" Peter's gruff voice snarled through the darkness of the courtyard, and heads turned to see what the commotion was all about.

Immediately, nearby, a rooster's crow resounded through the night air.

Peter stared at John, his eyes wide and bright in the firelight. John returned his gaze, then slowly shook his head and averted his eyes.

Another crow echoed clearly around the courtyard.

Peter remembered the Lord's warning that he would betray Him three times before the cock crowed twice. He bowed his shaggy head in shame.

At that very moment, Jesus was herded out into the courtyard. He raised his head and directed his gaze at Simon Peter. His wounded face was expressionless, but the one dark eye probed into Peter's very soul.

Stricken with guilt and regret, and sick at heart, Simon Peter began to cry bitterly. His body was seized by sobs coming so fast and hard that his chest ached as he stumbled blindly out the gate and into the frosty moonlight.

John remained behind, bowing his head and closing his eyes in sorrow and disbelief.

#

It was very early in the morning, and the first pale rays of sunlight peered over the horizon as Jesus stood before the Roman curator, Pontius Pilate.

Gloriel stood in her place beside him, but said not a word of encouragement or support. Unshed tears brimmed in her eyes, and a huge lump formed in her throat. *Oh, Father, I know I cannot, must not, help him now. Please give me the strength to persevere with him.*

The Father's voice was silent.

*I know this man possesses the power of life or death over Jesu, Father, and that this is all part of your Plan, but . . .*

Still the Most High spoke no word.

Gloriel glanced around at their surroundings. Pilate's palace-fortress, the Antonia, was almost indescribable in its lavishness.

Since the chief priests were not allowed to enter a gentile's residence, for fear of being defiled, Pilate came out to them. He sat down on the Bema, the seat of judgment, set up temporarily on the multi-colored mosaic pavement in front of the palace.

The procurator, a tall, slender, beardless man with close-cropped light brown hair, wore a white linen tunic under a bright red toga, the local fashion for a Roman citizen. Large, flawless emerald, ruby and sapphire rings sparkled on his long fingers. A golden circlet gleamed on his forehead. He peered curiously at the accused man standing quietly before him, head bowed, swaying slightly. The man appeared almost regal in his stance, despite his torn and sweat-stained robe and battered, swollen features.

Pilate was curious about this strange man, as he had heard many rumors about him and his purported miraculous deeds.

*Pontius Pilate has a fiery temper and he's very obstinate. But he is astute and perceptive, also,* Gloriel mused to herself.

The belligerent, rowdy crowd pushed and shoved themselves as far forward as they dared. Palace guards stood between them and Pilate, their javelins held at ready.

Caiaphas advanced and addressed Pilate, his voice trembling with hostility.

"Procurator, this rebel has been leading our people astray with his claims to be the Messiah. He has warned us not to give any kind of esteem or respect to

Caesar. He declares himself to be the Christ, a King," the high priest charged, pointing a long bony finger at the Lord.

Pilate turned his steely gray eyes on Jesus. "Are you the King of the Jews?" he asked curiously.

Jesus lifted his head and looked unwaveringly through his one eye into the procurator's face. "Yes, what you say is true," he said clearly.

More furious voices rang out, echoing in the early morning chill.

"He's been telling the people not to pay their taxes!"

"He wants to become King!"

"He is urging his followers to disobey the Roman government!"

The indignant accusations of the Sanhedrin and the teachers of religious law reverberated around the courtyard.

Pilate folded his hands in his lap and looked down at them. There was silence for a few minutes.

Finally, he looked up. Contemplating the crowd for a moment, he shook his head and spoke firmly, "I find no fault with this man."

The priests grew frantic in their quest to rid themselves of this nuisance who was threatening their power and authority over the people.

"He's a rabble rouser, an agitator causing disturbances everywhere he travels, whether in Judea, Galilee or Jerusalem!" Caiaphas declared in a disgusted tone, his face set like stone, and stern with wrath.

Pilate raised his eyebrows, pursed his thin lips and asked curiously, "Then he is a Galilean? Is that true?"

"Yes, yes, he is," said Caiaphas eagerly, his features coming to life. He stepped even farther forward from among the other priests.

"Then take him to your own authority, King Herod," Pilate replied impatiently. Without another word, he rose and turned on his heel, walking quickly back into the palace.

#

King Herod was overjoyed to see Jesus. He had heard so much about him, and was eager to see him perform a miracle. However, the pathetic figure standing before him looked nothing like a miracle-worker.

"So, are you Jesus of Nazareth, the worker of marvelous things?" Herod's fat face was wreathed in a smile of luminous good will. He rubbed his rotund belly in anticipation.

Jesus stood silently before the king, eyes downcast, and uttered not a word.

The Jewish leaders and teachers of the Law shouted out their false allegations.

"He says he is a King. He wants to usurp your throne, your majesty!"

"He stirs up trouble and sedition in cities and the towns all over Galilee and Judea, my lord!"

The king turned a sour look on the silent man standing motionless before him. "Is this true, Nazorean?" He asked sharply.

Jesus remained still as a statue, his muscles strong and lithe beneath the bloody linen robe. He uttered no sound.

Although nothing usually disturbed him very much, Herod was angered and disappointed by the Lord's silence. He regarded Jesus with frank exasperation, clucking his tongue.

He and his soldiers began to ridicule and mock the Lord, their strident laughter resounding around the palace walls.

But, they soon grew bored with this sport, and sent Jesus back to Pilate.

#

Back in the praetorium, the trial before Pontius Pilate resumed.

"Have you no defense to these accusations, Jesus of Nazareth?" Pilate asked the Lord, squinting his eyes, and steepling his long fingers.

Jesus bowed his head, and made no reply.

Gloriel stood close behind him, unable to either encourage or protect him.

She felt sick with compassion, aching to comfort him.

"Well, aren't you going to say anything?' Pilate urged sharply, growing increasingly angry and frustrated.

Jesus remained silent, closing his eye. Matted hair hung listlessly down his bruised cheeks, like pieces of dark hemp.

Pilate was amazed that Jesus would not respond to the accusations of the High Priest and the others.

The crowd began to push forward again, toward the Roman governor.

Gloriel noticed that Mary, Mary Magdalene and Susannah had followed the crowd to the praetorium.

"It is the custom to release a prisoner to you every year at Passover. Whoever you name will be freed. Do you want me to give you the King of the Jews?" Pilate asked the High Priest, pointing to Jesus.

"No! No! Not Jesus! Give us Barabbas!"

"Yes, Barabbas!"

"Barrabas!" The name of the notorious outlaw echoed through the courtyard.

Pilate stared at the crowd in amazement. "Barabbas is a murderer and an insurrectionist. Whereas I find no guilt in this man Jesus," he replied loudly, exasperated. And if I do release Barabbas, what do you want me to do with your King?"

The throng began yelling even more loudly, as the chief priests stirred them to frenzy.

"Crucify him! Crucify him!" The crowd's rumbling grew into a roar.

Pilate stood up and shouted "He has committed no crime! Why should I condemn him to death?" He paced back and forth with long strides, his face flushed with anger.

The people only howled more deafeningly.

"Crucify him!"

Weary of arguing, and wanting to please the people, Pilate then released the murderer Barabbas to them.

Still reluctant to sentence the Lord to death, he ordered him to be flogged; the legal preliminary to every crucifixion; hoping that would be enough to satisfy the blood-thirsty mob.

The guards took Jesus out of the praetorium, pulling him roughly by the rope binding his hands. They bound the rope to a short, stout whipping post outside the courtyard. Gloriel stayed close by his side, feeling nauseous, but unable to help him in any way.

There, Jesus was stripped of his clothing and bound to the column.

Gloriel longed to cover his nakedness, and gasped when she saw the flagrum, the instrument used for flogging. Several long, leather thongs, sharpened to a point, were attached to a short handle. At the end of the thongs were small balls of lead and sharp pieces of bone.

At the first stroke of the whip, the thongs cut deep into the flesh of Jesus' left shoulder and back, the lead balls and pieces of bone adding to his agony. He sucked in his breath through clenched teeth, and groaned deeply. Blood oozed from the wound and started to stream.

Thirteen violent stripes were laid on his shoulder, each one exacerbating his suffering. Groaning and panting for breath, the Lord received thirteen strokes to his other shoulder, and to his chest. Thirty-nine lashes tore into his body, down to the bone; and blood streamed freely to the ground, along with bits of the ripped tissue of his body. Flesh was torn from bone and slashed with a thousand cuts. His face was sliced, bruised, and swollen beyond recognition

Gloriel remained, unseen, at his side, praying to the Father that Jesu would survive this horrible desecration of his sacred flesh.

The Lord sank to his knees on the pavement, kneeling in his own blood, when the scourging was over. The soldiers who had perpetrated this dreadful punishment seized Jesus under his arms and dragged him, naked and bleeding profusely, into a hall where a crowd of other soldiers, mostly Syrians and Bedouins, waited eagerly; hoping to have some fun at the prisoner's expense.

Gloriel followed closely. *"Father, Most High God! Can't we help him even a little?"* she cried out in her mind. No saving answer came. No answer at all.

"This is the King of the Jews!" One of the soldiers from Mesopotamia shouted. "But look! He has no royal crown, or robe!"

A dark-faced Bedouin soldier replied, "Well, let's fix that problem. Poor fellow, we can't leave him in such a naked state! That would be disrespectful of us!"

He clapped Jesus on the shoulder, causing him to stagger and fall. The soldier laughed uproariously at his own joke, the rest of the gang of soldiers joining in. He jerked Jesus up onto his feet again. The Lord swayed and staggered a little, but stayed erect.

Someone fetched a royal purple velvet robe and threw it around Jesus' mutilated shoulders.

One of the soldiers placed a reed in his hands, jeering,

"Here is your scepter, O King!" He bowed low in ridicule. Another soldier fashioned a circlet of rushes, and tied it together. Then he took some thorny pieces from the branches of a jujube tree, carefully fastening them to the circlet of rushes, so as not to cut himself. Protecting his hands with a piece of leather, he walked up to Jesus and jammed the sharp thorns down viciously onto the Lord's already bloody head. Tears of blood flowed from the wounds and rolled down Jesus' cheeks.

Jesus cried out involuntarily from the massive pain, and fell once more to the shredded flesh of his knees.

His head felt as if it were encased in a great globe of flame, encased in crushing, darting, piercing, burning pain.

*Oh, Father, how much more can he endure? I want so desperately to help him, to comfort him, to ease his pain!*

Gloriel's cry echoed and re-echoed in her mind; but again, no answer came.

The blood-thirsty soldiers circled the suffering Lord, taunting him and bowing down in mock respect, shouting,

"Hail, King of the Jews!"

"Behold His Majesty!"

The mockery and humiliation continued for some time, until Pilate tired of waiting, and ordered Jesus brought back before him.

The soldiers dragged the Lord, still wearing the royal robe and the cruel crown, back into the praetorium.

Pilate stared at the wretched, unrecognizable figure swaying before him, head streaming blood, but still held erect.

Hoping to raise some modicum of pity for Jesus from the assembled mob, Pilate stood and addressed them. Bright drops of sweat beaded his upper lip as he spoke.

"Here, I bring the accused back before you. I can find no fault in him." He then pointed to the pitiable prisoner, and shouted, "Behold, the man!

The chief priests and Temple officers then howled, almost as one, "CRUCIFY HIM! CRUCIFY HIM!"

"You are no friend of Caesar if you release him!" one of the priests bellowed angrily, raising his fists in the air. "He claims to be the Son of God!"

Pilate sighed deeply, any hope of arousing pity gone now.

Walking down the steps separating him from Jesus, he approached the suffering man and asked quietly "Who are you? From where do you come?"

Jesus remained silent. Gloriel stood beside him, unseen.

Exasperated, Pilate said, "Don't you understand? Don't you know that I hold the power of life or death over you? I can either crucify you, or release you. Why do you not answer me?"

Jesus opened his one good eye and peered at Pilate.

"You would not have any power over me at all, unless my Father above gave it to you." He paused, searching for the strength to continue. "So, the one that delivered me into your hands bears the greater guilt," he said clearly, through swollen, cracked lips.

#

Lurking among the crowd, Judas Iscariot stood stock-still, struck to the heart by the Lord's words. Sickened, and filled with remorse, he slipped away and tried to return the blood money, the thirty pieces of silver, to the priests in the Temple. He pleaded with them to take back the coins, but they refused.

"I have sinned against the Lord, and betrayed him! He is innocent of any wrong-doing! I can't keep this money; it's tainted with his blood!" Judas shrieked, ridden with remorse and guilt.

"What is that to us?! Do what you want with it. It's out of our hands now." One of the priests declared. "Get out of here, you filthy piece of dung!"

"We cannot accept money that has been paid for murder. It is against our laws," another priest interjected.

In desperation and wild regret, Judas threw down the 30 pieces of silver on the Temple floor, and fled to the outskirts of the city, weeping bitterly and hysterically.

On the edge of a craggy cliff, Judas Iscariot, once one of the beloved twelve, hung himself from an ancient olive tree. The midday sun, the only witness, was a bloody thumbprint in a nimbus of dark clouds overhead.

#

Meanwhile, the Roman procurator, anxious to end the farce, gestured to one of his servants.

"Bring me a basin of water and a towel."

When the lad returned with the basin of water, Pilate washed his hands in front of the mob. "Behold! I wash my hands of any responsibility for this innocent man's death. This is your doing, so see to it," he said, glaring at the chief priests.

They only shouted back, "May his blood be on us, and on all our descendants, forever!"

Shaking his head in disgust, Pilate turned his back on them, and walked slowly into his palace.

# Chapter Thirty-Eight

The Lord stood silently outside the tribunal, bleeding and exhausted, head bowed, waiting. His hands were still bound together in front of his bloody body. A soldier approached, and brutally ripped off Jesus' bonds. Two others, bearing a patibulum, the piece of wood to which his arms would be fastened, dropped it roughly across his lacerated shoulders.

Jesus moaned, but did not look up. The soldiers balanced the beam and ordered him to hold it on his shoulders. Reaching up painfully, he grasped the rough wood.

Standing close behind him, Gloriel prayed to the Father.

"Most High, hear my prayer for Jesu. Grant him the strength to persevere, and to finish his mission."

#

Benjamin stood a short distance inside the Garden Gate, rubbing the round paunch under his brown tunic. He had enjoyed a fine breakfast of goat's milk, dark bread, and a bit of sweet honey-comb, after leaving his flock at the Temple gate. He stroked his grizzled beard, and patted the bag of coins hanging from his belt. Now he could return home to Bethlehem, and buy a few lambs to start the new flock for the coming year. His family would be happy with the money, which would support them comfortably. Most of the children were grown, now, some with families of their own.

Benjamin smiled to himself, his black eyes sparkling. *Here I am, an old man of fifty years, and God has blessed me with a fine family, and a decent living all this time.* He chuckled, and a pretty young girl passing by looked at him curiously.

It was almost noon, and Benjamin stood gazing up at a few white puffs of clouds wandering leisurely across the bright blue sky. "Kind of like my sheep grazing," he murmured to himself.

A disturbance down the cobbled street drew his attention. *What's happening?*

Peering through the crowd, he could see the red plumed hats of Roman soldiers approaching, a tall, middle-aged centurion leading the group. Hastily, Benjamin scooted off to one side of the street, scrunching himself up against the wall.

"Wha—Oh, Lord have mercy! Who is that?" he gasped under his breath.

A figure approached, stumbling and staggering under the weight of a heavy beam of rough-hewn wood. The man was clothed in a blood-stained tunic, his flesh hanging from him like scarlet rags under the weight of the wood. A vicious crown of thorns encircled his head, and deep red rivulets ran down his bruised and distorted face.

Benjamin's stomach churned, and vomit rose in his throat. He had seen crucifixions before, but this man . . .

Suddenly, a woman rushed to the man's side, tears streaming down her face, her veil clutched in both hands. Her chestnut brown hair, loosened from the confines of the veil, fell around her forehead and cheeks. Gently, she blotted away the blood oozing down the man's face.

One of the guards pushed her roughly away from the suffering man. "Get out of here! Stay away from him!" he growled petulantly.

The woman stumbled and almost fell, but never took her eyes off the Lord.

*Oh, it's Veronica!* Gloriel said to herself. *I know she will always be remembered for this act of kindness to Jesu.*

"Jesus!" Someone cried out from the crowd. "Jesus!"

The man lifted his head slightly and turned it toward the voice. His one open eye was filmed with pain and exhaustion.

*So, his name is Jesus,* Benjamin thought, as he joined the throng following the condemned.

There were many women among the mass of people, crying loudly, mourning and lamenting.

Painfully, lurching desperately under his burden, Jesus turned his head and spoke to the women in slurred Aramaic, his words jerking, and punctuated with groans. "Daughters of Jerusalem,—do not—weep for—me. It is—yourselves—and your children that—need your t-tears."

Jesus paused, gasping for breath. Bloody sweat poured down his battered and misshapen face. "There will—come a day when people—will be saying" he groaned, grimacing, "that those who have—no children are—blessed; Women who have—never borne a child,—those whose breasts—have never—nursed will be coun—ted as-fortun-ate." Jesus' voice cracked and he was unable to speak for a moment. He took a few more lurching steps.

*He can't continue talking, his strength is almost gone*, Gloriel thought, her heart aching for him.

"Every—one will-call up-on the moun—tains to fall down on them. For if—the things—you see are be-ing done when—the wood is—green, what will—h-hap-pen when it d-dries?" he continued, haltingly.

*What does he mean by that?* Benjamin wondered silently.

Just then, one of the soldiers shoved Jesus violently. "Shut up! Get going! Damn this mob!" he shouted.

Jesus staggered and nearly fell.

Benjamin elbowed forward to the front of the crowd. *I have to help him!* He thought frantically. *What's the matter with me? Why should I care? He's just another criminal getting what he deserves. But, Jesus . . .*

Vague memories began stirring in the back of the shepherd's mind. A bright light, the voices of angels, a babe lying in a manger; a young boy, holding a lamb gently in his arms . . .

Jesus stumbled again, dropping to his tattered knees. His shoulder muscles corded with agony, and he groaned loudly, gritting his teeth.

Two of the soldiers dragged him brutally to his feet. One of them looked around and spotted a tall, heavily muscled, dark-skinned man standing nearby, watching.

"You! You in the blue tunic! Come here!" he shouted.

The man looked around and then pointed to himself with a questioning expression. "Me? Are you talking to me?"

"Yes you, you idiot! Damn you! Come over here. You're needed to carry this man's cross. He can't go any farther!" the soldier shouted loudly.

"Why should I? I have nothing to do with him!" the man replied with annoyance.

The soldier approached the man, and pushed him roughly, jabbing his finger into his burly chest. "What's your name, scum?"

"I am Simon of Cyrene, and I don't know this criminal. Why should I help him?"

"Well," the soldier replied through clenched teeth, "How would you like to join him, then?" He scowled, staring unblinking into Simon's glittering black eyes.

"All right! All right! I'll do it!"

Swearing under his breath, Simon stalked over and crouched down while the soldiers untied the cords, and transferred the patibulum to his broad shoulders.

Jesus stood weaving from side to side, his slashed arms hanging limply at his sides. His once beautiful robe, tattered and stained with crimson, stuck to his torn and bleeding flesh. There was not a muscle anywhere that was not rent with anguish.

"Lord above, he hardly looks human," Benjamin whispered under his breath. "I should be helping him. He's exhausted." A nameless despair swept over the shepherd as he watched the ghastly scene.

Just then, Jesus tripped and fell to his knees again. His pale, swollen mouth gaped with agony.

Benjamin rushed forward, trying to push through the soldiers to get to the fallen Lord. They prodded the shepherd with the butt ends of their javelins, cursing, and knocking him to the pavement.

"The gods damn you! Get back, you stupid fool! Do you want us to nail you up there with him?!"

Heat waves shimmered up from the cobble-stone street. The sun glared whitely overhead, spotlighting the dreadful scene below.

"Get away from here, you filthy pig, unless you would like your head busted!" another guard shouted furiously.

Another shepherd standing among the crowd recognized Benjamin, rushed out and grabbed him, pulling him to his feet, and back into the mass of people.

"What's the matter with you, you brainless idiot? Do you want to die, too?" The other shepherd took hold of Benjamin's shoulders and shook him roughly.

*Benjamin, are you starting to remember?* Gloriel stood helplessly beside her bloodied charge, watching the guards jerk him once again to his bleeding feet, as the Father's Plan unfolded.

Faltering, staggering, reeling and lurching, the Lord of creation moved through the gate of Ephraim, toward his Destiny. For the third time, in his weakness and pain, he fell heavily to the ground, into the burning dust. His face was glimmering with sweat; his breath coming in quick gasps.

*The Creator lies prostrate in the dust!* Gloriel cried to herself, pain for her Lord sweeping over her. *How I wish I could tell them all that they can do nothing to him, unless he permits it!*

A hard brassy sky polished by the glaring sun stretched overhead. Jesus, the guards, and the crowd trod the narrow way, rising sharply to the Mount of Golgotha, the Place of the Skull.

Most of the people were quiet now, lost in their own thoughts as they trudged to the foot of the mound where the rough wooden pillar awaited the Lord. Here and there, some of the rabble began shrieking out their blood-lust. The acrid odor of sweat spread through the air.

Gloriel walked closely behind the Lord, praying silently. She yearned to whisper hope and encouragement in Jesu's ear. But she knew she could no longer help him.

"He has to do this by himself," she sobbed under her breath.

Finally, the awful procession reached its destination. Two crosses, already hung with their terrible onuses, stood starkly outlined against the white-hot sky. Two thieves, suffering terribly for their crimes, moaned, tossing their heads from side to side. One of them screamed obscenities at the guards and the crowd. The other spoke no words, but only whimpered pathetically.

Watching the two suffering men writhing in their agony, Gloriel's attention suddenly focused on the criminal on the left. She gasped in horror.

"Father! Father!" She lifted her voice to heaven, unheard by those around her. "Oh, dear God, it's Anthony! How did this happen? Oh, Most High, how did this happen?" she sobbed.

No answer came.

Time seemed to be suspended as Gloriel stared in dismay at the once handsome and innocent young man.

"Father, have mercy on him."

As the small angel waited, a strange calm crossed the threshold of her heart, and she focused once more on her role in the unfolding Drama of the Ages.

# Chapter Thirty-Nine

Jesus lay at the base of a small mound, on the pulp of bleeding, lacerated flesh of his back. Two crosses and a pillar stood outlined harshly against the blazing sky. The soldiers removed his blood-soaked robe and loincloth, leaving him starkly exposed in shameful nakedness.

Nearby, Mary, Mary Magdalene, John, and Susannah huddled together. His mother, trembling, and scarcely able to stand, leaned on John for support, her grief a raw, ragged wound to her heart.

Gloriel looked about for any of the other disciples, but none were in sight. A number of chief priests and Sadducees, their faces dark and voracious, milled about impatiently.

Pharisees with ornate phylacteries bound to their foreheads and left arms, nudged one another aside, trying to get the best view.

The shepherd Benjamin stood transfixed, a few feet behind Jesus' mother.

A tall Roman centurion called Nicolas stood to one side, gesturing silently to the soldiers, a strange expression moving over his striking features. Following his wordless directions, one of the guards brought a cup of wine mixed with bitter gall to Jesus. But when he tasted the drink, the Lord turned his parched lips aside, refusing to drink.

The patibulum lay on the ground directly above Jesus head. Knowing that the condemned's wrists would be easy to pierce, but the wood would not, one guard used a tool to bore two holes in the beam to help the nails enter the wood more easily.

Another soldier securely pinioned Jesus' left arm against the patibulum; while yet another took a heavy spike and a mallet, and drove the spike through Jesus' wrist.

The awful sound of hammering filled the air. Blood spurted, slowed, and poured in dark ripples over the rough wood and onto the ground.

The muscle in Jesus' hand contracted as the great sensory median nerve was smashed, and the pain became excruciating. He cried out, deep, rasping breaths of suffering drying his throat.

"Fa-ther, for-give them! They don't—know what they're doing!"

At these words, Nicolas' face drained of color, and a look of foreboding passed over his features. The shrieks of the blood-thirsty market rabble echoed in his ears. *This is not right, I know it's not right . . . what can I do?* He wondered silently, his breast heaving. The white-hot sky overhead darkened a little.

"The centurion knows there is something very sinful about this," Gloriel whispered to Sariel.

The rush of blood pulsing through Jesus' veins filled his head with a booming thunder, drowning out the sounds of the hammering. Soldiers then positioned his other arm and drove the cruel spike through his wrist.

With each blow of the hammer, Gloriel felt as if the spikes were piercing her heart.

The soldiers dragged Jesus to his feet and heaved him up, using the patibulum, which they then fixed to the coarse wood of the upright pillar.

The Lord's unrecognizable features contorted as bright arrows of pain shot out from his joints, and agony exploded from his very bowels. His body sagged, stretching out his arms.

The guards then bent Jesus' knees and positioned his left foot on top of the right, nailing them both to the pillar with one spike. Jesus cried out again, taking a deep, shuddering breath as pain twisted within him, wrenching him apart and snatching at his throat.

To prevent asphyxia, his body was then straightened out by the sweating soldiers, and he was suspended alone between Heaven and Earth.

Gloriel fought the pain spreading through her own breast, and the desperate longing to help her charge. She fell unseen to her knees, before the Lord fastened to his cross. She felt as if the spikes had been driven into her very soul.

*Jesu, my Jesu, the Lamb slain for sinners!* She cried out in her heart. She ached to cover his nakedness, to shelter him from the mocking eyes and voices, to soothe his anguish.

*Oh Father, I know Jesu has to do this alone. I know I cannot help him, but . . . my heart is shredded, and I yearn to call on your legions to carry him away from this terrible punishment. But nevertheless, your Plan must be fulfilled, and I must complete my mission, also. Forgive my weakness, Father.*

Urine and feces, loosed by deep anguish, slowly dripped down the cross. Purple bruises and wounds covered Jesus' naked body, now intersected with rivulets of scarlet. Hot torment filled every inch of his flesh, and his head rang with the shrieks of his pain.

Jesus bowed his head, still bearing the wicked crown of thorns. Dark hair matted with dirt and blood clung to his face in shreds. Breast heaving, he struggled for air. Pain twisted inside him, exploding from his very gut, snatching at his throat, and wrenching his body apart.

Mary cried out as the long-ago-predicted sword of sorrow pierced her very soul. Memories of a chubby, giggling toddler clinging to her knees seared her mind.

"Jeshua, my son, my precious boy . . ." she whispered raggedly. She collapsed, a grief-stricken mother prone in the dust, weeping. Her blue robe puddled in the dust around her.

Unseen, Sariel knelt beside her, placing her small hands on Mary's shuddering shoulders.

Stupefied with horror, Benjamin looked on the terrible scene, remembrance and recognition slowly flooding his mind.

*Jesus, I remember you now. I remember the days of your youth in Nazareth. I remember watching you cradle a baby lamb so gently in your arms. May the Most High have mercy on you, Jesus.*

He noticed that a crude sign had been secured to the cross, over Jesus' head. He turned to a well-dressed man standing nearby. "Sir, can you tell me what is written on the sign?" he asked pointing a shaky finger to the cross.

The man turned his glazed black eyes on Benjamin. "What? What did you say?" He rasped in an almost inaudible whisper.

"I asked what the sign over Jesus' head reads, sir," Benjamin replied.

"Jesus! Is that really Jesus of Nazareth?" The man's eyes grew huge in his white face.

"Yes, sir, so they say," Benjamin replied in a shaken voice. "But the sign, can you tell me what is written on it?"

The man was silent, his features stricken and shocked.

"Please, sir . . ." Benjamin's eyes filled with tears.

"'Jesus, King of the Jews.' It—it says 'Jesus, K-King of the Jews,'" the man whispered in a voice heavy with sorrow.

Benjamin sighed deeply, rubbing his eyes. "Thank you, sir. Thank you," he replied, gratefully.

The man appeared dazed and stunned, as his eyes wandered slowly over the crowd. His gaze fell on Mary, now collapsed in the arms of John.

"Mary! Is that you?"

Mary lifted her head and turned a ravaged face toward the man. Her streaming eyes widened. "Seth! Oh, Seth!" She cried out, her voice cracking. "See what they have done to our Jeshua!"

Seth returned his bewildered gaze to the cross, little trickles like ice water running over his flesh. The instrument of death was silhouetted crisply against the metallic sky.

"My friend, oh, my dear, dear friend. May the Most High have mercy on you," he whispered.

Moving closer to Mary, Mary Magdalene, Susannah and John, he watched numbly as the soldiers rattled their dice, gambling for the blood saturated clothing of the crucified Lord.

Gloriel, still kneeling at the foot of her Jesu's wooden throne, lifted her eyes to the figure hanging on the cross to his left.

*Anthony, how did your beauty and innocence come to this?* She wondered sorrowfully.

The other thief, hanging on Jesus' right, turned his face, groaning, toward the Lord. "You! If you are real-ly the—Messi-ah, save us, and your—self! Come—down from that cross!" He began to curse, saliva dripping from his twisted white mouth.

At that moment, Anthony cried out "Aren't you—even afraid of the Most-High? We deserve wh-what we are get-ting. This man—has done nothing to—deserve death!"

Robbed of its once youthful beauty, he turned his face, contorted with heavy pain and desperate longing, toward Jesus.

"Lord Jesus, p-please for-give my deser-tion, and my pride. Remem-ber me when you come into your heaven-ly King-dom," he sobbed, his voice growing weaker.

For a few moments, the Lord was silent. His breast heaved as he gazed at the penitent with a look kindled by compassion and love.

"Antho-ny, my son, I pro-mise you that this ve-ry day, you will join me in Para-dise."

One of the Pharisees, grim and sour-faced, approached the cross, staring up at Jesus with cold dark gray eyes glittering in anger.

"He thinks he saved others, but he cannot save himself! Come down from your 'throne' if you are truly the Christ!" He spat toward the tortured figure hanging in anguish before him.

Seconds, minutes, hours, an eternity passed, as the sufferers endured their fate. Jesus raised his head, light slanting on his unrecognizable face. His body crawled with flies.

"John, John, be-hold your mo-ther!" His gaze moved from John's stricken countenance to Mary's. "Emi, behold your son." His one open eye returned to John, his daily companion, his beloved friend.

"He's putting his mother in the care of his most beloved disciple," Gloriel whispered to Sariel.

"Yes," the little angel replied, her great blue-green eyes shining with tears. "Yes, I know, Gloriel. This was meant to be. John will take Mary into his own home and care for her tenderly, as long as she lives."

As he struggled for breath, Jesus' eye, filmed with pain and exhaustion, moved slowly over the crowd. His searching gaze fell on his boyhood friend. "S—Seth," he wheezed, his disfigured head twitching. "Ball" . . .

"Mary, what did he say? Did you hear?" Seth's trembling voice was hoarse with sorrow.

Mary laid a shaking hand on Seth's arm. "'Ball,' he said 'ball'," she whispered brokenly.

It was after two o'clock. A strange darkness fell over Golgotha and across the whole land, swallowing the light. People were frightened, and the crowd grew silent. The sun was gone, the still air heavy and oppressive.

"Father, it has been almost three hours. Merciful Lord, please let it end soon." Gloriel whispered a fervent prayer.

Suddenly, Jesus cried out in a loud voice, piercing and resonant," Eloi, Eloi, lama sabachthani?!"

"What is he saying?" Benjamin asked Seth, looking old and stricken and sick. "Is he calling for Elijah?"

Seth replied in a barely audible whisper, "He said "My God, My God, why have you forsaken me?" Overcome with compassion, Seth began to weep. Great globes of tears ran shining down his blanched cheeks. He felt drawn into the very heart of the cross. His own heart was so heavy it felt like a chunk of stone in his chest.

"He is taking the sins of mankind for all time upon himself at this very moment. He cannot communicate with the Most High, or even know that his Father is there. He's feeling utterly abandoned and covered with shame," Gloriel whispered to Sariel. She sighed raggedly, a choking fullness in her throat, like a silent cry.

"I am thirs-ty," Jesus breathed hoarsely, his voice growing weaker.

One of the soldiers soaked a sponge in sour wine and held it up to Jesus' lips on a hyssop branch.

Some of the watchers, gathered closely around the cross in the darkness, began to weep softly, beating their breasts and temples.

Two guards carrying heavy bars approached the two sufferers on either side of Jesus' cross. On Nicolas' orders, as was the custom, they swung the bars as hard as they could, breaking the legs of a screaming Anthony, and the unrepentant thief. No longer able to raise themselves up to breathe, they slipped quickly into unconsciousness as death approached. They succumbed within minutes, their terrible suffering ended at last.

Just then, Jesus shouted out, in a voice as full of power as the roaring of a desert lion. A cry that would echo down through the endless ages burst forth from the lips of the dying Savior.

"It is finished at last! Father! Into your hands I give my spirit!"

His bloodied head, adorned with its shameful crown, bowed to his chest. His body sagged as the Lord of Creation reached the end of his earthly journey, a victim of Man, the work of his own hands.

At that very moment, the great heavy curtain in the Temple split in two, from top to bottom. The earth began to roll and thunder underfoot, moaning, rising up and shaking its head, groaning as if in childbirth. Huge boulders cracked into pieces.

All over the city of Jerusalem, tombs were opened, and the dead walked the streets. An enormous roar of thunder shook the sky, as lightning split the air with powerful strokes.

A great gale of screaming wind beat itself against the gates of the Temple, and the earth shuddered, again and again, thundering underfoot. The very heavens shrieked and shouted with pain. The crowd began screaming in terror, as panic arose in the streets of Jerusalem.

The centurion and the other Roman soldiers, shaking and mindless with fright, struggled to stay on their feet.

"It must be true! This must have been the Son of God! Forgive us! Forgive us!" Nicolas cried out in a loud voice. His heart stammering with fear, he reached out to clutch at the feet of the Lord, bowed his head and wept bitterly. His tears traced courses whitely through the dirt and blood on Jesus' foot.

The priests and the Pharisees fled blindly down the hill, stumbling in the darkness, and speechless with panic. It seemed to them as if the darkness had fallen on the earth and swallowed it.

Gloriel sensed her bodily form taking shape. "Father! Father!" She cried out as a powerful force lifted her up above the cross.

Glancing back over her shoulder, she gasped in joyful amazement. Wings! Beautiful, magnificent, wonderful, glorious, soft pearly wings stretched out above and beyond her small form, lifting, lifting.

Leaving his ravaged remains behind, Jesus' spirit, ethereal in form, rose to meet Gloriel, and they ascended blissfully, hand in hand, to that special place reserved for the righteous dead, who had no permanent abode as yet.

Abruptly, the terrible screaming of the earth mourning its Creator, and the roaring winds, ceased. An unearthly quiet settled over Golgotha and the great city beyond.

Shaking from head to foot, like an aspen tree in a gale, Nicolas stepped forward and thrust his spear deep into the side of Jesus' body. Immediately, the gaping wound spewed water, and scarlet blood streamed.

"I'm sorry," he whispered, withdrawing the spear quickly. "I'm so sorry, but I have to be sure you are dead."

Mary, overcome with grief, withdrew from John's arms, and stumbled to the foot of her son's cross. She collapsed to her knees, reaching up with both arms, trying to touch Jesus' bloody feet. "Son, my son," she whispered weakly.

Nicolas stooped and raised her to her feet, handing her gently over to John. "Dear lady, please go home. This is no place for you. It is over," he said quietly.

John seated Mary on a large rock close to the foot of the cross.

The sun still hid its face from the earth as profound silence continued over Golgotha and the surrounding countryside.

*"It's as though the earth is holding its breath,"* Sariel thought to herself, sitting unseen next to her sorrowing charge.

Mary was quiet now, her head bowed, eyes closed.

"Mary . . ." Seth's voice rasped and broke.

Mary opened her weary, clouded eyes and looked up at her son's boyhood friend. "Oh, Seth, your heart must be broken, too," she replied quietly, taking his hand.

"Mary, do you know what Jesus meant when he said 'ball' just before he died?"

Tears still streamed unabated down Seth's pale cheeks. His reddened eyes were clouded with pain for his beloved childhood comrade.

Mary reached under her outer robe and brought out a cloth pouch and handed it carefully to Seth.

He slowly opened the pouch, hands trembling, and withdrew a small wooden ball, which he recognized immediately.

"Oh, Mary, it's the ball we played with when we were small, isn't it?" Blinded by his tears, he looked up as Jesus body was being released from its dreadful restraints.

Mary nodded, her gaze fixed on the mutilated corpse of her precious son. "Yes, yes," she whispered brokenly. "I know he wanted you to have it. Joseph made it for him, you know, and he loved it so."

Seth closed his swollen eyes and nodded silently.

Nicolas, watching with distress and regret in his eyes, instructed those removing Jesus' body to lay him in his mother's arms for a last farewell. He stepped forward to place a cloth over Jesus' naked loins. The brutal crown of thorns had been removed.

Seth was sobbing now, along with John, Mary Magdalene, Susannah, and those who had followed the Lord from Galilee. He stepped back to allow room for the men to approach with the body of his friend.

Sariel remained unseen, close behind Mary. Her hands rested upon the sorrowing mother's shoulders.

The unrecognizable body of the Lord Jesus was laid tenderly in his mother's arms, as she sat upon the rock at the foot of his cross.

Immediately, Mary's tears ceased, and an expression of peace, serenity, and dignity flowed over her alabaster features. Looking down into the beloved face, she cupped her hand on his bloodied cheek, and kissed his forehead tenderly. "Goodbye, my sweet boy. I know we will meet again. I love you."

Those gathered around sobbed aloud as they looked on the moving scene.

"Dear lady, please allow me to provide a place to lay your son to rest."

Mary looked up into the kind face of Joseph of Arimathea, a wealthy, but holy and righteous man. He belonged to the Jewish high council, but had not approved the decisions and actions of the other religious leaders regarding Jesus. He had obtained permission from Pontius Pilate to bury the body of the Lord in a new grave nearby. It was carved out of rock, with two chambers. Joseph had purchased it for his own last resting place.

"Thank you. Thank you, Sir." Mary replied quietly.

Gently, Joseph's servants took Jesus' body from the arms of his mother, wrapped it in a muslin cloth, and carried it to the tomb.

Susannah and Mary Magdalene followed closely behind, weeping, to find out where the body was being laid; while Mary, John and Seth waited at the foot of the empty wooden pillar.

When Mary Magdalene and Susannah returned, John and Seth lifted Jesus' sorrowing mother to her feet, and began walking her to an inn, where they would rest for the Sabbath day, and until Jesus' body was embalmed.

As they were on their way to the inn, walking along the edge of the silent crowd still gathered around, John noticed three figures huddled together. They were clutching one another and weeping softly.

"Lazarus! Mary! Martha!" The three raised their heads in unison, and looked around. "Over here, Lazarus!" John called out.

The three approached, their faces ravaged with sorrow. Embracing one another, sobbing softly, the friends stood circled together at the edge of the road.

John introduced Seth to Lazarus and his sisters.

"My friends, you must come and stay with us in Bethany, until the Sabbath is over," Lazarus insisted. "You, too, Seth." Mary and Martha nodded their heads in agreement.

"Thank you, my friends," John answered.

"I thank you, also, Lazarus," Seth murmured. "But my wife, Jamila, is resting at the inn where we are lodging. She is with child, and weary. I am so grateful to the Most High that she did not witness this terrible tragedy."

"Please, Seth, do bring her, too," Mary pleaded. "We all should be together tonight."

The little group of Jesus' friends, his mother, Mary Magdalene and Susannah walked slowly down the road, sorrowing, heading toward Bethany

#

Still standing beside the empty pillar, Benjamin, numb with shock, thought of his family in Bethlehem. He wished that he was with them now. *I was with him in the beginning and with him at the end. How mysterious are the ways of the Most High. It makes me want to be with my family, his gift to me,* he mused sadly.

Suddenly, whispering faintly into his consciousness, soft music and sweet voices came to him. He closed his eyes and remembered. Long years ago, the light, the heavenly voices, and the host of angels overhead . . . He remembered, and he knew without doubt. This Jesus, who had just suffered a shameful, horrifying, ghastly death, was that Good News of long ago; this Jesus was that small boy, holding the lamb so tenderly; this Jesus . . . Oh, dear God, this Jesus . . . Benjamin fell to his knees before the empty pillar, sobbing.

# Chapter Forty

Mary Magdalene lay sleepless on her bed. It was very early in the morning of the third day since the Lord had been crucified. Her violet eyes were bloodshot and swollen from weeping, her dark hair unkempt.

She felt overwhelmed with a sensation of profound sorrow and loss. *How can this be?* She asked herself for the hundredth time. *My Lord, my sweet Lord. I am heartsick. How can my heart be so wrung by grief and not burst? How could you leave us like this? How could you let this happen?*

She sat up in bed and buried her white face in her hands. "Oh, God, oh God, help me," she rasped, hoarse from shedding an ocean of tears.

A tumble of black hair hung limply about her face, as she rocked back and forth in the ancient motions of grief. Numbness began to cloud her mind. *I have to go to the tomb and pray. I have to go . . .*

Slowly she arose and washed her ravaged face in a basin of cold water, changed her clothing, and combed her hair. The tears lay just below the surface, waiting to brim and flow once more with her sorrow.

"No, I must go now. I cannot let another day go by," she spoke sharply to herself, aloud.

She lit a lantern, and swung a cloak around her shoulders, as it was still dark and chilly outside. Stepping out of the door, she felt a faint tremor underfoot, and thunder rolled across the heavens. Startled, she hesitated for a moment, but the neighboring countryside was sleeping, the air very quiet now. She breathed deeply of the crisp, early morning air. The eastern horizon edged the darkness with a pale gold-pink, luminous with a pearly tint.

Walking slowly through the quiet streets, Mary Magdalene headed toward the tomb where her beloved Lord lay. As she neared the garden, she wondered who would roll aside the huge stone blocking the entrance to the tomb. Someone had said that there were guards posted outside the entrance to make certain that no one could steal the body. Perhaps one of them would help her.

Gradually, as she walked, she became aware of a strange glow shimmering around the area of the tomb, turning the silver-leaved olive trees to gold. Frightened, she lowered her head and moved on. She picked her way slowly along the pathway, shivering, and drawing her cloak tightly around her slender body.

The ground at her feet began glowing softly. Glancing up, she drew in her breath sharply. "Dear God!" she whispered "Oh, my dear God!"

Directly ahead, the tomb was glowing, luminous with an unearthly radiance. Slowly, the fear abated, and a strange sense of peace pervaded Mary Magdalene's spirit. She looked around and realized that the guards whom Pilate had placed in front of the entrance were gone. She set the heavy lantern down on the rocky ground.

Gazing up at the entrance to the tomb, she gasped again. The huge stone had been rolled away from the opening, and the inside of the tomb glowed brightly in the pre-dawn shadows. There was no sound; not a leaf stirring, not a bird singing to the dawn. It was as though creation held its breath.

Mary Magdalene's body began trembling, and a faint nausea arose in her stomach as she cautiously approached the radiant tomb. Gathering her courage, she hesitantly stepped inside the opening. She shielded her eyes with one hand and stared in amazement as she realized the source of the light.

Two angels, dressed in brilliant white garments, their faces and bodies radiant, stood before her, smiling.

Fear chilled her, and she bowed down to the floor of the tomb, speechless with wonder and apprehension.

"Mary," said Gabriel, reaching out to raise her to her feet. "Mary Magdalene, why are you looking for the Lord in this place of the dead? Jesus is not here. He has risen from the grave!"

"Yes, Mary," Michael's deep voice interjected, "Don't you remember what he told you while he was still in Galilee?"

Mary shook her head, unable to speak. She felt blood rush to her face, as her great violet eyes reflected the glow from the two mighty archangels.

"He told you and his other followers that he had to be given over to sinners, that he would be crucified." Michael's voice became gentle and reassuring. "But he also said that on the third day, he would rise again."

"So, Mary of Magdala," Gabriel sang out, his smile a flash of brilliant benevolence. "Don't be looking for the living among the dead. He is risen, just as he promised!" he cried out joyfully.

Understanding flooded her soul, and Mary's heart filled with elation. Her beautiful countenance took on the same glow as that of the two angels. She clasped her hands together in excitement.

"Oh! Oh! I must go and tell the others!" Turning, she fled from the tomb, stumbling in her haste. Gathering up her skirts and running as fast as her legs would carry her, she arrived quickly at the house where the disciples were staying, hiding in fear from the authorities. Bursting in the door, she roused them in a loud voice, her face gleaming with tears of joy. Panting for breath, she burst out her news.

"Peter! John! James, Andrew! All of you! Our Lord is alive! His tomb is empty, and two shining angels told me that he is risen!"

"Mary, Mary, you're hysterical! That's impossible. Your grief has addled your brain. Calm down!" Peter grasped her arms and shook her slightly.

"No, no! You don't understand! I promise you, it's true!" Tears streamed down Mary Magdalene's face as she began to sob with frustration.

Peter turned to the other disciples and said "I'm going to see for myself. I'll be back soon."

John jumped to his feet. "I'll go with you, Peter."

Both men began running as soon as they exited the house. John, being more agile and younger, soon out-ran Peter, and reached the tomb just ahead of him.

Everything was exactly as Mary Magdalene had told them. The great stone was rolled away, and the grave clothes lay on the ground inside the tomb. Over in a corner, the cloth which had been used to cover the Lord's face lay carefully folded.

Mary Magdalene entered then, breathless, followed closely by Susannah and Joanna. Her great love for Jesus had overpowered her, and she could not stay away. She began weeping again as the other women stood open-mouthed with amazement.

The two magnificent angels were gone. Everything was quiet, except for the heavy breathing of the two apostles, and Mary Magdalene's sobs.

Peter and John, looked around dazedly, and then left the tomb to tell the other disciples what had happened.

Susannah and Joanna followed them, stunned and confused.

Sinking to her knees, Mary Magdalene wept softly with exhaustion from the emotional ordeal of the past three days.

"Mary." Peering through the blur of tears streaming from her eyes, Mary Magdalene saw that the two angels had returned. Michael stood where the head of Jesus had rested, and Gabriel stood at the foot.

"Mary Magdalene, why are you weeping?" Gabriel asked, gently, helping her to her feet.

"Do you know where our Lord has gone?" she sobbed. The air stirred behind the distraught woman, and she sensed someone standing behind her.

"Woman, why are you crying?" a low voice asked softly.

Turning around, she saw the figure of a man standing just inside the entrance, silhouetted starkly against the morning sky.

Thinking he must be the gardener, she stammered, "S-Sir, do you know where they have taken my Lord? If you do, please tell me so I can go to him."

Stepping back into the light, the man replied quietly, "Mary."

Stunned and bewildered, Mary Magdalene stared at him for a few moments. Her violet eyes widened, and she rose and stumbled toward him, crying "Rabboni! Master!" She fell to her knees in front of the Lord, overcome with elation.

Watching the joyful reunion, Gloriel smiled with delight. She stood unseen behind the risen Lord, her newly acquired wings folded closely around her small figure. *Oh, Father, thank you for this magnificent day of redemption for your earthly children. Thank you for the privilege of being a part of my Lord's life!* Her prayer rose to the throne of the Father, who rejoiced with her and the entire Heavenly Host.

Outside the tomb, the rising sun illuminated the countryside with brilliant color. Birds began to sing, trilling creation's joyful song to the risen Lord.

#

Two travelers, saddened and subdued by the events of the past few days, talked quietly together as they strolled along the dusty road from Jerusalem to the little village of Emmaus.

The day was warm with brilliant sunshine, and the surrounding fields smelled of new green grass. Wildflowers raised their bright multicolored heads to greet the bees and butterflies.

But the two disciples noticed none of the beauty around them. Their hearts were grieving as they discussed the awful incidents so vivid and fresh in their memories. Walking slowly, they heard footsteps approaching from behind. They both turned and saw a stranger coming up the pathway. They did not recognize the risen Lord.

Walking unseen behind Jesus, Gloriel thought to herself, *They don't recognize Jesu because of their lack of faith. They don't believe the account of the Lord's resurrection in the sacred writings, and this has blinded their eyes.*

"What are you talking about that leaves you with such mournful faces?" Jesus asked the two men when he caught up with them.

Cleopas, the younger of the two, peered at Jesus in amazement. "Haven't you heard what's happened in Jerusalem? You must be the only man in the city who doesn't know about these things!"

Jesus gazed deep into Cleopas' sad eyes. "What things? What has happened? He asked quietly.

"The things that happened to Jesus of Nazareth," Cleopas replied. "He was a prophet who did wonderful miracles. He was a wise teacher, highly regarded by all the people. But our leading priests and other religious leaders arrested him and handed him over to be condemned to death, and then they crucified him. Many of us believed he was the Messiah, come to rescue Israel." Cleopas paused, swallowed hard, and looked down at the ground.

"That all happened three days ago," Darius interjected. "Then some women from among his followers went to visit his tomb early this morning, and they came back with an amazing report. They said his body was missing, and they had seen two angels, who told them Jesus is alive! Some of the men ran out to see, and sure enough, Jesus' body was gone, just as the women had said." Darius looked out into the distance, his eyes bright with tears. "How is it that you have not heard of these happenings, sir? Have you been out of town? Have you not heard of Jesus of Nazareth?"

Responding to their questions as they walked along, Jesus explained to the two disciples why it was necessary for the Messiah to suffer, die, and rise again, according to the scriptural prophecies.

Darius and Cleopas were fascinated with Jesus' interpretations of the familiar passages, and before they realized it, they had arrived at their destination. Reluctant to part from this enthralling stranger, they invited Jesus to supper, and to stay overnight with them at their house.

When they settled down at the supper table, Gloriel stood behind Jesus, waiting to see if and when the two disciples would recognize him.

They enjoyed a good meal of boiled chicken, goat cheese, lentils, nuts and figs, along with earthen goblets brimming with wine.

Then Jesus took a piece of bread, blessed it, broke it, and gave it to Cleopas and Darius. When he placed the bread in their hands, suddenly, the veil was removed from their eyes, and they recognized their Lord.

Cleopas stared in amazement, and Darius' jaw dropped. Both of them started to speak, but suddenly, Jesus disappeared before their eyes.

They turned to one another, speechless for a moment, then both began to speak at once.

"Oh, dear God! Cleopas whispered.

"Cleopas, did you feel your heart burn within you as he was talking to us on the road?"

"Yes, yes, oh my Lord, yes! We must go back to Jerusalem right now and tell the others that we have seen him!" Cleopas replied, his voice quivering with emotion and excitement.

#

The two lost no time in returning to Jerusalem and began telling their brothers what had happened on the road to Emmaus. As they were still speaking, all of a sudden, Jesus was standing among them.

"Peace be with you!" he said, smiling broadly.

They were all petrified with fear. "It's a ghost!" Peter cried, backing away from the Lord.

"Don't touch it," Matthew whispered.

The rest of them were speechless with fright. The women there among them, Mary, his mother, Mary Magdalene, Susannah and Joanna, though momentarily stunned at his sudden appearance among them behind locked doors, stared at the Lord as joy gradually awakened in their spirits.

"Yes, yes, it's him," Sariel whispered in Mary's ear.

Jesus continued to grin from ear to ear, holding out his hands for them to see.

*He's having a bit of fun with them I think*, Gloriel mused, smiling to herself.

Though the doors were locked, Jesus had come to be with his friends. Looking around the room, he approached Thomas, his dark eyes penetrating deep into the doubter's puzzled gray ones.

"Thomas, my eternally skeptical one, come, put your fingers here where the nails pierced my wrists; Touch the wound in my side. You must stop doubting now. You must believe."

Thomas's eyes brimmed with tears. "My Lord and my God!" he exclaimed in a choked voice, sinking to his knees.

Then Jesus chided him gently. "Thomas, you believe now because you have seen me; but those who will believe without seeing me, are most blessed.

Jesus gaze swept the room as he addressed the other disciples, still smiling.

"It is really I, my dear friends. Come, touch me if you like. You can see the marks of the nails, and the wound in my side. I have risen to bring you all to eternal life! A ghost does not have flesh and bones. A ghost does not eat nor drink." He paused, waiting for his friends' reaction.

"So what's for breakfast?" How about some broiled fish? Do you have any honeycomb?"

"He's asking for food to show that he is real, and that they aren't seeing a vision, or a ghost," Gloriel whispered to Sariel.

Tremulous with awe and joy, John brought him a dish with the broiled fish and honeycomb he had requested. They all watched, wide-eyed, as he finished his breakfast with relish.

"Delicious! I was ravenous. Thank you, John."

The disciples began to relax, though still stunned. Mary was the first to approach her son and reach out to embrace him, tears of joy flooding her cheeks.

"Oh, my son, my son, it is really you! The Most High is so good; he has blessed me my whole life through, and is still blessing me! Blessed be God forever!"

Slowly, the room began to resound with joyful cries of celebration, as the disciples finally realized that they really were not dreaming, or hallucinating.

Radiant with delight, the risen Lord stretched out his long arms to bless his friends.

#

One morning a few days later, just as dawn was infusing the horizon with faint rose and gold, Jesus appeared on the shore of the Sea of Galilee. Peter and his brother Andrew, James and John, Nathaniel, and Thomas were standing together there, watching the sunrise. None of them noticed the Lord squatting on the sand a short distance down the beach, tending a fire.

"Well, brothers, I think I'll go fishing," Peter said suddenly.

"Wait, we'll go with you, Simon," one of the others replied.

"My friends! Wait, I have some fresh fish here. Come, I'll cook your breakfast! Jesus called.

*None of them dares to question him, because they know it's the Lord,* Gloriel thought. *It's still hard for them to understand, even though this is the third time he has shown himself to them . . .*

As soon as the meal was finished cooking, Jesus served his friends the fish and some fresh bread. Then he laid his hand on Peter's shoulder, beckoning him to walk with him down the beach. After they had strolled a short distance along the shore, the clear cool water lapping at their feet, Jesus paused and said quietly,

"Simon, do you love me more than the others do?"

"Oh, yes Lord, I do." Peter stopped walking and turned to face the Lord.

"Then you must feed my lambs." Jesus placed his arm around Peter's shoulder.

A bewildered look appeared on Peter's open face.

"Simon, son of John, do you love me?" Jesus repeated the question, looking deep into Peter's puzzled green eyes.

Peter hesitated, confused. "Uh-yes, yes, Lord. I do love you."

"Then tend my sheep." Jesus lowered his voice and drew Peter close, embracing him.

"Peter, do you love me?" This a mere whisper in Simon's ear.

Peter felt wounded that the Lord would ask him for a third time if he loved him. *Doesn't he believe me?* He thought to himself.

"My Lord, you must realize how much I love you. You know everything." Bright tears brimmed as a sob caught in his throat.

"All right, dear friend, then feed my sheep."

*Peter doesn't understand what's happening,* Gloriel mused, watching the exchange between Jesus and the brawny fisherman. *Being a leader, a shepherd, is so foreign to him. But he will learn. He will grasp what Jesu is asking of him, and why he asked him three times.*

#

It was a glorious morning. Jesus led his followers to the familiar little town of Bethany. Forty days had passed since he rose from the dead. Several times in those forty days, he appeared to them, encouraging and instructing them for the missions lying ahead.

He paused on the outskirts of Bethany, walked up a small hill, and turned to his apostles and disciples. Slowly, his clothing began radiating light.

"My dear ones, I must leave you now."

A murmur of protest arose immediately throughout this group of his closest followers.

Jesus raised his hand to quiet them. "But do not grieve. Soon I will send you a Comforter, the Holy Spirit. He will teach you everything you need to know to carry the Good News to the entire world. He will hearten and enlighten you, giving you wonderful Gifts to help you in your missions. He will also give you great joy, and bestow on you the greatest Gift of all, which is Love." Jesus' face glowed in exultation.

"Remember me always, in the breaking of the Bread, and the drinking of the Cup of my Blood. Behold, my brothers, I promise to be with you forever, even until the world ends."

Jesus raised his arms and blessed them. They watched in astonishment as he was lifted up before their eyes, ascending with power and glory into the clouds. Jaws agape, they stood gazing after him, overcome with emotion, awestricken.

Gloriel spread her wings, still unseen, and followed in her charge's wake, weeping with joy and gratitude that their missions were at last accomplished.

Suddenly, the disciples fell back in fear as Gabriel and Michael appeared; hovering just over their heads with splendid wings outspread.

"Men of Galilee! Why do you stand there staring after your Lord? Even though he ascends up into Heaven, he will return in the same way you saw him leave," Michael proclaimed in his powerful voice.

"Go now to Jerusalem, and wait for the Holy Spirit!" Gabriel instructed them, smiling.

Thus ended in power and glory, the Lord Jesus Christ's life on earth, and a small angel's unique and glorious mission.

### THE END

Or was it just the Beginning?

###

Printed in Great Britain
by Amazon